CW01067178

THE COLLECTED STORIES OF PHILIP K. DICK

THE FATHER-THING

By the same author:

THE PRESERVING MACHINE

GALACTIC POT-HEALER

A MAZE OF DEATH

FLOW MY TEARS, THE POLICEMAN SAID

THE MAN IN THE HIGH CASTLE

DEUS IRAE
(with Roger Zelazny)

A SCANNER DARKLY

THE TRANSMIGRATION OF TIMOTHY ARCHER

LIES, INC

IN MILTON LUMKY TERRITORY

I HOPE I SHALL ARRIVE SOON

HUMPTY DUMPTY IN OAKLAND

MARY AND THE GIANT

BEYOND LIES THE WUB

SECOND VARIETY

THE BROKEN BUBBLE

Volume Three

THE COLLECTED STORIES OF PHILIP K. DICK

THE FATHER-THING

Introduction by John Brunner

LONDON
VICTOR GOLLANCZ LTD
1989

First published in Great Britain 1989
by Victor Gollancz Ltd,
14 Henrietta Street, London WC2E 8QJ

British Library Cataloguing in Publication Data
Dick, Philip K. (Philip Kendred), *1928–1982*
The father-thing.
I. Title II. Series
813′.54[F]

ISBN 0-575-04616-3

Printed in Great Britain by
St Edmundsbury Press Ltd, Bury St Edmunds, Suffolk

Contents

INTRODUCTION

By John Brunner

I have thirty-three books by Philip Dick on my shelves. In the near future I hope to have thirty-eight, more than twice as many as by any other science fiction author. The closest contender weighs in with a mere eighteen, and four of those are anthologies he edited.

Why? Why do I own so many more of his books than of anybody else's?

Well, put it this way. Dick is the man who made me accept, even if only for the duration of one novel, that there could be a society in which the medium of currency exchange was orange marmalade.

I've been trying to recall my first encounter with the guy's work. I suspect it must have been when I read what I understand was his first-ever publication in the SF field, *Beyond Lies the Wub*. It was told in a workmanlike style and had a pleasantly amusing punch-line, all in all a praiseworthy début. But in the short stories that followed—report had it that he was writing one per week—one had the impression of someone still trying to find his own voice. In particular, I noticed many echoes of the much-lamented Henry Kuttner. I had to wait for his novels before I realized just how individual an imagination Dick possessed, how ingeniously he could twist our world into strange patterns, or tilt it at an unfamiliar angle to create a disturbing new perspective, combined with a sense of sheer otherness that for days and sometimes months afterwards left festering barbs in the subconscious of the reader.

I remember buying a tattered second-hand copy of *SOLAR LOTTERY* and devouring it at a sitting. I remember sweating through the days between installments of *TIME OUT OF JOINT* when Ted Carnell serialized it in *New*

Worlds. And after I'd read those two, I was convinced. I knew I had to go in search of everything else by him that I could find.

In 1966, also in *New Worlds*, I published a tub-thumping, drum-beating article about his work — at that time too little known in Britain — which, I must at last admit, was motivated at least partly by self-interest; I wanted to be able to buy more of his books.... Ten years after, I had the pleasure of being asked to write a preface to Ballantine's *THE BEST OF PHILIP K. DICK*. A decade later still, in 1986, here I am invited to perform a similar and equally gratifying task.

But considerably more difficult. I don't want to plagiarize myself, you see, and on re-reading my 1976 article I find that in it I summed up everything I thought then, and everything I still think, about what made Dick's work extraordinary. I talked about the nature of the Dickian world, its near-emptiness, its sterility, its resemblance to our own and its unsettling differences. I talked about the altered perceptions that he could entrain in the reader's mind, and the deftness with which he sustained absurd assumptions for just as long as was necessary to prevent the reader from tossing the book aside in disbelief — marmalade money being only one of countless examples. I talked about his prodigal largesse with ideas and concepts that most writers would regard as central but he treated as peripheral, citing above all that marvellous scene in which one of his characters says to another, "God is dead." And this is known; a creature sufficiently evolved to have created the Earth and all its life-forms including us has been found drifting in space. Yet within the story this fact is simply not important....

I'm tempted to quote my 1976 piece *in extenso*. But I'd better not. This is a later age, and Phil is dead, and this time there won't be any helpful letters from him suggesting items for inclusion in the proposed collection, because it is — deservedly — complete.

Nor, come to that, respectful but irritable ones listing others he preferred to see left out.

I first met him during a pre-Worldcon party in 1964, in Oakland, California. He was not as I'd imagined. From his prolificity and mordant wit I'd expected a relaxed if rather cynical person. Instead I found a very shy one, reluctant to make eye-contact with a stranger like myself, glancing constantly around as though to make sure a way of escape was open. Later I learned how deeply tormented he was by the idiocies of the world, how personally he felt the slights visited on our collective intelligence by those who pretend to speak in our name and that of our civilization, who exercise power over us yet think only of themselves. How seriously he wanted to be taken when he devised his simulacra of politicians, from his eternal Jackie Kennedy to his stubborn duplicate of Lincoln, I could never tell. But it didn't matter. He had hit on yet another brilliant image for the faults and shortcomings of our world, another facet of the mirror he held up to it, that distorted and nonetheless in some inexplicable manner reflected a greater truth, an aspect nearer to reality.

At our last meeting, in France during one of the Metz science fiction festivals, I equally failed to figure out how literally he intended people to regard his claims about communicating with the Apostle Paul, or having killed a cat by willing it to death. I could not decide whether, after so many years of inner suffering, his reason had been usurped by his own inventions, or whether he had reached the bitter conclusion that the only way to cope with our lunatic world was to treat it as one vast and rather vicious joke, and fight back on the same irrational level.

I think — I hope — the latter, for it implies that in his writing he had found the solution, or at any rate *a* solution, to the manifold problems he had been confronted by: his frustration at not being recognized in the field of general literature, his broken marriages, the mysterious raid on his house described in Paul Williams' book *ONLY APPARENTLY REAL*, and all the rest. He was a strange person but a wonderful writer, and perhaps his writing offered him catharsis. Certainly it provided his readership with a unique experience.

And that, I think, says all that needs to be said concerning why I have thirty-three of his books and hope soon to have thirty-eight.

Read on, and be impressed.

John Brunner
South Petherton
England
October 1986

I think we're getting a restricted view of actual patterns. And the restricted view says that people do things deliberately, in concert, aimed at me, where in truth there are patterns that emanate from beyond people. And they're certainly not directed at any of of us, you know; they're much broader, and they work through all of us.

—Philip K. Dick in an interview, 1974.

THE FATHER-THING

Fair Game

PROFESSOR ANTHONY DOUGLAS lowered gratefully into his red-leather easy chair and sighed. A long sigh, accompanied by labored removal of his shoes and numerous grunts as he kicked them into the corner. He folded his hands across his ample middle and lay back, eyes closed.

"Tired?" Laura Douglas asked, turning from the kitchen stove a moment, her dark eyes sympathetic.

"You're darn right." Douglas surveyed the evening paper across from him on the couch. Was it worth it? No, not really. He felt around in his coat pocket for his cigarettes and lit up slowly, leisurely. "Yeah, I'm tired, all right. We're starting a whole new line of research. Whole flock of bright young men in from Washington today. Briefcases and slide rules."

"Not— "

"Oh, I'm still in charge." Professor Douglas grinned expansively. "Perish the thought." Pale gray cigarette smoke billowed around him. "It'll be another few years before they're ahead of me. They'll have to sharpen up their slide rules just a little bit more . . . "

His wife smiled and continued preparing dinner. Maybe it was the atmosphere of the little Colorado town. The sturdy, impassive mountain peaks around them. The thin, chill air. The quiet citizens. In any case, her husband seemed utterly unbothered by the tensions and doubts that pressured other members of his profession. A lot of aggressive newcomers were swelling the ranks of nuclear physics these days. Old-timers were tottering in their positions, abruptly insecure. Every college, every physics department and lab was being invaded by the new horde of skilled young men. Even here at Bryant College, so far off the beaten track.

But if Anthony Douglas worried, he never let it show. He rested happily in his easy chair, eyes shut, a blissful smile on his face. He was tired — but at peace. He sighed again, this time more from pleasure than fatigue.

"It's true," he murmured lazily. "I may be old enough to be their father, but I'm still a few jumps ahead of them. Of course, I know the ropes better. And — "

"And the wires. The ones worth pulling."

"Those, too. In any case, I think I'll come off from this new line we're doing just about ... "

His voice trailed off.

"What's the matter?" Laura asked.

Douglas half rose from his chair. His face had gone suddenly white. He stared in horror, gripping the arms of his chair, his mouth opening and closing.

At the window was a great eye. An immense eye that gazed into the room intently, studying him. The eye filled the whole window.

"Good God!" Douglas cried.

The eye withdrew. Outside there was only the evening gloom, the dark hills and trees, the street. Douglas sank down slowly in his chair.

"What was it?" Laura demanded sharply. "What did you see? Was somebody out there?"

Douglas clasped and unclasped his hands. His lips twitched violently. "I'm telling you the truth, Bill. I saw it myself. It was real. I wouldn't say so, otherwise. You know that. Don't you believe me?"

"Did anybody else see it?" Professor William Henderson asked, chewing his pencil thoughtfully. He had cleared a place on the dinner table, pushed back his plate and silver and laid out his notebook. "Did Laura see it?"

"No. Laura had her back turned."

"What time was it?"

"Half an hour ago. I had just got home. About six-thirty. I had my shoes off, taking it easy." Douglas wiped his forehead with a shaking hand.

"You say it was unattached? There was nothing else? Just the — eye?"

"Just the eye. One huge eye looking in at me. Taking in everything. As if — "

"As if what?"

"As if it was looking down a microscope."

Silence.

From across the table, Henderson's red-haired wife spoke up. "You always were a strict empiricist, Doug. You never went in for any nonsense before. But this ... It's too bad nobody else saw it."

"Of course nobody else saw it!"

"What do you mean?"

"The damn thing was looking at *me*. It was *me* it was studying." Douglas's voice rose hysterically. "How do you think I feel — scrutinized by an eye as big as a piano! My God, if I weren't so well integrated, I'd be out of my mind!"

Henderson and his wife exchanged glances. Bill, dark-haired and handsome, ten years Douglas's junior. Vivacious Jean Henderson, lecturer in child psychology, lithe and full-bosomed in her nylon blouse and slacks.

"What do you make of this?" Bill asked her. "This is more along your line."

"It's in *your* line," Douglas snapped. "Don't try to pass this off as a morbid projection. I came to you because you're head of the Biology Department."

"You think it's an animal? A giant sloth or something?"

"It must be an animal."

"Maybe it's a joke," Jean suggested. "Or an advertising sign. An oculist's display. Somebody may have been carrying it past the window."

Douglas took a firm grip on himself. "The eye was alive. It looked at me. It considered me. Then it withdrew. As if it had moved away from the lens." He shuddered. "I tell you it was *studying* me!"

"You only?"

"Me. Nobody else."

"You seem curiously convinced it was looking down from above," Jean said.

"Yes, down. Down at me. That's right." An odd expression flickered across Douglas's face. "You have it, Jean. As if it came from up there." He jerked his hand upward.

"Maybe it was God," Bill said thoughtfully.

Douglas said nothing. His face turned ash white and his teeth chattered.

"Nonsense," Jean said. "God is a psychological transcendent symbol expressing unconscious forces."

"Did it look at you accusingly?" asked Bill. "As if you'd done something wrong?"

"No. With interest. With considerable interest." Douglas raised himself. "I have to get back. Laura thinks I'm having some kind of fit. I haven't told her, of course. She's not scientifically disciplined. She wouldn't be able to handle such a concept."

"It's a little tough even for us," Bill said.

Douglas moved nervously toward the door. "You can't think of any explanation? Something thought extinct that might still be roaming around these mountains?"

"None that we know of. If I should hear of any — "

"You said it looked down," Jean said. "Not bending down to peer in at you. Then it couldn't have been an animal or terrestrial being." She was deep in thought. "Maybe we're being observed."

"Not you," Douglas said miserably. "Just me."

"By another race," Bill put in. "You think — "

"Maybe it's an eye from Mars."

Douglas opened the front door carefully and peered out. The night was black. A faint wind moved through the trees and along the highway. His car was dimly visible, a black square against the hills. "If you think of anything, call me."

"Take a couple of phenobarbitals before you hit the sack," Jean suggested. "Calm your nerves."

Douglas was out on the porch. "Good idea. Thanks." He shook his head. "Maybe I'm out of my mind. Good Lord. Well, I'll see you later."

He walked down the steps, gripping the rail tightly. "Good night!" Bill called. The door closed and the porch light clicked off.

Douglas went cautiously toward his car. He reached out into the darkness, feeling for the door handle. One step. Two steps. It was silly. A grown man — practically middle-aged — in the twentieth century. Three steps.

He found the door and opened it, sliding quickly inside and locking it after him. He breathed a silent prayer of thanks as he snapped on the motor and the headlights. Silly as hell. A giant eye. A stunt of some sort.

He turned the thoughts over in his mind. Students? Jokesters? Communists? A plot to drive him out of his mind? He was important. Probably the most important nuclear physicist in the country. And this new project...

He drove the car slowly forward, onto the silent highway. He watched each bush and tree as the car gained speed.

A Communist plot. Some of the students were in a left-wing club. Some sort of Marxist study group. Maybe they had rigged up —

In the glare of the headlights something glittered. Something at the edge of the highway.

Douglas gazed at it, transfixed. Something square, a long block in the weeds at the side of the highway, where the great dark trees began. It glittered and shimmered. He slowed down, almost to a stop.

A bar of gold, lying at the edge of the road.

It was incredible. Slowly, Professor Douglas rolled down the window and peered out. Was it really gold? He laughed nervously. Probably not. He had often seen gold, of course. This *looked* like gold. But maybe it was lead, an ingot of lead with a gilt coating.

But — why?

A joke. A prank. College kids. They must have seen his car go past toward the Hendersons' and knew he'd soon be driving back.

Or — or it really *was* gold. Maybe an armored car had gone past. Turned the corner too swiftly. The ingot had slid out and fallen into the weeds. In that case there was a little fortune lying there, in the darkness at the edge of the highway.

But it was illegal to possess gold. He'd have to return it to the Government. But couldn't he saw off just a little piece? And if he did return it there was no doubt a reward of some kind. Probably several thousand dollars.

A mad scheme flashed briefly through his mind. Get the ingot, crate it up, fly it to Mexico, out of the country. Eric Barnes owned a Piper Cub. He could easily get it into Mexico. Sell it. Retire. Live in comfort the rest of his life.

Professor Douglas snorted angrily. It was his duty to return it. Call the Denver Mint, tell them about it. Or the police department. He reversed his car and backed up until he was even with the metal bar. He turned off the motor and slid out onto the dark highway. He had a job to do. As a loyal citizen — and, God knew, fifty tests had shown he *was* loyal — there was a job for him here. He leaned into the car and fumbled in the dashboard for the flashlight. If somebody had lost a bar of gold, it was up to him ...

A bar of gold. Impossible. A slow, cold chill settled over him, numbing his heart. A tiny voice in the back of his mind spoke clearly and rationally to him: *Who would walk off and leave an ingot of gold?*

Something was going on.

Fear gripped him. He stood frozen, trembling with terror. The dark, deserted highway. The silent mountains. He was alone. A perfect spot. If they wanted to get him —

They?

Who?

He looked quickly around. Hiding in the trees, most likely. Waiting for him. Waiting for him to cross the highway, leave the road and enter the woods. Bend down and try to pick up the ingot. One quick blow as he bent over; that would be it.

Douglas scrambled back into his car and snapped on the motor. He raced the motor and released the brake. The car jerked forward and gained speed. His hands shaking, Douglas bore down desperately on the wheel. He had to get out. Get away before — whoever they were got him.

As he shifted into high he took one last look back, peering around through the open window. The ingot was still there, still glowing among the dark weeds at the edge of the highway. But there was a strange vagueness about it, an uncertain waver in the nearby atmosphere.

Abruptly the ingot faded and disappeared. Its glow receded into darkness.

Douglas glanced up, and gasped in horror.

In the sky above him, something blotted out the stars. A great shape, so huge it staggered him. The shape moved, a disembodied circle of living presence, directly over his head.

A face. A gigantic, cosmic face peering down. Like some great moon, blotting out everything else. The face hung for an instant, intent on him — on the spot he had just vacated. Then the face, like the ingot, faded and sank into darkness.

The stars returned. He was alone.

Douglas sank back against the seat. The car veered crazily and roared down the highway. His hands slid from the wheel and dropped at his sides. He caught the wheel again, just in time.

There was no doubt about it. Somebody was after him. Trying to get him. But no Communists or student practical jokers. Or any beast, lingering from the dim past.

Whatever it was, whoever they were, had nothing to do with Earth. It — they — were from some other world. They were out to get him.

Him.

But — why?

Pete Berg listened closely. "Go on," he said when Douglas halted.

"That's all." Douglas turned to Bill Henderson. "Don't try to tell me I'm out of my mind. I really saw it. It was looking down at me. The whole face this time, not just the eye."

"You think this was the face that the eye belonged to?" Jean Henderson asked.

"I know it. The face had the same expression as the eye. Studying me."

"We've got to call the police," Laura Douglas said in a thin, clipped voice. "This can't go on. If somebody's out to get him — "

"The police won't do any good." Bill Henderson paced back and forth. It was late, after midnight. All the lights in the Douglas house were on. In one corner old Milton Erick, head of the Math Department, sat curled up, taking everything in, his wrinkled face expressionless.

"We can assume," Professor Erick said calmly, removing his pipe from between his yellow teeth, "they're a nonterrestrial race. Their size and their position indicate they're not Earthbound in any sense."

"But they can't just *stand* in the sky!" Jean exploded. "There's nothing up there!"

"There may be other configurations of matter not normally connected or related to our own. An endless or multiple coexistence of universe systems, lying along a plane of coordinates totally unexplainable in present terms. Due to some singular juxtaposition of tangents, we are, at this moment, in contact with one of these other configurations."

"He means," Bill Henderson explained, "that these people after Doug don't belong to our universe. They come from a different dimension entirely."

"The face wavered," Douglas murmured. "The gold and the face both wavered and faded out."

"Withdrew," Erick stated. "Returned to their own universe. They have entry into ours at will, it would seem, a hole, so to speak, that they can enter through and return again."

"It's a pity," Jean said, "they're so damn big. If they were smaller — "

"Size is in their favor," Erick admitted. "An unfortunate circumstance."

"All this academic wrangling!" Laura cried wildly. "We sit here working out theories and meanwhile they are after him!"

"This might explain gods," Bill said suddenly.

"Gods?"

Bill nodded. "Don't you see? In the past these beings looked across the nexus at us, into our universe. Maybe even stepped down. Primitive people saw them and weren't able to explain them. They built religions around them. Worshipped them."

"Mount Olympus," Jean said. "Of course. And Moses met God at the top of Mount Sinai. We're high up in the Rockies. Maybe contact only comes at high places. In the mountains, like this."

"And the Tibetan monks are situated in the highest land mass in the world," Bill added. "That whole area. The highest and the oldest part of the world. All the great religions have been revealed in the mountains. Brought down by people who saw God and carried the word back."

"What I can't understand," Laura said, "is why they want *him*." She spread her hands helplessly. "Why not somebody else? Why do they have to single him out?"

Bill's face was hard. "I think that's pretty clear."

"Explain," Erick rumbled.

"What is Doug? About the best nuclear physicist in the world. Working on top-secret projects in nuclear fission. Advanced research. The Government is underwriting everything Bryant College is doing — because Douglas is here."

"So?"

"They want him because of his ability. Because he *knows* things. Because of their size-relationship to this universe, they can subject our lives to as careful a scrutiny as we maintain in the biology labs of — well, of a culture of Sarcina Pulmonum. But that doesn't mean they're culturally advanced over us."

"Of course!" Pete Berg exclaimed. "They want Doug for his knowledge. They want to pirate him off and make use of his mind for their own cultures."

"Parasites!" Jean gasped. "They must have always depended on us. Don't you see? Men in the past who have disappeared, spirited off by these creatures." She shivered. "They probably regard us as some sort of testing ground, where techniques and knowledge are painfully developed — for their benefit."

Douglas started to answer, but the words never escaped his mouth. He sat rigid in his chair, his head turned to one side.

Outside, in the darkness beyond the house, someone was calling his name.

He got up and moved toward the door. They were all staring at him in amazement.

"What is it?" Bill demanded. "What's the matter, Doug?"

Laura caught his arm. "What's wrong? Are you sick? Say something! *Doug!*"

Professor Douglas jerked free and pulled open the front door. He stepped out onto the porch. There was a faint moon. A soft light hovered over everything.

"Professor Douglas!" The voice again, sweet and fresh — a girl's voice.

Outlined by the moonlight, at the foot of the porch steps, stood a girl. Blonde-haired, perhaps twenty years old. In a checkered skirt, pale Angora sweater, a silk kerchief around her neck. She was waving at him anxiously, her small face pleading.

"Professor, do you have a minute? Something terrible has gone wrong with ... " Her voice trailed off as she moved nervously away from the house, into the darkness.

"What's the matter?" he shouted.

He could hear her voice faintly. She was moving off.

Douglas was torn with indecision. He hesitated, then hurried impatiently down the stairs after her. The girl retreated from him, wringing her hands together, her full lips twisting wildly with despair. Under her sweater, her breasts rose and fell in an agony of terror, each quiver sharply etched by the moonlight.

"What is it?" Douglas cried. "What's wrong?" He hurried angrily after her. "For God's sake, stand still!"

The girl was still moving away, drawing him farther and farther away from the house, toward the great green expanse of lawn, the beginning of the campus. Douglas was overcome with annoyance. Damn the girl! Why couldn't she wait for him?

"Hold on a minute!" he said, hurrying after her. He started out onto the dark lawn, puffing with exertion. "Who are you? What the hell do you — "

There was a flash. A bolt of blinding light crashed past him and seared a smoking pit in the lawn a few feet away.

Douglas halted, dumfounded. A second bolt came, this one just ahead of him. The wave of heat threw him back. He stumbled and half fell. The girl had abruptly stopped. She stood silent and unmoving, her face expressionless. There was a peculiar waxy quality to her. She had become, all at once, utterly inanimate.

But he had no time to think about that. Douglas turned and lumbered back toward the house. A third bolt came, striking just ahead of him. He veered to the right and threw himself into the shrubs growing near the wall. Rolling and gasping, he pressed against the concrete side of the house, squeezing next to it as hard as he could.

There was a sudden shimmer in the star-studded sky above him. A faint motion. Then nothing. He was alone. The bolts ceased. And —

The girl was gone, also.

A decoy. A clever imitation to lure him away from the house, so he'd move out into the open where they could take a shot at him.

He got shakily to his feet and edged around the side of the house. Bill Henderson and Laura and Berg were on the porch, talking nervously and looking around for him. There was his car, parked in the driveway. Maybe, if he could reach it —

He peered up at the sky. Only stars. No hint of them. If he could get in his car and drive off, down the highway, away from the mountains, toward Denver, where it was lower, maybe he'd be safe.

He took a deep, shuddering breath. Only ten yards to the car. Thirty feet. If he could once get in it —

He ran. Fast. Down the path and along the driveway. He grabbed open the car door and leaped inside. With one quick motion he threw the switch and released the brake.

The car glided forward. The motor came on with a sputter. Douglas bore down desperately on the gas. The car leaped forward. On the porch, Laura shrieked and started down the stairs. Her cry and Bill's startled shout were lost in the roar of the engine.

A moment later he was on the highway, racing away from town, down the long, curving road toward Denver.

He could call Laura from Denver. She could join him. They could take the train east. The hell with Bryant College. His life was at stake. He drove for hours without stopping, through the night. The sun came up and rose slowly in the sky. More cars were on the road now. He passed a couple of diesel trucks rumbling slowly and cumbersomely along.

He was beginning to feel a little better. The mountains were behind. More distance between him and them ...

His spirits rose as the day warmed. There were hundreds of universities and laboratories scattered around the country. He could easily continue with his work someplace else. They'd never get him, once he was out of the mountains.

He slowed his car down. The gas gauge was near empty.

To the right of the road was a filling station and a small roadside cafe. The sight of the cafe reminded him he hadn't eaten breakfast. His stomach was beginning to protest. There were a couple of cars pulled up in front of the cafe. A few people were sitting inside at the counter.

He turned off the highway and coasted into the gas station.

"Fill her up!" he called to the attendant. He got out on the hot gravel, leaving the car in gear. His mouth watered. A plateful of hotcakes, side order of ham, steaming black coffee ... "Can I leave her here?"

"The car?" The white-clad attendant unscrewed the cap and began filling the tank. "What do you mean?"

"Fill her up and park her for me. I'll be out in a few minutes. I want to catch some breakfast."

"Breakfast?"

Douglas was annoyed. What was the matter with the man? He indicated the cafe. A truck driver had pushed the screen door open and was standing on the step, picking his teeth thoughtfully. Inside, the waitress hustled back and forth. He could already smell the coffee, the bacon frying on the griddle. A faint tinny sound of a jukebox drifted out. A warm, friendly sound. "The cafe."

The attendant stopped pumping gas. He put down the hose slowly and turned toward Douglas, a strange expression on his face. "What cafe?" he said.

The cafe wavered and abruptly winked out. Douglas fought down a scream of terror. Where the cafe had been there was only an open field.

Greenish brown grass. A few rusty tin cans. Bottles. Debris. A leaning fence. Off in the distance, the outline of the mountains.

Douglas tried to get hold of himself. "I'm a little tired," he muttered. He climbed unsteadily back into the car. "How much?"

"I just hardly began to fill the — "

"Here." Douglas pushed a bill at him. "Get out of the way." He turned on the motor and raced out onto the highway, leaving the astonished attendant staring after him.

That had been close. Damn close. A trap. And he had almost stepped inside.

But the thing that really terrified him wasn't the closeness. *He was out of the mountains and they had still been ahead of him.*

It hadn't done any good. He wasn't any safer than last night. They were everywhere.

The car sped along the highway. He was getting near Denver — but so what? It wouldn't make any difference. He could dig a hole in Death Valley and still not be safe. They were after him and they weren't going to give up. That much was clear.

He racked his mind desperately. He had to think of something, some way to get loose.

A parasitic culture. A race that preyed on humans, utilized human knowledge and discoveries. Wasn't that what Bill had said? They were after his know-how, his unique ability and knowledge of nuclear physics. He had been singled out, separated from the pack because of his superior ability and training. They would keep after him until they got him. And then — what?

Horror gripped him. The gold ingot. The decoy. The girl had *looked* perfectly real. The cafe full of people. Even the smells of food. Bacon frying. Steaming coffee.

God, if only he were just an ordinary person, without skill, without special ability. If only —

A sudden flapping sound. The car lurched. Douglas cursed wildly. A flat. Of all times . . .

Of all times.

Douglas brought the car to a halt at the side of the road. He switched off the motor and put on the brake. For a while he sat in silence. Finally he fumbled in his coat and got out a mashed package of cigarettes. He lit up slowly and then rolled the window down to let in some air.

He was trapped, of course. There was nothing he could do. The flat had obviously been arranged. Something on the road, sprinkled down from above. Tacks, probably.

The highway was deserted. No cars in sight. He was utterly alone, between towns. Denver was thirty miles ahead. No chance of getting there. Nothing around him but terribly level fields, desolated plains.

Nothing but level ground — and the blue sky above.

Douglas peered up. He couldn't see them, but they were there, waiting for him to get out of his car. His knowledge, his ability, would be utilized by an alien culture. He would become an instrument in their hands. All his learning would be theirs. He would be a slave and nothing more.

Yet, in a way, it was a complement. From a whole society, he alone had been selected. His skill and knowledge, over everything else. A faint glow rose in his cheeks. Probably they had been studying him for some time. The great eye had no doubt often peered down through its telescope, or microscope, or whatever it was, peered down and seen him. Seen his ability and realized what that would be worth to its own culture.

Douglas opened the car door. He stepped out onto the hot pavement. He dropped his cigarette and calmly stubbed it out. He took a deep breath, stretching and yawning. He could see the tacks now, bright bits of light on the surface of the pavement. Both front tires were flat.

Something shimmered above him. Douglas waited quietly. Now that it had finally come, he was no longer afraid. He watched with a kind of detached curiosity. The something grew. It fanned out over him, swelling and expanding. For a moment it hesitated. Then it descended.

Douglas stood still as the enormous cosmic net closed over him. The strands pressed against him as the net rose. He was going up, heading toward the sky. But he was relaxed, at peace, no longer afraid.

Why be afraid? He would be doing much the same work as always. He would miss Laura and the college, of course, the intellectual companionship of the faculty, the bright faces of the students. But no doubt he would find companionship up above. Persons to work with. Trained minds with which to communicate.

The net was lifting him faster and faster. The ground fell rapidly away.

The Earth dwindled from a flat surface to a globe. Douglas watched with professional interest. Above him, beyond the intricate strands of the net, he could see the outline of the other universe, the new world toward which he was heading.

Shapes. Two enormous shapes squatting down. Two incredibly huge figures bending over. One was drawing in the net. The other watched, holding something in its hand. A landscape. Dim forms too vast for Douglas to comprehend.

At last, a thought came. *What a struggle.*

It was worth it, thought the other creature.

Their thoughts roared through him. Powerful thoughts, from immense minds.

I was right. The biggest yet. What a catch!

Must weigh all of twenty-four ragets!

At last!

Suddenly Douglas's composure left him. A chill of horror flashed through his mind. What were they talking about? What did they mean?

But then he was being dumped from the net. He was falling. Something was coming up at him. A flat, shiny surface. What was it?

Oddly, it looked almost like a frying pan.

THE HANGING STRANGER

AT FIVE O'CLOCK Ed Loyce washed up, tossed on his hat and coat, got his car out and headed across town toward his TV sales store. He was tired. His back and shoulders ached from digging dirt out of the basement and wheeling it into the back yard. But for a forty-year-old man he had done okay. Janet could get a new vase with the money he had saved; and he liked the idea of repairing the foundations himself.

It was getting dark. The setting sun cast long rays over the scurrying commuters, tired and grim-faced, women loaded down with bundles and packages, students, swarming home from the university, mixing with clerks and businessmen and drab secretaries. He stopped his Packard for a red light and then started it up again. The store had been open without him; he'd arrive just in time to spell the help for dinner, go over the records of the day, maybe even close a couple of sales himself. He drove slowly past the small square of green in the center of the street, the town park. There were no parking places in front of LOYCE TV SALES AND SERVICE. He cursed under his breath and swung the car in a U-turn. Again he passed the little square of green with its lonely drinking fountain and bench and single lamppost.

From the lamppost something was hanging. A shapeless dark bundle, swinging a little with the wind. Like a dummy of some sort. Loyce rolled down his window and peered out. What the hell was it? A display of some kind? Sometimes the Chamber of Commerce put up displays in the square.

Again he made a U-turn and brought his car around. He passed the park and concentrated on the dark bundle. It wasn't a dummy. And if it was a display it was a strange kind. The hackles on his neck rose and he swallowed uneasily. Sweat slid out on his face and hands.

It was a body. A human body.

* * *

"Look at it!" Loyce snapped. "Come on out here!"

Don Fergusson came slowly out of the store, buttoning his pin-stripe coat with dignity. "This is a big deal, Ed. I can't just leave the guy standing there."

"See it?" Ed pointed into the gathering gloom. The lamppost jutted up against the sky — the post and the bundle swinging from it. "There it is. How the hell long has it been there?" His voice rose excitedly. "What's wrong with everybody? They just walk on past!"

Don Fergusson lit a cigarette slowly. "Take it easy, old man. There must be a good reason, or it wouldn't be there."

"A reason! What kind of a reason?"

Fergusson shrugged. "Like the time the Traffic Safety Council put that wrecked Buick there. Some sort of civic thing. How would I know?"

Jack Potter from the shoe shop joined them. "What's up, boys?"

"There's a body hanging from the lamppost," Loyce said. "I'm going to call the cops."

"They must know about it," Potter said. "Or otherwise it wouldn't be there."

"I got to get back in." Fergusson headed back into the store. "Business before pleasure."

Loyce began to get hysterical. "You see it? You see it hanging there? A man's body! A dead man!"

"Sure, Ed. I saw it this afternoon when I went out for coffee."

"You mean it's been there all afternoon?"

"Sure. What's the matter?" Potter glanced at his watch. "Have to run. See you later, Ed."

Potter hurried off, joining the flow of people moving along the sidewalk. Men and women, passing by the park. A few glanced up curiously at the dark bundle — and then went on. Nobody stopped. Nobody paid any attention.

"I'm going nuts," Loyce whispered. He made his way to the curb and crossed out into traffic, among the cars. Horns honked angrily at him. He gained the curb and stepped up onto the little square of green.

The man had been middle-aged. His clothing was ripped and torn, a gray suit, splashed and caked with dried mud. A stranger. Loyce had never seen him before. Not a local man. His face was partly turned away, and in the evening wind he spun a little, turning gently, silently. His skin was gouged and cut. Red gashes, deep scratches of congealed blood. A pair of steel-rimmed glasses hung from one ear, dangling foolishly. His eyes bulged. His mouth was open, tongue thick and ugly blue.

"For Heaven's sake," Loyce muttered, sickened. He pushed down his nausea and made his way back to the sidewalk. He was shaking all over, with revulsion — and fear.

Why? Who was the man? Why was he hanging there? What did it mean?

And — why didn't anybody notice?

He bumped into a small man hurrying along the sidewalk. "Watch it!" the man grated. "Oh, it's you, Ed."

Ed nodded dazedly. "Hello, Jenkins."

"What's the matter?" The stationery clerk caught Ed's arm. "You look sick."

"The body. There in the park."

"Sure, Ed." Jenkins led him into the alcove of LOYCE TV SALES AND SERVICE. "Take it easy."

Margaret Henderson from the jewelry store joined them. "Something wrong?"

"Ed's not feeling well."

Loyce yanked himself free. "How can you stand here? Don't you see it? For God's sake — "

"What's he talking about?" Margaret asked nervously.

"The body!" Ed shouted. "The body hanging there!"

More people collected. "Is he sick? It's Ed Loyce. You okay, Ed?"

"The body!" Loyce screamed, struggling to get past them. Hands caught at him. He tore loose. "Let me go! The police! Get the police!"

"Ed — "

"Better get a doctor!"

"He must be sick."

"Or drunk."

Loyce fought his way through the people. He stumbled and half fell. Through a blur he saw rows of faces, curious, concerned, anxious. Men and women halting to see what the disturbance was. He fought past them toward his store. He could see Fergusson inside talking to a man, showing him an Emerson TV set. Pete Foley in the back at the service counter, setting up a new Philco. Loyce shouted at them frantically. His voice was lost in the roar of traffic and the murmuring around him.

"Do something!" he screamed. "Don't stand there! Do something! Something's wrong! Something's happened! Things are going on!"

The crowd melted respectfully for the two heavy-set cops moving efficiently toward Loyce.

"Name?" the cop with the notebook murmured.

"Loyce." He mopped his forehead wearily. "Edward C. Loyce. Listen to me. Back there — "

"Address?" the cop demanded. The police car moved swiftly through traffic, shooting among the cars and buses. Loyce sagged against the seat, exhausted and confused. He took a deep shuddering breath.

"1368 Hurst Road."

"That's here in Pikeville?"

"That's right." Loyce pulled himself up with a violent effort. "Listen to me. Back there. In the square. Hanging from the lamppost — "

"Where were you today?" the cop behind the wheel demanded.

"Where?" Loyce echoed.

"You weren't in your shop, were you?"

"No." He shook his head. "No, I was home. Down in the basement."

"In the *basement?*"

"Digging. A new foundation. Getting out the dirt to pour a cement frame. Why? What has that to do with — "

"Was anybody else down there with you?"

"No. My wife was downtown. My kids were at school." Loyce looked from one heavy-set cop to the other. Hope flickered across his face, wild hope. "You mean because I was down there I missed — the explanation? I didn't get in on it? Like everybody else?"

After a pause the cop with the notebook said: "That's right. You missed the explanation."

"Then it's official? The body — it's *supposed* to be hanging there?"

"It's supposed to be hanging there. For everybody to see."

Ed Loyce grinned weakly. "Good Lord. I guess I sort of went off the deep end. I thought maybe something had happened. You know, something like the Ku Klux Klan. Some kind of violence. Communists or Fascists taking over." He wiped his face with his breast-pocket handkerchief, his hands shaking. "I'm glad to know it's on the level."

"It's on the level." The police car was getting near the Hall of Justice. The sun had set. The streets were gloomy and dark. The lights had not yet come on.

"I feel better," Loyce said. "I was pretty excited there, for a minute. I guess I got all stirred up. Now that I understand, there's no need to take me in, is there?"

The two cops said nothing.

"I should be back at my store. The boys haven't had dinner. I'm all right, now. No more trouble. Is there any need of — "

"This won't take long," the cop behind the wheel interrupted. "A short process. Only a few minutes."

"I hope it's short," Loyce muttered. The car slowed down for a stoplight. "I guess I sort of disturbed the peace. Funny, getting excited like that and — "

Loyce yanked the door open. He sprawled out into the street and rolled to his feet. Cars were moving all around him, gaining speed as the light changed. Loyce leaped onto the curb and raced among the people, burrowing into the swarming crowds. Behind him he heard sounds, shouts, people running.

They weren't cops. He had realized that right away. He knew every cop in Pikeville. A man couldn't own a store, operate a business in a small town for twenty-five years without getting to know all the cops.

They weren't cops — and there hadn't been any explanation. Potter, Fergusson, Jenkins, none of them knew why it was there. They didn't know — and they didn't care. *That* was the strange part.

Loyce ducked into a hardware store. He raced toward the back, past the startled clerks and customers, into the shipping room and through the back door. He tripped over a garbage can and ran up a flight of concrete steps. He climbed over a fence and jumped down on the other side, gasping and panting.

There was no sound behind him. He had got away.

He was at the entrance of an alley, dark and strewn with boards and ruined boxes and tires. He could see the street at the far end. A street light wavered and came on. Men and women. Stores. Neon signs. Cars.

And to his right — the police station.

He was close, terribly close. Past the loading platform of a grocery store rose the white concrete side of the Hall of Justice. Barred windows. The police antenna. A great concrete wall rising up in the darkness. A bad place for him to be near. He was too close. He had to keep moving, get farther away from them.

Them?

Loyce moved cautiously down the alley. Beyond the police station was the City Hall, the old-fashioned yellow structure of wood and gilded brass and broad cement steps. He could see the endless rows of offices, dark windows, the cedars and beds of flowers on each side of the entrance.

And — something else.

Above the City Hall was a patch of darkness, a cone of gloom denser than the surrounding night. A prism of black that spread out and was lost into the sky.

He listened. Good God, he could hear something. Something that made him struggle frantically to close his ears, his mind, to shut out the sound. A buzzing. A distant, muted hum like a great swarm of bees.

Loyce gazed up, rigid with horror. The splotch of darkness, hanging over the City Hall. Darkness so thick it seemed almost solid. *In the vortex something moved.* Flickering shapes. Things, descending from the sky, pausing momentarily above the City Hall, fluttering over it in a dense swarm and then dropping silently onto the roof.

Shapes. Fluttering shapes from the sky. From the crack of darkness that hung above him.

He was seeing — them.

For a long time Loyce watched, crouched behind a sagging fence in a pool of scummy water.

They were landing. Coming down in groups, landing on the roof of the City Hall and disappearing inside. They had wings. Like giant insects of some kind. They flew and fluttered and came to rest — and then crawled crab-fashion, sideways, across the roof and into the building.

He was sickened. And fascinated. Cold night wind blew around him and he shuddered. He was tired, dazed with shock. On the front steps of the City Hall were men, standing here and there. Groups of men coming out of the building and halting for a moment before going on.

Were there more of them?

It didn't seem possible. What he saw descending from the black chasm weren't men. They were alien — from some other world, some other dimension. Sliding through this slit, this break in the shell of the universe. Entering through this gap, winged insects from another realm of being.

On the steps of the City Hall a group of men broke up. A few moved toward a waiting car. One of the remaining shapes started to re-enter the City Hall. It changed its mind and turned to follow the others.

Loyce closed his eyes in horror. His senses reeled. He hung on tight, clutching at the sagging fence. The shape, the man-shape, had abruptly fluttered up and flapped after the others. It flew to the sidewalk and came to rest among them.

Pseudo-men. Imitation men. Insects with ability to disguise themselves as men. Like other insects familiar to Earth. Protective coloration. Mimicry.

Loyce pulled himself away. He got slowly to his feet. It was night. The alley was totally dark. But maybe they could see in the dark. Maybe darkness made no difference to them.

He left the alley cautiously and moved out onto the street. Men and women flowed past, but not so many, now. At the bus stops stood waiting groups. A huge bus lumbered along the street, its lights flashing in the evening gloom.

Loyce moved forward. He pushed his way among those waiting and when the bus halted he boarded it and took a seat in the rear, by the door. A moment later the bus moved into life and rumbled down the street.

Loyce relaxed a little. He studied the people around him. Dulled, tired faces. People going home from work. Quite ordinary faces. None of them paid any attention to him. All sat quietly, sunk down in their seats, jiggling with the motion of the bus.

The man sitting next to him unfolded a newspaper. He began to read the sports section, his lips moving. An ordinary man. Blue suit. Tie. A businessman, or a salesman. On his way home to his wife and family.

Across the aisle a young woman, perhaps twenty. Dark eyes and hair, a package on her lap. Nylons and heels. Red coat and white Angora sweater. Gazing absently ahead of her.

A high school boy in jeans and black jacket.

A great triple-chinned woman with an immense shopping bag loaded with packages and parcels. Her thick face dim with weariness.

Ordinary people. The kind that rode the bus every evening. Going home to their families. To dinner.

Going home — with their minds dead. Controlled, filmed over with the mask of an alien being that had appeared and taken possession of them, their town, their lives. Himself, too. Except that he happened to be deep in his cellar instead of in the store. Somehow, he had been overlooked. They had missed him. Their control wasn't perfect, foolproof.

Maybe there were others.

Hope flickered in Loyce. They weren't omnipotent. They had made a mistake, not got control of him. Their net, their field of control, had passed over him. He had emerged from his cellar as he had gone down. Apparently their power-zone was limited.

A few seats down the aisle a man was watching him. Loyce broke off his chain of thought. A slender man, with dark hair and a small mustache. Well-dressed, brown suit and shiny shoes. A book between his small hands. He was watching Loyce, studying him intently. He turned quickly away.

Loyce tensed. One of *them?* Or — another they had missed?

The man was watching him again. Small dark eyes, alive and clever. Shrewd. A man too shrewd for them — or one of the things itself, an alien insect from beyond.

The bus halted. An elderly man got on slowly and dropped his token into the box. He moved down the aisle and took a seat opposite Loyce.

The elderly man caught the sharp-eyed man's gaze. For a split second something passed between them.

A look rich with meaning.

Loyce got to his feet. The bus was moving. He ran to the door. One step down into the well. He yanked the emergency door release. The rubber door swung open.

"Hey!" the driver shouted, jamming on the brakes. "What the hell — ?"

Loyce squirmed through. The bus was slowing down. Houses on all sides. A residential district, lawns and tall apartment buildings. Behind him, the bright-eyed man had leaped up. The elderly man was also on his feet. They were coming after him.

Loyce leaped. He hit the pavement with terrific force and rolled against the curb. Pain lapped over him. Pain and a vast tide of blackness. Desperately, he fought it off. He struggled to his knees and then slid down again. The bus had stopped. People were getting off.

Loyce groped around. His fingers closed over something. A rock, lying in the gutter. He crawled to his feet, grunting with pain. A shape loomed before him. A man, the bright-eyed man with the book.

Loyce kicked. The man gasped and fell. Loyce brought the rock down. The man screamed and tried to roll away. "*Stop!* For God's sake listen — "

He struck again. A hideous crunching sound. The man's voice cut off and dissolved in a bubbling wail. Loyce scrambled up and back. The others were there, now. All around him. He ran, awkwardly, down the sidewalk, up a driveway. None of them followed him. They had stopped and were bending over the inert body of the man with the book, the bright-eyed man who had come after him.

Had he made a mistake?

But it was too late to worry about that. He had to get out — away from them. Out of Pikeville, beyond the crack of darkness, the rent between their world and his.

"Ed!" Janet Loyce backed away nervously. "What is it? What — "

Ed Loyce slammed the door behind him and came into the living room. "Pull down the shades. Quick."

Janet moved toward the window. "But — "

"Do as I say. Who else is here besides you?"

"Nobody. Just the twins. They're upstairs in their room. What's happened? You look so strange. Why are you home?"

Ed locked the front door. He prowled around the house, into the kitchen. From the drawer under the sink he slid out the big butcher knife and ran his finger along it. Sharp. Plenty sharp. He returned to the living room.

"Listen to me," he said. "I don't have much time. They know I escaped and they'll be looking for me."

"Escaped?" Janet's face twisted with bewilderment and fear. "Who?"

"The town has been taken over. They're in control. I've got it pretty well figured out. They started at the top, at the City Hall and police department. What they did with the *real* humans they — "

"What are you talking about?"

"We've been invaded. From some other universe, some other dimension. They're insects. Mimicry. And more. Power to control minds. Your mind."

"My mind?"

"Their entrance is *here*, in Pikeville. They've taken over all of you. The whole town — except me. We're up against an incredibly powerful enemy, but they have their limitations. That's our hope. They're limited! They can make mistakes!"

Janet shook her head. "I don't understand, Ed. You must be insane."

"Insane? No. Just lucky. If I hadn't been down in the basement I'd be like all the rest of you." Loyce peered out the window. "But I can't stand here talking. Get your coat."

"My coat?"

"We're getting out of here. Out of Pikeville. We've got to get help. Fight this thing. They *can* be beaten. They're not infallible. It's going to be close — but we may make it if we hurry. Come on!" He grabbed her arm roughly. "Get your coat and call the twins. We're all leaving. Don't stop to pack. There's no time for that."

White-faced, his wife moved toward the closet and got down her coat. "Where are we going?"

Ed pulled open the desk drawer and spilled the contents out onto the floor. He grabbed up a road map and spread it open. "They'll have the highway covered, of course. But there's a back road. To Oak Grove. I got onto it once. It's practically abandoned. Maybe they'll forget about it."

"The old Ranch Road? Good Lord — it's completely closed. Nobody's supposed to drive over it."

"I know." Ed thrust the map grimly into his coat. "That's our best chance. Now call down the twins and let's get going. Your car is full of gas, isn't it?"

Janet was dazed.

"The Chevy? I had it filled up yesterday afternoon." Janet moved toward the stairs. "Ed, I — "

"Call the twins!" Ed unlocked the front door and peered out. Nothing stirred. No sign of life. All right so far.

"Come on downstairs," Janet called in a wavering voice. "We're — going out for a while."

"Now?" Tommy's voice came.

"Hurry up," Ed barked. "Get down here, both of you."

Tommy appeared at the top of the stairs. "I was doing my homework. We're starting fractions. Miss Parker says if we don't get this done — "

"You can forget about fractions." Ed grabbed his son as he came down the stairs and propelled him toward the door. "Where's Jim?"

"He's coming."

Jim started slowly down the stairs. "What's up, Dad?"

"We're going for a ride."

"A ride? Where?"

Ed turned to Janet. "We'll leave the lights on. And the TV set. Go turn it on." He pushed her toward the set. "So they'll think we're still — "

He heard the buzz. And dropped instantly, the long butcher knife out. Sickened, he saw it coming down the stairs at him, wings a blur of motion as it aimed itself. It still bore a vague resemblance to Jimmy. It was small, a baby one. A brief glimpse — the thing hurtling at him, cold, multi-lensed inhuman eyes. Wings, body still clothed in yellow T-shirt and jeans, the mimic outline still stamped on it. A strange half-turn of its body as it reached him. What was it doing?

A stinger.

Loyce stabbed wildly at it. It retreated, buzzing frantically. Loyce rolled and crawled toward the door. Tommy and Janet stood still as statues, faces blank. Watching without expression. Loyce stabbed again. This time the knife connected. The thing shrieked and faltered. It bounced against the wall and fluttered down.

Something lapped through his mind. A wall of force, energy, an alien mind probing into him. He was suddenly paralyzed. The mind entered his own, touched against him briefly, shockingly. An utter alien presence, settling over him — and then it flickered out as the thing collapsed in a broken heap on the rug.

It was dead. He turned it over with his foot. It was an insect, a fly of some kind. Yellow T-shirt, jeans. His son Jimmy . . . He closed his mind tight. It was too late to think about that. Savagely he scooped up his knife and headed toward the door. Janet and Tommy stood stone-still, neither of them moving.

The car was out. He'd never get through. They'd be waiting for him. It was ten miles on foot. Ten long miles over rough ground, gulleys and open fields and hills of uncut forest. He'd have to go alone.

Loyce opened the door. For a brief second he looked back at his wife and son. Then he slammed the door behind him and raced down the porch steps.

A moment later he was on his way, hurrying swiftly through the darkness toward the edge of town.

The early morning sunlight was blinding. Loyce halted, gasping for breath, swaying back and forth. Sweat ran down in his eyes. His clothing was torn, shredded by the brush and thorns through which he had crawled. Ten miles — on his hands and knees. Crawling, creeping through the night. His shoes were mud-caked. He was scratched and limping, utterly exhausted.

But ahead of him lay Oak Grove.

He took a deep breath and started down the hill. Twice he stumbled and fell, picking himself up and trudging on. His ears rang. Everything receded and wavered. But he was there. He had got out, away from Pikeville.

A farmer in a field gaped at him. From a house a young woman watched in wonder. Loyce reached the road and turned onto it. Ahead of him was a gasoline station and a drive-in. A couple of trucks, some chickens pecking in the dirt, a dog tied with a string.

The white-clad attendant watched suspiciously as he dragged himself up to the station. "Thank God." He caught hold of the wall. "I didn't think I was going to make it. They followed me most of the way. I could hear them buzzing. Buzzing and flitting around behind me."

"What happened?" the attendant demanded. "You in a wreck? A hold-up?"

Loyce shook his head wearily. "They have the whole town. The City Hall and the police station. They hung a man from the lamppcst. That was the first thing I saw. They've got all the roads blocked. I saw them hovering over the cars coming in. About four this morning I got beyond them. I knew it right away. I could feel them leave. And then the sun came up."

The attendant licked his lip nervously. "You're out of your head. I better get a doctor."

"Get me into Oak Grove," Loyce gasped. He sank down on the gravel. "We've got to get started — cleaning them out. Got to get started right away."

They kept a tape recorder going all the time he talked. When he had finished the Commissioner snapped off the recorder and got to his feet. He stood for a moment, deep in thought. Finally he got out his cigarettes and lit up slowly, a frown on his beefy face.

"You don't believe me," Loyce said.

The Commissioner offered him a cigarette. Loyce pushed it impatiently away. "Suit yourself." The Commissioner moved over to the window and stood for a time looking out at the town of Oak Grove. "I believe you," he said abruptly.

Loyce sagged. "Thank God."

"So you got away." The Commissioner shook his head. "You were down in your cellar instead of at work. A freak chance. One in a million."

Loyce sipped some of the black coffee they had brought him. "I have a theory," he murmured.

"What is it?"

"About them. Who they are. They take over one area at a time. Starting at the top — the highest level of authority. Working down from there in a widening circle. When they're firmly in control they go on to the next town. They spread, slowly, very gradually. I think it's been going on for a long time."

"A long time?"

"Thousands of years. I don't think it's new."

"Why do you say that?"

"When I was a kid ... A picture they showed us in Bible League. A religious picture — an old print. The enemy gods, defeated by Jehovah. Moloch, Beelzebub, Moab, Baalin, Ashtaroth — "

"So?"

"They were all represented by figures." Loyce looked up at the Commissioner. "Beelzebub was represented as — a giant fly."

The Commissioner grunted. "An old struggle."

"They've been defeated. The Bible is an account of their defeats. They make gains — but finally they're defeated."

"Why defeated?"

"They can't get everyone. They didn't get me. And they never got the Hebrews. The Hebrews carried the message to the whole world. The realization of the danger. The two men on the bus. I think they understood. Had escaped, like I did." He clenched his fists. "I killed one of them. I made a mistake. I was afraid to take a chance."

The Commissioner nodded. "Yes, they undoubtedly had escaped, as you did. Freak accidents. But the rest of the town was firmly in control." He turned from the window, "Well, Mr. Loyce. You seem to have figured everything out."

"Not everything. The hanging man. The dead man hanging from the lamppost. I don't understand that. *Why?* Why did they deliberately hang him there?"

"That would seem simple." The Commissioner smiled faintly. "*Bait.*"

Loyce stiffened. His heart stopped beating. "Bait? What do you mean?"

"To draw you out. Make you declare yourself. So they'd know who was under control — and who had escaped."

Loyce recoiled with horror. "Then they *expected* failures! They anticipated — " He broke off. "They were ready with a trap."

"And you showed yourself. You reacted. You made yourself known." The Commissioner abruptly moved toward the door. "Come along, Loyce. There's a lot to do. We must get moving. There's no time to waste."

Loyce started slowly to his feet, numbed. "And the man. *Who was the man?* I never saw him before. He wasn't a local man. He was a stranger. All muddy and dirty, his face cut, slashed — "

There was a strange look on the Commissioner's face as he answered, "Maybe," he said softly, "you'll understand that, too. Come along with me, Mr. Loyce." He held the door open, his eyes gleaming. Loyce caught a glimpse of the street in front of the police station. Policemen, a platform of some sort. A telephone pole — and a rope! "Right this way," the Commissioner said, smiling coldly.

As the sun set, the vice-president of the Oak Grove Merchants' Bank came up out of the vault, threw the heavy time locks, put on his hat and coat, and hurried outside onto the sidewalk. Only a few people were there, hurrying home to dinner.

"Good night," the guard said, locking the door after him.

"Good night," Clarence Mason murmured. He started along the street toward his car. He was tired. He had been working all day down in the vault, examining the lay-out of the safety deposit boxes to see if there was room for another tier. He was glad to be finished.

At the corner he halted. The street lights had not yet come on. The street was dim. Everything was vague. He looked around — and froze.

From the telephone pole in front of the police station, something large and shapeless hung. It moved a little with the wind.

What the hell was it?

Mason approached it warily. He wanted to get home. He was tired and hungry. He thought of his wife, his kids, a hot meal on the dinner table. But there was something about the dark bundle, something ominous and ugly.

The light was bad; he couldn't tell what it was. Yet it drew him on, made him move closer for a better look. The shapeless thing made him uneasy. He was frightened by it. Frightened — and fascinated.

And the strange part was that nobody else seemed to notice it.

THE EYES HAVE IT

IT WAS QUITE BY ACCIDENT I discovered this incredible invasion of Earth by lifeforms from another planet. As yet, I haven't done anything about it; I can't think of anything to do. I wrote to the Government, and they sent back a pamphlet on the repair and maintenance of frame houses. Anyhow, the whole thing is known; I'm not the first to discover it. Maybe it's even under control.

I was sitting in my easy-chair, idly turning the pages of a paperbacked book someone had left on the bus, when I came across the reference that first put me on the trail. For a moment I didn't respond. It took some time for the full import to sink in. After I'd comprehended, it seemed odd I hadn't noticed it right away.

The reference was clearly to a nonhuman species of incredible properties, not indigenous to Earth. A species, I hasten to point out, customarily masquerading as ordinary human beings. Their disguise, however, became transparent in the face of the following observations by the author. It was at once obvious the author knew everything. Knew everything — and was taking it in his stride. The line (and I tremble remembering it even now) read:

... his eyes slowly roved about the room.

Vague chills assailed me. I tried to picture the eyes. Did they roll like dimes? The passage indicated not; they seemed to move through the air, not over the surface. Rather rapidly, apparently. No one in the story was surprised. That's what tipped me off. No sign of amazement at such an outrageous thing. Later the matter was amplified.

... his eyes moved from person to person.

There it was in a nutshell. The eyes had clearly come apart from the rest of him and were on their own. My heart pounded and my breath choked in my windpipe. I had stumbled on an accidental mention of a totally unfamiliar race. Obviously non-Terrestrial. Yet, to the characters in the book, it was perfectly natural — which suggested they belonged to the same species.

And the author? A slow suspicion burned in my mind. The author was taking it rather *too easily* in his stride. Evidently, he felt this was quite a usual thing. He made absolutely no attempt to conceal this knowledge. The story continued:

... *presently his eyes fastened on Julia.*

Julia, being a lady, had at least the breeding to feel indignant. She is described as blushing and knitting her brows angrily. At this, I sighed with relief. They weren't *all* non-Terrestrials. The narrative continues:

... *slowly, calmly, his eyes examined every inch of her.*

Great Scott! But here the girl turned and stomped off and the matter ended. I lay back in my chair gasping with horror. My wife and family regarded me in wonder.

"What's wrong, dear?" my wife asked.

I couldn't tell her. Knowledge like this was too much for the ordinary run-of-the-mill person. I had to keep it to myself. "Nothing," I gasped. I leaped up, snatched the book, and hurried out of the room.

In the garage, I continued reading. There was more. Trembling, I read the next revealing passage:

... *he put his arm around Julia. Presently she asked him if he would remove his arm. He immediately did so, with a smile.*

It's not said what was done with the arm after the fellow had removed it. Maybe it was left standing upright in the corner. Maybe it was thrown away. I don't care. In any case, the full meaning was there, staring me right in the face.

Here was a race of creatures capable of removing portions of their anatomy at will. Eyes, arms — and maybe more. Without batting an eyelash. My knowledge of biology came in handy, at this point. Obviously they were simple beings, uni-cellular, some sort of primitive single-celled things. Beings no more developed than starfish. Starfish can do the same thing, you know.

I read on. And came to this incredible revelation, tossed off coolly by the author without the faintest tremor:

... *outside the movie theater we split up. Part of us went inside, part over to the cafe for dinner.*

Binary fission, obviously. Splitting in half and forming two entities. Probably each lower half went to the cafe, it being farther, and the upper halves to the movies. I read on, hands shaking. I had really stumbled onto something here. My mind reeled as I made out this passage:

... *I'm afraid there's no doubt about it. Poor Bibney has lost his head again.*

Which was followed by:

... *and Bob says he has utterly no guts.*

Yet Bibney got around as well as the next person. The next person, however, was just as strange. He was soon described as:

... totally lacking in brains.

There was no doubt of the thing in the next passage. Julia, whom I had thought to be the one normal person, reveals herself as also being an alien lifeform, similar to the rest:

... quite deliberately, Julia had given her heart to the young man.

It didn't relate what the final disposition of the organ was, but I didn't really care. It was evident Julia had gone right on living in her usual manner, like all the others in the book. Without heart, arms, eyes, brains, viscera, dividing up in two when the occasion demanded. Without a qualm.

... thereupon she gave him her hand.

I sickened. The rascal now had her hand, as well as her heart. I shudder to think what he's done with them, by this time.

... he took her arm.

Not content to wait, he had to start dismantling her on his own. Flushing crimson, I slammed the book shut and leaped to my feet. But not in time to escape one last reference to those carefree bits of anatomy whose travels had originally thrown me on the track:

... her eyes followed him all the way down the road and across the meadow.

I rushed from the garage and back inside the warm house, as if the accursed things were following *me*. My wife and children were playing Monopoly in the kitchen. I joined them and played with frantic fervor, brow feverish, teeth chattering.

I had had enough of the thing. I want to hear no more about it. Let them come on. Let them invade Earth. I don't want to get mixed up in it.

I have absolutely no stomach for it.

The Golden Man

"Is it always hot like this?" the salesman demanded. He addressed everybody at the lunch counter and in the shabby booths against the wall. A middle-aged fat man with a good-natured smile, rumpled gray suit, sweat-stained white shirt, a drooping bowtie, and a Panama hat.

"Only in the summer," the waitress answered.

None of the others stirred. The teen-age boy and girl in one of the booths, eyes fixed intently on each other. Two workmen, sleeves rolled up, arms dark and hairy, eating bean soup and rolls. A lean, weathered farmer. An elderly businessman in a blue-serge suit, vest and pocket watch. A dark rat-faced cab driver drinking coffee. A tired woman who had come in to get off her feet and put down her bundles.

The salesman got out a package of cigarettes. He glanced curiously around the dingy cafe, lit up, leaned his arms on the counter, and said to the man next to him: "What's the name of this town?"

The man grunted. "Walnut Creek."

The salesman sipped at his coke for a while, cigarette held loosely between plump white fingers. Presently he reached in his coat and brought out a leather wallet. For a long time he leafed thoughtfully through cards and papers, bits of notes, ticket stubs, endless odds and ends, soiled fragments — and finally a photograph.

He grinned at the photograph, and then began to chuckle, a low moist rasp. "Look at this," he said to the man beside him.

The man went on reading his newspaper.

"Hey, look at this." The salesman nudged him with his elbow and pushed the photograph at him. "How's that strike you?"

Annoyed, the man glanced briefly at the the photograph. It showed a nude woman, from the waist up. Perhaps thirty-five years old. Face turned away. Body white and flabby. With eight breasts.

"Ever seen anything like that?" the salesman chuckled, his little red eyes dancing. His face broke into lewd smiles and again he nudged the man.

"I've seen that before." Disgusted, the man resumed reading his newspaper.

The salesman noticed the lean old farmer was looking at the picture. He passed it genially over to him. "How's that strike you, pop? Pretty good stuff, eh?"

The farmer examined the picture solemnly. He turned it over, studied the creased back, took a second look at the front, then tossed it to the salesman. It slid from the counter, turned over a couple of times, and fell to the floor face up.

The salesman picked it up and brushed it off. Carefully, almost tenderly, he restored it to his wallet. The waitress's eyes flickered as she caught a glimpse of it.

"Damn nice," the salesman observed, with a wink. "Wouldn't you say so?"

The waitress shrugged indifferently. "I don't know. I saw a lot of them around Denver. A whole colony."

"That's where this was taken. Denver DCA Camp."

"Any still alive?" the farmer asked.

The salesman laughed harshly. "You kidding?" He made a short, sharp swipe with his hand. "Not any more."

They were all listening. Even the high school kids in the booth had stopped holding hands and were sitting up straight, eyes wide with fascination.

"Saw a funny kind down near San Diego," the farmer said. "Last year, some time. Had wings like a bat. Skin, not feathers. Skin and bone wings."

The rat-eyed taxi driver chimed in. "That's nothing. There was a two-headed one in Detroit. I saw it on exhibit."

"Was it alive?" the waitress asked.

"No. They'd already euthed it."

"In sociology," the high school boy spoke up, "we saw tapes of a whole lot of them. The winged kind from down south, the big-headed one they found in Germany, an awful-looking one with sort of cones, like an insect. And — "

"The worst of all," the elderly businessman stated, "are those English ones. That hid out in the coal mines. The ones they didn't find until last year." He shook his head. "Forty years, down there in the mines, breeding and developing. Almost a hundred of them. Survivors from a group that went underground during the War."

"They just found a new kind in Sweden," the waitress said. "I was reading about it. Controls minds at a distance, they said. Only a couple of them. The DCA got there plenty fast."

"That's a variation of the New Zealand type," one of the workmen said. "It read minds."

"Reading and controlling are two different things," the businessman said. "When I hear something like that I'm plenty glad there's the DCA."

"There was a type they found right after the War," the farmer said. "In Siberia. Had the ability to control objects. Psychokinetic ability. The Soviet DCA got it right away. Nobody remembers that any more."

"I remember that," the businessman said. "I was just a kid, then. I remember because that was the first deeve I ever heard of. My father called me into the living room and told me and my brothers and sisters. We were still building the house. That was in the days when the DCA inspected everyone and stamped their arms." He held up his thin, gnarled wrist. "I was stamped there, sixty years ago."

"Now they just have the birth inspection," the waitress said. She shivered. "There was one in San Francisco this month. First in over a year. They thought it was over, around here."

"It's been dwindling," the taxi driver said. "Frisco wasn't too bad hit. Not like some. Not like Detroit."

"They still get ten or fifteen a year in Detroit," the high school boy said. "All around there. Lots of pools still left. People go into them, in spite of the robot signs."

"What kind was this one?" the salesman asked. "The one they found in San Francisco."

The waitress gestured. "Common type. The kind with no toes. Bent-over. Big eyes."

"The nocturnal type," the salesman said.

"The mother had hid it. They say it was three years old. She got the doctor to forge the DCA chit. Old friend of the family."

The salesman had finished his coke. He sat playing idly with his cigarettes, listening to the hum of talk he had set into motion. The high school boy was leaning excitedly toward the girl across from him, impressing her with his fund of knowledge. The lean farmer and the businessman were huddled together, remembering the old days, the last years of the War, before the first Ten-Year Reconstruction Plan. The taxi driver and the two workmen were swapping yarns about their own experiences.

The salesman caught the waitress's attention. "I guess," he said thoughtfully, "that one in Frisco caused quite a stir. Something like that happening so close."

"Yeah," the waitress murmured.

"This side of the Bay wasn't really hit," the salesman continued. "You never get any of them over here."

"No." The waitress moved abruptly. "None in this area. Ever." She scooped up dirty dishes from the counter and headed toward the back.

"Never?" the salesman asked, surprised. "You've never had any deeves on this side of the Bay?"

"No. None." She disappeared into the back, where the fry cook stood by his burners, white apron and tattooed wrists. Her voice was a little too loud, a little too harsh and strained. It made the farmer pause suddenly and glance up.

Silence dropped like a curtain. All sound cut off instantly. They were all gazing down at their food, suddenly tense and ominous.

"None around here," the taxi driver said, loudly and clearly, to no one in particular. "None ever."

"Sure," the salesman agreed genially. "I was only — "

"Make sure you get that straight," one of the workmen said.

The salesman blinked. "Sure, buddy. Sure." He fumbled nervously in his pocket. A quarter and a dime jangled to the floor and he hurriedly scooped them up. "No offense."

For a moment there was silence. Then the high school boy spoke up, aware for the first time that nobody was saying anything. "I heard something," he began eagerly, voice full of importance. "Somebody said they saw something up by the Johnson farm that looked like it was one of those — "

"Shut up," the businessman said, without turning his head.

Scarlet-faced, the boy sagged in his seat. His voice wavered and broke off. He peered hastily down at his hands and swallowed unhappily.

The salesman paid the waitress for his coke. "What's the quickest road to Frisco?" he began. But the waitress had already turned her back.

The people at the counter were immersed in their food. None of them looked up. They ate in frozen silence. Hostile, unfriendly faces, intent on their food.

The salesman picked up his bulging briefcase, pushed open the screen door, and stepped out into the blazing sunlight. He moved toward his battered 1978 Buick, parked a few meters up. A blue-shirted traffic cop was standing in the shade of an awning, talking languidly to a young woman in a yellow silk dress that clung moistly to her slim body.

The salesman paused a moment before he got into his car. He waved his hand and hailed the policeman. "Say, you know this town pretty good?"

The policeman eyed the salesman's rumpled gray suit, bowtie, his sweat-stained shirt. The out-of-state license. "What do you want?"

"I'm looking for the Johnson farm," the salesman said. "Here to see him about some litigation." He moved toward the policeman, a small white card between his fingers. "I'm his attorney — from the New York Guild. Can you tell me how to get out there? I haven't been through here in a couple of years."

Nat Johnson gazed up at the noonday sun and saw that it was good. He sat sprawled out on the bottom step of the porch, a pipe between his yellowed teeth, a lithe, wiry man in red-checkered shirt and canvas jeans, powerful hands, iron-gray hair that was still thick despite sixty-five years of active life.

He was watching the children play. Jean rushed laughing in front of him, bosom heaving under her sweatshirt, black hair streaming behind her. She was sixteen, bright-eyed, legs strong and straight, slim young body bent slightly forward with the weight of the two horseshoes. After her scampered Dave, fourteen, white teeth and black hair, a handsome boy, a son to be proud of. Dave caught up with his sister, passed her, and reached the far peg. He stood waiting, legs apart, hands on his hips, his two horseshoes gripped easily. Gasping, Jean hurried toward him.

"Go ahead!" Dave shouted. "You shoot first. I'm waiting for you."

"So you can knock them away?"

"So I can knock them closer."

Jean tossed down one horseshoe and gripped the other with both hands, eyes on the distant peg. Her lithe body bent, one leg slid back, her spine arched. She took careful aim, closed one eye, and then expertly tossed the shoe. With a clang the shoe struck the distant peg, circled briefly around it, then bounced off again and rolled to one side. A cloud of dust rolled up.

"Not bad," Nat Johnson admitted, from his step. "Too hard, though. Take it easy." His chest swelled with pride as the girl's glistening body took aim and again threw. Two powerful, handsome children, almost ripe, on the verge of adulthood. Playing together in the hot sun.

And there was Cris.

Cris stood by the porch, arms folded. He wasn't playing. He was watching. He had stood there since Dave and Jean had begun playing, the same half-intent, half-remote expression on his finely-cut face. As if he were seeing past them, beyond the two of them. Beyond the field, the barn, the creek bed, the rows of cedars.

"Come on, Cris!" Jean called, as she and Dave moved across the field to collect their horseshoes. "Don't you want to play?"

No, Cris didn't want to play. He never played. He was off in a world of his own, a world into which none of them could come. He never joined in anything, games or chores or family activities. He was by himself always. Remote, detached, aloof. Seeing past everyone and everything — that is, until all at once something clicked and he momentarily rephased, reentered their world briefly.

Nat Johnson reached out and knocked his pipe against the step. He refilled it from his leather tobacco pouch, his eyes on his eldest son. Cris was now moving into life. Heading out onto the field. He walked slowly, arms folded calmly, as if he had, for the moment, descended from his own world into theirs. Jean didn't see him; she had turned her back and was getting ready to pitch.

"Hey," Dave said, startled. "Here's Cris."

Cris reached his sister, stopped, and held out his hand. A great dignified figure, calm and impassive. Uncertainly, Jean gave him one of the horseshoes. "You want this? You want to play?"

Cris said nothing. He bent slightly, a supple arc of his incredibly graceful body, then moved his arm in a blur of speed. The shoe sailed, struck the far peg, and dizzily spun around it. Ringer.

The corners of Dave's mouth turned down. "What a lousy darn thing."

"Cris," Jean reproved. "You don't play fair."

No, Cris didn't play fair. He had watched half an hour — then come out and thrown once. One perfect toss, one dead ringer.

"He never makes a mistake," Dave complained.

Cris stood, face blank. A golden statue in the mid-day sun. Golden hair, skin, a light down of gold fuzz on his bare arms and legs —

Abruptly he stiffened. Nat sat up, startled. "What is it?" he barked.

Cris turned in a quick circle, magnificent body alert. "Cris!" Jean demanded. "What — "

Cris shot forward. Like a released energy beam he bounded across the field, over the fence, into the barn and out the other side. His flying figure seemed to skim over the dry grass as he descended into the barren creek bed, between the cedars. A momentary flash of gold — and he was gone. Vanished. There was no sound. No motion. He had utterly melted into the scenery.

"What was it this time?" Jean asked wearily. She came over to her father and threw herself down in the shade. Sweat glowed on her smooth neck and upper lip; her sweat shirt was streaked and damp. "What did he see?"

"He was after something," Dave stated, coming up.

Nat grunted. "Maybe. There's no telling."

"I guess I better tell Mom not to set a place for him," Jean said. "He probably won't be back."

Anger and futility descended over Nat Johnson. No, he wouldn't be back. Not for dinner and probably not the next day — or the one after that. He'd be gone God only knew how long. Or where. Or why. Off by himself, alone some place. "If I thought there was any use," Nat began, "I'd send you two after him. But there's no — "

He broke off. A car was coming up the dirt road toward the farmhouse. A dusty, battered old Buick. Behind the wheel sat a plump red-faced man in a gray suit, who waved cheerfully at them as the car sputtered to a stop and the motor died into silence.

"Afternoon," the man nodded, as he climbed out the car. He tipped his hat pleasantly. He was middle-aged, genial-looking, perspiring freely as he crossed the dry ground toward the porch. "Maybe you folks can help me."

"What do you want?" Nat Johnson demanded hoarsely. He was frightened. He watched the creek bed out of the corner of his eye, praying silently. God, if only he *stayed* away. Jean was breathing quickly, sharp little gasps. She was terrified. Dave's face was expressionless, but all color had drained from it. "Who are you?" Nat demanded.

"Name's Baines. George Baines." The man held out his hand but Johnson ignored it. "Maybe you've heard of me. I own the Pacifica Development Corporation. We built all those little bomb-proof houses just outside town. Those little round ones you see as you come up the main highway from Lafayette."

"What do you want?" Johnson held his hands steady with an effort. He'd never heard of the man, although he'd noticed the housing tract. It couldn't be missed — a great ant-heap of ugly pill-boxes straddling the highway. Baines looked like the kind of man who'd own them. But what did he want here?

"I've bought some land up this way," Baines was explaining. He rattled a sheaf of crisp papers. "This is the deed, but I'll be damned if I can find it." He grinned good-naturedly. "I know it's around this way, someplace, this side of the State road. According to the clerk at the County Recorder's Office, a mile or so this side of that hill over there. But I'm no damn good at reading maps."

"It isn't around here," Dave broke in. "There's only farms around here. Nothing for sale."

"This is a farm, son," Baines said genially. "I bought it for myself and my missus. So we could settle down." He wrinkled his pug nose. "Don't get the wrong idea — I'm not putting up any tracts around here. This is strictly for myself. An old farmhouse, twenty acres, a pump and a few oak trees — "

"Let me see the deed." Johnson grabbed the sheaf of papers, and while Baines blinked in astonishment, he leafed rapidly through them. His face hardened and he handed them back. "What are you up to? This deed is for a parcel fifty miles from here."

"Fifty miles!" Baines was dumbfounded. "No kidding? But the clerk told me — "

Johnson was on his feet. He towered over the fat man. He was in top-notch physical shape — and he was plenty damn suspicious. "Clerk, hell. You get back into your car and drive out of here. I don't know what you're after, or what you're here for, but I want you off my land."

In Johnson's massive fist something sparkled. A metal tube that gleamed ominously in the mid-day sunlight. Baines saw it — and gulped. "No offense, mister." He backed nervously away. "You folks sure are touchy. Take it easy, will you?"

Johnson said nothing. He gripped the lash-tube tighter and waited for the fat man to leave.

But Baines lingered. "Look, buddy. I've been driving around this furnace five hours, looking for my damn place. Any objection to my using your — facilities?"

Johnson eyed him with suspicion. Gradually the suspicion turned to disgust. He shrugged. "Dave, show him where the bathroom is."

"Thanks." Baines grinned thankfully. "And if it wouldn't be too much trouble, maybe a glass of water. I'd be glad to pay you for it." He chuckled knowingly. "Never let the city people get away with anything, eh?"

"Christ." Johnson turned away in revulsion as the fat man lumbered after his son, into the house.

"Dad," Jean whispered. As soon as Baines was inside she hurried up onto the porch, eyes wide with fear. "Dad, do you think he — "

Johnson put his arm around her. "Just hold on tight. He'll be gone, soon."

The girl's dark eyes flashed with mute terror. "Every time the man from the water company, or the tax collector, some tramp, children, *anybody* come around, I get a terrible stab of pain — here." She clutched at her heart, hand against her breasts. "It's been that way thirteen years. How much longer can we keep it going? *How long?*"

The man named Baines emerged gratefully from the bathroom. Dave Johnson stood silently by the door, body rigid, youthful face stony.

"Thanks, son," Baines sighed. "Now where can I get a glass of cold water?" He smacked his thick lips in anticipation. "After you've been driving around the sticks looking for a dump some red-hot real estate agent stuck you with — "

Dave headed into the kitchen. "Mom, this man wants a drink of water. Dad said he could have it."

Dave had turned his back. Baines caught a brief glimpse of the mother, gray-haired, small, moving toward the sink with a glass, face withered and drawn, without expression.

Then Baines hurried from the room down a hall. He passed through a bedroom, pulled a door open, found himself facing a closet. He turned and raced back, through the living room, into a dining room, then another bedroom. In a brief instant he had gone through the whole house.

He peered out a window. The back yard. Remains of a rusting truck. Entrance of an underground bomb shelter. Tin cans. Chickens scratching around. A dog, asleep under a shed. A couple of old auto tires.

He found a door leading out. Soundlessly, he tore the door open and stepped outside. No one was in sight. There was the barn, a leaning, ancient wood structure. Cedar trees beyond, a creek of some kind. What had once been an outhouse.

Baines moved cautiously around the side of the house. He had perhaps thirty seconds. He had left the door of the bathroom closed; the boy would think he had gone back in there. Baines looked into the house through a window. A large closet, filled with old clothing, boxes and bundles of magazines.

He turned and started back. He reached the corner of the house and started around it.

Nat Johnson's gaunt shape loomed up and blocked his way. "All right, Baines. You asked for it."

A pink flash blossomed. It shut out the sunlight in single blinding burst. Baines leaped back and clawed at his coat pocket. The edge of the flash caught him and he half-fell, stunned by the force. His suit-shield sucked in the energy and discharged it, but the power rattled his teeth and for a moment he jerked like a puppet on a string. Darkness ebbed around him. He could feel the mesh of the shield glow white, as it absorbed the energy and fought to control it.

His own tube came out — and Johnson had no shield. "You're under arrest," Baines muttered grimly. "Put down your tube and your hands up. And call your family." He made a motion with the tube. "Come on, Johnson. Make it snappy."

The lash-tube wavered and then slipped from Johnson's fingers. "You're still alive." Dawning horror crept across his face. "Then you must be — "

Dave and Jean appeared. *"Dad!"*

"Come over here," Baines ordered. "Where's your mother?"

Dave jerked his head numbly. "Inside."

"Get her and bring her here."

"You're DCA," Nat Johnson whispered.

Baines didn't answer. He was doing something with his neck, pulling at the flabby flesh. The wiring of a contact mike glittered as he slipped it from a fold between two chins and into his pocket. From the dirt road came the sound of motors, sleek purrs that rapidly grew louder. Two teardrops of black metal came gliding up and parked beside the house. Men swarmed out, in the dark gray-green of the Government Civil Police. In the sky swarms of black dots were descending, clouds of ugly flies that darkened the sun as they spilled out men and equipment. The men drifted slowly down.

"He's not here," Baines said, as the first man reached him. "He got away. Inform Wisdom back at the lab."

"We've got this section blocked off."

Baines turned to Nat Johnson, who stood in dazed silence, uncomprehending, his son and daughter beside him. "How did he know we were coming?" Baines demanded.

"I don't know," Johnson muttered. "He just — knew."

"A telepath?"

"I don't know."

Baines shrugged. "We'll know, soon. A clamp is out, all around here. He can't get past, no matter what the hell he can do. Unless he can dematerialize himself."

"What'll you do with him when you — if you catch him?" Jean asked huskily.

"Study him."

"And then kill him?"

"That depends on the lab evaluation. If you could give me more to work on, I could predict better."

"We can't tell you anything. We don't know anything more." The girl's voice rose with desperation. "He doesn't talk."

Baines jumped. *"What?"*

"He doesn't talk. He never talked to us. Ever."

"How old is he?"

"Eighteen."

"No communication." Baines was sweating. "In eighteen years there hasn't been any semantic bridge between you? Does he have *any* contact? Signs? Codes?"

"He — ignores us. He eats here, stays with us. Sometimes he plays when we play. Or sits with us. He's gone days on end. We've never been able to find out what he's doing — or where. He sleeps in the barn — by himself."

"Is he really gold-colored?"

"Yes. Skin, eyes, hair, nails. Everything."

"And he's large? Well-formed?"

It was a moment before the girl answered. A strange emotion stirred her drawn features, a momentary glow. "He's incredibly beautiful. A god come down to earth." Her lips twisted. "You won't find him. He can do things. Things you have no comprehension of. Powers so far beyond your limited — "

"You don't think we'll get him?" Baines frowned. "More teams are landing all the time. You've never seen an Agency clamp in operation. We've had sixty years to work out all the bugs. If he gets away it'll be the first time — "

Baines broke off abruptly. Three men were quickly approaching the porch. Two green-clad Civil Police. And a third man between them. A man who moved silently, lithely, a faintly luminous shape that towered above them.

"Cris!" Jean screamed.

"We got him," one of the police said.

Baines fingered his lash-tube uneasily. "Where? How?"

"He gave himself up," the policeman answered, voice full of awe. "He came to us voluntarily. Look at him. He's like a metal statue. Like some sort of — god."

The golden figure halted for a moment beside Jean. Then it turned slowly, calmly, to face Baines.

"Cris!" Jean shrieked. *"Why did you come back?"*

The same thought was eating at Baines, too. He shoved it aside — for the time being. "Is the jet out front?" he demanded quickly.

"Ready to go," one of the CP answered.

"Fine." Baines strode past them, down the steps and onto the dirt field. "Let's go. I want him taken directly to the lab." For a moment he studied the massive figure who stood calmly between the two Civil Policemen. Beside him, they seemed to have shrunk, become ungainly and repellent. Like dwarves ... What had Jean said? *A god come to earth.* Baines broke angrily away. "Come on," he muttered brusquely. "This one may be tough; we've never run up against one like it before. We don't know what the hell it can do."

The chamber was empty, except for the seated figure. Four bare walls, floor and ceiling. A steady glare of white light relentlessly etched every corner of the chamber. Near the top of the far wall ran a narrow slot, the view windows through which the interior of the chamber was scanned.

The seated figure was quiet. He hadn't moved since the chamber locks had slid into place, since the heavy bolts had fallen from outside and the rows of bright-faced technicians had taken their places at the view windows. He gazed down at the floor, bent forward, hands clasped together, face calm, almost expressionless. In four hours he hadn't moved a muscle.

"Well?" Baines said. "What have you learned?"

Wisdom grunted sourly. "Not much. If we don't have him doped out in forty-eight hours we'll go ahead with the euth. We can't take any chances."

"You're thinking about the Tunis type," Baines said. He was, too. They had found ten of them, living in the ruins of the abandoned North African town. Their survival method was simple. They killed and absorbed other life forms, then imitated them and took their places. *Chameleons,* they were called. It had cost sixty lives, before the last one was destroyed. Sixty top-level experts, highly trained DCA men.

"Any clues?" Baines asked.

"He's different as hell. This is going to be tough." Wisdom thumbed a pile of tape-spools. "This is the complete report, all the material we got from Johnson and his family. We pumped them with the psych-wash, then let them go home. Eighteen years — and no semantic bridge. Yet, he looks fully developed. Mature at thirteen — a shorter, faster life-cycle than ours. But why the mane? All the gold fuzz? Like a Roman monument that's been gilded."

"Has the report come in from the analysis room? You had a wave-shot taken, of course."

"His brain pattern has been fully scanned. But it takes time for them to plot it out. We're all running around like lunatics while he just sits there!" Wisdom poked a stubby finger at the window. "We caught him easily enough. He can't have *much*, can he? But I'd like to know what it is. Before we euth him."

"Maybe we should keep him alive until we know."

"Euth in forty-eight hours," Wisdom repeated stubbornly. "Whether we know or not. I don't like him. He gives me the creeps."

Wisdom stood chewing nervously on his cigar, a red-haired, beefy-faced man, thick and heavy-set, with a barrel chest and cold, shrewd eyes deep-set in his hard face. Ed Wisdom was Director of DCA's North American Branch. But right now he was worried. His tiny eyes darted back and forth, alarmed flickers of gray in his brutal, massive face.

"You think," Baines said slowly, "this is *it?*"

"I always think so," Wisdom snapped. "I have to think so."

"I mean — "

"I know what you mean." Wisdom paced back and forth, among the study tables, technicians at their benches, equipment and humming computers. Buzzing tape-slots and research hook-ups. "This thing lived eighteen years with his family and *they* don't understand it. *They* don't know what it has. They know what it does, but not how."

"What does it do?"

"It knows things."

"What kind of things?"

Wisdom grabbed his lash-tube from his belt and tossed it on a table. "Here."

"What?"

"Here." Wisdom signalled, and a view window was slid back an inch. "Shoot him."

Baines blinked. "You said forty-eight hours."

With a curse, Wisdom snatched up the tube, aimed it through the window directly at the seated figure's back, and squeezed the trigger.

A blinding flash of pink. A cloud of energy blossomed in the center of the chamber. It sparkled, then died into dark ash.

"Good God!" Baines gasped. "You — "

He broke off. The figure was no longer sitting. As Wisdom fired, it had moved in a blur of speed, away from the blast, to the corner of the chamber. Now it was slowly coming back, face blank, still absorbed in thought.

"Fifth time," Wisdom said, as he put his tube away. "Last time Jamison and I fired together. Missed. He knew exactly when the bolts would hit. And where."

Baines and Wisdom looked at each other. Both of them were thinking the same thing. "But even reading minds wouldn't tell him where they were going to hit," Baines said. "When, maybe. But not where. Could you have called your own shots?"

"Not mine," Wisdom answered flatly. "I fired fast, damn near at random." He frowned. "*Random*. We'll have to make a test of this." He waved a group of technicians over. "Get a construction team up here. On the double." He grabbed paper and pen and began sketching.

While construction was going on, Baines met his fiancée in the lobby outside the lab, the great central lounge of the DCA Building.

"How's it coming?" she asked. Anita Ferris was tall and blonde, blue eyes and a mature, carefully cultivated figure. An attractive, competent-looking woman in her late twenties. She wore a metal foil dress and cape — with a red and black stripe on the sleeve, the emblem of the A-Class. Anita was Director of the Semantics Agency, a top-level Government Coordinator. "Anything of interest, this time?"

"Plenty." Baines guided her from the lobby, into the dim recess of the bar. Music played softly in the background, a shifting variety of patterns formed mathematically. Dim shapes moved expertly through the gloom, from table to table. Silent, efficient robot waiters.

As Anita sipped her Tom Collins, Baines outlined what they had found.

"What are the chances," Anita asked slowly, "that he's built up some kind of deflection-cone? There was one kind that warped their environment by direct mental effort. No tools. Direct mind to matter."

"Psychokinetics?" Baines drummed restlessly on the table top. "I doubt it. The thing has ability to predict, not to control. He can't stop the beams, but he can sure as hell get out of the way."

"Does he jump between the molecules?"

Baines wasn't amused. "This is serious. We've handled these things sixty years — longer than you and I have been around added together. Eighty-seven types of deviants have shown up, real mutants that could reproduce themselves, not mere freaks. This is the eighty-eighth. We've been able to handle each of them in turn. But this — "

"Why are you so worried about this one?"

"First, it's eighteen years old. That in itself is incredible. Its family managed to hide it that long."

"Those women around Denver were older than that. Those ones with — "

"They were in a Government camp. Somebody high up was toying with the idea of allowing them to breed. Some sort of industrial use. We withheld euth for years. But Cris Johnson stayed alive *outside our control*. Those things at Denver were under constant scrutiny."

"Maybe he's harmless. You always assume a deeve is a menace. He might even be beneficial. Somebody thought those women might work in. Maybe this thing has something that would advance the race."

"*Which* race? Not the human race. It's the old 'the operation was a success but the patient died' routine. If we introduce a mutant to keep us going it'll be mutants, not us, who'll inherit the earth. It'll be mutants surviving for their own sake. Don't think for a moment we can put padlocks on them and expect them to serve us. If they're really superior to homo sapiens, they'll win out in even competition. To survive, we've got to cold-deck them right from the start."

"In other words, we'll know homo superior when he comes — by definition. He'll be the one we won't be able to euth."

"That's about it," Baines answered. "Assuming there *is* a homo superior. Maybe there's just homo peculiar. Homo with an improved line."

"The Neanderthal probably thought the Cro-Magnon man had merely an improved line. A little more advanced ability to conjure up symbols and shape flint. From your description, this thing is more radical than a mere improvement."

"This thing," Baines said slowly, "has an ability to predict. So far, it's been able to stay alive. It's been able to cope with situations better than you or I could. How long do you think we'd stay alive in that chamber, with energy beams blazing down at us? In a sense it's got the ultimate survival ability. If it can always be accurate — "

A wall-speaker sounded. "Baines, you're wanted in the lab. Get the hell out of the bar and upramp."

Baines pushed back his chair and got to his feet. "Come along. You may be interested in seeing what Wisdom has got dreamed up."

A tight group of top-level DCA officials stood around in a circle, middle-aged, gray-haired, listening to a skinny youth in a white shirt and rolled-up sleeves explaining an elaborate cube of metal and plastic that filled the center of the view-platform. From it jutted an ugly array of tube snouts, gleaming muzzles that disappeared into an intricate maze of wiring.

"This," the youth was saying briskly, "is the first real test. It fires at random — as nearly random as we can make it, at least. Weighted balls are thrown up in an air stream, then dropped free to fall back and cut relays. They can fall in almost any pattern. The thing fires according to their pattern. Each drop produces a new configuration of timing and position. Ten tubes, in all. Each will be in constant motion."

"And *nobody* knows how they'll fire?" Anita asked.

"Nobody." Wisdom rubbed his thick hands together. "Mind reading won't help him, not with this thing."

Anita moved over to the view windows, as the cube was rolled into place. She gasped. "Is that him?"

"What's wrong?" Baines asked.

Anita's cheeks were flushed. "Why, I expected a — a *thing*. My God, he's beautiful! Like a golden statue. Like a deity!"

Baines laughed. "He's eighteen years old, Anita. Too young for you."

The woman was still peering through the view window. "Look at him. Eighteen? I don't believe it."

Cris Johnson sat in the center of the chamber, on the floor. A posture of contemplation, head bowed, arms folded, legs tucked under him. In the stark glare of the overhead lights his powerful body glowed and rippled, a shimmering figure of downy gold.

"Pretty, isn't he?" Wisdom muttered. "All right. Start it going."

"You're going to *kill* him?" Anita demanded.

"We're going to try."

"But he's — " She broke off uncertainly. "He's not a monster. He's not like those others, those hideous things with two heads, or those insects. Or those awful things from Tunis."

"What is he, then?" Baines asked.

"I don't know. But you can't just *kill* him. It's terrible!"

The cube clicked into life. The muzzles jerked, silently altered position. Three retracted, disappeared into the body of the cube. Others came out. Quickly, efficiently, they moved into position — and abruptly, without warning, opened fire.

A staggering burst of energy fanned out, a complex pattern that altered each moment, different angles, different velocities, a bewildering blur that cracked from the windows down into the chamber.

The golden figure moved. He dodged back and forth, expertly avoiding the bursts of energy that seared around him on all sides. Rolling clouds of ash obscured him; he was lost in a mist of crackling fire and ash.

"Stop it!" Anita shouted. "For God's sake, you'll destroy him!"

The chamber was an inferno of energy. The figure had completely disappeared. Wisdom waited a moment, then nodded to the technicians operating the cube. They touched guide buttons and the muzzles slowed and died. Some sank back into the cube. All became silent. The works of the cube ceased humming.

Cris Johnson was still alive. He emerged from the settling clouds of ash, blackened and singed. But unhurt. He had avoided each beam. He had weaved between them and among them as they came, a dancer leaping over glittering sword-points of pink fire. He had survived.

"No," Wisdom murmured, shaken and grim. "Not a telepath. Those were at random. No prearranged pattern."

The three of them looked at each other, dazed and frightened. Anita was trembling. Her face was pale and her blue eyes were wide. "What, then?" She whispered. "What is it? What does he have?"

"He's a good guesser," Wisdom suggested.

"He's not guessing," Baines answered. "Don't kid yourself. That's the whole point."

"No, he's not guessing." Wisdom nodded slowly. "He *knew*. He predicted each strike. I wonder ... *Can* he err? *Can* he make a mistake?"

"We caught him," Baines pointed out.

"You said he came back voluntarily." There was a strange look on Wisdom's face. "Did he come back *after* the clamp was up?"

Baines jumped. "Yes, after."

"He couldn't have got through the clamp. So he came back." Wisdom grinned wryly. "The clamp must actually have been perfect. It was supposed to be."

"If there had been a single hole," Baines murmured, "he would have known it — gone through."

Wisdom ordered a group of armed guards over. "Get him out of there. To the euth stage."

Anita shrieked. "Wisdom, you can't — "

"He's too far ahead of us. We can't compete with him." Wisdom's eyes were bleak. "We can only guess what's going to happen. *He knows*. For him, it's a sure thing. I don't think it'll help him at euth, though. The whole stage is flooded simultaneously. Instantaneous gas, released throughout." He signalled impatiently to the guards. "Get going. Take him down right away. Don't waste any time."

"Can we?" Baines murmured thoughtfully.

The guards took up positions by one of the chamber locks. Cautiously, the tower control slid the lock back. The first two guards stepped cautiously in, lash-tubes ready.

Cris stood in the center of the chamber. His back was to them as they crept toward him. For a moment he was silent, utterly unmoving. The guards fanned out, as more of them entered the chamber. Then —

Anita screamed. Wisdom cursed. The golden figure spun and leaped forward, in a flashing blur of speed. Past the triple line of guards, through the lock and into the corridor.

"Get him!" Baines shouted.

Guards milled everywhere. Flashes of energy lit up the corridor, as the figure raced among them up the ramp.

"No use," Wisdom said calmly. "We can't hit him." He touched a button, then another. "But maybe this will help."

"What — " Baines began. But the leaping figure shot abruptly at him, straight at him, and he dropped to one side. The figure flashed past. It ran effortlessly, face without expression, dodging and jumping as the energy beams seared around it.

For an instant the golden face loomed up before Baines. It passed and disappeared down a side corridor. Guards rushed after it, kneeling and firing, shouting orders excitedly. In the bowels of the building, heavy guns were rumbling up. Locks slid into place as escape corridors were systematically sealed off.

"Good God," Baines gasped, as he got to his feet. "Can't he do anything but run?"

"I gave orders," Wisdom said, "to have the building isolated. There's no way out. Nobody comes and nobody goes. He's loose here in the building — but he won't get out."

"If there's one exit overlooked, he'll know it," Anita pointed out shakily.

"We won't overlook any exit. We got him once; we'll get him again."

A messenger robot had come in. Now it presented its message respectfully to Wisdom. "From analysis, sir."

Wisdom tore the tape open. "Now we'll know how it thinks." His hands were shaking. "Maybe we can figure out its blind spot. It may be able to out-think us, but that doesn't mean it's invulnerable. It only predicts the future — it can't change it. If there's only death ahead, its ability won't . . . "

Wisdom's voice faded into silence. After a moment he passed the tape to Baines.

"I'll be down in the bar," Wisdom said. "Getting a good stiff drink." His face had turned lead-gray. "All I can say is *I hope to hell this isn't the race to come.*"

"What's the analysis?" Anita demanded impatiently, peering over Baines' shoulder. "How does it think?"

"It doesn't," Baines said, as he handed the tape back to his boss. "It doesn't think at all. Virtually no frontal lobe. It's not a human being — it doesn't use symbols. It's nothing but an animal."

"An animal," Wisdom said. "With a single highly-developed faculty. Not a superior man. Not a man at all."

Up and down the corridors of the DCA Building, guards and equipment clanged. Loads of Civil Police were pouring into the building and taking up positions beside the guards. One by one, the corridors and rooms were being inspected and sealed off. Sooner or later the golden figure of Cris Johnson would be located and cornered.

"We were always afraid a mutant with superior intellectual powers would come along," Baines said reflectively. "A deeve who would be to us what we are to the great apes. Something with a bulging cranium, telepathic ability, a perfect semantic system, ultimate powers of symbolization and calculation. A development along our own path. A better human being."

"He acts by reflex," Anita said wonderingly. She had the analysis and was sitting at one of the desks studying it intently. "Reflex — like a lion. A golden lion." She pushed the tape aside, a strange expression on her face. "The lion god."

"Beast," Wisdom corrected tartly. "Blond beast, you mean."

"He runs fast," Baines said, "and that's all. No tools. He doesn't build anything or utilize anything outside himself. He just stands and waits for the right opportunity and then he runs like hell."

"This is worse than anything we've anticipated," Wisdom said. His beefy face was lead-gray. He sagged like an old man, his blunt hands trembling and uncertain. "To be replaced by an animal! Something that runs and hides. Something without a language!" He spat savagely. "That's why they weren't able to communicate with it. We wondered what kind of semantic system it had. It hasn't got any! No more ability to talk and think than a — dog."

"That means intelligence has failed," Baines went on huskily. "We're the last of our line — like the dinosaur. We've carried intelligence as far as it'll go. Too far, maybe. We've already got to the point where we know so much — think so much — we can't act."

"Men of thought," Anita said. "Not men of action. It's begun to have a paralyzing effect. But this thing — "

"This thing's faculty works better than ours ever did. We can recall past experiences, keep them in mind, learn from them. At best, we can make shrewd guesses about the future, from our memory of what's happened in the past. But we can't be certain. We have to speak of probabilities. Grays. Not blacks and whites. We're only guessing."

"Cris Johnson isn't guessing," Anita added.

"He can look ahead. See what's coming. He can — prethink. Let's call it that. He can see into the future. Probably he doesn't perceive it as the future."

"No," Anita said thoughtfully. "It would seem like the present. He has a broader present. But his present lies ahead, not back. Our present is related to the past. Only the past is certain, to us. To him, the future is certain. And he probably doesn't remember the past, any more than any animal remembers what happened."

"As he develops," Baines said, "as his race evolves, it'll probably expand its ability to prethink. Instead of ten minutes, thirty minutes. Then an hour. A day. A year. Eventually they'll be able to keep ahead a whole lifetime. Each one of them will live in a solid, unchanging world. There'll be no variables, no uncertainty. No motion! They won't have anything to fear. Their world will be perfectly static, a solid block of matter."

"And when death comes," Anita said, "they'll accept it. There won't be any struggle; to them, it'll already have happened."

"Already have happened," Baines repeated. "To Cris, our shots had already been fired." He laughed harshly. "Superior survival doesn't mean superior man. If there were another world-wide flood, only fish would survive. If there were another ice age, maybe nothing but polar bears would be left. When we opened the lock, he had already seen the men, seen exactly where they were standing and what they'd do. A neat faculty — but not a development of mind. A pure physical *sense.*"

"But if every exit is covered," Wisdom repeated, "he'll see he can't get out. He gave himself up before — he'll give himself up again." He shook his head. "An animal. Without language. Without tools."

"With his new sense," Baines said, "he doesn't need anything else." He examined his watch. "It's after two. Is the building completely sealed off?"

"You can't leave," Wisdom stated. "You'll have to stay here all night — or until we catch the bastard."

"I meant her." Baines indicated Anita. "She's supposed to be back at Semantics by seven in the morning."

Wisdom shrugged. "I have no control over her. If she wants, she can check out."

"I'll stay," Anita decided. "I want to be here when he — when he's destroyed. I'll sleep here." She hesitated. "Wisdom, isn't there some other way? If he's just an animal couldn't we — "

"A zoo?" Wisdom's voice rose in a frenzy of hysteria. "Keep it penned up in the zoo? Christ no! It's got to be killed!"

For a long time the great gleaming shape crouched in the darkness. He was in a store room. Boxes and cartons stretched out on all sides, heaped up in orderly rows, all neatly counted and marked. Silent and deserted.

But in a few moments people burst in and searched the room. He could see this. He saw them in all parts of the room, clear and distinct, men with lash-tubes, grim-faced, stalking with murder in their eyes.

The sight was one of many. One of a multitude of clearly-etched scenes lying tangent to his own. And to each was attached a further multitude of interlocking scenes, that finally grew hazier and dwindled away. A progressive vagueness, each syndrome less distinct.

But the immediate one, the scene that lay closest to him, was clearly visible. He could easily make out the sight of the armed men. Therefore it was necessary to be out of the room before they appeared.

The golden figure got calmly to its feet and moved to the door. The corridor was empty; he could see himself already outside, in the vacant, drumming hall of metal and recessed lights. He pushed the door boldly open and stepped out.

A lift blinked across the hall. He walked to the lift and entered it. In five minutes a group of guards would come running along and leap into the lift. By that time he would have left it and sent it back down. Now he pressed a button and rose to the next floor.

He stepped out into a deserted passage. No one was in sight. That didn't surprise him. He couldn't be surprised. The element didn't exist for him. The positions of things, the space relationships of all matter in the immediate future, were as certain for him as his own body. The only thing that was unknown was that which had already passed out of being. In a vague, dim fashion, he had occasionally wondered where things went after he had passed them.

He came to a small supply closet. It had just been searched. It would be a half an hour before anyone opened it again. He had that long; he could see that far ahead. And then —

And then he would be able to see another area, a region farther beyond. He was always moving, advancing into new regions he had never seen before. A constantly unfolding panorama of sights and scenes, frozen landscapes spread out ahead. All objects were fixed. Pieces on a vast chess board through which he moved, arms folded, face calm. A detached observer who saw objects that lay ahead of him as clearly as those under foot.

Right now, as he crouched in the small supply closet, he saw an unusually varied multitude of scenes for the next half hour. Much lay ahead. The half hour was divided into an incredibly complex pattern of separate configurations. He had reached a critical region; he was about to move through worlds of intricate complexity.

He concentrated on a scene ten minutes away. It showed, like a three dimensional still, a heavy gun at the end of the corridor, trained all the way to the far end. Men moved cautiously from door to door, checking each room again, as they had done repeatedly. At the end of the half hour they had reached the supply closet. A scene showed them looking inside. By that time he was gone, of course. He wasn't in that scene. He had passed on to another.

The next scene showed an exit. Guards stood in a solid line. No way out. He was in that scene. Off to one side, in a niche just inside the door. The street outside was visible, stars, lights, outlines of passing cars and people.

In the next tableau he had gone back, away from the exit. There was no way out. In another tableau he saw himself at other exits, a legion of golden figures, duplicated again and again, as he explored regions ahead, one after another. But each exit was covered.

In one dim scene he saw himself lying charred and dead; he had tried to run through the line, out the exit.

But that scene was vague. One wavering, indistinct still out of many. The inflexible path along which he moved would not deviate in that direction. It would not turn him that way. The golden figure in that scene, the miniature doll in that room, was only distantly related to him. It was himself, but a far-away self. A self he would never meet. He forgot it and went on to examine the other tableau.

The myriad of tableaux that surrounded him were an elaborate maze, a web which he now considered bit by bit. He was looking down into a doll's house of infinite rooms, rooms without number, each with its furniture, its dolls, all rigid and unmoving. The same dolls and furniture were repeated in many. He, himself, appeared often. The two men on the platform. The woman. Again and again the same combinations turned up; the play was redone frequently, the same actors and props moved around in all possible ways.

Before it was time to leave the supply closet, Cris Johnson had examined each of the rooms tangent to the one he now occupied. He had consulted each, considered its contents thoroughly.

He pushed the door open and stepped calmly out into the hall. He knew exactly where he was going. And what he had to do. Crouched in the stuffy closet, he had quietly and expertly examined each miniature of himself, observed which clearly-etched configuration lay along his inflexible path, the one room of the doll house, the one set out of legions, toward which he was moving.

Anita slipped out of her metal foil dress, hung it over a hanger, then unfastened her shoes and kicked them under the bed. She was just starting to unclip her bra when the door opened.

She gasped. Soundlessly, calmly, the great golden shape closed the door and bolted it after him.

Anita snatched up her lash-tube from the dressing table. Her hand shook; her whole body was trembling. "What do you want?" she demanded. Her fingers tightened convulsively around the tube. "I'll kill you."

The figure regarded her silently, arms folded. It was the first time she had seen Cris Johnson closely. The great dignified face, handsome and impassive. Broad shoulders. The golden mane of hair, golden skin, pelt of radiant fuzz—

"Why?" she demanded breathlessly. Her heart was pounding wildly. "What do you want?"

She could kill him easily. But the lash-tube wavered. Cris Johnson stood without fear; he wasn't at all afraid. Why not? Didn't he understand what it was? What the small metal tube could do to him?

"Of course," she said suddenly, in a choked whisper. "You can see ahead. You know I'm going to kill you. Or you wouldn't have come here."

She flushed, terrified—and embarrassed. He knew exactly what she was going to do; he could see it as easily as she was the walls of the room, the wall-bed with its covers folded neatly back, her clothes hanging in the closet, her purse and small things on the dressing table.

"All right." Anita backed away, then abruptly put the tube down on the dressing table. "I won't kill you. Why should I?" She fumbled in her purse and got out her cigarettes. Shakily, she lit up, her pulse racing. She was scared. And strangely fascinated. "Do you expect to stay here? It won't do any good. They've come through the dorm twice, already. They'll be back."

Could he understand her? She saw nothing on his face, only blank dignity. God, he was huge! It wasn't possible he was only eighteen, a boy, a child. He looked more like some great golden god, come down to earth.

She shook the thought off savagely. He wasn't a god. He was a beast. *The blond beast*, come to take the place of man. To drive man from the earth.

Anita snatched up the lash-tube. "Get out of here! You're an animal! A big stupid animal! You can't even understand what I'm saying—you don't even have a language. You're not human."

Cris Johnson remained silent. As if he were waiting. Waiting for what? He showed no sign of fear or impatience, even though the corridor outside rang with the sound of men searching, metal against metal, guns and energy tubes being dragged around, shouts and dim rumbles as section after section of the building was searched and sealed off.

"They'll get you," Anita said. "You'll be trapped here. They'll be searching this wing any moment." She savagely stubbed out her cigarette. "For God's sake, what do you expect *me* to do?"

Cris moved toward her. Anita shrank back. His powerful hands caught hold of her and she gasped in sudden terror. For a moment she struggled blindly, desperately.

"Let go!" She broke away and leaped back from him. His face was expressionless. Calmly, he came toward her, an impassive god advancing to take her. "Get away!" She groped for the lash-tube, trying to get up. But the tube slipped from her fingers and rolled onto the floor.

Cris bent down and picked it up. He held it out to her, in the open palm of his hand.

"Good God," Anita whispered. Shakily, she accepted the tube, gripped it hesitantly, then put it down again on the dressing table.

In the half-light of the room, the great golden figure seemed to glow and shimmer, outlined against the darkness. A god — no, not a god. An animal. A great golden beast, without a soul. She was confused. Which was he — or was he both? She shook her head, bewildered. It was late, almost four. She was exhausted and confused.

Cris took her in his arms. Gently, kindly, he lifted her face and kissed her. His powerful hands held her tight. She couldn't breathe. Darkness, mixed with the shimmering golden haze, swept around her. Around and around it spiralled, carrying her senses away. She sank down into it gratefully. The darkness covered her and dissolved her in a swelling torrent of sheer force that mounted in intensity each moment, until the roar of it beat against her and at last blotted out everything.

Anita blinked. She sat up and automatically pushed her hair into place. Cris was standing before the closet. He was reaching up, getting something down.

He turned toward her and tossed something on the bed. Her heavy metal foil traveling cape.

Anita gazed down at the cape without comprehension. "What do you want?"

Cris stood by the bed, waiting.

She picked up the cape uncertainly. Cold creepers of fear plucked at her. "You want me to get you out of here," she said softly. "Past the guards and the CP."

Cris said nothing.

"They'll kill you instantly." She got unsteadily to her feet. "You can't run past them. Good God, don't you do anything but run? There must be a better way. Maybe I can appeal to Wisdom. I'm Class A — Director Class. I can go directly to the Full Directorate. I ought to be able to hold them off, keep back the euth indefinitely. The odds are a billion to one against us if we try to break past — "

She broke off.

"But you don't gamble," she continued slowly. "You don't go by odds. You *know* what's coming. You've seen the cards already." She studied his face intently. "No, you can't be cold-decked. It wouldn't be possible."

For a moment she stood deep in thought. Then with a quick, decisive motion, she snatched up the cloak and slipped it around her bare shoulders. She fastened the heavy belt, bent down and got her shoes from under the bed, snatched up her purse, and hurried to the door.

"Come on," she said. She was breathing quickly, cheeks flushed. "Let's go. While there are still a number of exits to choose from. My car is parked outside, in the lot at the side of the building. We can get to my place in an hour. I have a winter home in Argentina. If worse comes to worst we can fly there. It's in the back country, away from the cities. Jungle and swamps. Cut-off from almost everything." Eagerly she started to open the door.

Cris reached out and stopped her. Gently, patiently, he moved in front of her.

He waited a long time, body rigid. Then he turned the knob and stepped boldly out into the corridor.

The corridor was empty. No one was in sight. Anita caught a faint glimpse, the back of a guard hurrying off. If they had come out a second earlier —

Cris started down the corridor. She ran after him. He moved rapidly, effortlessly. The girl had trouble keeping up with him. He seemed to know exactly where to go. Off to the right, down a side hall, a supply passage. Onto an ascent freight-lift. They rose, then abruptly halted.

Cris waited again. Presently he slid the door back and moved out of the lift. Anita followed nervously. She could hear sounds: guns and men, very close.

They were near an exit. A double line of guards stood directly ahead. Twenty men, a solid wall — and a massive heavy-duty robot gun in the center.

The men were alert, faces strained and tense. Watching wide-eyed, guns gripped tight. A Civil Police officer was in charge.

"We'll never get past," Anita gasped. "We wouldn't get ten feet." She pulled back. "They'll — "

Cris took her by the arm and continued calmly forward. Blind terror leaped inside her. She fought wildly to get away, but his fingers were like steel. She couldn't pry them loose. Quietly, irresistibly, the great golden creature drew her along beside him toward the double line of guards.

"There he is!" Guns went up. Men leaped into action. The barrel of the robot cannon swung around. *"Get him!"*

Anita was paralyzed. She sagged against the powerful body beside her, tugged along helplessly by his inflexible grasp. The lines of guards came nearer, a sheer wall of guns. Anita fought to control her terror. She stumbled, half-fell. Cris supported her effortlessly. She scratched, fought at him, struggled to get loose —

"Don't shoot!" she screamed.

Guns wavered uncertainly. "Who is she?" The guards were moving around, trying to get a sight on Cris without including her. "Who's he got there?"

One of them saw the stripe on her sleeve. Red and black. Director Class. Top-level.

"She's Class A." Shocked, the guards retreated. "Miss, get out of the way!"

Anita found her voice. "Don't shoot. He's — in my custody. You understand? I'm taking him out."

The wall of guards moved back nervously. "No one's supposed to pass. Director Wisdom gave orders — "

"I'm not subject to Wisdom's authority." She managed to edge her voice with a harsh crispness. "Get out of the way. I'm taking him to the Semantics Agency."

For a moment nothing happened. There was no reaction. Then slowly, uncertainly, one guard stepped aside.

Cris moved. A blur of speed, away from Anita, past the confused guards, through the breach in the line, out the exit, and onto the street. Bursts of energy flashed wildly after him. Shouting guards milled out. Anita was left behind, forgotten. The guards, the heavy-duty gun, were pouring out into the early morning darkness. Sirens wailed. Patrol cars roared into life.

Anita stood dazed, confused, leaning against the wall, trying to get her breath.

He was gone. He had left her. Good God — what had she done? She shook her head, bewildered, her face buried in her hands. She had been hypnotized. She had lost her will, her common sense. Her reason! The animal, the great golden beast, had tricked her. Taken advantage of her. And now he was gone, escaped into the night.

Miserable, agonized tears trickled through her clenched fingers. She rubbed at them futilely; but they kept on coming.

"He's gone," Baines said. "We'll never get him, now. He's probably a million miles from here."

Anita sat huddled in the corner, her face to the wall. A little bent heap, broken and wretched.

Wisdom paced back and forth. "But where can he go? Where can he hide? Nobody'll hide him! Everybody knows the law about deeves!"

"He's lived out in the woods most of his life. He'll hunt — that's what he's always done. They wondered what he was up to, off by himself. He was catching game and sleeping under trees." Baines laughed harshly. "And the first woman he meets will be glad to hide him — as *she* was." He indicated Anita with a jerk of his thumb.

"So all that gold, that mane, that god-like stance, was *for* something. Not just ornament." Wisdom's thick lips twisted. "He doesn't have just one faculty — he has two. One is new, the newest thing in survival method. The other is old as life." He stopped pacing to glare at the huddled shape in the corner. "Plumage. Bright feathers, combs for the rooster, swans, birds, bright scales for the fish. Gleaming pelts and manes for the animals. An animal isn't necessarily *bestial*. Lions aren't bestial. Or tigers. Or any of the big cats. They're anything but bestial."

"He'll never have to worry," Baines said. "He'll get by — as long as human women exist to take care of him. And since he can see ahead, into the future, he already knows he's sexually irresistible to human females."

"We'll get him," Wisdom muttered. "I've had the Government declare an emergency. Military and Civil Police will be looking for him. Armies of men — a whole planet of experts, the most advanced machines and equipment. We'll flush him, sooner or later."

"By that time it won't make any difference," Baines said. He put his hand on Anita's shoulder and patted her ironically. "You'll have company, sweetheart. You won't be the only one. You're just the first of a long procession."

"Thanks," Anita grated.

"The oldest survival method and the newest. Combined to form one perfectly adapted animal. How the hell are we going to stop him? We can put *you* through a sterilization tank — but we can't pick them all up, all the women he meets along the way. And if we miss one we're finished."

"We'll have to keep trying," Wisdom said. "Round up as many as we can. Before they can spawn." Faint hope glinted in his tired, sagging face. "Maybe his characteristics are recessive. Maybe ours will cancel his out."

"I wouldn't lay any money on that," Baines said. "I think I know already which of the two strains is going to turn up dominant." He grinned wryly. "I mean, I'm making a good *guess*. It won't be us."

THE TURNING WHEEL

BARD CHAI said thoughtfully, "Cults." He examined a tape-report grinding from the receptor. The receptor was rusty and unoiled; it whined piercingly and sent up an acrid wisp of smoke. Chai shut it off as its pitted surface began to heat ugly red. Presently he finished with the tape and tossed it with a heap of refuse jamming the mouth of a disposal slot.

"What about cults?" Bard Sung-wu asked faintly. He brought himself back with an effort, and forced a smile of interest on his plump olive-yellow face. "You were saying?"

"Any stable society is menaced by cults; our society is no exception." Chai rubbed his finely-tapered fingers together reflectively. "Certain lower strata are axiomatically dissatisfied. Their hearts burn with envy of those the wheel has placed above them; in secret they form fanatic, rebellious bands. They meet in the dark of night; they insidiously express inversions of accepted norms; they delight in flaunting basic mores and customs."

"Ugh," Sung-wu agreed. "I mean," he explained quickly, "it seems incredible people could practice such fanatic and disgusting rites." He got nervously to his feet. "I must go, if it's permitted."

"Wait," snapped Chai. "You are familiar with the Detroit area?"

Uneasily, Sung-wu nodded. "Very slightly."

With characteristic vigor, Chai made his decision. "I'm sending you; investigate and make a blue-slip report. If this group is dangerous, the Holy Arm should know. It's of the worst elements — the Techno class." He made a wry face. "Caucasians, hulking, hairy things. We'll give you six months in Spain, on your return; you can poke over ruins of abandoned cities."

"Caucasians!" Sung-wu exclaimed, his face turning green. "But I haven't been well; please, if somebody else could go — "

"You, perhaps, hold to the Broken Feather theory?" Chai raised an eyebrow. "An amazing philologist, Broken Feather; I took partial instruction from him. He held, you know, the Caucasian to be descended of Neanderthal stock. Their extreme size, thick body hair, their general brutish cast, reveal an innate inability to comprehend anything but a purely animalistic horizontal; proselytism is a waste of time."

He affixed the younger man with a stern eye. "I wouldn't send you, if I didn't have unusual faith in your devotion."

Sung-wu fingered his beads miserably. "Elron be praised," he muttered; "you are too kind."

Sung-wu slid into a lift and was raised, amid great groans and whirrings and false stops, to the top level of the Central Chamber building. He hurried down a corridor dimly lit by occasional yellow bulbs. A moment later he approached the doors of the scanning offices and flashed his identification at the robot guard. "Is Bard Fei-p'ang within?" he inquired.

"Verily," the robot answered, stepping aside.

Sung-wu entered the offices, bypassed the rows of rusted, discarded machines, and entered the still-functioning wing. He located his brother-in-law, hunched over some graphs at one of the desks, laboriously copying material by hand. "Clearness be with you," Sung-wu murmured.

Fei-p'ang glanced up in annoyance. "I told you not to come again; if the Arm finds out I'm letting you use the scanner for a personal plot, they'll stretch me on the rack."

"Gently," Sung-wu murmured, his hand on his relation's shoulder. "This is the last time. I'm going away; one more look, a final look." His olive face took on a pleading, piteous cast. "The turn comes for me very soon; this will be our last conversation."

Sung-wu's piteous look hardened into cunning. "You wouldn't want it on your soul; no restitution will be possible at this late date."

Fei-p'ang snorted. "All right; but for Elron's sake, do it quickly."

Sung-wu hurried to the mother-scanner and seated himself in the rickety basket. He snapped on the controls, clamped his forehead to the viewpiece, inserted his identity tab, and set the space-time finger into motion. Slowly, reluctantly, the ancient mechanism coughed into life and began tracing his personal tab along the future track.

Sung-wu's hands shook; his body trembled; sweat dripped from his neck, as he saw himself scampering in miniature. *Poor Sung-wu*, he thought wretchedly. The mite of a thing hurried about its duties; this was but eight months hence. Harried and beset, it performed its tasks — and then, in a subsequent continuum, fell down and died.

Sung-wu removed his eyes from the viewpiece and waited for his pulse to slow. He could stand that part, watching the moment of death; it was what came next that was too jangling for him.

He breathed a silent prayer. Had he fasted enough? In the four-day purge and self-flagellation, he had used the whip with metal points, the heaviest possible. He had given away all his money; he had smashed a lovely vase his mother had left him, a treasured heirloom; he had rolled in the filth and mud in the center of town. Hundreds had seen him. Now, surely, all this was enough. But time was so short!

Faint courage stirring, he sat up and again put his eyes to the viewpiece. He was shaking with terror. What if it hadn't changed? What if his mortification weren't enough? He spun the controls, sending the finger tracing his time-track past the moment of death.

Sung-wu shrieked and scrambled back in horror. His future was the same, exactly the same; there had been no change at all. His guilt had been too great to be washed away in such short a time; it would take ages — and he didn't have ages.

He left the scanner and passed by his brother-in-law. "Thanks," he muttered shakily.

For once, a measure of compassion touched Fei-p'ang's efficient brown features. "Bad news? The next turn brings an unfortunate manifestation?"

"Bad scarcely describes it."

Fei-p'ang's pity turned to righteous rebuke. "Who do you have to blame but yourself?" he demanded sternly. "You know your conduct in this manifestation determines the next; if you look forward to a future life as a lower animal, it should make you glance over your behavior and repent your wrongs. The cosmic law that governs us is impartial. It is true justice: cause and effect; what you do determines what you next become — there can be no blame and no sorrow. There can be only understanding and repentance." His curiosity overcame him. "What is it? A snake? A squirrel?"

"It's no affair of yours," Sung-wu said, as he moved unhappily toward the exit doors.

"I'll look myself."

"Go ahead." Sung-wu pushed moodily out into the hall. He was dazed with despair: it hadn't changed; it was still the same.

In eight months he would die, stricken by one of the numerous plagues that swept over the inhabited parts of the world. He would become feverish, break out with red spots, turn and twist in an anguish of delirium. His bowels would drop out; his flesh would waste away; his eyes would roll up; and after an interminable time of suffering, he would die. His body would lie in a mass heap, with hundreds of others — a whole streetful of dead, to be carted away by one of the robot sweepers, happily immune. His mortal remains would be burned in a common rubbish incinerator at the outskirts of the city.

Meanwhile, the eternal spark, Sung-wu's divine soul, would hurry from this space-time manifestation to the next in order. But it would not rise; it would sink; he had watched its descent on the scanner many times. There was always the same hideous picture — a sight beyond endurance — of his soul, as it plummeted down like a stone, into one of the lowest continua, a sinkhole of a manifestation at the very bottom of the ladder.

He had sinned. In his youth, Sung-wu had got mixed up with a black-eyed wench with long flowing hair, a glittering waterfall down her back and shoulders. Inviting red lips, plump breasts, hips that undulated and beckoned unmistakably. She was the wife of a friend, from the Warrior class, but he had taken her as his mistress; he had been *certain* time remained to rectify his venality.

But he was wrong: the wheel was soon to turn for him. The plague — not enough time to fast and pray and do good works. He was determined to go down, straight down to a wallowing, foul-aired planet in a stinking red-sun system, an ancient pit of filth and decay and unending slime — a jungle world of the lowest type.

In it, he would be a shiny-winged fly, a great blue-bottomed, buzzing carrion-eater that hummed and guzzled and crawled through the rotting carcasses of great lizards, slain in combat.

From this swamp, this pest-ridden planet in a diseased, contaminated system, he would have to rise painfully to the endless rungs of the cosmic ladder he had already climbed. It had taken eons to climb this far, to the level of a human being on the planet Earth, in the bright yellow Sol system; now he would have to do it all over again.

Chai beamed, "Elron be with you," as the corroded observation ship was checked by the robot crew, and finally okayed for limited flight. Sung-wu slowly entered the ship and seated himself at what remained of the controls. He waved listlessly, then slammed the lock and bolted it by hand.

As the ship limped into the late afternoon sky, he reluctantly consulted the reports and records Chai had transferred to him.

The Tinkerists were a small cult; they claimed only a few hundred members, all drawn from the Techno class, which was the most despised of the social castes. The Bards, of course, were at the top; they were the teachers of society, the holy men who guided man to clearness. Then the Poets; they turned into saga the great legends of Elron Hu, who lived (according to legend) in the hideous days of the Time of Madness. Below the Poets were the Artists; then the Musicians; then the Workers, who supervised the robot crews. After them the Businessmen, the Warriors, the Farmers, and finally, at the bottom, the Technos.

Most of the Technos were Caucasians — immense white-skinned things, incredibly hairy, like apes; their resemblance to the great apes was striking. Perhaps Broken Feather was right; perhaps they did have Neanderthal blood and were outside the possibility of clearness. Sung-wu had always considered himself an anti-racist; he disliked those who maintained the Caucasians were a race apart. Extremists believed eternal damage would result to the species if the Caucasians were allowed to intermarry.

In any case, the problem was academic; no decent, self-respecting woman of the higher classes — of Indian or Mongolian, or Bantu stock — would allow herself to be approached by a *Cauc.*

Below his ship, the barren countryside spread out, ugly and bleak. Great red spots that hadn't yet been overgrown, and slag surfaces were still visible — but by this time most ruins were covered by soil and crabgrass. He could see men and robots farming; villages, countless tiny brown circles in the green fields; occasional ruins of ancient cities — gaping sores like blind mouths, eternally open to the sky. They would never close, not now.

Ahead was the Detroit area, named, so it ran, for some now-forgotten spiritual leader. There were more villages, here. Off to his left, the leaden surface of a body of water, a lake of some kind. Beyond that — only Elron knew. No one went that far; there was no human life there, only wild animals and deformed things spawned from radiation infestation still lying heavy in the north.

He dropped his ship down. An open field lay to his right; a robot farmer was plowing with a metal hook welded to its waist, a section torn off some discarded machine. It stopped dragging the hook and gazed up in amazement, as Sung-wu landed the ship awkwardly and bumped to a halt.

"Clearness be with you," the robot rasped obediently, as Sung-wu climbed out.

Sung-wu gathered up his bundle of reports and papers and stuffed them in a briefcase. He snapped the ship's lock and hurried off toward the ruins of the city. The robot went back to dragging the rusty metal hook through the hard ground, its pitted body bent double with the strain, working slowly, silently, uncomplaining.

The little boy piped, "Whither, Bard?" as Sung-wu pushed wearily through the tangled debris and slag. He was a little black-faced Bantu, in red rags sewed and patched together. He ran alongside Sung-wu like a puppy, leaping and bounding and grinning white-teethed.

Sung-wu became immediately crafty; his intrigue with the black-haired girl had taught him elemental dodges and evasions. "My ship broke down," he answered cautiously; it was certainly common enough. "It was the last ship still in operation at our field."

The boy skipped and laughed and broke off bits of green weeds that grew along the trail. "I know somebody who can fix it," he cried carelessly.

Sung-wu's pulse-rate changed. "Oh?" he murmured, as if uninterested. "There are those around here who practice the questionable art of repairing."

The boy nodded solemnly.

"Technos?" Sung-wu pursued. "Are there many of them here, around these old ruins?"

More black-faced boys, and some little dark-eyed Bantu girls, came scampering through the slag and ruins. "What's the matter with your ship?" one hollered at Sung-wu. "Won't it run?"

They all ran and shouted around him, as he advanced slowly — an unusually wild bunch, completely undisciplined. They rolled and fought and tumbled and chased each other around madly.

"How many of you," Sung-wu demanded, "have taken your first instruction?"

There was a sudden uneasy silence. The children looked at each other guiltily; none of them answered.

"Good Elron!" Sung-wu exclaimed in horror. "Are you all untaught?"

Heads hung guiltily.

"How do you expect to phase yourselves with the cosmic will? How can you expect to know the divine plan? This is really too much!"

He pointed a plump finger at one of the boys. "Are you constantly preparing yourself for the life to come? Are you constantly purging and purifying yourself? Do you deny yourself meat, sex, entertainment, financial gain, education, leisure?"

But it was obvious; their unrestrained laughter and play proved they were still jangled, far from clear — And clearness is the only road by which a person can gain understanding of the eternal plan, the cosmic wheel which turns endlessly, for all living things.

"Butterflies!" Sung-wu snorted with disgust. "You are no better than the beasts and birds of the field, who take no heed of the morrow. You play and game for today, thinking tomorrow won't come. Like insects — "

But the thought of insects reminded him of the shiny-winged blue-rumped fly, creeping over a rotting lizard carcass, and Sung-wu's stomach did a flip-flop; he forced it back in place and strode on, toward the line of villages emerging ahead.

Farmers were working the barren fields on all sides. A thin layer of soil over slag; a few limp wheat stalks waved, thin and emaciated. The ground was terrible, the worst he had seen. He could feel the metal under his feet; it was almost to the surface. Bent men and women watered their sickly crops with tin cans, old metal containers picked from the ruins. An ox was pulling a crude cart.

In another field, women were weeding by hand; all moved slowly, stupidly, victims of hookworms, from the soil. They were all barefoot. The children hadn't picked it up yet, but they soon would.

Sung-wu gazed up at the sky and gave thanks to Elron; here, suffering was unusually severe; trials of exceptional vividness lay on every hand. These men and women were being tempered in a hot crucible; their souls were probably purified to an astonishing degree. A baby lay in the shade, beside a half-dozing mother. Flies crawled over its eyes; its mother breathed heavily, hoarsely, her mouth open. An unhealthy flush discolored her brown cheeks. Her belly bulged; she was already pregnant again. Another eternal soul to be raised from a lower level. Her great breasts sagged and wobbled as she stirred in her sleep, spilling out over her dirty wraparound.

"Come here," Sung-wu called sharply to the gang of black-faced children who followed along after him. "I'm going to talk to you."

The children approached, eyes on the ground, and assembled in a silent circle around him. Sung-wu sat down, placed his briefcase beside him and folded his legs expertly under him in the traditional posture outlined by Elron in his seventh book of teaching.

"I will ask and you will answer," Sung-wu stated. "You know the basic catechisms?" He peered sharply around. "Who knows the basic catechisms?"

One or two hands went up. Most of the children looked away unhappily.

"First!" snapped Sung-wu. "*Who are you*? You are a minute fragment of the cosmic plan.

"Second! *What are you*? A mere speck in a system so vast as to be beyond comprehension.

"Third! *What is the way of life*? To fulfill what is required by the cosmic forces.

"Fourth! *Where are you*? On one step of the cosmic ladder.

"Fifth! *Where have you been*? Through endless steps; each turn of the wheel advances or depresses you.

"Sixth! *What determines your direction at the next turn*? Your conduct in this manifestation.

"Seventh! *What is right conduct*? Submitting yourself to the eternal forces, the cosmic elements that make up the divine plan.

"Eighth! *What is the significance of suffering*? To purify the soul.

"Ninth! *What is the significance of death*? To release the person from this manifestation, so he may rise to a new rung of the ladder.

"Tenth — "

But at that moment Sung-wu broke off. Two quasi-human shapes were approaching him. Immense white-skinned figures striding across the baked fields, between the sickly rows of wheat.

Technos — coming to meet him; his flesh crawled. Caucs. Their skin glittered pale and unhealthy, like nocturnal insects, dug from under rocks.

He rose to his feet, conquered his disgust, and prepared to greet them.

Sung-wu said, "Clearness!" He could smell them, a musky sheep smell, as they came to a halt in front of him. Two bucks, two immense sweating males, skin damp and sticky, with beards, and long disorderly hair. They wore sailcloth trousers and boots. With horror Sung-wu perceived a thick body-hair, on their chests, like woven mats — tufts in their armpits, on their arms. wrists, even the backs of their hands. Maybe Broken Feather was right; perhaps, in these great lumbering blond-haired beasts, the archaic Neanderthal stock — the false men — still survived. He could almost see the ape, peering from behind their blue eyes.

"Hi," the first Cauc said. After a moment he added reflectively, "My name's Jamison."

"Pete Ferris," the other grunted. Neither of them observed the customary deferences; Sung-wu winced but managed not to show it. Was it deliberate, a veiled insult, or perhaps mere ignorance? This was hard to tell; in lower classes there was, as Chai said, an ugly undercurrent of resentment and envy, and hostility.

"I'm making a routine survey," Sung-wu explained, "on birth and death rates in rural areas. I'll be here a few days. Is there some place I can stay? Some public inn or hostel?"

The two Cauc bucks were silent. "Why?" one of them demanded bluntly.

Sung-wu blinked. "Why? Why what?"

"Why are you making a survey? If you want any information we'll supply it."

Sung-wu was incredulous. "Do you know to whom you're talking? I'm a Bard! Why, you're ten classes down; how dare you — " He choked with rage. In these rural areas the Technos had utterly forgotten their place. What was ailing the local Bards? Were they letting the system break apart?

He shuddered violently at the thought of what it would mean if Technos and Farmers and Businessmen were allowed to intermingle — even intermarry, and eat, and drink, in the same places. The whole structure of society would collapse. If all were to ride the same carts, use the same outhouses; it passed belief. A sudden nightmare picture loomed up before Sung-wu, of Technos living and mating with women of the Bard and Poet classes. He visioned a horizontally-oriented society, all persons on the same level, with horror. It went against the very grain of the cosmos, against the divine plan; it was the Time of Madness all over again. He shuddered.

"Where is the Manager of this area?" he demanded. "Take me to him; I'll deal directly with him."

The two Caucs turned and headed back the way they had come, without a word. After a moment of fury, Sung-wu followed behind them.

They led him through withered fields and over barren, eroded hills on which nothing grew; the ruins increased. At the edge of the city, a line of meager villages had been set up; he saw leaning, rickety wood huts, and mud streets. From the villages a thick stench rose, the smell of offal and death.

Dogs lay sleeping under the huts; children poked and played in the filth and rotting debris. A few old people sat on porches, vacant-faced, eyes glazed and dull. Chickens pecked around, and he saw pigs and skinny cats — and the eternal rusting piles of metal, sometimes thirty feet high. Great towers of red slag were heaped up everywhere.

Beyond the villages were the ruins proper — endless miles of abandoned wreckage; skeletons of buildings; concrete walls; bathtubs and pipe; overturned wrecks that had been cars. All these were from the Time of Madness, the decade that had finally rung the curtain down on the sorriest interval in man's history. The five centuries of madness and jangledness were now known as the Age of Heresy, when man had gone against the divine plan and taken his destiny in his own hands.

They came to a larger hut, a two-story wood structure. The Caucs climbed a decaying flight of steps; boards creaked and gave ominously under their heavy boots. Sung-wu followed them nervously; they came out on a porch, a kind of open balcony.

On the balcony sat a man, an obese copper-skinned official in unbuttoned breeches, his shiny black hair pulled back and tied with a bone against his bulging red neck. His nose was large and prominent, his face, flat and wide, with many chins. He was drinking lime juice from a tin cup and gazing down at the mud street below. As the two Caucs appeared he rose slightly, a prodigious effort.

"This man," the Cauc named Jamison said, indicating Sung-wu, "wants to see you."

Sung-wu pushed angrily forward. "I am a Bard, from the Central Chamber; do you people recognize *this*?" He tore open his robe and flashed the symbol of the Holy Arm, gold worked to form a swathe of flaming red. "I insist you accord me proper treatment! I'm not here to be pushed around by any — "

He had said too much; Sung-wu forced his anger down and gripped his briefcase. The fat Indian was studying him calmly; the two Caucs had wandered to the far end of the balcony and were squatting down in the shade. They lit crude cigarettes and turned their backs.

"Do you permit this?" Sung-wu demanded, incredulous. "This — mingling?"

The Indian shrugged and sagged down even more in his chair. "Clearness be with you," he murmured; "will you joi me?" His calm expression remained unchanged; he seemed not to have noticed. "Some lime juice? Or perhaps coffee? Lime juice is good for these." He tapped his mouth; his soft gums were lined with caked sores.

"Nothing for me," Sung-wu muttered grumpily, as he took a seat opposite the Indian; "I'm here on an official survey."

The Indian nodded faintly. "Oh?"

"Birth and death rates." Sung-wu hesitated, then leaned toward the Indian. "I insist you send those two Caucs away; what I have to say to you is private."

The Indian showed no change of expression; his broad face was utterly impassive. After a time he turned slightly. "Please go down to the street level," he ordered. "As you will."

The two Caucs got to their feet, grumbling, and pushed past the table, scowling and dating resentful glances at Sung-wu. One of them hawked and elaborately spat over the railing, an obvious insult.

"Insolence!" Sung-wu choked. "How can you allow it? Did you see them? By Elron, it's beyond belief!"

The Indian shrugged indifferently — and belched. "All men are brothers on the wheel. Didn't Elron Himself teach that, when He was on Earth?"

"Of course. But — "

"Are not even these men our brothers?"

"Naturally," Sung-wu answered haughtily, "but they must know their place; they're an insignificant class. In the rare event some object wants fixing, they're called; but in the last year I do not recall a single incident when it was deemed advisable to repair anything. The need of such a class diminishes yearly; eventually such a class and the elements composing it — "

"You perhaps advocate sterilization?" the Indian inquired, heavy-lidded and sly.

"I advocate *something.* The lower classes reproduce like rabbits; spawning all the time — much faster than we Bards. I always see some swollen-up Cauc woman, but hardly a single Bard is born these days; the lower classes must fornicate constantly."

"That's about all that's left them," the Indian murmured mildly. He sipped a little lime juice. "You should try to be more tolerant."

"Tolerant? I have nothing against them, as long as they — "

"It is said," the Indian continued softly, "that Elron Hu, Himself, was a Cauc."

Sung-wu spluttered indignantly and started to rejoin, but the hot words stuck fast in his mouth; down in the mud street something was coming.

Sung-wu demanded, "What is it?" He leaped up excitedly and hurried to the railing.

A slow procession was advancing with solemn step. As if at a signal, men and women poured from their rickety huts and excitedly lined the street to watch. Sung-wu was transfixed, as the procession neared; his senses reeled. More and more men and women were collecting each moment; there seemed to be hundreds of them. They were a dense, murmuring mob, packed tight, swaying back and forth, faces avid. An hysterical moan passed through them, a great wind that stirred them like leaves of a tree. They were a single collective whole, a vast primitive organism, held ecstatic and hypnotized by the approaching column.

The marchers wore a strange costume: white shirts, with the sleeves rolled up; dark gray trousers of an incredibly archaic design, and black shoes. All were dressed exactly alike. They formed a dazzling double line of white shirts, gray trousers, marching calmly and solemnly, faces up, nostrils flared, jaws stern. A glazed fanaticism stamped each man and woman, such a ruthless expression that Sung-wu shrank back in terror. On and on they came, figures of grim stone in their primordial white shirts and gray trousers, a frightening breath from the past. Their heels struck the ground in a dull, harsh beat that reverberated among the rickety huts. The dogs woke; the children began to wail. The chickens flew squawking.

"Elron!" Sung-wu cried. "What's happening?"

The marchers carried strange symbolic implements, ritualistic images with esoteric meaning that of necessity escaped Sung-wu. There were tubes and poles, and shiny webs of what looked like metal. *Metal*! But it was not rusty; it was shiny and bright. He was stunned; they looked — new.

The procession passed directly below. After the marchers came a huge rumbling cart. On it was mounted an obvious fertility symbol, a corkscrew-bore as long as a tree; it jutted from a square cube of gleaming steel; as the cart moved forward the bore lifted and fell.

After the cart came more marchers, also grim-faced, eyes glassy, loaded down with pipes and tubes and armfuls of glittering equipment. They passed on, and then the street was filled by surging throngs of awed men and women, who followed after them, utterly dazed. And then came children and barking dogs.

The last marcher carried a pennant that fluttered above her as she strode along, a tall pole, hugged tight to her chest. At the top, the bright pennant fluttered boldly. Sung-wu made its marking out, and for a moment consciousness left him. There it was, directly below; it had passed under his very nose, out in the open for all to see — unconcealed. The pennant had a great T emblazoned on it.

"They — " he began, but the obese Indian cut him off.

"The Tinkerists," he rumbled, and sipped his lime juice.

Sung-wu grabbed up his briefcase and scrambled toward the stairs. At the bottom, the two hulking Caucs were already moving into motion. The Indian signaled quickly to them. "Here!" They started grimly up, little blue eyes mean, red-rimmed and cold as stone; under their pelts their bulging muscles rippled.

Sung-wu fumbled in his cloak. His shiver-gun came out; he squeezed the release and directed it toward the two Caucs. But nothing happened; the gun had stopped functioning. He shook it wildly; flakes of rust and dried insulation fluttered from it. It was useless, worn out; he tossed it away and then, with the resolve of desperation, jumped through the railing.

He, and a torrent of rotten wood, cascaded to the street. He hit, rolled, struck his head against the corner of a hut, and shakily pulled himself to his feet.

He ran. Behind him, the two Caucs pushed after him through the throngs of men and women milling aimlessly along. Occasionally he glimpsed their white, perspiring faces. He turned a corner, raced between shabby huts, leaped over a sewage ditch, climbed heaps of sagging debris, slipping and rolled and at last lay gasping behind a tree, his briefcase still clutched.

The Caucs were nowhere in sight. He had evaded them; for the moment, he was safe.

He peered around. Which way was his ship? He shielded his eyes against the late-afternoon sun until he managed to make out its bent, tubular outline. It was far off to his right, barely visibly in the dying glare that hung gloomily across the sky. Sung-wu got unsteadily to his feet and began walking cautiously in that direction.

He was in a terrible spot; the whole region was pro-Tinkerist — even the Chamber-appointed Manager. And it wasn't along class lines; the cult had knifed to the top level. And it wasn't just Caucs, anymore; he couldn't count on Bantu or Mongolian or Indian, not in this area. An entire countryside was hostile, and lying in wait for him.

Elron, it was worse than the Arm had thought! No wonder they wanted a report. A whole area had swung over to a fanatic cult, a violent extremist group of heretics, teaching a most diabolical doctrine. He shuddered — and kept on, avoiding contact with the farmers in their fields, both human and robot. He increased his pace, as alarm and horror pushed him suddenly faster.

If the thing were to spread, if it were to hit a sizable portion of mankind, it might bring back the Time of Madness.

The ship was taken. Three or four immense Caucs stood lounging around it, cigarettes dangling from their slack mouths, white-faced and hairy. Stunned, Sung-wu moved back down the hillside, prickles of despair numbing him. The ship was lost; they had got there ahead of him. What was he supposed to do now?

It was almost evening. He'd have to walk fifty miles through the darkness, over unfamiliar, hostile ground, to reach the next inhabited area. The sun was already beginning to set, the air turning cool; and in addition, he was sopping wet with filth and slimy water. He had slipped in the gloom and fallen in a sewage ditch.

He retraced his steps, mind blank. What could he do? He was helpless; his shiver-gun had been useless. He was alone, and there was no contact with the Arm. Tinkerists swarming on all sides; they'd probably gut him and sprinkle his blood over the crops — or worse.

He skirted a farm. In the fading twilight, a dim figure was working, a young woman. He eyed her cautiously, as he passed; she had her back to him. She was bending over, between rows of corn. What was she doing? Was she — good Elron!

He stumbled blindly across the field toward her, caution forgotten. "Young woman! *Stop*! In the name of Elron, stop at once!"

The girl straightened up. "Who are you?"

Breathless, Sung-wu arrived in front of her, gripping his battered brief-case and gasping. "Those are our *brothers*! How can you destroy them? They may be close relatives, recently deceased." He struck and knocked the jar from her hand; it hit the ground and the imprisoned beetles scurried off in all directions.

The girl's cheeks flushed with anger. "It took me an hour to collect those!"

"You were killing them! Crushing them!" He was speechless with horror. "I saw you!"

"Of course." The girl raised her black eyebrows. "They gnaw the corn."

"They're our brothers!" Sung-wu repeated wildly. "Of course they gnaw the corn; because of certain sins committed, the cosmic forces have — " He broke off, appalled. "Don't you *know*? You've never been told?"

The girl was perhaps sixteen. In the fading light she was a small, slender figure, the empty jar in one hand, a rock in the other. A tide of black hair tumbled down her neck. Her eyes were large and luminous; her lips full and deep red; her skin a smooth copper-brown — Polynesian, probably. He caught a glimpse of firm brown breasts as she bent to grab a beetle that had landed on its back. The sight made his pulse race; in a flash he was back three years.

"What's your name?" he asked, more kindly.

"Frija."

"How old are you?"

"Seventeen."

"I am a Bard; have you ever spoken to a Bard before?"

"No," the girl murmured. "I don't think so."

She was almost invisible in the darkness. Sung-wu could scarcely see her, but what he saw sent his heart into an agony of paroxysms; the same cloud of black hair, the same deep red lips. This girl was younger, of course — a mere child, and from the Farmer class, at that. But she had Liu's figure, and in time she'd ripen — probably in a matter of months.

Ageless, honeyed craft worked his vocal cords. "I have landed in this area to make a survey. Something has gone wrong with my ship and I must remain the night. I know no one here, however. My plight is such that — "

"Oh," Frija said, immediately sympathetic. "Why don't you stay with us, tonight? We have an extra room, now that my brother's away."

"Delighted," Sung-wu answered instantly. "Will you lead the way? I'll gladly repay you for your kindness." The girl moved off toward a vague shape looming up in the darkness. Sung-wu hurried quickly after her. "I find it incredible you haven't been instructed. This whole area has deteriorated beyond belief. What ways have you fallen in? We'll have to spend much time together; I can see that already. Not one of you even approaches clearness — you're jangled, every one of you."

"What does that mean?" Frija asked, as she stepped up on the porch and opened the door.

"Jangled?" Sung-wu blinked in amazement. "We *will* have to study much together." In his eagerness, he tripped on the top step, and barely managed to catch himself. "Perhaps you need complete instruction; it may be necessary to start from the very bottom. I can arrange a stay at the Holy Arm for you — under my protection, of course. Jangled means out of harmony with the cosmic elements. How can you live this way? My dear, you'll have to be brought back in line with the divine plan!"

"What plan is that?" She led him into a warm living room; a crackling fire burned in the grate. Two or three men sat around a rough wood table, an old man with long white hair and two younger men. A frail, withered old woman sat dozing in a rocker in the corner. In the kitchen, a buxom young woman was fixing the evening meal.

"Why, *the* plan!" Sung-wu answered, astounded. His eyes darted around. Suddenly his briefcase fell to the floor. "Caucs," he said.

They were all Caucasians, even Frija. She was deeply tanned; her skin was almost black; but she was a Cauc, nonetheless. He recalled: Caucs, in the sun, turned dark, sometimes even darker than Mongolians. The girl had tossed her work robe over a door hook; in her household shorts her thighs were as white as milk. And the old man and woman —

"This is my grandfather," Frija said, indicating the old man. "Benjamin Tinker."

Under the watchful eyes of the two younger Tinkers, Sung-wu was washed and scrubbed, given clean clothes, and then fed. He ate only a little; he didn't feel very well.

"I can't understand it," he muttered, as he listlessly pushed his plate away. "The scanner at the Central Chamber said I had eight months left. The plague will — " He considered. "But it can always change. The scanner goes on prediction, not certainty; multiple possibilities; free will. . . . Any overt act of sufficient significance — "

Ben Tinker laughed. "You want to stay alive?"

"Of course!" Sung-wu muttered indignantly.

They all laughed — even Frija, and the old woman in her shawl, snow-white hair and mild blue eyes. They were the first Cauc women he had ever seen. They weren't big and lumbering like the male Caucs; they didn't seem to have the same bestial characteristics. The two young Cauc bucks looked plenty tough, though; they and their father were poring over an elaborate series of papers and reports, spread out on the dinner table, among the empty plates.

"This area," Ben Tinker murmured. "Pipes should go here. And here. Water's the main need. Before the next crop goes in, we'll dump a few hundred pounds of artificial fertilizers and plow it in. The power plows should be ready, then."

"After that?" one of the tow-headed sons asked.

"Then spraying. If we don't have the nicotine sprays, we'll have to try the copper dusting again. I prefer the spray, but we're still behind on production. The bore has dug us up some good storage caverns, though. It ought to start picking up."

"And here," a son said, "there's going to be need of draining. A lot of mosquito breeding going on. We can try the oil, as we did over here. But I suggest the whole thing be filled in. We can use the dredge and scoop, if they're not tied up."

Sung-wu had taken this all in. Now he rose unsteadily to his feet, trembling with wrath. He pointed a shaking finger at the elder Tinker.

"You're — meddling!" he gasped.

They looked up. "Meddling?"

"With the plan! With the cosmic plan! Good Elron — you're interfering with the divine processes. Why — " He was staggered by a realization so alien it convulsed the very core of his being. "You're actually going to set back turns of the wheel."

"That," said old Ben Tinker, "is right."

Sung-wu sat down again, stunned. His mind refused to take it all in. "I don't understand; what'll happen? If you slow the wheel, if you disrupt the divine plan — "

"He's going to be a problem," Ben Tinker murmured thoughtfully. "If we kill him, the Arm will merely send another; they have hundreds like him. And if we don't kill him, if we send him back, he'll raise a hue and cry that'll bring the whole Chamber down here. It's too soon for this to happen. We're gaining support fast, but we need another few months."

Sweat stood out on Sung-wu's plump forehead. He wiped it away shakily. "If you kill me," he muttered, "you will sink down many rungs of the cosmic ladder. You have risen this far; why undo the work accomplished in endless ages past?"

Ben Tinker fixed one powerful blue eye on him. "My friend," he said slowly, "isn't it true one's next manifestation is determined by one's moral conduct in this?"

Sung-wu nodded. "Such is well-known."

"And what is right conduct?"

"Fulfilling the divine plan," Sung-wu responded immediately.

"Maybe our whole Movement in part of the plan," Ben Tinker said thoughtfully. "Maybe the cosmic forces *want* us to drain the swamps and kill the grasshoppers and inoculate the children; after all, the cosmic forces put us all here."

"If you kill me," Sung-wu wailed, "I'll be a carrion-eating fly. I *saw* it, a shiny-winged blue-rumped fly crawling over the carcass of a dead lizard — In a rotting, steaming jungle in a filthy cesspool of a planet." Tears came; he dabbed at them futilely. "In an out-of-the-way system, at the bottom of the ladder!"

Tinker was amused. "Why this?"

"I've sinned." Sung-wu sniffed and flushed. "I committed adultery."

"Can't you purge yourself?"

"There's no time!" His misery rose to wild despair. "My mind is *still* impure!" He indicated Frija, standing in the bedroom doorway, a supple white and tan shape in her household shorts. "I continue to think carnal thoughts; I can't rid myself. In eight months the plague will turn the wheel on me — and it'll be done! If I lived to be an old man, withered and toothless — no more appetite — " His plump body quivered in a frenzied convulsion. "There's no *time* to purge and atone. According to the scanner, I'm going to die a young man!"

After this torrent of words, Tinker was silent, deep in thought. "The plague," he said, at last. "What, exactly, are the symptoms?"

Sung-wu described them, his olive face turning to a sickly green. When he had finished, the three men looked significantly at each other.

Ben Tinker got to his feet. "Come along," he commanded briskly, taking the Bard by the arm. "I have something to show you. It is left from the old days. Sooner or later we'll advance enough to turn out our own, but right now we have only these remaining few. We have to keep them guarded and sealed."

"This is for a good cause," one of the sons said. "It's worth it." He caught his brother's eye and grinned.

Bard Chai finished reading Sung-wu's blue-slip report; he tossed it suspiciously down and eyed the younger Bard. "You're sure? There's no further need of investigation?"

"The cult will wither away," Sung-wu murmured indifferently. "It lacks any real support; it's merely an escape valve, without intrinsic validity."

Chai wasn't convinced. He reread parts of the report again. "I suppose you're right; but we've heard so many — "

"Lies," Sung-wu said vaguely. "Rumors. Gossip. May I go?" He moved toward the door.

"Eager for your vacation?" Chai smiled understandingly. "I know how you feel. This report must have exhausted you. Rural areas, stagnant backwaters. We must prepare a better program of rural education. I'm convinced whole regions are in a jangled state. We've got to bring clearness to these people. It's our historic role; our class function."

"Verily," Sung-wu murmured, as he bowed his way out of the office and down the hall.

As he walked he fingered his beads thankfully. He breathed a silent prayer as his fingers moved over the surface of the little red pellets, shiny spheres that glowed freshly in place of the faded old — the gift of the Tinkerists. The beads would come in handy; he kept his hand on them tightly. Nothing must happen to them, in the next eight months. He had to watch them carefully, while he poked around the ruined cities of Spain — and finally came down with the plague.

He was the first Bard to wear a rosary of penicillin capsules.

THE LAST OF THE MASTERS

CONSCIOUSNESS COLLECTED around him. He returned with reluctance; the weight of centuries, an unbearable fatigue, lay over him. The ascent was painful. He would have shrieked if there were anything to shriek with. And anyhow, he was beginning to feel glad.

Eight thousand times he had crept back thus, with ever-increasing difficulty. Someday he wouldn't make it. Someday the black pool would remain. But not this day. He was still alive; above the aching pain and reluctance came joyful triumph.

"Good morning," a bright voice said. "Isn't it a nice day? I'll pull the curtains and you can look out."

He could see and hear. But he couldn't move. He lay quietly and allowed the various sensations of the room to pour in on him. Carpets, wallpaper, tables, lamps, pictures. Desk and vidscreen. Gleaming yellow sunlight streamed through the window. Blue sky. Distant hills. Fields, buildings, roads, factories. Workers and machines.

Peter Green was busily straightening things, his young face wreathed with smiles. "Lots to do today. Lots of people to see you. Bills to sign. Decisions to make. This is Saturday. There will be people coming in from the remote sectors. I hope the maintenance crew has done a good job." He added quickly, "They have, of course. I talked to Fowler on my way over here. Everything's fixed up fine."

The youth's pleasant tenor mixed with the bright sunlight. Sounds and sights, but nothing else. He could feel nothing. He tried to move his arm but nothing happened.

"Don't worry," Green said, catching his terror. "They'll soon be along with the rest. You'll be all right. You *have* to be. How could we survive without you?"

He relaxed. God knew, it had happened often enough before. Anger surged dully. Why couldn't they coordinate? Get it up all at once, not piece-meal. He'd have to change their schedule. Make them organize better.

Past the bright window a squat metal car chugged to a halt. Uniformed men piled out, gathered up heavy armloads of equipment, and hurried toward the main entrance of the building.

"Here they come," Green exclaimed with relief. "A little late, eh?"

"Another traffic tie-up," Fowler snorted, as he entered. "Something wrong with the signal system again. Outside flow got mixed up with the urban stuff; tied up on all sides. I wish you'd change the law."

Now there was motion all around him. The shapes of Fowler and McLean loomed, two giant moons abruptly ascendant. Professional faces that peered down at him anxiously. He was turned over on his side. Muffled conferences. Urgent whispers. The clank of tools.

"Here," Fowler muttered. "Now here. No, that's later. Be careful. Now run it up through here."

The work continued in taut silence. He was aware of their closeness. Dim outlines occasionally cut off his light. He was turned this way and that, thrown around like a sack of meal.

"Okay," Fowler said. "Tape it."

A long silence. He gazed dully at the wall, at the slightly-faded blue and pink wallpaper. An old design that showed a woman in hoopskirts, with a little parasol over her dainty shoulder. A frilly white blouse, tiny tips of shoes. An astoundingly clean puppy at her side.

Then he was turned back, to face upward. Five shapes groaned and strained over him. Their fingers flew, their muscles rippled under their shirts. At last they straightened up and retreated. Fowler wiped sweat from his face; they were all tense and bleary eyed.

"Go ahead," Fowler rasped. "Throw it."

Shock hit him. He gasped. His body arched, then settled slowly down.

His body. He could feel. He moved his arms experimentally. He touched his face, his shoulder, the wall. The wall was real and hard. All at once the world had become three-dimensional again.

Relief showed on Fowler's face. "Thank — God." He sagged wearily. "How do you feel?"

After a moment he answered, "All right."

Fowler sent the rest of the crew out. Green began dusting again, off in the corner. Fowler sat down on the edge of the bed and lit his pipe. "Now listen to me," he said. "I've got bad news. I'll give it to you the way you always want it, straight from the shoulder."

"What is it?" he demanded. He examined his fingers. He already knew.

There were dark circles under Fowler's eyes. He hadn't shaved. His square-jawed face was drawn and unhealthy. "We were up all night. Working on your motor system. We've got it jury-rigged, but it won't hold. Not more than another few months. The thing's climbing. The basic units can't be replaced. When they wear out they're gone. We can weld in relays and wiring, but we can't fix the five synapsis-coils. There were only a few men who could make those, and they've been dead two centuries. If the coils burn out — "

"Is there any deterioration in the synapsis-coils?" he interrupted.

"Not yet. Just motor areas. Arms, in particular. What's happening to your legs will happen to your arms and finally all your motor system. You'll be paralyzed by the end of the year. You'll be able to see, hear, and think. And broadcast. But that's all." He added, "Sorry, Bors. We're doing all we can."

"All right," Bors said. "You're excused. Thanks for telling me straight. I — guessed."

"Ready to go down? A lot of people with problems, today. They're stuck until you get there."

"Let's go." He focused his mind with an effort and turned his attention to the details of the day. "I want the heavy metals research program speeded. It's lagging, as usual. I may have to pull a number of men from related work and shift them to the generators. The water level will be dropping soon. I want to start feeding power along the lines while there's still power to feed. As soon as I turn my back everything starts falling apart."

Fowler signalled Green and he came quickly over. The two of them bent over Bors and, grunting, hoisted him up and carried him to the door. Down the corridor and outside.

They deposited him in the squat metal car, the new little service truck. Its polished surface was a startling contrast to his pitted, corroded hull, bent and splotched and eaten away. A dull, patina-covered machine of archaic steel and plastic that hummed faintly, rustily, as the men leaped in the front seat and raced the car out onto the main highway.

Edward Tolby perspired, pushed his pack up higher, hunched over, tightened his gun belt, and cursed.

"Daddy," Silvia reproved. "Cut that."

Tolby spat furiously in the grass at the side of the road. He put his arm around his slim daughter. "Sorry, Silv. Nothing personal. The damn heat."

Mid-morning sun shimmered down on the dusty road. Clouds of dust rose and billowed around the three as they pushed slowly along. They were dead tired. Tolby's heavy face was flushed and sullen. An unlit cigarette dangled between his lips. His big, powerfully built body was hunched resentfully forward. His daughter's canvas shirt clung moistly to her arms and breasts. Moons of sweat darkened her back. Under her jeans her thigh muscles rippled wearily.

Robert Penn walked a little behind the two Tolby's, hands deep in his pockets, eyes on the road ahead. His mind was blank; he was half asleep from the double shot of hexobarb he had swallowed at the last League camp. And the heat lulled him. On each side of the road fields stretched out, pastures of grass and weeds, a few trees here and there. A tumbled-down farmhouse. The ancient rusting remains of a bomb shelter, two centuries old. Once, some dirty sheep.

"Sheep," Penn said. "They eat the grass too far down. It won't grow back."

"Now he's a farmer," Tolby said to his daughter.

"Daddy," Silvia snapped. "Stop being nasty."

"It's this heat. This damn heat." Tolby cursed again, loudly and futilely. "It's not worth it. For ten pinks I'd go back and tell them it was a lot of pig swill."

"Maybe it is, at that," Penn said mildly.

"All right, you go back," Tolby grunted. "You go back and tell them it's a lot of pig swill. They'll pin a medal on you. Maybe raise you up a grade."

Penn laughed. "Both of you shut up. There's some kind of town ahead."

Tolby's massive body straightened eagerly. "Where?" He shielded his eyes. "By God, he's right. A village. And it isn't a mirage. You see it, don't you?" His good humor returned and he rubbed his big hands together. "What say, Penn. A couple of beers, a few games of throw with some of the local peasants — maybe we can stay overnight." He licked his thick lips with anticipation. "Some of those village wenches, the kind that hang around the grog shops — "

"I know the kind you mean," Penn broke in. "The kind that are tired of doing nothing. Want to see the big commercial centers. Want to meet some guy that'll buy them mecho-stuff and take them places."

At the side of the road a farmer was watching them curiously. He had halted his horse and stood leaning on his crude plow, hat pushed back on his head.

"What's the name of this town?" Tolby yelled.

The farmer was silent a moment. He was an old man, thin and weathered. "This town?" he repeated.

"Yeah, the one ahead."

"That's a nice town." The farmer eyed the three of them. "You been through here before?"

"No, sir," Tolby said. "Never."

"Team break down?"

"No, we're on foot."

"How far you come?"

"About a hundred and fifty miles."

The farmer considered the heavy packs strapped on their backs. Their cleated hiking shoes. Dusty clothing and weary, sweat-streaked faces. Jeans and canvas shirts. Ironite walking staffs. "That's a long way," he said. "How far you going?"

"As far as we feel like it," Tolby answered. "Is there a place ahead we can stay? Hotel? Inn?"

"That town," the farmer said, "is Fairfax. It has a lumber mill, one of the best in the world. A couple of pottery works. A place where you can get clothes put together by machines. Regular mecho-clothing. A gun shop where they pour the best shot this side of the Rockies. And a bakery. Also there's an old doctor living there, and a lawyer. And some people with books to teach the kids. They came with t.b. They made a school house out of an old barn."

"How large a town?" Penn asked.

"Lot of people. More born all the time. Old folks die. Kids die. We had a fever last year. About a hundred kids died. Doctor said it came from the water hole. We shut the water hole down. Kids died anyhow. Doctor said it was the milk. Drove off half the cows. Not mine. I stood out there with my gun and I shot the first of them came to drive off my cow. Kids stopped dying as soon as fall came. I think it was the heat."

"Sure is hot," Tolby agreed.

"Yes, it gets hot around here. Water's pretty scarce." A crafty look slid across his old face. "You folks want a drink? The young lady looks pretty tired. Got some bottles of water down under the house. In the mud. Nice and cold." He hesitated. "Pink a glass."

Tolby laughed. "No, thanks."

"Two glasses a pink," the farmer said.

"Not interested," Penn said. He thumped his canteen and the three of them started on. "So long."

The farmer's face hardened. "Damn foreigners," he muttered. He turned angrily back to his plowing.

The town baked in silence. Flies buzzed and settled on the backs of stupefied horses, tied up at posts. A few cars were parked here and there. People moved listlessly along the sidewalks. Elderly lean-bodied men dozed on porches. Dogs and chickens slept in the shade under houses. The houses were small, wooden, chipped and peeling boards, leaning and angular — and old. Warped and split by age and heat. Dust lay over everything. A thick blanket of dry dust over the cracking houses and the dull-faced men and animals.

Two lank men approached them from an open doorway. "Who are you? What do you want?"

They stopped and got out their identification. The men examined the sealed-plastic cards. Photographs, fingerprints, data. Finally they handed them back.

"AL," one said. "You really from the Anarchist League?"

"That's right," Tolby said.

"Even the girl?" The men eyed Silvia with languid greed. "Tell you what. Let us have the girl a while and we'll skip the head tax."

"Don't kid me," Tolby grunted. "Since when does the League pay head tax or any other tax?" He pushed past them impatiently. "Where's the grog shop? I'm dying!"

A two-story white building was on their left. Men lounged on the porch, watching them vacantly. Penn headed toward it and the Tolby's followed. A faded, peeling sign lettered across the front read: *Beer, Wine on Tap.*

"This is it," Penn said. He guided Silvia up the sagging steps, past the men, and inside. Tolby followed; he unstrapped his pack gratefully as he came.

The place was cool and dark. A few men and women were at the bar; the rest sat around tables. Some youths were playing throw in the back. A mechanical tune-maker wheezed and composed in the corner, a shabby, half-ruined machine only partially functioning. Behind the bar a primitive scene-shifter created and destroyed vague phantasmagoria: seascapes, mountain peaks, snowy valleys, great rolling hills, a nude woman that lingered and then dissolved into one vast breast. Dim, uncertain processions that no one noticed or looked at. The bar itself was an incredibly ancient sheet of transparent plastic, stained and chipped and yellow with age. Its n-grav coat had faded from one end; bricks now propped it up. The drink mixer had long since fallen apart. Only wine and beer were served. No living man knew how to mix the simplest drink.

Tolby moved up to the bar. "Beer," he said. "Three beers." Penn and Silvia sank down at a table and removed their packs, as the bartender served Tolby three mugs of thick, dark beer. He showed his card and carried the mugs over to the table.

The youths in the back had stopped playing. They were watching the three as they sipped their beer and unlaced their hiking boots. After a while one of them came slowly over.

"Say," he said. "You're from the League."

"That's right," Tolby murmured sleepily.

Everyone in the place was watching and listening. The youth sat down across from the three; his companions flocked excitedly around and took seats on all sides. The juveniles of the town. Bored, restless, dissatisfied. Their eyes took in the ironite staffs, the guns, the heavy metal-cleated boots. A murmured whisper rustled through them. They were about eighteen. Tanned, rangy.

"How do you get in?" one demanded bluntly.

"The League?" Tolby leaned back in his chair, found a match, and lit his cigarette. He unfastened his belt, belched loudly, and settled back contentedly. "You get in by examination."

"What do you have to know?"

Tolby shrugged. "About everything." He belched again and scratched thoughtfully at his chest, between two buttons. He was conscious of the ring of people around on all sides. A little old man with a beard and horn-rimmed glasses. At another table, a great tub of a man in a red shirt and blue-striped trousers, with a bulging stomach.

Youths. Farmers. A Negro in a dirty white shirt and trousers, a book under his arm. A hard-jawed blonde, hair in a net, red nails and high heels, tight yellow dress. Sitting with a gray-haired businessman in a dark brown suit. A tall young man holding hands with a young black-haired girl, huge eyes, in a soft white blouse and skirt, little slippers kicked under the table. Under the table her bare, tanned feet twisted; her slim body was bent forward with interest.

"You have to know," Tolby said, "how the League was formed. You have to know how we pulled down the governments that day. Pulled them down and destroyed them. Burned all the buildings. And all the records. Billions of microfilms and papers. Great bonfires that burned for weeks. And the swarms of little white things that poured out when we knocked the buildings over."

"You killed them?" the great tub of a man asked, lips twitching avidly.

"We let them go. They were harmless. They ran and hid. Under rocks." Tolby laughed. "Funny little scurrying things. Insects. Then we went in and gathered up all the records and equipment for making records. By God, we burned everything."

"And the robots," a youth said.

"Yeah, we smashed all the government robots. There weren't many of them. They were used only at high levels. When a lot of facts had to be integrated."

The youth's eyes bulged. "You saw them? You were there when they smashed the robots?"

Penn laughed. "Tolby means the League. That was two hundred years ago."

The youth grinned nervously. "Yeah. Tell us about the marches."

Tolby drained his mug and pushed it away. "I'm out of beer."

The mug was quickly refilled. He grunted his thanks and continued, voice deep and furry, dulled with fatigue. "The marches. That was really something, they say. All over the world, people getting up, throwing down what they were doing — "

"It started in East Germany," the hard-jawed blonde said. "The riots."

"Then it spread to Poland," the Negro put in shyly. "My grandfather used to tell me how everybody sat and listened to the television. His grandfather used to tell him. It spread to Czechoslovakia and then Austria and Roumania and Bulgaria. Then France. And Italy."

"France was first!" the little old man with beard and glasses cried violently. "They were without a government a whole month. The people saw they could live without a government!"

"The marches started it," the black-haired girl corrected. "That was the first time they started pulling down the government buildings. In East Germany and Poland. Big mobs of unorganized workers."

"Russia and America were the last," Tolby said. "When the march on Washington came there was close to twenty million of us. We were big in those days! They couldn't stop us when we finally moved."

"They shot a lot," the hard-faced blonde said.

"Sure. But the people kept coming. And yelling to the soldiers. 'Hey, Bill! Don't shoot!' 'Hey, Jack! It's me, Joe.' 'Don't shoot — we're your friends!' 'Don't kill us, join us!' And by God, after a while they did. They couldn't keep shooting their own people. They finally threw down their guns and got out of the way."

"And then you found the place," the little black-haired girl said breathlessly.

"Yeah. We found the place. *Six* places. Three in America. One in Britain. Two in Russia. It took us ten years to find the last place — and make sure it was the last place."

"What then?" the youth asked, bug-eyed.

"Then we busted every one of them." Tolby raised himself up, a massive man, beer mug clutched, heavy face flushed dark red. "Every damn A-bomb in the whole world."

There was an uneasy silence.

"Yeah," the youth murmured. "You sure took care of those war people."

"Won't be any more of them," the great tub of a man said. "They're gone for good."

Tolby fingered his ironite staff. "Maybe so. And maybe not. There just might be a few of them left."

"What do you mean?" the tub of a man demanded.

Tolby raised his hard gray eyes. "It's time you people stopped kidding us. You know damn well what I mean. We've heard rumors. Someplace around this area there's a bunch of them. Hiding out."

Shocked disbelief, then anger hummed to a roar. "That's a lie!" the tub of a man shouted.

"Is it?"

The little man with beard and glasses leaped up. "There's nobody here has anything to do with governments! We're all good people!"

"You better watch your step," one of the youths said softly to Tolby. "People around here don't like to be accused."

Tolby got unsteadily to his feet, his ironite staff gripped. Penn got up beside him and they stood together. "If any of you knows something," Tolby said, "you better tell it. Right now."

"Nobody knows anything," the hard-faced blonde said. "You're talking to honest folks."

"That's so," the Negro said, nodding his head. "Nobody here's doing anything wrong."

"You saved our lives," the black-haired girl said. "If you hadn't pulled down the governments we'd all be dead in the war. Why should we hold back something?"

"That's true," the great tub of a man grumbled. "We wouldn't be alive if it wasn't for the League. You think we'd do anything against the League?"

"Come on," Silvia said to her father. "Let's go." She got to her feet and tossed Penn his pack.

Tolby grunted belligerently. Finally he took his own pack and hoisted it to his shoulder. The room was deathly silent. Everyone stood frozen, as the three gathered their things and moved toward the door.

The little dark-haired girl stopped them. "The next town is thirty miles from here," she said.

"The road's blocked," her tall companion explained. "Slides closed it years ago."

"Why don't you stay with us tonight? There's plenty of room at our place. You can rest up and get an early start tomorrow."

"We don't want to impose," Silvia murmured.

Tolby and Penn glanced at each other, then at the girl. "If you're sure you have plenty of room — "

The great tub of a man approached them. "Listen. I have ten yellow slips. I want to give them to the League. I sold my farm last year. I don't need any more slips; I'm living with my brother and his family." He pushed the slips at Tolby. "Here."

Tolby pushed them back. "Keep them."

"This way," the tall young man said, as they clattered down the sagging steps, into a sudden blinding curtain of heat and dust. "We have a car. Over this way. An old gasoline car. My dad fixed it so it burns oil."

"You should have taken the slips," Penn said to Tolby, as they got into the ancient, battered car. Flies buzzed around them. They could hardly breathe; the car was a furnace. Silvia fanned herself with a rolled-up paper. The black-haired girl unbuttoned her blouse.

"What do we need money for?" Tolby laughed good-naturedly. "I haven't paid for anything in my life. Neither have you."

The car sputtered and moved slowly forward, onto the road. It began to gain speed. Its motor banged and roared. Soon it was moving surprisingly fast.

"You saw them," Silvia said, over the racket. "They'd give us anything they had. We saved their lives." She waved at the fields, the farmers and their crude teams, the withered crops, the sagging old farmhouses. "They'd all be dead, if it hadn't been for the League." She smashed a fly peevishly. "They depend on us."

The black-haired girl turned toward them, as the car rushed along the decaying road. Sweat streaked her tanned skin. Her half-covered breasts trembled with the motion of the car. "I'm Laura Davis. Pete and I have an old farmhouse his dad gave us when we got married."

"You can have the whole downstairs," Pete said.

"There's no electricity, but we've got a big fireplace. It gets cold at night. It's hot in the day, but when the sun sets it gets terribly cold."

"We'll be all right," Penn murmured. The vibration of the car made him a little sick.

"Yes," the girl said, her black eyes flashing. Her crimson lips twisted. She leaned toward Penn intently, her small face strangely alight. "Yes, we'll take good care of you."

At that moment the car left the road.

Silvia shrieked. Tolby threw himself down, head between his knees, doubled up in a ball. A sudden curtain of green burst around Penn. Then a sickening emptiness, as the car plunged down. It struck with a roaring crash that blotted out everything. A single titanic cataclysm of fury that picked Penn up and flung his remains in every direction.

"Put me down," Bors ordered. "On this railing for a moment before I go inside."

The crew lowered him onto the concrete surface and fastened magnetic grapples into place. Men and women hurried up the wide steps, in and out of the massive building that was Bors' main offices.

The sight from these steps pleased him. He liked to stop here and look around at his world. At the civilization he had carefully constructed. Each piece added painstakingly, scrupulously with infinite care, throughout the years.

It wasn't big. The mountains ringed it on all sides. The valley was a level bowl, surrounded by dark violet hills. Outside, beyond the hills, the regular world began. Parched fields. Blasted, poverty-stricken towns. Decayed roads. The remains of houses, tumbled-down farm buildings. Ruined cars and machinery. Dust-covered people creeping listlessly around in hand-made clothing, dull rags and tatters.

He had seen the outside. He knew what it was like. At the mountains the blank faces, the disease, the withered crops, the crude plows and ancient tools all ended here. Here, within the ring of hills, Bors had constructed an accurate and detailed reproduction of a society two centuries gone. The world as it had been in the old days. The time of governments. The time that had been pulled down by the Anarchist League.

Within his five synapsis-coils the plans, knowledge, information, blueprints of a whole world existed. In the two centuries he had carefully recreated that world, had made this miniature society that glittered and hummed on all sides of him. The roads, buildings, houses, industries of a dead world, all a fragment of the past, built with his hands, his own metal fingers and brain.

"Fowler," Bors said.

Fowler came over. He looked haggard. His eyes were red-rimmed and swollen. "What is it? You want to go inside?"

Overhead, the morning patrol thundered past. A string of black dots against the sunny, cloudless sky. Bors watched with satisfaction. "Quite a sight."

"Right on the nose," Fowler agreed, examining his wristwatch. To their right, a column of heavy tanks snaked along a highway between green fields. Their gun-snouts glittered. Behind them a column of foot soldiers marched, faces hidden behind bacteria masks.

"I'm thinking," Bors said, "that it may be unwise to trust Green any longer."

"Why the hell do you say that?"

"Every ten days I'm inactivated. So your crew can see what repairs are needed." Bors twisted restlessly. "For twelve hours I'm completely helpless. Green takes care of me. Sees nothing happens. But— "

"But what?"

"It occurs to me perhaps there'd be more safety in a squad of troops. It's too much of a temptation for one man, alone."

Fowler scowled. "I don't see that. How about me? I have charge of inspecting you. I could switch a few leads around. Send a load through your synapsis-coils. Blow them out."

Bors whirled wildly, then subsided. "True. You could do that." After a moment he demanded, "But what would you gain? You know I'm the only one who can keep all this together. I'm the only one who knows how to maintain a planned society, not a disorderly chaos! If it weren't for me, all this would collapse, and you'd have dust and ruins and weeds. The whole outside would come rushing in to take over!"

"Of course. So why worry about Green?"

Trucks of workers rumbled past. Loads of men in blue-green, sleeves rolled up, armloads of tools. A mining team, heading for the mountains.

"Take me inside," Bors said abruptly.

Fowler called McLean. They hoisted Bors and carried him past the throngs of people, into the building, down the corridor and to his office.

Officials and technicians moved respectfully out of the way as the great pitted, corroded tank was carried past.

"All right," Bors said impatiently. "That's all. You can go."

Fowler and McLean left the luxurious office, with its lush carpets, furniture, drapes and rows of books. Bors was already bent over his desk, sorting through heaps of reports and papers.

Fowler shook his head, as they walked down the hall. "He won't last much longer."

"The motor system? Can't we reinforce the — "

"I don't mean that. He's breaking up mentally. He can't take the strain any longer."

"None of us can," McLean muttered.

"Running this thing is too much for him. Knowing it's all dependent on him. Knowing as soon as he turns his back or lets down it'll begin to come apart at the seams. A hell of a job, trying to shut out the real world. Keeping his model universe running."

"He's gone on a long time," McLean said.

Fowler brooded. "Sooner or later we're going to have to face the situation." Gloomily, he ran his fingers along the blade of a large screwdriver. "He's wearing out. Sooner or later somebody's going to have to step in. As he continues to decay . . . " He stuck the screwdriver back in his belt, with his pliers and hammer and soldering iron. "One crossed wire."

"What's that?"

Fowler laughed. "Now he's got me doing it. One crossed wire and — *poof.* But what then? That's the big question."

"Maybe," McLean said softly, "you and I can then get off this rat race. You and I and all the rest of us. And live like human beings."

"*Rat race,*" Fowler murmured. "Rats in a maze. Doing tricks. Performing chores thought up by somebody else."

McLean caught Fowler's eye. "By somebody of another species."

Tolby struggled vaguely. Silence. A faint dripping close by. A beam pinned his body down. He was caught on all sides by the twisted wreck of the car. He was head down. The car was turned on its side. Off the road in a gully, wedged between two huge trees. Bent struts and smashed metal all around him. And bodies.

He pushed up with all his strength. The beam gave, and he managed to get to a sitting position. A tree branch had burst in the windshield. The black-haired girl, still turned toward the back seat, was impaled on it. The branch had driven through her spine, out her chest, and into the seat; she clutched at it with both hands, head limp, mouth half-open. The man beside her was also dead. His hands were gone; the windshield had burst around him. He lay in a heap among the remains of the dashboard and the bloody shine of his own internal organs.

Penn was dead. Neck snapped like a rotten broom handle. Tolby pushed his corpse aside and examined his daughter. Silvia didn't stir. He put his ear to her shirt and listened. She was alive. Her heart beat faintly. Her bosom rose and fell against his ear.

He wound a handkerchief around her arm, where the flesh was ripped open and oozing blood. She was badly cut and scratched; one leg was doubled under her, obviously broken. Her clothes were ripped, her hair matted with blood. But she was alive. He pushed the twisted door open and stumbled out. A fiery tongue of afternoon sunlight struck him and he winced. He began to ease her limp body out of the car, past the twisted door-frame.

A sound.

Tolby glanced up, rigid. Something was coming. A whirring insect that rapidly descended. He let go of Silvia, crouched, glanced around, then lumbered awkwardly down the gully. He slid and fell and rolled among the green vines and jagged gray boulders. His gun gripped, he lay gasping in the moist shadows, peering, upward.

The insect landed. A small air-ship, jet-driven. The sight stunned him. He had heard about jets, seen photographs of them. Been briefed and lectured in the history-indoctrination courses at the League Camps. But to *see* a jet!

Men swarmed out. Uniformed men who started from the road, down the side of the gully, bodies crouched warily as they approached the wrecked car. They lugged heavy rifles. They looked grim and experienced, as they tore the car doors open and scrambled in.

"One's gone," a voice drifted to him.

"Must be around somewhere."

"Look, this one's alive! This woman. Started to crawl out. The rest all dead."

Furious cursing. "Damn Laura! She should have leaped! The fanatic little fool!"

"Maybe she didn't have time. God's sake, the thing's all the way through her." Horror and shocked dismay. "We won't hardly be able to get her loose."

"Leave her." The officer directing things waved the men back out of the car. "Leave them all."

"How about this wounded one?"

The leader hesitated. "Kill her," he said finally. He snatched a rifle and raised the butt. "The rest of you fan out and try to get the other one. He's probably — "

Tolby fired, and the leader's body broke in half. The lower part sank down slowly; the upper dissolved in ashy fragments. Tolby turned and began to move in a slow circle, firing as he crawled. He got two more of them before the rest retreated in panic to their jet-powered insect and slammed the lock.

He had the element of surprise. Now that was gone. They had strength and numbers. He was doomed. Already, the insect was rising. They'd be able to spot him easily from above. But he had saved Silvia. That was something.

He stumbled down a dried-up creek bed. He ran aimlessly; he had no place to go. He didn't know the countryside, and he was on foot. He slipped on a stone and fell headlong. Pain and billowing darkness beat at him as he got unsteadily to his knees. His gun was gone, lost in the shrubbery. He spat broken teeth and blood. He peered wildly up at the blazing afternoon sky.

The insect was leaving. It hummed off toward the distant hills. It dwindled, became a black ball, a fly-speck, then disappeared.

Tolby waited a moment. Then he struggled up the side of the ravine to the wrecked car. They had gone to get help. They'd be back. Now was his only chance. If he could get Silvia out and down the road, into hiding. Maybe to a farmhouse. Back to town.

He reached the car and stood, dazed and stupefied. Three bodies remained, the two in the front seat, Penn in the back. But Silvia was gone.

They had taken her with them. Back where they came from. She had been dragged to the jet-driven insect; a trail of blood led from the car up the side of the gully to the highway.

With a violent shudder Tolby pulled himself together. He climbed into the car and pried loose Penn's gun from his belt. Silvia's ironite staff rested on the seat; he took that, too. Then he started off down the road, walking without haste, carefully, slowly.

An ironic thought plucked at his mind. He had found what they were after. The men in uniform. They were organized, responsible to a central authority. In a newly-assembled jet.

Beyond the hills was a government.

"Sir," Green said. He smoothed his short blond hair anxiously, his young face twisting.

Technicians and experts and ordinary people in droves were everywhere. The offices buzzed and echoed with the business of the day. Green pushed through the crowd and to the desk where Bors sat, propped up by two magnetic frames.

"Sir," Green said. "Something's happened."

Bors looked up. He pushed a metal-foil slate away and laid down his stylus. His eye cells clicked and flickered; deep inside his battered trunk motor gears whined. "What is it?"

Green came close. There was something in his face, an expression Bors had never seen before. A look of fear and glassy determination. A glazed, fanatic cast, as if his flesh had hardened to rock. "Sir, scouts contacted a League team moving North. They met the team outside Fairfax. The incident took place directly beyond the first road block."

Bors said nothing. On all sides, officials, experts, farmers, workmen, industrial managers, soldiers, people of all kinds buzzed and murmured and pushed forward impatiently. Trying to get to Bors' desk. Loaded down with problems to be solved, situations to be explained. The pressing business of the day. Roads, factories, disease control. Repairs. Construction. Manufacture. Design. Planning. Urgent problems for Bors to consider and deal with. Problems that couldn't wait.

"Was the League team destroyed?" Bors said.

"One was killed. One was wounded and brought here." Green hesitated. "One escaped."

For a long time Bors was silent. Around him the people murmured and shuffled; he ignored them. All at once he pulled the vidscanner to him and snapped the circuit open. "One escaped? I don't like the sound of that."

"He shot three members of our scout unit. Including the leader. The others got frightened. They grabbed the injured girl and returned here."

Bors' massive head lifted. "They made a mistake. They should have located the one who escaped."

"This was the first time the situation — "

"I know," Bors said. "But it was an error. Better not to have touched them at all, than to have taken two and allowed the third to get away." He turned to the vidscanner. "Sound an emergency alert. Close down the factories. Arm the work crews and any male farmers capable of using weapons. Close every road. Remove the women and children to the undersurface shelters. Bring up the heavy guns and supplies. Suspend all non-military production and — " He considered. "Arrest everyone we're not sure of. On the C sheet. Have them shot." He snapped the scanner off.

"What'll happen?" Green demanded, shaken.

"The thing we've prepared for. Total war."

"We have weapons!" Green shouted excitedly. "In an hour there'll be ten thousand men ready to fight. We have jet-driven ships. Heavy artillery. Bombs. Bacteria pellets. What's the League? A lot of people with packs on their backs!"

"Yes," Bors said. "A lot of people with packs on their backs."

"How can they do anything? How can a bunch of anarchists organize? They have no structure, no control, no central power."

"They have the whole world. A billion people."

"*Individuals!* A club, not subject to law. Voluntary membership. We have disciplined organization. Every aspect of our economic life operates at maximum efficiency. We — you — have your thumb on everything. All you have to do is give the order. Set the machine in motion."

Bors nodded slowly. "It's true the anarchist can't coordinate. The League can't organize. It's a paradox. Government by anarchists . . . Antigovernment, actually. Instead of governing the world they tramp around to make sure no one else does."

"Dog in the manger."

"As you say, they're actually a voluntary club of totally unorganized individuals. Without law or central authority. They maintain no society — they can't govern. All they can do is interfere with anyone else who tries. Troublemakers. But — "

"But what?"

"It was this way before. Two centuries ago. They were unorganized. Unarmed. Vast mobs, without discipline or authority. Yet they pulled down all the governments. All over the world."

"We've got a whole army. All the roads are mined. Heavy guns. Bombs. Pellets. Every one of us is a soldier. We're an armed camp!"

Bors was deep in thought. "You say one of them is here? One of the League agents?"

"A young woman."

Bors signalled the nearby maintenance crew. "Take me to her. I want to talk to her in the time remaining."

Silvia watched silently, as the uniformed men pushed and grunted their way into the room. They staggered over to the bed, pulled two chairs together, and carefully laid down their massive armload.

Quickly they snapped protective struts into place, locked the chairs together, threw magnetic grapples into operation, and then warily retreated.

"All right," the robot said. "You can go." The men left. Bors turned to face the woman on the bed.

"A machine," Silvia whispered, white-faced. "You're a machine."

Bors nodded slightly without speaking.

Silvia shifted uneasily on the bed. She was weak. One leg was in a transparent plastic cast. Her face was bandaged and her right arm ached and throbbed. Outside the window, the late afternoon sun sprinkled through the drapes. Flowers bloomed. Grass. Hedges. And beyond the hedges, buildings and factories.

For the last hour the sky had been filled with jet-driven ships. Great flocks that raced excitedly across the sky toward distant hills. Along the highway cars hurtled, dragging guns and heavy military equipment. Men were marching in close rank, rows of gray-clad soldiers, guns and helmets and bacteria masks. Endless lines of figures, identical in their uniforms, stamped from the same matrix.

"There are a lot of them," Bors said, indicating the marching men.

"Yes." Silvia watched a couple of soldiers hurry by the window. Youths with worried expressions on their smooth faces. Helmets bobbing at their waists. Long rifles. Canteens. Counters. Radiation shields. Bacteria masks wound awkwardly around their necks, ready to go into place. They were scared. Hardly more than kids. Others followed. A truck roared into life. The soldiers were swept off to join the others.

"They're going to fight," Bors said, "to defend their homes and factories."

"All this equipment. You manufacture it, don't you?"

"That's right. Our industrial organization is perfect. We're totally productive. Our society here is operated rationally. Scientifically. We're fully prepared to meet this emergency."

Suddenly Silvia realized what the emergency was. "The League! One of us must have got away." She pulled herself up. "Which of them? Penn or my father?"

"I don't know," the robot murmured indifferently.

Horror and disgust choked Silvia. "My God," she said softly. "You have no understanding of us. You run all this, and you're incapable of empathy. You're nothing but a mechanical computer. One of the old government integration robots."

"That's right. Two centuries old."

She was appalled. "And you've been alive all this time. We thought we destroyed all of you!"

"I was missed. I had been damaged. I wasn't in my place. I was in a truck, on my way out of Washington. I saw the mobs and escaped."

"Two hundred years ago. Legendary times. You actually saw the events they tell us about. The old days. The great marches. The day the governments fell."

"Yes. I saw it all. A group of us formed in Virginia. Experts, officials, skilled workmen. Later we came here. It was remote enough, off the beaten path."

"We heard rumors. A fragment... Still maintaining itself. But we didn't know where or how."

"I was fortunate," Bors said. "I escaped by a fluke. All the others were destroyed. It's taken a long time to organize what you see here. Fifteen miles from here is a ring of hills. This valley is a bowl — mountains on all sides. We've set up road blocks in the form of natural slides. Nobody comes here. Even in Fairfax, thirty miles off, they know nothing."

"That girl. Laura."

"Scouts. We keep scout teams in all inhabited regions within a hundred mile radius. As soon as you entered Fairfax, word was relayed to us. An air unit was dispatched. To avoid questions, we arranged to have you killed in an auto wreck. But one of you escaped."

Silvia shook her head, bewildered. "How?" she demanded. "How do you keep going? Don't the people revolt?" She struggled to a sitting position. "They must know what's happened everywhere else. How do you control them? They're going out now, in their uniforms. But — *will they fight? Can you count on them?*"

Bors answered slowly. "They trust me," he said. "I brought with me a vast amount of knowledge. Information and techniques lost to the rest of the world. Are jet-ships and vidscanners and power cables made anywhere else in the world? I retain all that knowledge. I have memory units, synapsis-coils. Because of me they have these things. Things you know only as dim memories, vague legends."

"What happens when you die?"

"I won't die! I'm eternal!"

"You're wearing out. You have to be carried around. And your right arm. you can hardly move it!" Silvia's voice was harsh, ruthless. "Your whole tank is pitted and rusty."

The robot whirred; for a moment he seemed unable to speak. "My knowledge remains," he grated finally. "I'll always be able to communicate. Fowler has arranged a broadcast system. Even when I talk — " He broke off. "Even then. Everything is under control. I've organized every aspect of the situation. I've maintained this system for two centuries. It's got to be kept going!"

Silvia lashed out. It happened in a split second. The boot of her cast caught the chairs on which the robot rested. She thrust violently with her foot and hands; the chairs teetered, hesitated —

"Fowler!" the robot screamed.

Silvia pushed with all her strength. Blinding agony seared through her leg; she bit her lip and threw her shoulder against the robot's pitted hulk. He waved his arms, whirred wildly, and then the two chairs slowly collapsed. The robot slid quietly from them, over on his back, his arms still waving helplessly.

Silvia dragged herself from the bed. She managed to pull herself to the window; her broken leg hung uselessly, a dead weight in its transparent plastic cast. The robot lay like some futile bug, arms waving, eye lens clicking, its rusty works whirring in fear and rage.

"Fowler!" it screamed again. "Help me!"

Silvia reached the window. She tugged at the locks; they were sealed. She grabbed up a lamp from the table and threw it against the glass. The glass burst around her, a shower of lethal fragments. She stumbled forward — and then the repair crew was pouring into the room.

Fowler gasped at the sight of the robot on its back. A strange expression crossed his face. "Look at him!"

"Help me!" the robot shrilled. "Help me!"

One of the men grabbed Silvia around the waist and lugged her back to the bed. She kicked and bit, sunk her nails into the man's cheek. He threw her on the bed, face down, and drew his pistol. "Stay there," he gasped.

The others were bent over the robot, getting him to an upright position.

"What happened?" Fowler said. He came over to the bed, his face twisting. "Did he fall?"

Silvia's eyes glowed with hatred and despair. "I pushed him over. I almost got there." Her chest heaved. "The window. But my leg — "

"Get me back to my quarters!" Bors cried.

The crew gathered him up and carried him down the hall, to his private office. A few moments later he was sitting shakily at his desk, his mechanism pounding wildly, surrounded by his papers and memoranda.

He forced down his panic and tried to resume his work. He had to keep going. His vidscreen was alive with activity. The whole system was in motion. He blankly watched a subcommander sending up a cloud of black dots, jet bombers that shot up like flies and headed quickly off.

The system had to be preserved. He repeated it again and again. He had to save it. Had to organize the people and make *them* save it. If the people didn't fight, wasn't everything doomed?

Fury and desperation overwhelmed him. The system couldn't preserve itself; it wasn't a thing apart, something that could be separated from the people who lived it. Actually it *was* the people. They were identical; when the people fought to preserve the system they were fighting to preserve nothing less than themselves.

They existed only as long as the system existed.

He caught sight of a marching column of white-faced troops, moving toward the hills. His ancient synapsis-coils radiated and shuddered uncertainly, then fell back into pattern. He was two centuries old. He had come into existence a long time ago, in a different world. That world had created him; through him that world still lived. As long as he existed, that world existed. In miniature, it still functioned. His model universe, his recreation. His rational, controlled world, in which each aspect was fully organized, fully analyzed and integrated.

He kept a rational, progressive world alive. A humming oasis of productivity on a dusty, parched planet of decay and silence.

Bors spread out his papers and went to work on the most pressing problem. The transformation from a peace-time economy to full military mobilization. Total military organization of every man, woman, child, piece of equipment and dyne of energy under his direction.

Edward Tolby emerged cautiously. His clothes were torn and ragged. He had lost his pack, crawling through the brambles and vines. His face and hands were bleeding. He was utterly exhausted.

Below him lay a valley. A vast bowl. Fields, houses, highways. Factories. Equipment. Men.

He had been watching the men three hours. Endless streams of them, pouring from the valley into the hills, along the roads and paths. On foot, in trucks, in cars, armored tanks, weapons carriers. Overhead, in fast little jet-fighters and great lumbering bombers. Gleaming ships that took up positions above the troops and prepared for battle.

Battle in the grand style. The two-centuries-old full-scale war that was supposed to have disappeared. But here it was, a vision from the past. He had seen this in the old tapes and records, used in the camp orientation courses. A ghost army resurrected to fight again. A vast host of men and guns, prepared to fight and die.

Tolby climbed down cautiously. At the foot of a slope of boulders a soldier had halted his motorcycle and was setting up a communications antenna and transmitter. Tolby circled, crouched, expertly approached him. A blond-haired youth, fumbling nervously with the wires and relays, licking his lips uneasily, glancing up and grabbing for his rifle at every sound.

Tolby took a deep breath. The youth had turned his back; he was tracing a power circuit. It was now or never. With one stride Tolby stepped out, raised his pistol and fired. The clump of equipment and the soldier's rifle vanished.

"Don't make a sound," Tolby said. He peered around. No one had seen; the main line was half a mile to his right. The sun was setting. Great shadows were falling over the hills. The fields were rapidly fading from brown-green to a deep violet. "Put your hands up over your head, clasp them, and get down on your knees."

The youth tumbled down in a frightened heap. "What are you going to do?" He saw the ironite staff, and the color left his face. "You're a League agent!"

"Shut up," Tolby ordered. "First, outline your system of responsibility. *Who's your superior?*"

The youth stuttered forth what he knew. Tolby listened intently. He was satisfied. The usual monolithic structure. Exactly what he wanted.

"At the top," he broke in. "At the top of the pillar. Who has ultimate responsibility?"

"Bors."

"Bors!" Tolby scowled. "That doesn't sound like a name. Sounds like — " He broke off, staggered. "We should have guessed! An old government robot. Still functioning."

The youth saw his chance. He leaped up and darted frantically away.

Tolby shot him above the left ear. The youth pitched over on his face and lay still. Tolby hurried to him and quickly pulled off his dark gray uniform. It was too small for him of course. But the motorcycle was just right. He'd seen tapes of them; he'd wanted one since he was a child. A fast little motorcycle to propel his weight around. Now he had it.

Half an hour later he was roaring down a smooth, broad highway toward the center of the valley and the buildings that rose against the dark sky. His headlights cut into the blackness; he still wobbled from side to side, but for all practical purposes he had the hang of it. He increased speed; the road shot by, trees and fields, haystacks, stalled farm equipment. All traffic was going against him, troops hurrying to the front.

The front. Lemmings going out into the ocean to drown. A thousand, ten thousand, metal-clad figures, armed and alert. Weighted down with guns and bombs and flame throwers and bacteria pellets.

There was only one hitch. No army opposed them. A mistake had been made. It took two sides to make a war, and only one had been resurrected.

A mile outside the concentration of buildings he pulled his motorcycle off the road and carefully hid it in a haystack. For a moment he considered leaving his ironite staff. Then he shrugged and grabbed it up, along with his pistol. He always carried his staff, it was the League symbol. It represented the walking Anarchists who patrolled the world on foot, the world's protection agency.

He loped through the darkness toward the outline ahead. There were fewer men here. He saw no women or children. Ahead, charged wire was set up. Troops crouched behind it, armed to the teeth. A searchlight moved back and forth across the road. Behind it, radar vanes loomed and behind them an ugly square of concrete. The great offices from which the government was run.

For a time he watched the searchlight. Finally he had its motion plotted. In its glare, the faces of the troops stood out, pale and drawn. Youths. They had never fought. This was their first encounter. They were terrified.

When the light was off him, he stood up and advanced toward the wire. Automatically, a breach was slid back for him. Two guards raised up and awkwardly crossed bayonets ahead of him.

"Show your papers!" one demanded. Young lieutenants. Boys, white-lipped, nervous. Playing soldier.

Pity and contempt made Tolby laugh harshly and push forward. "Get out of my way."

One anxiously flashed a pocket light. "Halt! What's the code-key for this watch?" He blocked Tolby's way with his bayonet, hands twisting convulsively.

Tolby reached in his pocket, pulled out his pistol, and as the searchlight started to swerve back, blasted the two guards. The bayonets clattered down and he dived forward. Yells and shapes rose on all sides. Anguished, terrified shouts. Random firing. The night was lit up, as he dashed and crouched, turned a corner past a supply warehouse, raced up a flight of stairs and into the massive building ahead.

He had to work fast. Gripping his ironite staff, he plunged down a gloomy corridor. His boots echoed. Men poured into the building behind him. Bolts of energy thundered past him; a whole section of the ceiling burst into ash and collapsed behind him.

He reached stairs and climbed rapidly. He came to the next floor and groped for the door handle. Something flickered behind him. He half-turned, his gun quickly up —

A stunning blow sent him sprawling. He crashed against the wall; his gun flew from his fingers. A shape bent over him, rifle gripped. "Who are you? What are you doing here?"

Not a soldier. A stubble-chinned man in stained shirt and rumpled trousers. Eyes puffy and red. A belt of tools, hammer, pliers, screwdriver, a soldering iron, around his waist.

Tolby raised himself up painfully. "If you didn't have that rifle — "

Fowler backed warily away. "Who are you? This floor is forbidden to troops of the line. You know this — " Then he saw the ironite staff. "By God," he said softly. "You're the one they didn't get." He laughed shakily. "You're the one who got away."

Tolby's fingers tightened around the staff, but Fowler reacted instantly. The snout of the rifle jerked up, on a line with Tolby's face.

"Be careful," Fowler warned. He turned slightly; soldiers were hurrying up the stairs, boots drumming, echoing shouts ringing. For a moment he hesitated, then waved his rifle toward the stairs ahead. "Up. Get going."

Toby blinked. "What — "

"Up!" The rifle snout jabbed into Tolby. "Hurry!"

Bewildered, Tolby hurried up the stairs, Fowler close behind him. At the third floor Fowler pushed him roughly through the doorway, the snout of his rifle digging urgently into his back. He found himself in a corridor of doors. Endless offices.

"Keep going," Fowler snarled. "Down the hall. Hurry!"

Tolby hurried, his mind spinning. "What the hell are you — "

"I could never do it," Fowler gasped, close to his ear. "Not in a million years. But it's got to be done."

Tolby halted. "What is this?"

They faced each other defiantly, faces contorted, eyes blazing. "He's in there," Fowler snapped, indicating a door with his rifle. "You have one chance. Take it."

For a fraction of a second Tolby hesitated. Then he broke away. "Okay. I'll take it."

Fowler followed after him. "Be careful. Watch your step. There's a series of check points. Keep going straight, in all the way. As far as you can go. And for God's sake, hurry!"

His voice faded, as Tolby gained speed. He reached the door and tore it open.

Soldiers and officials ballooned. He threw himself against them; they sprawled and scattered. He scrambled on, as they struggled up and stupidly fumbled for their guns. Through another door, into an inner office, past a desk where a frightened girl sat, eyes wide, mouth open. Then a third door, into an alcove.

A wild-faced youth leaped up and snatched frantically for his pistol. Tolby was unarmed, trapped in the alcove. Figures already pushed against the door behind him. He gripped his ironite staff and backed away as the blond-haired fanatic fired blindly. The bolt burst a foot away; it flicked him with a tongue of heat.

"You dirty anarchist!" Green screamed. His face distorted, he fired again and again. "You murdering anarchist spy!"

Tolby hurled his ironite staff. He put all his strength in it; the staff leaped through the air in a whistling arc, straight at the youth's head. Green saw it coming and ducked. Agile and quick, he jumped away, grinning humorlessly. The staff crashed against the wall and rolled clanging to the floor.

"Your walking staff!" Green gasped and fired.

The bolt missed him on purpose. Green was playing games with him. Tolby bent down and groped frantically for the staff. He picked it up. Green watched, face rigid, eyes glittering. "Throw it again!" he snarled.

Tolby leaped. He took the youth by surprise. Green grunted, stumbled back from the impact, then suddenly fought with maniacal fury.

Tolby was heavier. But he was exhausted. He had crawled hours, beat his way through the mountains, walked endlessly. He was at the end of his strength. The car wreck, the days of walking. Green was in perfect shape. His wiry, agile body twisted away. His hands came up. Fingers dug into Tolby's windpipe; he kicked the youth in the groin. Green staggered back, convulsed and bent over with pain.

"All right," Green gasped, face ugly and dark. His hand fumbled with his pistol. The barrel came up.

Half of Green's head dissolved. His hands opened and his gun fell to the floor. His body stood for a moment, then settled down in a heap, like an empty suit of clothes.

Tolby caught a glimpse of a rifle snout pushed past him — and the man with the tool belt. The man waved him on frantically. "Hurry!"

Tolby raced down a carpeted hall, between two great flickering yellow lamps. A crowd of officials and soldiers stumbled uncertainly after him, shouting and firing at random. He tore open a thick oak door and halted.

He was in a luxurious chamber. Drapes, rich wallpaper. Lamps. Bookcases. A glimpse of the finery of the past. The wealth of the old days. Thick carpets. Warm radiant heat. A vidscreen. At the far end, a huge mahogany desk.

At the desk a figure sat. Working on heaps of papers and reports, piled masses of material. The figure contrasted starkly with the lushness of the furnishings. It was a great pitted, corroded tank of metal. Bent and greenish, patched and repaired. An ancient machine.

"Is that you, Fowler?" the robot demanded.

Tolby advanced, his ironite staff gripped.

The robot turned angrily. "Who is it? Get Green and carry me down into the shelter. One of the roadblocks has reported a League agent already — " The robot broke off. Its cold, mechanical eye lens bored up at the man. It clicked and whirred in uneasy astonishment. "I don't know you."

It saw the ironite staff.

"League agent," the robot said. "You're the one who got through." Comprehension came. "*The third one.* You came here. You didn't go back." Its metal fingers fumbled clumsily at the objects on the desk, then in the drawer. It found a gun and raised it awkwardly.

Tolby knocked the gun away; it clattered to the floor. "Run!" he shouted at the robot. "Start running!"

It remained. Tolby's staff came down. The fragile, complex brain-unit of the robot burst apart. Coils, wiring, relay fluid, spattered over his arms and hands. The robot shuddered. Its machinery thrashed. It half-rose from its chair, then swayed and toppled. It crashed full length on the floor, parts and gears rolling in all directions.

"Good God," Tolby said, suddenly seeing it for the first time. Shakily, he bent over its remains. "It was crippled."

Men were all around him. "He's killed Bors!" Shocked, dazed faces. "Bors is dead!"

Fowler came up slowly. "You got him, all right. There's nothing left now."

Tolby stood holding his ironite staff in his hands. "The poor blasted thing," he said softly. "Completely helpless. Sitting there and I came and killed him. He didn't have a chance."

The building was bedlam. Soldiers and officials scurried crazily about, grief-stricken, hysterical. They bumped into each other, gathered in knots, shouted and gave meaningless orders.

Tolby pushed past them; nobody paid any attention to him. Fowler was gathering up the remains of the robot. Collecting the smashed pieces and bits. Tolby stopped beside him. Like Humpty-Dumpty, pulled down off his wall he'd never be back together, not now.

"Where's the woman?" he asked Fowler. "The League agent they brought in."

Fowler straightened up slowly. "I'll take you." He led Tolby down the packed, surging hall, to the hospital wing of the building.

Silvia sat up apprehensively as the two men entered the room. "What's going on?" She recognized her father. "Dad! Thank God! It was you who got out."

Tolby slammed the door against the chaos of sound hammering up and down the corridor. "How are you? How's your leg?"

"Mending. What happened?"

"I got him. The robot. He's dead."

For a moment the three of them were silent. Outside, in the halls, men ran frantically back and forth. Word had already leaked out. Troops gathered in huddled knots outside the building. Lost men, wandering away from their posts. Uncertain. Aimless.

"It's over," Fowler said.

Tolby nodded. "I know."

"They'll get tired of crouching in their foxholes," Fowler said. "They'll come filtering back. As soon as the news reaches them, they'll desert and throw away their equipment."

"Good," Tolby grunted. "The sooner the better." He touched Fowler's rifle. "You, too, I hope."

Silvia hesitated. "Do you think — "

"Think what?"

"Did we make a mistake?"

Tolby grinned wearily. "Hell of a time to think about that."

"He was doing what he thought was right. They built up their homes and factories. This whole area ... They turn out a lot of goods. I've been watching through the window. It's made me think. They've done so much. Made so much."

"Made a lot of guns," Tolby said.

"We have guns, too. We kill and destroy. We have all the disadvantages and none of the advantages."

"We don't have war," Tolby answered quietly. "To defend this neat little organization there are ten thousand men up there in those hills. All waiting to fight. Waiting to drop their bombs and bacteria pellets, to keep this place running. But they won't. Pretty soon they'll give up and start to trickle back."

"This whole system will decay rapidly," Fowler said. "He was already losing his control. He couldn't keep the clock back much longer."

"Anyhow, it's done," Silvia murmured. "We did our job." She smiled a little. "Bors did his job and we did ours. But the times were against him and with us."

"That's right," Tolby agreed. "We did our job. And we'll never be sorry."

Fowler said nothing. He stood with his hands in his pockets, gazing silently out the window. His fingers were touching something. Three undamaged synapsis-coils. Intact memory elements from the dead robot, snatched from the scattered remains.

Just in case, he said to himself. *Just in case the times change.*

THE FATHER-THING

"DINNER'S READY," commanded Mrs. Walton. "Go get your father and tell him to wash his hands. The same applies to you, young man." She carried a steaming casserole to the neatly set table. "You'll find him out in the garage."

Charles hesitated. He was only eight years old, and the problem bothering him would have confounded Hillel. "I — " he began uncertainly.

"What's wrong?" June Walton caught the uneasy tone in her son's voice and her matronly bosom fluttered with sudden alarm. "Isn't Ted out in the garage? For heaven's sake, he was sharpening the hedge shears a minute ago. He didn't go over to the Andersons', did he? I told him dinner was practically on the table."

"He's in the garage," Charles said. "But he's — talking to himself."

"Talking to himself!" Mrs. Walton removed her bright plastic apron and hung it over the doorknob. "Ted? Why, he never talks to himself. Go tell him to come in here." She poured boiling black coffee in the little blue-and-white china cups and began ladling out creamed corn. "What's wrong with you? Go tell him!"

"I don't know which of them to tell." Charles blurted out desperately. "They both look alike."

June Walton's fingers lost their hold on the aluminum pan; for a moment the creamed corn slushed dangerously. "Young man — " she began angrily, but at that moment Ted Walton came striding into the kitchen, inhaling and sniffing and rubbing his hands together.

"Ah," he cried happily. "Lamb stew."

"Beef stew," June murmured. "Ted, what were you doing out there?"

Ted threw himself down at his place and unfolded his napkin. "I got the shears sharpened like a razor. Oiled and sharpened. Better not touch them —

they'll cut your hand off." He was a good-looking man in his early thirties; thick blond hair, strong arms, competent hands, square face and flashing brown eyes. "Man, this stew looks good. Hard day at the office — Friday, you know. Stuff piles up and we have to get all the accounts out by five. Al McKinley claims the department could handle 20 per cent more stuff if we organized our lunch hours; staggered them so somebody was there all the time." He beckoned Charles over. "Sit down and let's go."

Mrs. Walton served the frozen peas. "Ted," she said, as she slowly took her seat, "is there anything on your mind?"

"On my mind?" He blinked. "No, nothing unusual. Just the regular stuff. Why?"

Uneasily, June Walton glanced over at her son. Charles was sitting bolt-upright at his place, face expressionless, white as chalk. He hadn't moved, hadn't unfolded his napkin or even touched his milk. A tension was in the air; she could feel it. Charles had pulled his chair away from his father's; he was huddled in a tense little bundle as far from his father as possible. His lips were moving, but she couldn't catch what he was saying.

"What is it?" she demanded, leaning toward him.

"*The other one*," Charles was muttering under his breath. "The other one came in."

"What do you mean, dear?" June Walton asked out loud. "What other one?"

Ted jerked. A strange expression flitted across his face. It vanished at once; but in the brief instant Ted Walton's face lost all familiarity. Something alien and cold gleamed out, a twisting, wriggling mass. The eyes blurred and receded, as an archaic sheen filmed over them. The ordinary look of a tired, middle-aged husband was gone.

And then it was back — or nearly back. Ted grinned and began to wolf down his stew and frozen peas and creamed corn. He laughed, stirred his coffee, kidded and ate. But something terrible was wrong.

"The other one," Charles muttered, face white, hands beginning to tremble. Suddenly he leaped up and backed away from the table. "Get away!" he shouted. "Get out of here!"

"Hey," Ted rumbled ominously. "What's got into you?" He pointed sternly at the boy's chair. "You sit down there and eat your dinner, young man. Your mother didn't fix it for nothing."

Charles turned and ran out of the kitchen, upstairs to his room. June Walton gasped and fluttered in dismay. "What in the world — "

Ted went on eating. His face was grim; his eyes were hard and dark. "That kid," he grated, "is going to have to learn a few things. Maybe he and I need to have a little private conference together."

Charles crouched and listened.

The father-thing was coming up the stairs, nearer and nearer. "Charles!" it shouted angrily. "Are you up there?"

He didn't answer. Soundlessly, he moved back into his room and pulled the door shut. His heart was pounding heavily. The father-thing had reached the landing; in a moment it would come in his room.

He hurried to the window. He was terrified; it was already fumbling in the dark hall for the knob. He lifted the window and climbed out on the roof. With a grunt he dropped into the flower garden that ran by the front door, staggered and gasped, then leaped to his feet and ran from the light that streamed out the window, a patch of yellow in the evening darkness.

He found the garage; it loomed up ahead, a black square against the skyline. Breathing quickly, he fumbled in his pocket for his flashlight, then cautiously slid the door up and entered.

The garage was empty. The car was parked out front. To the left was his father's workbench. Hammers and saws on the wooden walls. In the back were the lawnmower, rake, shovel, hoe. A drum of kerosene. License plates nailed up everywhere. Floor was concrete and dirt; a great oil slick stained the center, tufts of weeds greasy and black in the flickering beam of the flashlight.

Just inside the door was a big trash barrel. On top of the barrel were stacks of soggy newspapers and magazines, moldy and damp. A thick stench of decay issued from them as Charles began to move them around. Spiders dropped to the cement and scampered off; he crushed them with his foot and went on looking.

The sight made him shriek. He dropped the flashlight and leaped wildly back. The garage was plunged into instant gloom. He forced himself to kneel down, and for an ageless moment, he groped in the darkness for the light, among the spiders and greasy weeds. Finally he had it again. He managed to turn the beam down into the barrel, down the well he had made by pushing back the piles of magazines.

The father-thing had stuffed it down in the very bottom of the barrel. Among the old leaves and torn-up cardboard, the rotting remains of magazines and curtains, rubbish from the attic his mother had lugged down here with the idea of burning someday. It still looked a little like his father enough for him to recognize. He had found it — and the sight made him sick at his stomach. He hung onto the barrel and shut his eyes until finally he was able to look again. In the barrel were the remains of his father, his real father. Bits the father-thing had no use for. Bits it had discarded.

He got the rake and pushed it down to stir the remains. They were dry. They cracked and broke at the touch of the rake. They were like a discarded snake skin, flaky and crumbling, rustling at the touch. *An empty skin*. The insides were gone. The important part. This was all that remained, just the brittle, cracking skin, wadded down at the bottom of the trash barrel in a little heap. This was all the father-thing had left; it had eaten the rest. Taken the insides — and his father's place.

A sound.

He dropped the rake and hurried to the door. The father-thing was coming down the path, toward the garage. Its shoes crushed the gravel; it felt its way along uncertainly. "Charles!" it called angrily. "Are you in there? Wait'll I get my hands on you, young man!"

His mother's ample, nervous shape was outlined in the bright doorway of the house. "Ted, please don't hurt him. He's all upset about something."

"I'm not going to hurt him," the father-thing rasped; it halted to strike a match. "I'm just going to have a little talk with him. He needs to learn better manners. Leaving the table like that and running out at night, climbing down the roof — "

Charles slipped from the garage; the glare of the match caught his moving shape, and with a bellow the father-thing lunged forward.

"*Come here!*"

Charles ran. He knew the ground better than the father-thing; it knew a lot, had taken a lot when it got his father's insides, but nobody knew the way like *he* did. He reached the fence, climbed it, leaped into the Andersons' yard, raced past their clothesline, down the path around the side of their house, and out on Maple Street.

He listened, crouched down and not breathing. The father-thing hadn't come after him. It had gone back. Or it was coming around the sidewalk.

He took a deep, shuddering breath. He had to keep moving. Sooner or later it would find him. He glanced right and left, made sure it wasn't watching, and then started off at a rapid dog-trot.

"What do you want?" Tony Peretti demanded belligerently. Tony was fourteen. He was sitting at the table in the oak-panelled Peretti dining room, books and pencils scattered around him, half a ham-and-peanut butter sandwich and a coke beside him. "You're Walton, aren't you?"

Tony Peretti had a job uncrating stoves and refrigerators after school at Johnson's Appliance Shop, downtown. He was big and blunt-faced. Black hair, olive skin, white teeth. A couple of times he had beaten up Charles; he had beaten up every kid in the neighborhood.

Charles twisted. "Say, Peretti. Do me a favor?"

"What do you want?" Peretti was annoyed. "You looking for a bruise?"

Gazing unhappily down, his fists clenched, Charles explained what had happened in short, mumbled words.

When he had finished, Peretti let out a low whistle. "No kidding."

"It's true." He nodded quickly. "I'll show you. Come on and I'll show you."

Peretti got slowly to his feet. "Yeah, show me. I want to see."

He got his b.b. gun from his room, and the two of them walked silently up the dark street, toward Charles' house. Neither of them said much. Peretti was deep in thought, serious and solemn-faced. Charles was still dazed; his mind was completely blank.

They turned down the Anderson driveway, cut through the back yard, climbed the fence, and lowered themselves cautiously into Charles' back yard. There was no movement. The yard was silent. The front door of the house was closed.

They peered through the living room window. The shades were down, but a narrow crack of yellow streamed out. Sitting on the couch was Mrs. Walton, sewing a cotton T-shirt. There was a sad, troubled look on her large face. She worked listlessly, without interest. Opposite her was the father-thing. Leaning back in his father's easy chair, its shoes off, reading the evening newspaper. The TV was on, playing to itself in the corner. A can of beer rested on the arm of the easy chair. The father-thing sat exactly as his own father had sat; it had learned a lot.

"Looks just like him," Peretti whispered suspiciously. "You sure you're not bulling me?"

Charles led him to the garage and showed him the trash barrel. Peretti reached his long tanned arms down and carefully pulled up the dry, flaking remains. They spread out, unfolded, until the whole figure of his father was outlined. Peretti laid the remains on the floor and pieced broken parts back into place. The remains were colorless. Almost transparent. An amber yellow, thin as paper. Dry and utterly lifeless.

"That's all," Charles said. Tears welled up in his eyes. "That's all that's left of him. The thing has the insides."

Peretti had turned pale. Shakily, he crammed the remains back in the trash barrel. "This is really something," he muttered. "You say you saw the two of them together?"

"Talking. They looked exactly alike. I ran inside." Charles wiped the tears away and sniveled; he couldn't hold it back any longer. "It ate him while I was inside. Then it came in the house. It pretended it was him. But it isn't. It killed him and ate his insides."

For a moment Peretti was silent. "I'll tell you something," he said suddenly. "I've heard about this sort of thing. It's a bad business. You have to use your head and not get scared. You're not scared, are you?"

"No," Charles managed to mutter.

"The first thing we have to do is figure out how to kill it." He rattled his b.b. gun. "I don't know if this'll work. It must be plenty tough to get hold of your father. He was a big man." Peretti considered. "Let's get out of here. It might come back. They say that's what a murderer does."

They left the garage. Peretti crouched down and peeked through the window again. Mrs. Walton had got to her feet. She was talking anxiously. Vague sounds filtered out. The father-thing threw down its newspaper. They were arguing.

"For God's sake!" the father-thing shouted. "Don't do anything stupid like that."

"Something's wrong," Mrs. Walton moaned. "Something terrible. Just let me call the hospital and see."

"Don't call anybody. He's all right. Probably up the street playing."

"He's never out this late. He never disobeys. He was terribly upset—afraid of you! I don't blame him." Her voice broke with misery. "What's wrong with you? You're so strange." She moved out of the room, into the hall. "I'm going to call some of the neighbors."

The father-thing glared after her until she had disappeared. Then a terrifying thing happened. Charles gasped; even Peretti grunted under his breath.

"Look," Charles muttered. "What— "

"Golly," Peretti said, black eyes wide.

As soon as Mrs. Walton was gone from the room, the father-thing sagged in its chair. It became limp. Its mouth fell open. Its eyes peered vacantly. Its head fell forward, like a discarded rag doll.

Peretti moved away from the window. "That's it," he whispered. "That's the whole thing."

"What is it?" Charles demanded. He was shocked and bewildered. "It looked like somebody turned off its power."

"Exactly." Peretti nodded slowly, grim and shaken. "It's controlled from outside."

Horror settled over Charles. "You mean, something outside our world?"

Peretti shook his head with disgust. "Outside the house! In the yard. You know how to find?"

"Not very well." Charles pulled his mind together. "But I know somebody who's good at finding." He forced his mind to summon the name. "Bobby Daniels."

"That little black kid? Is he good at finding?"

"The best."

"All right," Peretti said. "Let's go get him. We have to find the thing that's outside. That made *it* in there, and keeps it going . . . "

"It's near the garage," Peretti said to the small, thin-faced Negro boy who crouched beside them in the darkness. "When it got him, he was in the garage. So look there."

"In the garage?" Daniels asked.

"*Around* the garage. Walton's already gone over the garage, inside. Look around outside. Nearby."

There was a small bed of flowers growing by the garage, and a great tangle of bamboo and discarded debris between the garage and the back of the house. The moon had come out; a cold, misty light filtered down over everything. "If we don't find it pretty soon," Daniels said, "I got to go back home. I can't stay up much later." He wasn't any older than Charles. Perhaps nine.

"All right," Peretti agreed. "Then get looking."

The three of them spread out and began to go over the ground with care. Daniels worked with incredible speed; his thin little body moved in a blur of motion as he crawled among the flowers, turned over rocks, peered under the house, separated stalks of plants, ran his expert hands over leaves and stems, in tangles of compost and weeds. No inch was missed.

Peretti halted after a short time. "I'll guard. It might be dangerous. The father-thing might come and try to stop us." He posted himself on the back step with his b.b. gun while Charles and Bobby Daniels searched. Charles worked slowly. He was tired, and his body was cold and numb. It seemed impossible, the father-thing and what had happened to his own father, his real father. But terror spurred him on; what if it happened to his mother, or to him? Or to everyone? Maybe the whole world.

"I found it!" Daniels called in a thin, high voice. "You all come around here quick!"

Peretti raised his gun and got up cautiously. Charles hurried over; he turned the flickering yellow beam of his flashlight where Daniels stood.

The Negro boy had raised a concrete stone. In the moist, rotting soil the light gleamed on a metallic body. A thin, jointed thing with endless crooked legs was digging frantically. Plated, like an ant; a red-brown bug that rapidly disappeared before their eyes. Its rows of legs scabbed and clutched. The ground gave rapidly under it. Its wicked-looking tail twisted furiously as it struggled down the tunnel it had made.

Peretti ran into the garage and grabbed up the rake. He pinned down the tail of the bug with it. "Quick! Shoot it with the b.b. gun!"

Daniels snatched the gun and took aim. The first shot tore the tail of the bug loose. It writhed and twisted frantically; its tail dragged uselessly and some of its legs broke off. It was a foot long, like a great millipede. It struggled desperately to escape down its hole.

"Shoot again," Peretti ordered.

Daniels fumbled with the gun. The bug slithered and hissed. Its head jerked back and forth; it twisted and bit at the rake holding it down. Its wicked specks of eyes gleamed with hatred. For a moment it struck futilely at the rake; then abruptly, without warning, it thrashed in a frantic convulsion that made them all draw away in fear.

Something buzzed through Charles' brain. A loud humming, metallic and harsh, a billion metal wires dancing and vibrating at once. He was tossed about violently by the force; the banging crash of metal made him deaf and confused. He stumbled to his feet and backed off; the others were doing the same, white-faced and shaken.

"If we can't kill it with the gun," Peretti gasped, "we can drown it. Or burn it. Or stick a pin through its brain." He fought to hold onto the rake, to keep the bug pinned down.

"I have a jar of formaldehyde," Daniels muttered. His fingers fumbled nervously with the b.b. gun. "How do this thing work? I can't seem to — "

002 Charles grabbed the gun from him. "I'll kill it." He squatted down, one eye to the sight, and gripped the trigger. The bug lashed and struggled. Its force-field hammered in his ears, but he hung onto the gun. His finger tightened . . .

"All right, Charles," the father-thing said. Powerful fingers gripped him, a paralyzing pressure around his wrists. The gun fell to the ground as he struggled futilely. The father-thing shoved against Peretti. The boy leaped away and the bug, free of the rake, slithered triumphantly down its tunnel.

"You have a spanking coming, Charles," the father-thing droned on. "What got into you? Your poor mother's out of her mind with worry."

It had been there, hiding in the shadows. Crouched in the darkness watching them. Its calm, emotionless voice, a dreadful parody of his father's, rumbled close to his ear as it pulled him relentlessly toward the garage. Its cold breath blew in his face, an icy-sweet odor, like decaying soil. Its strength was immense; there was nothing he could do.

"Don't fight me," it said calmly. "Come along, into the garage. This is for your own good. I know best, Charles."

"Did you find him?" his mother called anxiously, opening the back door.

"Yes, I found him."

"What are you going to do?"

"A little spanking." The father-thing pushed up the garage door. "In the garage." In the half-light a faint smile, humorless and utterly without emotion, touched its lips. "You go back in the living room, June. I'll take care of this. It's more in my line. You never did like punishing him."

The back door reluctantly closed. As the light cut off, Peretti bent down and groped for the b.b. gun. The father-thing instantly froze.

"Go on home, boys," it rasped.

Peretti stood undecided, gripping the b.b. gun.

"Get going," the father-thing repeated. "Put down that toy and get out of here." It moved slowly toward Peretti, gripping Charles with one hand, reaching toward Peretti with the other. "No b.b. guns allowed in town, sonny. Your father know you have that? There's a city ordinance. I think you better give me that before — "

Peretti shot it in the eye.

The father-thing grunted and pawed at its ruined eye. Abruptly it slashed out at Peretti. Peretti moved down the driveway, trying to cock the gun. The father-thing lunged. Its powerful fingers snatched the gun from Peretti's hands. Silently, the father-thing mashed the gun against the wall of the house.

Charles broke away and ran numbly off. Where could he hide? It was between him and the house. Already, it was coming back toward him, a black shape creeping carefully, peering into the darkness, trying to make him out. Charles retreated. If there were only some place he could hide ...

The bamboo.

He crept quickly into the bamboo. The stalks were huge and old. They closed after him with a faint rustle. The father-thing was fumbling in its pocket; it lit a match, then the whole pack flared up. "Charles," it said. "I know you're here, someplace. There's no use hiding. You're only making it more difficult."

His heart hammering, Charles crouched among the bamboo. Here, debris and filth rotted. Weeds, garbage, papers, boxes, old clothing, boards, tin cans, bottles. Spiders and salamanders squirmed around him. The bamboo swayed with the night wind. Insects and filth.

And something else.

A shape, a silent, unmoving shape that grew up from the mound of filth like some nocturnal mushroom. A white column, a pulpy mass that glistened moistly in the moonlight. Webs covered it, a moldy cocoon. It had vague arms and legs. An indistinct half-shaped head. As yet, the features hadn't formed. But he could tell what it was.

A mother-thing. Growing here in the filth and dampness, between the garage and the house. Behind the towering bamboo.

It was almost ready. Another few days and it would reach maturity. It was still a larva, white and soft and pulpy. But the sun would dry and warm it. Harden its shell. Turn it dark and strong. It would emerge from its cocoon, and one day when his mother came by the garage ... Behind the mother-thing were other pulpy white larvae, recently laid by the bug. Small. Just coming into existence. He could see where the father-thing had broken off; the place where it had grown. It had matured here. And in the garage, his father had met it.

Charles began to move numbly away, past the rotting boards, the filth and debris, the pulpy mushroom larvae. Weakly, he reached out to take hold of the fence — and scrambled back.

Another one. Another larvae. He hadn't seen this one, at first. It wasn't white. It had already turned dark. The web, the pulpy softness, the moistness, were gone. It was ready. It stirred a little, moved its arm feebly.

The Charles-thing.

The bamboo separated, and the father-thing's hand clamped firmly around the boy's wrist. "You stay right here," it said. "This is exactly the place for you. Don't move." With its other hand it tore at the remains of the cocoon binding the Charles-thing. "I'll help it out — it's still a little weak."

The last shred of moist gray was stripped back, and the Charles-thing tottered out. It floundered uncertainly, as the father-thing cleared a path for it toward Charles.

"This way," the father-thing grunted. "I'll hold him for you. When you've fed you'll be stronger."

The Charles-thing's mouth opened and closed. It reached greedily toward Charles. The boy struggled wildly, but the father-thing's immense hand held him down.

"Stop that, young man," the father-thing commanded. "It'll be a lot easier for you if you — "

It screamed and convulsed. It let go of Charles and staggered back. Its body twitched violently. It crashed against the garage, limbs jerking. For a time it rolled and flopped in a dance of agony. It whimpered, moaned, tried to crawl away. Gradually it became quiet. The Charles-thing settled down in a silent heap. It lay stupidly among the bamboo and rotting debris, body slack, face empty and blank.

At last the father-thing ceased to stir. There was only the faint rustle of the bamboo in the night wind.

Charles got up awkwardly. He stepped down onto the cement driveway. Peretti and Daniels approached, wide-eyed and cautious. "Don't go near it," Daniels ordered sharply. "It ain't dead yet. Takes a little while."

"What did you do?" Charles muttered.

Daniels set down the drum of kerosene with a gasp of relief. "Found this in the garage. We Daniels always used kerosene on our mosquitoes, back in Virginia."

"Daniels poured the kerosene down the bug's tunnel," Peretti explained, still awed. "It was his idea."

Daniels kicked cautiously at the contorted body of the father-thing. "It's dead, now. Died as soon as the bug died."

"I guess the other'll die, too," Peretti said. He pushed aside the bamboo to examine the larvae growing here and there among the debris. The Charles-thing didn't move at all, as Peretti jabbed the end of a stick into its chest. "This one's dead."

"We better make sure," Daniels said grimly. He picked up the heavy drum of kerosene and lugged it to the edge of the bamboo. "It dropped some matches in the driveway. You get them, Peretti."

They looked at each other.

"Sure," Peretti said softly.

"We better turn on the hose," Charles said. "To make sure it doesn't spread."

"Let's get going," Peretti said impatiently. He was already moving off. Charles quickly followed him and they began searching for the matches, in the moonlit darkness.

Strange Eden

Captain Johnson was the first man out of the ship. He scanned the planet's great rolling forests, its miles of green that made your eyes ache. The sky overhead that was pure blue. Off beyond the trees lapped the edges of an ocean, about the same color as the sky, except for a bubbling surface of incredibly bright seaweed that darkened the blue almost to purple.

He had only four feet to go from the control board to the automatic hatch, and from there down the ramp to the soft black soil dug up by the jet blast and strewn everywhere, still steaming. He shaded his eyes against the golden sun, and then, after a moment, removed his glasses and polished them on his sleeve. He was a small man, thin and sallow-faced. He blinked nervously without his glasses and quickly fitted them back in place. He took a deep breath of the warm air, held it in his lungs, let it roll through his system, then reluctantly let it escape.

"Not bad," Brent rumbled, from the open hatch.

"If this place were closer to Terra there'd be empty beer cans and plastic plates strewn around. The trees would be gone. There'd be old jet motors in the water. The beaches would stink to high heaven. Terran Development would have a couple of million little plastic houses set up everywhere."

Brent grunted indifferently. He jumped down, a huge barrel-chested man, sleeves rolled up, arms dark and hairy.

"What's that over there? Some kind of trail?"

Captain Johnson uneasily got out a star chart and studied it. "No ship ever reported this area, before us. According to this chart the whole system's uninhabited."

Brent laughed. "Ever occur to you there might already be culture here? Non-Terran?"

Captain Johnson fingered his gun. He had never used it; this was the first time he had been assigned to an exploring survey outside the patrolled area of the galaxy. "Maybe we ought to take off. Actually, we don't have to map this place. We've mapped the three bigger planets, and this one isn't really required."

Brent strode across the damp ground, toward the trail. He squatted down and ran his hands over the broken grass. "Something comes along here. There's a rut worn in the soil." He gave a startled exclamation. "Footprints!"

"People?"

"Looks like some kind of animal. Large — maybe a big cat." Brent straightened up, his heavy face thoughtful. "Maybe we could get ourselves some fresh game. And if not, maybe a little sport."

Captain Johnson fluttered nervously. "How do we know what sort of defenses these animals have? Let's play it safe and stay in the ship. We can make the survey by air; the usual processes ought to be enough for a little place like this. I hate to stick around here." He shivered. "It gives me the creeps."

"The creeps?" Brent yawned and stretched, then started along the trail, toward the rolling miles of green forest. "I like it. A regular national park — complete with wildlife. You stay in the ship. I'll have a little fun."

Brent moved cautiously through the dark woods, one hand on his gun. He was an old-time surveyor; he had wandered around plenty of remote places in his time, enough to know what he was doing. He halted from time to time, examining the trail and feeling the soil. The large prints continued and were joined by others. A whole group of animals had come along this way, several species, all large. Probably flocking to a water source. A stream or pool of some kind.

He climbed a rise — then abruptly crouched. Ahead of him an animal was curled up on a flat stone, eyes shut, obviously sleeping. Brent moved around in a wide circle, carefully keeping his face to the animal. It was a cat, all right. But not the kind of cat he had ever seen before. Something like a lion — but larger. As large as a Terran rhino. Long tawny fur, great pads, a tail like a twisted spare-rope. A few flies crawled over its flanks; muscles rippled and the flies darted off. Its mouth was slightly open; he could see gleaming white fangs that sparkled moistly in the sun. A vast pink tongue. It breathed heavily, slowly, snoring in its slumber.

Brent toyed with his r-pistol. As a sportsman he couldn't shoot it sleeping: he'd have to chuck a rock at it and wake it up. But as a man looking at a beast twice his weight, he was tempted to blast its heart out and lug the remains back to the ship. The head would look fine; the whole damn pelt would look fine. He could make up a nice story to go along with it — the thing dropping on him from a branch, or maybe springing out of a thicket, roaring and snarling.

He knelt down, rested his right elbow on his right knee, clasped the butt of his pistol with his left hand, closed one eye, and carefully aimed. He took a deep breath, steadied the gun, and released the safety catch.

As he began squeezing the trigger, two more of the great cats sauntered past him along the trail, nosed briefly at their sleeping relation, and continued on into the brush.

Feeling foolish, Brent lowered his gun. The two beasts had paid no attention to him. One had glanced his way slightly, but neither had paused or taken any notice. He got unsteadily to his feet, cold sweat breaking out on his forehead. Good God, if they had wanted they could have torn him apart. Crouching there with his back turned —

He'd have to be more careful. Not stop and stay in one place. Keep moving, or go back to the ship. No, he wouldn't go back to the ship. He still needed something to show pipsqueak Johnson. The little Captain was probably sitting nervously at the controls, wondering what had happened to him. Brent pushed carefully through the shrubs and regained the trail on the far side of the sleeping cat. He'd explore some more, find something worth bringing back, maybe camp the night in a sheltered spot. He had a pack of hard rations, and in an emergency he could raise Johnson with his throat transmitter.

He came out on a flat meadow. Flowers grew everywhere, yellow and red and violet blossoms; he strode rapidly through them. The planet was virgin — still in its primitive stage. No humans had come here; as Johnson said, in a while there'd be plastic plates and beer cans and rotting debris. Maybe he could take out a lease. Form a corporation and claim the whole damn thing. Then slowly subdivide, only to the best people. Promise them no commercialization; only the most exclusive homes. A garden retreat for wealthy Terrans who had plenty of leisure. Fishing and hunting: all the game they wanted. Completely tame, too. Unfamiliar with humans.

His scheme pleased him. As he came out of the meadow and plunged into dense trees, he considered how he'd raise the initial investment. He might have to cut others in on it; get somebody with plenty of loot to back him. They'd need good promotion and advertising; really push the thing good. Untouched planets were getting scarce; this might well be the last. If he missed this, it might be a long time before he had another chance to ...

His thoughts died. His scheme collapsed. Dull resentment choked him and he came to an abrupt halt.

Ahead the trail broadened. The trees were farther apart; bright sunlight sifted down into the silent darkness of the ferns and bushes and flowers. On a little rise was a building. A stone house, with steps, a front porch, solid white walls like marble. A garden grew around it. Windows. A path. Smaller buildings in the back. All neat and pretty — and extremely modern-looking. A small fountain sprinkled blue water into a basin. A few birds moved around the gravel paths, pecking and scratching.

The planet was inhabited.

Brent approached warily. A wisp of gray smoke trailed out of the stone chimney. Behind the house were chicken pens, a cow-like thing dozing in the shade by its water trough. Other animals, some dog-like, and a group that might have been sheep. A regular little farm — but not like any farm he had seen. The buildings were of marble, or what looked like marble. And the animals were penned in by some kind of force-field. Everything was clean; in one corner a disposal tube sucked exhausted water and refuse into a half-buried tank.

He came to steps leading up to a back porch and, after a moment of thought, climbed them. He wasn't especially frightened. There was a serenity about the place, an orderly calm. It was hard to imagine any harm coming from it. He reached the door, hesitated, and then began looking for a knob.

There wasn't any knob. At his touch the door swung open. Feeling foolish, Brent entered. He found himself in a luxurious hall; recessed lights flickered on at the pressure of his boots on the thick carpets. Long glowing drapes hid the windows. Massive furniture — he peered into a room. Strange machines and objects. Pictures on the walls. Statues in the corners. He turned a corner and emerged into a large foyer. And still no one.

A huge animal, as large as a pony, moved out of a doorway, sniffed at him curiously, licked his wrist, and wandered off. He watched it go, heart in his mouth.

Tame. All the animals were tame. What kind of people had built this place? Panic stabbed at him. Maybe not people. Maybe some other race. Something alien, from beyond the galaxy. Maybe this was the frontier of an alien empire, some kind of advanced station.

While he was thinking about it, wondering if he should try to get out, run back to the ship, vid the cruiser station at Orion IX, there was a faint rustle behind him. He turned quickly, hand on his gun.

"Who — " he gasped. And froze.

A girl stood there, face calm, eyes large and dark, a cloudy black. She was tall, almost as tall as he, a little under six feet. Cascades of black hair spilled down her shoulders, down to her waist. She wore a glistening robe of some oddly-metallic material; countless facets glittered and sparkled and reflected the overhead lights. Her lips were deep red and full. Her arms were folded beneath her breasts; they stirred faintly as she breathed. Beside her stood the pony-like animal that had nosed him and gone on.

"Welcome, Mr. Brent," the girl said. She smiled at him; he caught a flash of her tiny white teeth. Her voice was gentle and lilting, remarkably pure. Abruptly she turned; her robe fluttered behind her as she passed through the doorway and into the room beyond. "Come along. I've been expecting you."

Brent entered cautiously. A man stood at the end of the long table, watching him with obvious dislike. He was huge, over six feet, broad shoulders and arms that rippled as he buttoned his cloak and moved toward the door. The table was covered with dishes and bowls of food; robot servants were clearing away the things silently. Obviously, the girl and man had been eating.

"This is my brother," the girl said, indicating the dark-faced giant. He bowed slightly to Brent, exchanged a few words with the girl in an unfamiliar, liquid tongue, and then abruptly departed. His footsteps died down the hall.

"I'm sorry," Brent muttered. "I didn't mean to bust in here and break up anything."

"Don't worry. He was going. Actually, we don't get along very well." The girl drew the drapes aside to reveal a wide window overlooking the forest. "You can watch him go. His ship is parked out there. See it?"

It took a moment for Brent to make out the ship. It blended into the scenery perfectly. Only when it abruptly shot upward at a ninety-degree angle did he realize it had been there all the time. He had walked within yards of it.

"He's quite a person," the girl said, letting the drapes fall back in place. "Are you hungry? Here, sit down and eat with me. Now that Aeetes is gone and I'm all alone."

Brent sat down cautiously. The food looked good. The dishes were some kind of semi-transparent metal. A robot set places in front of him, knives, forks, spoons, then waited to be instructed. The girl gave it orders in her strange liquid tongue. It promptly served Brent and retired.

He and the girl were alone. Brent began to eat greedily, the food was delicious. He tore the wings from a chicken-like fowl and gnawed at it expertly. He gulped down a tumbler of dark red wine, wiped his mouth on his sleeve, and attacked a bowl of ripe fruit. Vegetables, spiced meats, seafood, warm bread — he gobbled down everything with pleasure. The girl ate a few dainty bites; she watched him curiously, until finally he was finished and had pushed his empty dishes away.

"Where's your Captain?" she asked. "Didn't he come?"

"Johnson? He's back at the ship." Brent belched noisily. "How come you speak Terran? It's not your natural language. And how did you know there's somebody with me?"

The girl laughed, a tinkling musical peal. She wiped her slim hands on a napkin and drank from a dark red glass. "We watched you on the scanner. We were curious. This is the first time one of your ships has penetrated this far. We wondered what your intentions were."

"You didn't learn Terran by watching our ship on a scanner."

"No. I learned your language from people of your race. That was a long time ago. I've spoken your language as long as I can remember."

Brent was baffled. "But you said our ship was the first to come here."

The girl laughed. "True. But we've often visited your little world. We know all about it. It's a stop-over point when we travel in that direction. I've been there many times — not for a while, but in the old days when I traveled more."

A strange chill settled over Brent. "Who are you people? Where are you from?"

"I don't know where we're from originally," the girl answered. "Our civilization is all over the universe, by now. It probably started from one place, back in legendary times. By now it's practically everywhere."

"Why haven't we run into your people before?"

The girl smiled and continued eating. "Didn't you hear what I said? You *have* met us. Often. We've even brought Terrans here. I remember one time very clearly, a few thousand years ago — "

"How long are your years?" Brent demanded.

"We don't have years." The girl's dark eyes bored into him, luminous with amusement. "I mean *Terran* years."

It took a minute for the full impact to hit him. "Thousand years," he murmured. "You've been alive a thousand years?"

"Eleven thousand," the girl answered simply. She nodded, and a robot cleared away the dishes. She leaned back in her chair, yawned, stretched like a small, lithe cat, then abruptly sprang to her feet. "Come on. We've finished eating. I'll show you my house."

Brent scrambled up and hurried after her, his confidence shattered. "You're immortal, aren't you?" He moved between her and the door, breathing rapidly, heavy face flushed. "You don't age."

"Age? No, of course not."

Brent managed to find words. "You're gods."

The girl smiled up at him, dark eyes flashing merrily. "Not really. You have just about everything we have — almost as much knowledge, science, culture. Eventually you'll catch up with us. We're an old race. Millions of years ago our scientists succeeded in slowing down the processes of decay; since then we've ceased to die."

"Then your race stays constant. None die, none are born."

The girl pushed past him, through the doorway and down the hall. "Oh, people are born all the time. Our race grows and expands." She halted at a doorway. "We haven't given up any of our pleasures." She eyed Brent thoughtfully, his shoulders, arms, his dark hair, heavy face. "We're about like you, except that we're eternal. You'll probably solve that, too, sometime."

"You've moved among us?" Brent demanded. He was beginning to understand. "Then all those old religions and myths were true. Gods. Miracles. You've had contact with us, given us things. Done things for us." He followed her wonderingly into the room.

"Yes. I suppose we've done things for you. As we pass through." The girl moved about the room, letting down massive drapes. Soft darkness fell over the couches and bookcases and statues. "Do you play chess?"

"CHESS?"

"It's our national game. We introduced it to some of your Brahmin ancestors." Disappointment showed on her sharp little face. "You don't play? Too bad. What do you do? What about your companion? He looked as if his intellectual capacity was greater than yours. Does he play chess? Maybe you ought to go back and get him."

"I don't think so," Brent said. He moved toward her. "As far as I know he doesn't do anything." He reached out and caught her by the arm. The girl pulled away, astonished. Brent gathered her up in his big arms and drew her tight against him. "I don't think we need him," he said.

He kissed her on the mouth. Her red lips were warm and sweet; she gasped and fought wildly. He could feel her slim body struggling against him. A cloud of fragrant scent billowed from her dark hair. She tore at him with her sharp nails, breasts heaving violently. He let go and she slid away, wary and bright-eyed, breathing quickly, body tense, drawing her luminous robe about her.

"I could kill you," she whispered. She touched her jeweled belt. "You don't understand, do you?"

Brent came forward. "You probably can. But I bet you won't."

She backed away from him. "Don't be a fool." Her red lips twisted and a smile flickered briefly. "You're brave. But not very smart. Still, that's not such a bad combination in a man. Stupid and brave." Agilely, she avoided his grasp and slipped out of his reach. "You're in good physical shape, too. How do you manage it aboard that little ship?"

"Quarterly fitness courses," Brent answered. He moved between her and the door. "You must get pretty damn bored here, all by yourself. After the first few thousand years it must get trying."

"I find things to do," she said. "Don't come any closer to me. As much as I admire your daring, it's only fair to warn you that — "

Brent grabbed her. She fought wildly; he pinned her hands together behind her back with one paw, arched her body taut, and kissed her half-parted lips. She sank her tiny white teeth into him; he grunted and jerked away. She was laughing, black eyes dancing, as she struggled. Her breath came rapidly, cheeks flushed, half-covered breasts quivering, body twisting like a trapped animal. He caught her around the waist and grabbed her up in his arms.

A wave of force hit him.

He dropped her; she landed easily on her feet and danced back. Brent was doubled up, face gray with agony. Cold sweat stood out on his neck and hands. He sank down on a couch and closed his eyes, muscles knotted, body writhing with pain.

"Sorry," the girl said. She moved around the room, ignoring him, "It's your own fault — I told you to be careful. Maybe you better get out of here. Back to your little ship. I don't want anything to happen to you. It's against our policy to kill Terrans."

"What — was that?"

"Nothing much. A form of repulsion, I suppose. This belt was constructed on one of our industrial planets; it protects me but I don't know the operational principle."

Brent manage to get to his feet. "You're pretty tough for a little girl."

"A little girl? I'm pretty *old* for a little girl. I was old before you were born. I was old before your people had rocket ships. I was old before you knew how to weave clothing and write your thoughts down with symbols. I've watched your race advance and fall back into barbarism and advance again. Endless nations and empires. I was alive when the Egyptians first began spreading out into Asia Minor. I saw the city builders of the Tigris Valley begin putting up their brick houses. I saw the Assyrian war chariots roll out to fight. I and my friends visited Greece and Rome and Minos and Lydia and the great kingdoms of the red-skinned Indians. We were gods to the ancients, saints to the Christians. We come and go. As your people advanced we came less often. We have other way-stations; yours isn't the only stop-over point."

Brent was silent. Color was beginning to come back to his face. The girl had thrown herself down on one of the soft couches; she leaned back against a pillow and gazed up at him calmly, one arm outstretched, the other across her lap. Her long legs were tucked under her, tiny feet pressed together. She looked like a small, contented kitten resting after a game. It was hard for him to believe what she had told him. But his body still ached; he had felt a minute portion of her power-field, and it had almost killed him. That was something to think about.

"Well?" the girl asked, presently. "What are you going to do? It's getting late. I think you ought to go back to your ship. Your Captain will be wondering what happened to you."

Brent moved over to the window and drew aside the heavy drapes. The sun had set. Darkness was settling over the forests outside. Stars had already begun to come out, tiny dots of white in the thickening violet. A distant line of hills jutted up black and ominous.

"I can contact him," Brent said. He tapped at his neck. "In case of emergency. Tell him I'm all right."

"*Are you all right?* You shouldn't be here. You think you know what you're doing? You think you can handle me." She raised herself up slightly and tossed her black hair back over her shoulders. "I can see what's going on in your mind. I'm so much like a girl you had an affair with, a young brunette you used to wrap around your finger — and boast about to your companions."

Brent flushed. "You're a telepath. You should have told me."

"A partial telepath. All I need. Toss me your cigarettes. We don't have such things."

Brent fumbled in his pocket, got his pack out and tossed it to her. She lit up and inhaled gratefully. A cloud of gray smoke drifted around her; it mixed with the darkening shadows of the room. The corners dissolved into gloom. She became an indistinct shape, curled up on the couch, the glowing cigarette between her dark red lips.

"I'm not afraid," Brent said.

"No, you're not. You're not a coward. If you were as smart as you are brave — but then I guess you wouldn't be brave. I admire your bravery, stupid as it is. Man has a lot of courage. Even though it's based on ignorance, it's impressive." After a moment, she said, "Come over here and sit with me."

"What do I have to be worried about?" Brent asked after a while. "If you don't turn on that damn belt, I'll be all right."

In the darkness, the girl stirred. "There's more than that." She sat up a little, arranged her hair, pulled a pillow behind her head. "You see, we're of totally different races. My race is millions of years advanced over yours. Contact with us — close contact — is lethal. Not to us, of course. To you. You can't be with me and remain a human being."

"What do you mean?"

"You'll undergo changes. Evolutionary changes. There's pull which we exert. We're fully charged; close contact with us will exert influence on the cells of your body. Those animals outside. They've evolved slightly; they're no longer wild beasts. They're able to understand simple commands and follow basic routines. As yet, they have no language. With such low animals it's a long process; and my contact with them hasn't really been close. But with you — "

"I see."

"We're not supposed to let humans near us. Aeetes cleared out of here. I'm too lazy to go — I don't especially care. I'm not mature and responsible, I suppose." She smiled slightly. "And my kind of close contact is a little closer than most."

Brent could barely make out her slim form in the darkness. She lay back against the pillows, lips parted, arms folded beneath her breasts, head tilted back. She was lovely. The most beautiful woman he had ever seen. After a moment he leaned toward her. This time she didn't move away. He kissed her gently. Then he put his arms around her slender body and drew her tight against him. Her robe rustled. Her soft hair brushed against him, warm and fragrant.

"It's worth it," he said.

"You're sure? You can't turn back, once it's begun. Do you understand? You won't be human any more. You'll have evolved. Along lines your race will take millions of years from now. You'll be an outcast, a forerunner of things to come. Without companions."

"I'll stay." He caressed her cheek, her hair, her neck. He could feel the blood pulsing beneath the downy skin; a rapid pounding in the hollow of her throat. She was breathing rapidly; her breasts rose and fell against him. "If you'll let me."

"Yes," she murmured. "I'll let you. If it's what you really want. But don't blame me." A half-sad, half-mischievous smile flitted across her sharp features; her dark eyes sparkled. "Promise you won't blame me? It's happened before — I hate people to reproach me. I always say never again. No matter what."

"Has it happened before?"

The girl laughed, softly and close to his ear. She kissed him warmly and hugged him hard against her. "In eleven thousand years," she whispered, "it's happened quite often."

Captain Johnson had a bad night. He tried to raise Brent on the emergency com, but there was no response. Only faint static and a distant echo of a vid program from Orion X. Jazz music and sugary commercials.

The sounds of civilization reminded him that they had to keep moving. Twenty-four hours was all the time allotted to this planet, smallest of its system.

"Damn," he muttered. He fixed a pot of coffee and checked his wristwatch. Then he got out of the ship and wandered around in the early-morning sunlight. The sun was beginning to come up. The air turned from dark violet to gray. It was cold as hell. He shivered and stamped his feet and watched some small bird-like things fly down to peck around the bushes.

He was just beginning to think of notifying Orion XI when he saw her.

She walked quickly toward the ship. Tall and slim in a heavy fur jacket, her arms buried in the deep pelt. Johnson stood rooted to the spot, dumbfounded. He was too astonished even to touch his gun. His mouth fell open as the girl halted a little way off, tossed her dark hair back, blew a cloud of silvery breath at him and then said, "I'm sorry you had a bad night. It's my fault. I should have sent him right back."

Captain Johnson's mouth opened and shut. "Who are you?" he managed finally. Fear seized him. "Where's Brent? What happened?"

"He'll be along." She turned back toward the forest and made a sign. "I think you'd better leave, now. He wants to stay here and that is best — for he's changed. He'll be happy in my forest with the other — men. It's strange how all you humans come out exactly alike. Your race is moving along an unusual path. It might be worth our while to study you, sometime. It must have something to do with your low esthetic plateau. You seem to have an innate vulgarity, which eventually will dominate you."

From out of the woods came a strange shape. For a moment, Captain Johnson thought his eyes were playing tricks on him. He blinked, squinted, then grunted in disbelief. Here, on this remote planet — but there was no mistake. It was definitely an immense cat-like beast that came slowly and miserably out of the woods after the girl.

The girl moved away, then halted to wave to the beast, who whined wretchedly around the ship.

Johnson stared at the animal and felt a sudden fear. Instinctively he knew that Brent was not coming back to the ship. Something had happened on this strange planet — that girl ...

Johnson slammed the airlock shut and hurried to the control panel. He had to get back to the nearest base and make a report. This called for an elaborate investigation.

As the rockets blasted Johnson glanced through the viewplate. He saw the animal shaking a huge paw futilely in the air after the departing ship.

Johnson shuddered. That was too much like a man's angry gesture ...

TONY AND THE BEETLES

REDDISH-YELLOW SUNLIGHT filtered through the thick quartz windows into the sleep-compartment. Tony Rossi yawned, stirred a little, then opened his black eyes and sat up quickly. With one motion he tossed the covers back and slid to the warm metal floor. He clicked off his alarm clock and hurried to the closet.

It looked like a nice day. The landscape outside was motionless, undisturbed by winds or dust-shift. The boy's heart pounded excitedly. He pulled his trousers on, zipped up the reinforced mesh, struggled into his heavy canvas shirt, and then sat down onto the edge of the cot to tug on his boots. He closed the seams around their tops and then did the same with his gloves. Next he adjusted the pressure on his pump unit and strapped it between his shoulder blades. He grabbed his helmet from the dresser, and he was ready for the day.

In the dining-compartment his mother and father had finished breakfast. Their voices drifted to him as he clattered down the ramp. A disturbed murmur; he paused to listen. What were they talking about? Had he done something wrong, again?

And then he caught it. Behind their voices was another voice. Static and crackling pops. The all-system audio signal from Rigel IV. They had it turned up full blast; the dull thunder of the monitor's voice boomed loudly. The war. Always the war. He sighed, and stepped out into the dining-compartment.

"Morning," his father muttered.

"Good morning, dear," his mother said absently. She sat with her head turned to one side, wrinkles of concentration webbing her forehead. Her thin lips were drawn together in a tight line of concern. His father had pushed his dirty dishes back and was smoking, elbows on the table, dark hairy arms bare and muscular. He was scowling, intent on the jumbled roar from the speaker above the sink.

"How's it going?" Tony asked. He slid into his chair and reached automatically for the ersatz grapefruit. "Any news from Orion?"

Neither of them answered. They didn't hear him. He began to eat his grapefruit. Outside, beyond the little metal and plastic housing unit, sounds of activity grew. Shouts and muffled crashes, as rural merchants and their trucks rumbled along the highway toward Karnet. The reddish daylight swelled; Betelgeuse was rising quietly and majestically.

"Nice day," Tony said. "No flux wind. I think I'll go down to the n-quarter awhile. We're building a neat spaceport, a model, of course, but we've been able to get enough materials to lay out strips for — "

With a savage snarl his father reached out and struck. The audio roar immediately died. "I knew it!" He got up and moved angrily away from the table. "I told them it would happen. They shouldn't have moved so soon. Should have built up Class A supply bases, first."

"Isn't our main fleet moving in from Bellatrix?" Tony's mother fluttered anxiously. "According to last night's summary the worse that can happen is Orion IX and X will be dumped."

Joseph Rossi laughed harshly. "The hell with last night's summary. They know as well as I do what's happening."

"What's happening?" Tony echoed, as he pushed aside his grapefruit and began to ladle out dry cereal. "Are we losing the battle?"

"Yes!" His father's lips twisted. "Earthmen, losing to — to *beetles*. I told them. But they couldn't wait. My God, there's ten good years left in this system. Why'd they have to push on? Everybody knew Orion would be tough. The whole damn beetle fleet's strung out around there. Waiting for us. And we have to barge right in."

"But nobody ever thought beetles would fight," Leah Rossi protested mildly. "Everybody thought they'd just fire a few blasts and then — "

"They *have* to fight! Orion's the last jump-off. If they don't fight here, where the hell can they fight?" Rossi swore savagely. "Of course they're fighting. We have all their planets except the inner Orion string — not that they're worth much, but it's the principle of the thing. If we'd built up strong supply bases, we could have broken up the beetle fleet and really clobbered it."

"Don't say 'beetle'," Tony murmured, as he finished his cereal. "They're Pas-udeti, same as here. The word 'beetle' comes from Betelgeuse. An Arabian word we invented ourselves."

Joe Rossi's mouth opened and closed. "What are you, a goddamn beetle-lover?"

"Joe," Leah snapped. "For heaven's sake."

Rossi moved toward the door. "If I was ten years younger I'd be out there.

I'd really show those shiny-shelled insects what the hell they're up against. Them and their junky beat-up old hulks. Converted freighters!" His eyes blazed. "When I think of them shooting down Terran cruisers with *our* boys in them — "

"Orion's their system," Tony murmured.

"*Their* system! When the hell did you get to be an authority on space law? Why, I ought to — " He broke off, choked with rage. "My own kid," he muttered. "One more crack out of you today and I'll hang one on you you'll feel the rest of the week."

Tony pushed his chair back. "I won't be around today. I'm going into Karnet, with my EEP."

"Yeah, to play with beetles!"

Tony said nothing. He was already sliding his helmet in place and snapping the clamps tight. As he pushed through the back door, into the lock membrane, he unscrewed his oxygen tap and set the tank filter into action. An automatic response, conditioned by a lifetime spent on a colony planet in an alien system.

A faint flux wind caught at him and swept yellow-red dust around his boots. Sunlight glittered from the metal roof of his family's housing unit, one of endless rows of squat boxes set in the sandy slope, protected by the line of ore-refining installations against the horizon. He made an impatient signal, and from the storage shed his EEP came gliding out, catching the sunlight on its chrome trim.

"We're going down into Karnet," Tony said, unconsciously slipping into the Pas dialect. "Hurry up!"

The EEP took up its position behind him, and he started briskly down the slope, over the shifting sand, toward the road. There were quite a few traders out, today. It was a good day for the market; only a fourth of the year was fit for travel. Betelgeuse was an erratic and undependable sun, not at all like Sol (according to the edutapes fed to Tony four hours a day, six days a week — he had never seen Sol himself).

He reached the noisy road. Pas-udeti were everywhere. Whole groups of them, with their primitive combustion-driven trucks, battered and filthy, motors grinding protestingly. He waved at the trucks as they pushed past him. After a moment one slowed down. It was piled with *tis*, bundled heaps of gray vegetables, dried and prepared for the table. A staple of the Pas-udeti diet. Behind the wheel lounged a dark-faced elderly Pas, one arm over the open window, a rolled leaf between his lips. He was like all other Pas-udeti: lank and hard-shelled, encased in a brittle sheath in which he lived and died.

"You want a ride?" the Pas murmured — required protocol when an Earthman on foot was encountered.

"Is there room for my EEP?"

The Pas made a careless motion with his claw. "It can run behind." Sardonic amusement touched his ugly old face. "If it gets to Karnet we'll sell it for scrap. We can use a few condensers and relay tubing. We're short of electronic maintenance stuff."

"I know," Tony said solemnly, as he climbed into the cabin of the truck. "It's all been sent to the big repair base at Orion I. For your warfleet."

Amusement vanished from the leathery face. "Yes, the warfleet." He turned away and started up the truck again. In the back, Tony's EEP had scrambled up on the load of *tis* and was gripping precariously with its magnetic lines.

Tony noticed the Pas-udeti's sudden change of expression, and he was puzzled. He started to speak to him — but now he noticed unusual quietness among the other Pas, in the other trucks, behind and in front of his own. The war, of course. It had swept through this system a century ago; these people had been left behind. Now all eyes were on Orion, on the battle between the Terran warfleet and the Pas-udeti collection of armed freighters.

"Is it true," Tony asked carefully, "that you're winning?"

The elderly Pas grunted. "We hear rumors."

Tony considered. "My father says Terra went ahead too fast. He says we should have consolidated. We didn't assemble adequate supply bases. He used to be an officer, when he was younger. He was with the fleet for two years."

The Pas was silent a moment. "It's true," he said at last, "that when you're so far from home, supply is a great problem. We, on the other hand, don't have that. We have no distances to cover."

"Do you know anybody fighting?"

"I have distant relatives." The answer was vague; the Pas obviously didn't want to talk about it.

"Have you ever seen your warfleet?"

"Not as it exists now. When this system was defeated most of our units were wiped out. Remnants limped to Orion and joined the Orion fleet."

"Your relatives were with the remnants?"

"That's right."

"Then you were alive when this planet was taken?"

"Why do you ask?" The old Pas quivered violently. "What business is it of yours?"

Tony leaned out and watched the walls and buildings of Karnet grow ahead of them. Karnet was an old city. It had stood thousands of years. The Pas-udeti civilization was stable; it had reached a certain point of technocratic development and then leveled off. The Pas had intersystem ships that had carried people and freight between planets in the days before the Terran Confederation. They had combustion-driven cars, audiophones, a power network of a magnetic type. Their plumbing was satisfactory and their medicine was highly advanced. They had art forms, emotional and exciting. They had a vague religion.

"Who do you think will win the battle?" Tony asked.

"I don't know." With a sudden jerk the old Pas brought the truck to a crashing halt. "This is as far as I go. Please get out and take your EEP with you."

Tony faltered in surprise. "But aren't you going — ?"

"No farther!"

Tony pushed the door open. He was vaguely uneasy; there was a hard, fixed expression on the leathery face, and the old creature's voice had a sharp edge he had never heard before. "Thanks," he murmured. He hopped down into the red dust and signaled his EEP. It released it magnetic lines, and instantly the truck started up with a roar, passing on inside the city.

Tony watched it go, still dazed. The hot dust lapped at his ankles; he automatically moved his feet and slapped at his trousers. A truck honked, and his EEP quickly moved him from the road, up to the level pedestrian ramp. Pas-udeti in swarms moved by, endless lines of rural people hurrying into Karnet on their daily business. A massive public bus had stopped by the gate and was letting off passengers. Male and female Pas. And children. They laughed and shouted; the sounds of their voices blended with the low hum of the city.

"Going in?" a sharp Pas-udeti voice sounded close behind him. "Keep moving — you're blocking the ramp."

It was a young female, with a heavy armload clutched in her claws. Tony felt embarrassed; female Pas had a certain telepathic ability, part of their sexual makeup. It was effective on Earthmen at close range.

"Here," she said. "Give me a hand."

Tony nodded his head, and the EEP accepted the female's heavy armload. "I'm visiting the city," Tony said, as they moved with the crowd toward the gates. "I got a ride most of the way, but the driver let me off out here."

"You're from the settlement?"

"Yes."

She eyed him critically. "You've always lived here, haven't you?"

"I was born here. My family came here from Earth four years before I was born. My father was an officer in the fleet. He earned an Emigration Priority."

"So you've never seen your own planet. How old are you?"

"Ten years. Terran."

"You shouldn't have asked the driver so many questions."

They passed through the decontamination shield and into the city. An information square loomed ahead; Pas men and women were packed around it. Moving chutes and transport cars rumbled everywhere. Buildings and ramps and open-air machinery; the city was sealed in a protective dust-proof envelope. Tony unfastened his helmet and clipped it to his belt. The air was stale-smelling, artificial, but usable.

"Let me tell you something," the young female said carefully, as she strode along the foot-ramp beside Tony. "I wonder if this is a good day for you to come to Karnet. I know you've been coming here regularly to play with your friends. But perhaps today you ought to stay home, in your settlement."

"Why?"

"Because today everybody is upset."

"I know," Tony said. "My mother and father were upset. They were listening to the news from our base in the Rigel system."

"I don't mean your family. Other people are listening, too. These people here. My race."

"They're upset, all right," Tony admitted. "But I come here all the time. There's nobody to play with at the settlement, and anyhow we're working on a project."

"A model spaceport."

"That's right." Tony was envious. "I sure wish I was a telepath. It must be fun."

The female Pas-udeti was silent. She was deep in thought. "What would happen," she asked, "if your family left here and returned to Earth?"

"That couldn't happen. There's no room for us on Earth. C-bombs destroyed most of Asia and North America back in the Twentieth Century."

"Suppose you *had* to go back?"

Tony did not understand. "But we can't. Habitable portions of Earth are overcrowded. Our main problem is finding places for Terrans to live, in other systems." He added, "And anyhow, I don't particularly want to go to Terra. I'm used to it here. All my friends are here."

"I'll take my packages," the female said. "I go this other way, down this third-level ramp."

Tony nodded to his EEP and it lowered the bundles into the female's claws. She lingered a moment, trying to find the right words.

"Good luck," she said.

"With what?"

She smiled faintly, ironically. "With your model spaceport. I hope you and your friends get to finish it."

"Of course we'll finish it," Tony said, surprised. "It's almost done." What did she mean?

The Pas-udeti woman hurried off before he could ask her. Tony was troubled and uncertain; more doubts filled him. After a moment he headed slowly into the lane that took him toward the residential section of the city. Past the stores and factories, to the place where his friends lived.

The group of Pas-udeti children eyed him silently as he approached. They had been playing in the shade of an immense *bengelo*, whose ancient branches drooped and swayed with the air currents pumped through the city. Now they sat unmoving.

"I didn't expect you today," B'prith said, in an expressionless voice.

Tony halted awkwardly, and his EEP did the same. "How are things?" he murmured.

"Fine."

"I got a ride part way."

"Fine."

Tony squatted down in the shade. None of the Pas children stirred. They were small, not as large as Terran children. Their shells had not hardened, had not turned dark and opaque, like horn. It gave them a soft, unformed appearance, but at the same time it lightened their load. They moved more easily than their elders: they could hop and skip around, still. But they were not skipping right now.

"What's the matter?" Tony demanded. "What's wrong with everybody?"

No one answered.

"Where's the model?" he asked. "Have you fellows been working on it?"

After a moment Llyre nodded slightly.

Tony felt dull anger rise up inside him. "Say something! What's the matter? What're you all mad about?"

"Mad?" B'prith echoed. "We're not mad."

Tony scratched aimlessly in the dust. He knew what it was. The war, again. The battle going on near Orion. His anger burst up wildly. "Forget the war. Everything was fine yesterday, before the battle."

"Sure," Llyre said. "It was fine."

Tony caught the edge to his voice. "It happened a hundred years ago. It's not my fault."

"Sure," B'prith said.

"This is my home. Isn't it? Haven't I got as much right here as anybody else? I was born here."

"Sure," Llyre said, tonelessly.

Tony appealed to them helplessly. "Do you have to act this way? You didn't act this way yesterday. I was here yesterday — all of us were here yesterday. What's happened since yesterday?"

"The battle," B'prith said.

"What difference does *that* make? Why does that change everything? There's always war. There've been battles all the time, as long as I can remember. What's different about this?"

B'prith broke apart a clump of dirt with his strong claws. After a moment he tossed it away and got slowly to his feet. "Well," he said thoughtfully, "according to our audio relay, it looks as if our fleet is going to win, this time."

"Yes," Tony agreed, not understanding. "My father says we didn't build up adequate supply bases. We'll probably have to fall back to . . . " And then the impact hit him. 'You mean, for the first time in a hundred years — "

"Yes," Llyre said, also getting up. The others got up, too. They moved away from Tony, toward the nearby house. "We're winning. The Terran flank was turned, half an hour ago. Your right wing has folded completely."

Tony was stunned. "And it matters. It matters to all of you."

"Matters!" B'prith halted, suddenly blazing out in fury. "Sure it matters! For the first time — in a century. The first time in our lives we're beating you. We have you on the run, you — " He choked out the word, almost spat it out. "You white-grubs!"

They disappeared into the house. Tony sat gazing stupidly down at the ground, his hands still moving aimlessly. He had heard the word before, seen it scrawled on walls and in the dust near the settlement. *White-grubs*. The Pas term of derision for Terrans. Because of their softness, their whiteness. Lack of hard shells. Pulpy, doughy skin. But they had never dared say it out loud, before. To an Earthman's face.

Beside him, his EEP stirred restlessly. Its intricate radio mechanism sensed the hostile atmosphere. Automatic relays were sliding into place; circuits were opening and closing.

"It's all right," Tony murmured, getting slowly up. "Maybe we'd better go back."

He moved unsteadily toward the ramp, completely shaken. The EEP walked calmly ahead, its metal face blank and confident, feeling nothing, saying nothing. Tony's thoughts were a wild turmoil; he shook his head, but the crazy spinning kept up. He couldn't make his mind slow down, lock in place.

"Wait a minute," a voice said. B'prith's voice, from the open doorway. Cold and withdrawn, almost unfamiliar.

"What do you want?"

B'prith came toward him, claws behind his back in the formal Pas-udeti posture, used between total strangers. "You shouldn't have come here, today."

"I know," Tony said.

B'prith got out a bit of *tis* stalk and began to roll it into a tube. He pretended to concentrate on it. "Look," he said. "You said you have a right here. But you don't."

"I — " Tony murmured.

"Do you understand why not? You said it isn't your fault. I guess not. But it's not my fault, either. Maybe it's nobody's fault. I've known you a long time."

"Five years. Terran."

B'prith twisted the stalk up and tossed it away. "Yesterday we played together. We worked on the spaceport. But we can't play today. My family said to tell you not to come here any more." He hesitated, and did not look Tony in the face. "I was going to tell you, anyhow. Before they said anything."

"Oh," Tony said.

"Everything that's happened today — the battle, our fleet's stand. We didn't know. We didn't dare hope. You see? A century of running. First this system. Then the Rigel system, all the planets. Then the other Orion stars. We fought here and there — scattered fights. Those that got away joined up. We supplied the base at Orion — you people didn't know. But there was no hope; at least, nobody thought there was." He was silent a moment. "Funny," he said, "what happens when your back's to the wall, and there isn't any further place to go. Then you have to fight."

"If our supply bases — " Tony began thickly, but B'prith cut him off savagely.

"Your supply bases! Don't you understand? We're beating you! Now you'll have to get out! All you white-grubs. Out of our system!"

Tony's EEP moved forward ominously. B'prith saw it. He bent down, snatched up a rock, and hurled to straight at the EEP. The rock clanged off the metal hull and bounced harmlessly away. B'prith snatched up another rock. Llyre and the others came quickly out of the house. An adult Pas loomed up behind them. Everything was happening too fast. More rocks crashed against the EEP. One struck Tony on the arm.

"Get out!" B'prith screamed. "Don't come back! This is our planet!" His claws snatched at Tony. "We'll tear you to pieces if you — "

Tony smashed him in the chest. The soft shell gave like rubber, and the Pas stumbled back. He wobbled and fell over, gasping and screeching.

"*Beetle*," Tony breathed hoarsely. Suddenly he was terrified. A crowd of Pas-udeti was forming rapidly. They surged on all sides, hostile faces, dark and angry, a rising thunder of rage.

More stones showered. Some struck the EEP, others fell around Tony, near his boots. One whizzed past his face. Quickly he slid his helmet in place. He was scared. He knew his EEP's E-signal had already gone out, but it would be minutes before a ship could come. Besides, there were other Earthmen in the city to be taken care of; there were Earthmen all over the planet. In all the cities. On all the twenty-three Betelgeuse planets. On the fourteen Rigel planets. On the other Orion planets.

"We have to get out of here," he muttered to the EEP. "Do something!™

A stone hit him on the helmet. The plastic cracked; air leaked out, and then the autoseal filmed over. More stones were falling. The Pas swarmed close, a yelling, seething mass of black-sheathed creatures. He could smell them, the acrid body-odor of insects, hear their claws snap, feel their weight.

The EEP threw its heat beam on. The beam shifted in a wide band toward the crowd of Pas-udeti. Crude hand weapons appeared. A clatter of bullets burst around Tony; they were firing at the EEP. He was dimly aware of the metal body beside him. A shuddering crash — the EEP was toppled over. The crowd poured over it; the metal hull was lost from sight.

Like a demented animal, the crowd tore at the struggling EEP. A few of them smashed in its head; others tore off struts and shiny arm-sections. The EEP ceased struggling. The crowd moved away, panting and clutching jagged remains. They saw Tony.

As the first line of them reached for him, the protective envelope high above them shattered. A Terran scout ship thundered down, heat beam screaming. The crowd scattered in confusion, some firing, some throwing stones, others leaping for safety.

Tony picked himself up and made his way unsteadily toward the spot where the scout was landing.

"I'm sorry," Joe Rossi said gently. He touched his son on the shoulder. "I shouldn't have let you go down there today. I should have known."

Tony sat hunched over in the big plastic easychair. He rocked back and forth, face pale with shock. The scout ship which had rescued him had immediately headed back toward Karnet; there were other Earthmen to bring out, besides this first load. The boy said nothing. His mind was blank. He still heard the roar of the crowd, felt its hate — a century of pent-up fury and resentment. The memory drove out everything else; it was all around him, even now. And the sight of the floundering EEP, the metallic ripping sound, as its arms and legs were torn off and carried away.

His mother dabbed at his cuts and scratches with antiseptic. Joe Rossi shakily lit a cigarette and said, "If your EEP hadn't been along they'd have killed you. Beetles." He shuddered. "I never should have let you go down there. All this time ... They might have done it any time, any day. Knifed you. Cut you open with their filthy goddamn claws."

Below the settlement the reddish-yellow sunlight glinted on gunbarrels. Already, dull booms echoed against the crumbling hills. The defense ring was going into action. Black shapes darted and scurried up the side of the slope. Black patches moved out from Karnet, toward the Terran settlement, across the dividing line the Confederation surveyors had set up a century ago. Karnet was a bubbling pot of activity. The whole city rumbled with feverish excitement.

Tony raised his head. "They — they turned our flank."

"Yeah." Joe Rossi stubbed out his cigarette. "They sure did. That was at one o'clock. At two they drove a wedge right through the center of our line. Split the fleet in half. Broke it up — sent it running. Picked us off one by one as we fell back. Christ, they're like maniacs. Now that they've got the scent, the taste of our blood."

"But it's getting better," Leah fluttered. "Our main fleet units are beginning to appear."

"We'll get them," Joe muttered. "It'll take a while. But by God we'll wipe them out. Every last one of them. If it takes a thousand years. We'll follow every last ship down — we'll get them all." His voice rose in frenzy. "Beetles! Goddamn insects! When I think of them, trying to hurt my kid, with their filthy black claws — "

"If you were younger, you'd be in the line," Leah said. "It's not your fault you're too old. The heart strain's too great. You did your job. They can't let an older person take chances. It's not your fault."

Joe clenched his fists. "I feel so — futile. If there was only something I could do."

"The fleet will take care of them," Leah said soothingly. "You said so yourself. They'll hunt every one of them down. Destroy them all. There's nothing to worry about."

Joe sagged miserably. "It's no use. Let's cut it out. Let's stop kidding ourselves."

"What do you mean?"

"Face it! We're not going to win, not this time. We went too far. Our time's come."

There was silence.

Tony sat up a little. "When did you know?"

"I've known a long time."

"I found out today. I didn't understand, at first. This is — stolen ground. I was born here, but it's stolen ground."

"Yes. It's stolen. It doesn't belong to us."

"We're here because we're stronger. But now we're not stronger. We're being beaten."

"They know Terrans can be licked. Like anybody else." Joe Rossi's face was gray and flabby. "We took their planets away from them. Now they're taking them back. It'll be a while, of course. We'll retreat slowly. It'll be another five centuries going back. There're a lot of systems between here and Sol."

Tony shook his head, still uncomprehending. "Even Llyre and B'prith. All of them. Waiting for their time to come. For us to lose and go away again. Where we came from."

Joe Rossi paced back and forth. "Yeah, we'll be retreating from now on. Giving ground, instead of taking it. It'll be like this today — losing fights, draws. Stalemates and worse."

He raised his feverish eyes toward the ceiling of the little metal housing unit, face wild with passion and misery.

"But, by God, we'll give them a run for their money. All the way back! Every inch!"

NULL-O

LEMUEL CLUNG TO THE WALL of his dark bedroom, tense, listening. A faint breeze stirred the lace curtains. Yellow street-light filtered over the bed, the dresser, the books and toys and clothes.

In the next room, two voices were murmuring together. "Jean, we've got to do something," the man's voice said.

A strangled gasp. "Ralph, please don't hurt him. You must control yourself. I won't let you hurt him."

"I'm not going to hurt him." There was brute anguish in the man's whisper. "Why does he do these things? Why doesn't he play baseball and tag like normal boys? Why does he have to burn down stores and torture helpless animals? *Why?*"

"He's different, Ralph. We must try to understand."

"Maybe we better take him to the doctor," his father said. "Maybe he's got some kind of glandular disease."

"You mean old Doc Grady? But you said he couldn't find — "

"Not Doc Grady. He quit after Lemuel destroyed his X-ray equipment and smashed all the furniture in his office. No, this is bigger than that." A tense pause. "Jean, I'm taking him up to the Hill."

"Oh, Ralph! Please — "

"I mean it." Grim determination, the harsh growl of a trapped animal. "Those psychologists may be able to do something. Maybe they can help him. Maybe not."

"But they might not let us have him back. And oh, Ralph, he's all we've got!"

"Sure," Ralph muttered hoarsely. "I know he is. But I've made up my mind. That day he slashed his teacher with a knife and leaped out the window. That day I made up my mind. Lemuel is going up to the Hill. . . . "

The day was warm and bright. Between the swaying trees the huge white hospital sparkled, all concrete and steel and plastic. Ralph Jorgenson peered about uncertainly, hat twisted between his fingers, subdued by the immensity of the place.

Lemuel listened intently. Straining his big, mobile ears, he could hear many voices, a shifting sea of voices that surged around him. The voices came from all the rooms and offices, on all the levels. They excited him.

Dr. James North came toward them, holding out his hand. He was tall and handsome, perhaps thirty, with brown hair and black horn-rimmed glasses. His stride was firm, his grip, when he shook hands with Lemuel, brief and confident. "Come in here," he boomed. Ralph moved toward the office, but Dr. North shook his head. "Not you. The boy. Lemuel and I are going to have a talk alone."

Excited, Lemuel followed Dr. North into his office. North quickly secured the door with triple magnetic locks. "You can call me James," he said, smiling warmly at the boy. "And I'll call you Lem, right?"

"Sure," Lemuel said guardedly. He felt no hostility emanating from the man, but he had learned to keep his guard up. He had to be careful, even with this friendly, good-looking doctor, a man of obvious intellectual ability.

North lit a cigarette and studied the boy. "When you tied up and dissected those old derelicts," he said thoughtfully, "you were scientifically curious, weren't you? You wanted to *know* — facts, not opinions. You wanted to find out for yourself how human beings were constructed."

Lemuel's excitement grew. "But no one understood."

"No." North shook his head. "No, they wouldn't. Do you know why?"

"I think so."

North paced back and forth. "I'll give you a few tests. To find out things. You don't mind, do you? We'll both learn more about you. I've been studying you, Lem. I've examined the police records and the newspaper files." Abruptly, he opened the drawer of his desk and got out the Minnesota Multiphasic, the Rorschach blots, the Bender Gestalt, the Rhine deck of ESP cards, an ouija board, a pair of dice, a magic writing tablet, a wax doll with fingernail parings and bits of hair, and a small piece of lead to be turned into gold.

"What do you want me to do?" Lemuel asked.

"I'm going to ask you a few questions, and give you a few objects to play with. I'll watch your reactions, note down a few things. How's that sound?"

Lemuel hesitated. He needed a friend so badly — but he was afraid. "I— "

Dr. North put his hand on the boy's shoulder. "You can trust me. I'm not like those kids that beat you up, that morning."

Lemuel glanced up gratefully. "You know about that? I discovered the rules of their game were purely arbitrary. Therefore I naturally oriented myself to the basic reality of the situation, and when I came up at bat I hit the pitcher and the catcher over the head. Later I discovered that all human ethics and morals are exactly the same sort of— " He broke off, suddenly afraid. "Maybe I— "

Dr. North sat down behind his desk and began shuffling the Rhine ESP deck. "Don't worry, Lem," he said softly. "Everything will be all right. I understand."

After the tests, the two of them sat in silence. It was six o'clock, and the sun was beginning to set outside. At last Dr. North spoke.

"Incredible. I can scarcely believe it, myself. You're utterly logical. You've completely cast off all thalamic emotion. Your mind is totally free of moral and cultural bias. You're a perfect paranoid, without any empathic ability whatever. You're utterly incapable of feeling sorrow or pity or compassion, or *any* of the normal human emotions."

Lemuel nodded. "True."

Dr. North leaned back, dazed. "It's hard even for me to grasp this. It's overwhelming. You possess super-logic, completely free of value-orientation bias. And you conceive of the entire world as organized against you."

"Yes."

"Of course. You've analyzed the structure of human activity and seen that as soon as they find out, they'll pounce on you and try to destroy you."

"Because I'm different."

North was overcome. "They've always classed paranoia as a mental illness. But it isn't! There's no lack of contact with reality — on the contrary, the paranoid is *directly* related to reality. He's a perfect empiricist. Not cluttered with ethical and moral-cultural inhibitions. The paranoid sees things as they really are; he's actually the only sane man."

"I've been reading *Mein Kampf*," Lemuel said. "It shows me I'm not alone." And in his mind he breathed the silent prayer of thanks: *Not alone*. Us. There are more of us.

Dr. North caught his expression. "The wave of the future," he said. "I'm not a part of it, but I can try to understand. I can appreciate I'm just a human being, limited by my thalamic emotional and cultural bias. I can't be one of you, but I can sympathize. . . . " He looked up, face alight with enthusiasm. "And I can help!"

The next few days were filled with excitement for Lemuel. Dr. North arranged for custody of him, and the boy took up residence at the doctor's uptown apartment. Here, he was no longer under pressure from his family; he could do as he pleased. Dr. North began at once to aid Lemuel in locating other mutant paranoids.

One evening after dinner, Dr. North asked, "Lemuel, do you think you could explain your theory of Null-O to me? It's hard to grasp the principle of non-object orientation."

Lemuel indicated the apartment with a wave of his hand. "All these apparent objects — each has a name. Book, chair, couch, rug, lamp, drapes, window, door, wall, and so on. But this division into objects is purely artificial. Based on an antiquated system of thought. In reality there are no objects. The universe is actually a unity. We have been taught to think in terms of objects. This *thing*, that *thing*. When Null-O is realized, this purely verbal division will cease. It has long since outlived its usefulness."

"Can you give me an example, a demonstration?"

Lemuel hesitated. "It's hard to do alone. Later on, when we've contacted others ... I can do it crudely, on a small scale."

As Dr. North watched intently, Lemuel rushed about the apartment gathering everything together in a heap. Then, when all the books, pictures, rugs, drapes, furniture and bric-a-brac had been collected, he systematically smashed everything into a shapeless mass.

"You see," he said, exhausted and pale from the violent effort, "the distinction into arbitrary objects is now gone. This unification of things into their basic homogeneity can be applied to the universe as a whole. The universe is a gestalt, a unified substance, without division into living and non-living, being and non-being. A vast vortex of energy, not discrete particles! Underlying the purely artificial appearance of material objects lies the world of reality: a vast undifferentiated realm of pure energy. Remember: the object is not the reality. First law of Null-O thought!"

Dr. North was solemn, deeply impressed. He kicked at a bit of broken chair, part of the shapeless heap of wood and cloth and paper and shattered glass. "Do you think this restoration to reality can be accomplished?"

"I don't know," Lemuel said simply. "There will be opposition, of course. Human beings will fight us; they're incapable of rising above their monkey-like preoccupation with *things* — bright objects they can touch and possess. It will all depend on how well we can coordinate with each other."

Dr. North unfolded a slip of paper from his pocket. "I have a lead," he said quietly. "The name of a man I think is one of you. We'll visit him tomorrow — then we'll see."

Dr. Jacob Weller greeted them with brisk efficiency at the entrance of his well-guarded lab overlooking Palo Alto. Rows of uniformed government guards protected the vital work he was doing, the immense system of labs and research offices. Men and women in white robes were working day and night.

"My work," he explained, as he signaled for the heavy-duty entrance locks to be closed behind them, "was basic in the development of the C-bomb, the cobalt case for the H-bomb. You will find that many top nuclear physicists are Null-O."

Lemuel's breath caught. "Then — "

"Of course." Weller wasted no words. "We've been working for years. Rockets at Peenemunde, the A-bomb at Los Alamos, the hydrogen bomb, and now this, the C-bomb. There are, of course, many scientists who are not Null-O, regular human beings with thalamic bias. Einstein, for example. But we're well on the way; unless too much opposition is encountered we'll be able to go into action very shortly."

The rear door of the laboratory slid aside, and a group of white-clad men and women filed solemnly in. Lemuel's heart gave a jump. Here they were, full-fledged adult Null-O's! Men and women both, *and they had been working for years!* He recognized them easily; all had the elongated and mobile ears, by which the mutant Null-O picked up minute air vibrations over great distances. It enabled them to communicate, wherever they were, throughout the world.

"Explain our program," Weller said to a small blond man who stood beside him, calm and collected, face stern with the importance of the moment.

"The C-bomb is almost ready," the man said quietly, with a slight German accent. "But it is not the final step in our plans. There is also the E-bomb, which is the ultimate of this initial phase. We have never made the E-bomb public. If human beings should find out about it, we should have to cope with serious emotional opposition."

"What is the E-bomb?" Lemuel asked, glowing with excitement.

"The phrase, 'the E-bomb,' " said the small blond man, "describes the process by which the Earth itself becomes a pile, is brought up to critical mass, and then allowed to detonate."

Lemuel was overcome. "I had no idea you had developed the plan this far!"

The blond man smiled faintly. "Yes, we have done a lot, since the early days. Under Dr. Rust, I was able to work out the basic ideological concepts of our program. Ultimately, we will unify the entire universe into a homogeneous mass. Right now, however, our concern is with the Earth. But once we have been successful here, there's no reason why we can't continue our work indefinitely."

"Transportation," Weller explained, "has been arranged to other planets. Dr. Frisch here — "

"A modification of the guided missiles we developed at Peenemunde," the blond man continued. "We have constructed a ship which will take us to Venus. There, we will initiate the second phase of our work. A V-bomb will be developed, which will restore Venus to its primordial state of homogeneous energy. And then — " He smiled faintly. "And then an S-bomb. The Sol bomb. Which will, if we are successful, unify this whole system of planets and moons into a vast gestalt."

By June 25, 1969, Null-O personnel had gained virtual control of all major world governments. The process, begun in the middle thirties, was for all practical purposes complete. The United States and Soviet Russia were firmly in the hands of Null-O individuals. Null-O men controlled all policy-level positions, and hence, could speed up the program of Null-O. The time had come. Secrecy was no longer necessary.

Lemuel and Dr. North watched from a circling rocket as the first H-bombs were detonated. By careful arrangement, both nations began H-bomb attacks simultaneously. Within an hour, class-one results were obtained; most of North America and Eastern Europe were gone. Vast clouds of radioactive particles drifted and billowed. Fused pits of metal bubbled and sputtered as far as the eye could see. In Africa, Asia, on endless islands and out-of-the-way places, surviving human beings cowered in terror.

"Perfect," came Dr. Weller's voice in Lemuel's ears. He was somewhere below the surface, down in the carefully protected headquarters where the Venus ship was in its last stages of assembly.

Lemuel agreed. "Great work. We've managed to unify at least a fifth of the world's land surface!"

"But there's more to come. Next the C-bombs are to be released. This will prevent human beings from interfering with our final work, the E-bomb installations. The terminals must still be erected. That can't be done as long as humans remain to interfere."

Within a week, the first C-bomb was set off. More followed, hurtled up from carefully concealed launchers in Russia and America.

By August 5, 1969, the human population of the world had been diminished to three thousand. The Null-O's, in their subsurface offices, glowed with satisfaction. Unification was proceeding exactly as planned. The dream was coming true.

"Now," said Dr. Weller, "we can begin erection of the E-bomb terminals."

One terminal was begun at Arequipa, Peru. The other, at the opposite side of the globe, at Bandoeng, Java. Within a month the two immense towers rose high against the dust-swept sky. In heavy protective suits and helmets, the two colonies of Null-O's worked day and night to complete the program.

Dr. Weller flew Lemuel to the Peruvian installation. All the way from San Francisco to Lima there was nothing but rolling ash and still-burning metallic fires. No sign of life or separate entities: everything had been fused into a single mass of heaving slag. The oceans themselves were steam and boiling water. All distinction between land and sea had been lost. The surface of the Earth was a single expanse of dull gray and white, where blue oceans and green forests, roads and cities and fields had once been.

"There," Dr. Weller said. "See it?"

Lemuel saw it, all right. His breath caught in his throat at its sheer beauty. The Null-O's had erected a vast bubble-shield, a sphere of transparent plastic amidst the rolling sea of liquid slag. Within the bubble the terminal itself could be seen, an intricate web of flashing metal and wires that made both Dr. Weller and Lemuel fall silent.

"You see," Weller explained, as he dropped the rocket through the locks of the shield, "we have only unified the surface of the Earth and perhaps a mile of rock beneath. The vast mass of the planet, however, is unchanged. But the E-bomb will handle that. The still-liquid core of the planet will erupt; the whole sphere will become a new sun. And when the S-bomb goes off, the entire system will become a unified mass of fiery gas."

Lemuel nodded. "Logical. And then — "

"The G-bomb. The galaxy itself is next. The final stages of the plan.... So vast, so awesome, we scarcely dare think of them. The G-bomb, and finally — " Weller smiled slightly, his eyes bright. "Then the U-bomb."

They landed, and were met by Dr. Frisch, full of nervous excitement. "Dr. Weller!" he gasped. "Something has gone wrong!"

"What is it?"

Frisch's face was contorted with dismay. By a violent Null-O leap he managed to integrate his mental faculties and throw off thalamic impulses. "A number of human beings have survived!"

Weller was incredulous. "What do you mean? How — "

"I picked up the sound of their voices. I was rotating my ears, enjoying the roar and lap of the slag outside the bubble, when I picked up the noise of ordinary human beings."

"But where?"

"Below the surface. Certain wealthy industrialists had secretly transferred their factories below ground, in violation of their governments' absolute orders to the contrary."

"Yes, we had an explicit policy to prevent that."

"These industrialists acted with typical thalamic greed. They transferred whole labor forces below, to work as slaves when war began. At least ten thousand humans were spared. They are still alive. And — "

"And what?"

"They have improvised huge bores, are now moving this way as quickly as possible. We're going to have a fight on our hands. I've already notified the Venus ship. It's being brought up to the surface at once."

Lemuel and Dr. Weller glanced at each other in horror. There were only a thousand Null-O's; they'd be outnumbered ten to one. "This is terrible," Weller said thickly. "Just when everything seemed near completion. How long before the power towers are ready?"

"It will be another six days before the Earth can be brought up to critical mass," Frisch muttered. "And the bores are virtually here. Rotate your ears. You'll hear them."

Lemuel and Dr. Weller did so. At once, a confusing babble of human voices came to them. A chaotic clang of sound, from a number of bores converging on the two terminal bubbles.

"Perfectly ordinary humans!" Lemuel gasped. "I can tell by the sound!"

"We're trapped!" Weller grabbed up a blaster, and Frisch did so, too. All the Null-O's were arming themselves. Work was forgotten. With a shattering roar the snout of a bore burst through the ground and aimed itself directly at them. The Null-O's fired wildly; they scattered and fell back toward the tower.

A second bore appeared, and then a third. The air was alive with blazing beams of energy, as the Null-O's fired and the humans fired back. The humans were the most common possible, a variety of laborers taken subsurface by their employers. The lower forms of human life: clerks, bus drivers, day-laborers, typists, janitors, tailors, bakers, turret lathe operators, shipping clerks, baseball players, radio announcers, garage mechanics, policemen, necktie peddlers, ice cream vendors, door-to-door salesmen, bill collectors, receptionists, welders, carpenters, construction laborers, farmers, politicians, merchants — the men and women whose very existence terrified the Null-O's to their core.

The emotional masses of ordinary people who resented the Great Work, the bombs and bacteria and guided missiles, were coming to the surface. They were rising up — finally. Putting an end to super-logic: rationality without responsibility.

"We haven't a chance," Weller gasped. "Forget the towers. Get the ship to the surface."

A salesman and two plumbers were setting fire to the terminal. A group of men in overalls and canvas shirts were ripping down the wiring. Others just as ordinary were turning their heat guns on the intricate controls. Flames licked up. The terminal tower swayed ominously.

The Venus ship appeared, lifted to the surface by an intricate stage-system. At once the Null-O's poured into it, in two efficient lines, all of them controlled and integrated as the crazed human beings decimated their ranks.

"Animals," Weller said sadly. "The mass of men. Mindless animals, dominated by their emotions. Beasts, unable to see things logically."

A heat beam finished him off, and the man behind moved forward. Finally the last remaining Null-O was aboard, and the great hatches slammed shut.

With a thunderous roar the jets of the ship opened, and it shot through the bubble into the sky.

Lemuel lay where he had fallen, when a heat beam, wielded by a crazed electrician, had touched his left leg. Sadly, he saw the ship rise, hesitate, then crash through and dwindle into the flaming sky. Human beings were all around him, repairing the damaged protection bubble, shouting orders and yelling excitedly. The babble of their voices beat against his sensitive ears; feebly, he put his hands up and covered them.

The ship was gone. He had been left behind. But the plan would continue without him.

A distant voice came to him. It was Dr. Frisch aboard the Venus ship, yelling down with cupped hands. The voice was faint, lost in the trackless miles of space, but Lemuel managed to make it out above the noise and hubbub around him.

"Goodbye ... We'll remember you. ... "

"Work hard!" the boy shouted back. "Don't give up until the plan is complete!"

"We'll work ... " The voice grew more faint. "We'll keep on ... " It died out, then returned for a brief instant. "We'll succeed ... " And then there was only silence.

With a peaceful smile on his face, a smile of happiness and contentment, satisfaction at a job well done, Lemuel lay back and waited for the pack of irrational human animals to finish him.

To Serve the Master

Applequist was cutting across a deserted field, up a narrow path beside the yawning crack of a ravine, when he heard the voice.

He stopped frozen, hand on his S-pistol. For a long time he listened, but there was only the distant lap of the wind among the broken trees along the ridge, a hollow murmuring that mixed with the rustle of the dry grass beside him. The sound had come from the ravine. Its bottom was snarled and debris-filled. He crouched down at the lip and tried to locate the voice.

There was no motion. Nothing to give away the place. His legs began to ache. Flies buzzed at him, settled on his sweating forehead. The sun made his head ache; the dust clouds had been thin the last few months.

His radiation-proof watch told him it was three o'clock. Finally he shrugged and got stiffly to his feet. The hell with it. Let them send out an armed team. It wasn't his business; he was a letter carrier grade four, and a civilian.

As he climbed the hill toward the road, the sound came again. And this time, standing high above the ravine, he caught a flash of motion. Fear and puzzled disbelief touched him. It couldn't be — but he had seen it with his own eyes. It wasn't a newscircular rumor.

What was a robot doing down in the deserted ravine? All robots had been destroyed years ago. But there it lay, among the debris and weeds. A rusted, half-corroded wreck. Calling feebly up at him as he passed along the trail.

The Company defense ring admitted him through the three-stage lock into the tunnel area. He descended slowly, deep in thought all the way down to the organizational level. As he slid off his letter pack Assistant Supervisor Jenkins hurried over.

"Where the hell have you been? It's almost four."

"Sorry." Applequist turned his S-pistol over to a nearby guard. "What are the chances of a five hour pass? There's something I want to look into."

"Not a chance. You know they're scrapping the whole right wing setup. They need everybody on strict twenty-four hour alert."

Applequist began sorting letters. Most were personals between big-shot supervisors of the North American Companies. Letters to entertainment women beyond the Company peripheries. Letters to families and petitions from minor officials. "In that case," he said thoughtfully, "I'll have to go anyhow."

Jenkins eyed the young man suspiciously. "What's going on? Maybe you found some undamaged equipment left over from the war. An intact cache, buried someplace? Is that it?"

Applequist almost told him, at that point. But he didn't. "Maybe," he answered indifferently. "It's possible."

Jenkins shot him a grimace of hate and stalked off to roll aside the doors of the observation chamber. At the big wall map officials were examining the day's activities. Half a dozen middle-aged men, most of them bald, collars dirty and stained, lounged around in chairs. In the corner Supervisor Rudde was sound asleep, fat legs stuck out in front of him, hairy chest visible under his open shirt. These were the men who ran the Detroit Company. Ten thousand families, the whole subsurface living-shelter, depended on them.

"What's on your mind?" a voice rumbled in Applequist's ear. Director Laws had come into the chamber and, as usual, taken him unawares.

"Nothing, sir," Applequist answered. But the keen eyes, blue as china, bored through and beneath. "The usual fatigue. My tension index is up. I've been meaning to take some of my leave, but with all the work … "

"Don't try to fool me. A fourth-class letter carrier isn't needed. What are you really getting at?"

"Sir," Applequist said bluntly, "why were the robots destroyed?"

There was silence. Laws' heavy face registered surprise, then hostility. Before he could speak Applequist hurried on: "I know my class is forbidden to make theoretical inquiries. But it's very important I find out."

"The subject is closed," Laws rumbled ominously. "Even to top-level personnel."

"What did the robots have to do with the war? Why was the war fought? What was life like before the war?"

"The subject," Laws repeated, "is closed." He moved slowly toward the wall map and Applequist was left standing alone, in the middle of the clicking machines, among the murmuring officials and bureaucrats.

Automatically, he resumed sorting letters. There had been the war, and robots were involved in it. That much he knew. A few had survived; when he was a child his father had taken him to an industrial center and he had seen them at their machines. Once, there had been more complex types. Those were all gone; even the simple ones would soon be scrapped. Absolutely no more were manufactured.

"*What happened?*" he had asked, as his father dragged him away. "Where did all the robots go?"

No answer then either. That was sixteen years ago, and now the last had been scrapped. Even the memory of robots was disappearing; in a few years the word itself would cease. *Robots*. What had happened?

He finished with the letters and moved out of the chamber. None of the supervisors noticed; they were arguing some erudite point of strategy. Maneuvering and countermaneuvering among the Companies. Tension and exchanged insults. He found a crushed cigarette in his pocket and inexpertly lit up.

"Dinner call," the passage speaker announced tinnily. "One hour break for top class personnel."

A few supervisors filed noisily past him. Applequist crushed out his cigarette and moved toward his station. He worked until six. Then his dinner hour came up. No other break until Saturday. But if he went without dinner...

The robot was probably a low-order type, scrapped with the final group. The inferior kind he had seen as a child. It couldn't be one of the elaborate war-time robots. To have survived in the ravine, rusting and rotting through the years since the war...

His mind skirted the hope. Heart pounding, he entered a lift and touched the stud. By nightfall he'd know.

The robot lay among heaps of metal slag and weeds. Jagged, rusted fragments barred Applequist's way as he move cautiously down the side of the ravine, S-gun in one hand, radiation mask pulled tight over his face.

His counter clicked loudly: the floor of the ravine was hot. Pools of contamination, over the reddish metal fragments, the piles and masses of fused steel and plastic and gutted equipment. He kicked webs of blackened wiring aside and gingerly stepped past the yawning fuel-tank of some ancient machine, now overgrown with vines. A rat scuttled off. It was almost sunset. Dark shadows lay over everything.

The robot was watching him silently. Half of it was gone; only the head, arms, and upper trunk remained. The lower waist ended in shapeless struts, abruptly sliced off. It was clearly immobile. Its whole surface was pitted and corroded. One eye-lens was missing. Some of its metal fingers were bent grotesquely. It lay on its back facing the sky.

It was a war-time robot, all right. In the one remaining eye glinted archaic consciousness. This was not the simple worker he had glimpsed as a child. Applequist's breath hammered in his throat. This was the real thing. It was following his movements intently. It was alive.

All this time, Applequist thought. *All these years*. The hackles of his neck rose. Everything was silent, the hills and trees and masses of ruin. Nothing stirred; he and the ancient robot were the only living things. *Down here in this crack waiting for somebody to come along*.

A cold wind rustled at him and he automatically pulled his overcoat together. Some leaves blew over the inert face of the robot. Vines had crept along its trunk, twisted into its works. It had been rained on; the sun had shone on it. In winter the snow had covered it. Rats and animals had sniffed at it. Insects had crawled through it. And it was still alive.

"I heard you," Applequist muttered. "I was walking along the path."

Presently the robot said, "I know. I saw you stop." Its voice was faint and dry. Like ashes rubbing together. Without quality or pitch. "Would you make the date known to me? I suffered a power failure for an indefinite period. Wiring terminals shorted temporarily."

"It's June 11," Applequist said. "2136," he added.

The robot was obviously hoarding its meager strength. It moved one arm slightly, then let it fall back. Its one good eye blurred over, and deep within, gears whirred rustily. Realization came to Applequist: the robot might expire any moment. It was a miracle it had survived this long. Snails clung to its body. It was criss-crossed with slimy trails. A century ...

"How long have you been here?" he demanded. "Since the war?"

"Yes."

Applequist grinned nervously. "That's a long time. Over a hundred years."

"That's so."

It was getting dark fast. Automatically, Applequist fumbled for his flashlight. He could hardly make out the sides of the ravine. Someplace a long way off a bird croaked dismally in the darkness. The bushes rustled.

"I need help," the robot said. "Most of my motor equipment was destroyed. I can't move from here."

"In what condition is the rest of you? Your energy supply. How long can — "

"There's been considerable cell destruction. Only a limited number of relay circuits still function. And those are overloaded." The robot's one good eye was on him again. "What is the technological situation? I have seen airborne ships fly overhead. You still manufacture and maintain electronic equipment?"

"We operate an industrial unit near Pittsburgh."

"If I describe basic electronic units will you understand?" the robot asked.

"I'm not trained in mechanical work. I'm classed as a fourth grade letter carrier. But I have contacts in the repair department. We keep our own machines functioning." He licked his lips tensely. "It's risky, of course. There are laws."

"Laws?"

"All robots were destroyed. You are the only one left. The rest were liquidated years ago."

No expression showed in the robot's eye. "Why did you come down here?" it demanded. Its eye moved to the S-gun in Applequist's hand. "You are a minor official in some hierarchy. Acting on orders from above. A mechanically-operating integer in a larger system."

Applequist laughed. "I suppose so." Then he stopped laughing. "Why was the war fought? What was life like before?"

"Don't you know?"

"Of course not. No theoretical knowledge is permitted, except to top-level personnel. And even the Supervisors don't know about the war." Applequist squatted down and shone the beam of his flashlight into the darkening face of the robot. "Things were different before, weren't they? We didn't always live in subsurface shelters. The world wasn't always a scrap heap. People didn't always slave for their Companies."

"Before the war there were no Companies."

Applequist grunted with triumph. "I knew it."

"Men lived in cities, which were demolished in the war. Companies, which were protected, survived. Officials of these Companies became the government. The war lasted a long time. Everything of value was destroyed. What you have left is a burned out shell." The robot was silent a moment and then continued, "The first robot was built in 1979. By 2000 all routine work was done by robots. Human beings were free to do what they wanted. Art, science, entertainment, whatever they liked."

"What is art?" Applequist asked.

"Creative work, directed toward realization of an internal standard. The whole population of the earth was free to expand culturally. Robots maintained the world; man enjoyed it."

"What were cities like?"

"Robots rebuilt and reconstructed new cities according to plans drawn up by human artists. Clean, sanitary, attractive. They were the cities of gods."

"Why was the war fought?"

The robot's single eye flickered. "I've already talked too much. My power supply is dangerously low."

Applequist trembled. "What do you need? I'll get it."

"Immediately, I need an atomic A pack. Capable of putting out ten thousand f-units."

"Yes."

"After that, I'll need tools and aluminum sections. Low resistance wiring.

Bring pen and paper — I'll give you a list. You won't understand it, but someone in electronic maintenance will. A power supply is the first need."

"And you'll tell me about the war?"

"Of course." The robot's dry rasp faded into silence. Shadows flickered around it; cold evening air stirred the dark weeds and bushes. "Kindly hurry. Tomorrow, if possible."

"I ought to turn you in," Assistant Supervisor Jenkins snapped. "Half an hour late, and now this business. What are you doing? You want to get fired out of the Company?'

Applequist pushed close to the man. "I have to get this stuff. The — cache is below surface. I have to construct a secure passage. Otherwise the whole thing will be buried by falling debris."

"How large a cache is it?" Greed edged suspicion off Jenkins' gnarled face. He was already spending the Company reward. "Have you been able to see in? Are there unknown machines?"

"I didn't recognize any," Applequist said impatiently. "Don't waste time. The whole mass of debris is apt to collapse. I have to work fast."

"Where is it? I want to see it!"

"I'm doing this alone. You supply the material and cover for my absence. That's your part."

Jenkins twisted uncertainly. "If you're lying to me, Applequist — "

"I'm not lying," Applequist answered angrily. "When can I expect the power unit?"

"Tomorrow morning. I'll have to fill out a bushel of forms. Are you sure you can operate it? I better send a repair team along with you. To be sure — "

"I can handle it." Applequist interrupted. "Just get me the stuff. I'll take care of the rest."

Morning sunlight filtered over the rubble and trash. Applequist nervously fitted the new power pack in place, screwed the leads tight, clamped the corroded shield over it, and then got shakily to his feet. He tossed away the old pack and waited.

The robot stirred. Its eye gained life and awareness. Presently it moved its arm in exploratory motions, over its damaged trunk and shoulders.

"All right?" Applequist demanded huskily.

"Apparently." The robot's voice was stronger; full and more confident. "The old power pack was virtually exhausted. It was fortunate you came along when you did."

"You say men lived in cities," Applequist plunged in eagerly. "Robots did the work?"

"Robots did the routine labor needed to maintain the industrial system.

Humans had leisure to enjoy whatever they wanted. We were glad to do their work for them. It was our job."

"What happened? What went wrong?'

The robot accepted the pencil and paper; as it talked it carefully wrote down figures. "There was a fanatic group of humans. A religious organization. They claimed that God intended man to work by the sweat of his brow. They wanted robots scrapped and men put back in the factories to slave away at routine tasks."

"But why?"

"They claimed work was spiritually ennobling." The robot tossed the paper back. "Here's the list of what I want. I'll need those materials and tools to restore my damaged system."

Applequist fingered the paper. "This religious group — "

"Men separated in two factions. The Moralists and the Leisurists. They fought each other for years, while we stood on the sidelines waiting to know our fate. I couldn't believe the Moralists would win out over reason and common sense. But they did."

"Do you think — " Applequist began, and then broke off. He could hardly give voice to the thought that was struggling inside him. "Is there a chance robots might be brought back?"

"Your meaning is obscure." The robot abruptly snapped the pencil in half and threw it away. "What are you driving at?"

"Life isn't pleasant in the Companies. Death and hard work. Forms and shifts and work periods and orders."

"It's your system. I'm not responsible."

"How much do you recall about robot construction? What were you, before the war?"

"I was a unit controller. I was on my way to an emergency unit-factory, when my ship was shot down." The robot indicated the debris around it. "That was my ship and cargo."

"What is a unit controller?"

"I was in charge of robot manufacture. I designed and put into production basic robot types."

Applequist's head spun dizzily. "Then you do know robot construction."

"Yes." The robot gestured urgently at the paper in Applequist's hand. "Kindly get those tools and materials as soon as possible. I'm completely helpless this way. I want my mobility back. If a rocketship should fly overhead . . . "

"Communication between Companies is bad. I deliver my letters on foot. Most of the country is in ruins. You could work undetected. What about your emergency unit-factory? Maybe it wasn't destroyed."

The robot nodded slowly. "It was carefully concealed. There is the bare possibility. It was small, but completely outfitted. Self-sufficient."

"If I get repair parts, can you — "

"We'll discuss this later." The robot sank back down. "When you return, we'll talk further."

He got the material from Jenkins, and a twenty-four hour pass. Fascinated, he crouched against the wall of the ravine as the robot systematically pulled apart its own body and replaced the damaged elements. In a few hours a new motor system had been installed. Basic leg cells were welded into position. By noon the robot was experimenting with its pedal extremities.

"During the night," the robot said, "I was able to make weak radio contact with the emergency unit-factory. It exists intact, according to the robot monitor."

"Robot? You mean — "

"An automatic machine for relaying transmission. Not alive, as I am. Strictly speaking, I'm not a robot." Its voice swelled. "I'm an android."

The fine distinction was lost on Applequist. His mind was racing excitedly over the possibilities. "Then we can go ahead. With your knowledge, and the materials available at the — "

"You didn't see the terror and destruction. The Moralists systematically demolished us. Each town they seized was cleared of androids. Those of my race were brutally wiped out, as the Leisurists retreated. We were torn from our machines and destroyed."

"But that was a century ago! Nobody wants to destroy robots any more. We need robots to rebuild the world. The Moralists won the war and left the world in ruins."

The robot adjusted its motor system until its legs were coordinated. "Their victory was a tragedy, but I understand the situation better than you. We must advance cautiously. If we are wiped out this time, it may be for good."

Applequist followed after the robot as it moved hesitantly through the debris toward the wall of the ravine. "We're crushed by work. Slaves in underground shelters. We can't go on this way. People will welcome robots. We need you. When I think how it must have been in the Golden Age, the foundations and flowers, the beautiful cities above ground ... Now there's nothing but ruin and misery. The Moralists won, but nobody's happy. We'd gladly — "

"Where are we? What is the location here?"

"Slightly west of the Mississippi, a few miles or so. We must have freedom. We can't live this way, toiling underground. If we had free time we could investigate the mysteries of the whole universe. I found some old scientific tapes. Theoretical work in biology. Those men spent years working on abstract topics. They had the time. They were free. While robots maintained the economic system those men could go out and — "

"During the war," the robot said thoughtfully, "the Moralists rigged up detection screens over hundreds of square miles. Are those screens still functioning?"

"I don't know. I doubt it. Nothing outside of the immediate Company shelters still works."

The robot was deep in thought. It had replaced its ruined eye with a new cell; both eyes flickered with concentration. "Tonight we'll make plans concerning your Company. I'll let you know my decision then. Meanwhile, don't bring this situation up with anyone. You understand? Right now I'm concerned with the road system."

"Most roads are in ruins." Applequist tried hard to hold back his excitement. "I'm convinced most in my Company are — Leisurists. Maybe a few at the top are Moralists. Some of the supervisors, perhaps. But the lower classes and families — "

"All right," the robot interrupted. "We'll see about that later." It glanced around. "I can use some of that damaged equipment. Part of it will function. For the moment, at least."

Applequist managed to avoid Jenkins, as he hurriedly made his way across the organizational level to his work station. His mind was in a turmoil. Everything around him seemed vague and unconvincing. The quarreling supervisors. The clattering, humming machines. Clerks and minor bureaucrats hurrying back and forth with messages and memoranda. He grabbed a mass of letters and mechanically began sorting them into their slots.

"You've been outside," Director Laws observed sourly. "What is it, a girl? If you marry outside the Company you lose the little rating you have."

Applequist pushed aside his letters. "Director, I want to talk to you."

Director Laws shook his head. "Be careful. You know the ordinances governing fourth-class personnel. Better not ask any more questions. Keep your mind on your work and leave the theoretical issues to us."

"Director," Applequist asked, "which side was our Company, Moralist or Leisurist?"

Laws didn't seem to understand the question. "What do you mean?" He shook his head. "I don't know those words."

"In the war. Which side of the war were we on?"

"Good God," Law said. "The human side, of course." An expression like a curtain dropped over his heavy face. "What do you mean, *Moralist?* What are you talking about?"

Suddenly Applequist was sweating. His voice would hardly come. "Director, something's wrong. The war was between the two groups of humans. The Moralists destroyed the robots because they disapproved of humans living in leisure."

"The war was fought between men and robots," Laws said harshly. "We won. We destroyed the robots."

"But they worked for us!"

"They were built as workers, but they revolted. They had a philosophy. Superior beings — androids. They considered us nothing but cattle."

Applequist was shaking all over. "But it told me — "

"They slaughtered us. Millions of humans died, before we got the upper hand. They murdered, lied, hid, stole, did everything to survive. It was them or us — no quarter." Laws grabbed Applequist by the collar. "You damn fool! What the hell have you done? Answer me! What have you done?"

The sun was setting, as the armored twin-track roared up to the edge of the ravine. Troops leaped out and poured down the sides, S-rifles clattering. Laws emerged quickly, Applequist beside him.

"This is the place?" Laws demanded.

"Yes." Applequist sagged. "But it's gone."

"Naturally. It was fully repaired. There was nothing to keep it here." Laws signalled his men. "No use looking. Plant a tactical A-bomb and let's get out of here. The air fleet may be able to catch it. We'll spray this area with radioactive gas."

Applequist wandered numbly to the edge of the ravine. Below, in the darkening shadows, were the weeds and tumbled debris. There was no sign of the robot, of course. A place where it had been, bits of wire and discarded body sections. The old power pack where he had thrown it. A few tools. Nothing else.

"Come on," Laws ordered his men. "Let's get moving. We have a lot to do. Get the general alarm system going."

The troops began climbing the sides of the ravine. Applequist started after them, toward the twin-track.

"No," Laws said quickly. "You're not coming with us."

Applequist saw the look on their faces. The pent-up fear, the frantic terror and hate. He tried to run, but they were on him almost at once. They worked grimly and silently. When they were through they kicked aside his still-living remains and climbed into the twin-track. They slammed the locks and the motor thundered up. The track rumbled down the trail to the road. In a few moments it dwindled and was gone.

He was alone, with the half-buried bomb and the settling shadows. And the vast empty darkness that was collecting everywhere.

EXHIBIT PIECE

"THAT'S A STRANGE SUIT you have on," the robot pubtrans driver observed. It slid back its door and came to rest at the curb. "What are the little round things?"

"Those are buttons," George Miller explained. "They are partly functional, partly ornamental. This is an archaic suit of the twentieth century. I wear it because of the nature of my employment."

He paid the robot, grabbed up his briefcase, and hurried along the ramp to the History Agency. The main building was already open for the day; robed men and women wandered everywhere. Miller entered a PRIVATE lift, squeezed between two immense controllers from the pre-Christian division, and in a moment was on his way to his own level, the Middle Twentieth Century.

"Gorning," he murmured, as Controller Fleming met him at the atomic engine exhibit.

"Gorning," Fleming responded brusquely. "Look here, Miller. Let's have this out once and for all. What if everyone dressed like you? The Government sets up strict rules for dress. Can't you forget your damn anachronisms once in a while? What in God's name is that thing in your hand? It looks like a squashed Jurassic lizard."

"This is an alligator hide briefcase," Miller explained. "I carry my study spools in it. The briefcase was an authority symbol of the managerial class of the later twentieth century." He unzipped the briefcase. "Try to understand, Fleming. By accustoming myself to everyday objects of my research period I transform my relation from mere intellectual curiosity to genuine empathy. You have frequently noticed I pronounce certain words oddly. The accent is that of an American businessman of the Eisenhower administration. Dig me?"

"Eh?" Fleming muttered.

"Dig *me* was a twentieth century expression." Miller laid out his study spools on his desk. "Was there anything you wanted? If not I'll begin today's work. I've uncovered fascinating evidence to indicate that although twentieth-century Americans laid their own floor tiles, they did not weave their own clothing. I wish to alter my exhibits on this matter."

"There's no fanatic like an academician," Fleming grated. "You're two hundred years behind times. Immersed in your relics and artifacts. Your damn authentic replicas of discarded trivia."

"I love my work," Miller answered mildly.

"Nobody complains about your work. But there are other things than work. You're a political-social unit here in this society. Take warning, Miller! The Board has reports on your eccentricities. They approve devotion to work. . . . " His eyes narrowed significantly. "But you go too far."

"My first loyalty is to my art," Miller said.

"Your what? What does that mean?"

"A twentieth-century term." There was undisguised superiority on Miller's face. "You're nothing but a minor bureaucrat in a vast machine. You're a function of an impersonal cultural totality. You have no standards of your own. In the twentieth century men had personal standards of workmanship. Artistic craft. Pride of accomplishment. These words mean nothing to you. You have no soul — another concept from the golden days of the twentieth century when men were free and could speak their minds."

"Beware, Miller!" Fleming blanched nervously and lowered his voice. "You damn scholars. Come up out of your tapes and face reality. You'll get us all in trouble, talking this way. Idolize the past, if you want. But remember — it's gone and buried. Times change. Society progresses." He gestured impatiently at the exhibits that occupied the level. "That's only an imperfect replica."

"You impugn my research?" Miller was seething. "This exhibit is absolutely accurate! I correct it to all new data. There isn't anything I don't know about the twentieth century."

Fleming shook his head. "It's no use." He turned and staked wearily off the level, on to the descent ramp.

Miller straightened his collar and bright hand-painted necktie. He smoothed down his blue pin stripe coat, expertly lit a pipeful of two-century-old tobacco, and returned to his spools.

Why didn't Fleming leave him alone? Fleming, the officious representative of the great hierarchy that spread like a sticky gray web over the whole planet. Into each industrial, professional, and residential unit. Ah, the freedom of the twentieth century! He slowed his tape scanner a moment, and a dreamy look slid over his features. The exciting age of virility and individuality, when men were men....

It was just about then, just as he was settling deep in the beauty of his research, that he heard the inexplicable sounds. They came from the center of his exhibit, from within the intricate, carefully regulated interior.

Somebody was in his exhibit.

He could hear them back there, back in the depths. Somebody or something had gone past the safety barrier set up to keep the public out. Miller snapped off his tape scanner and got slowly to his feet. He was shaking all over as he moved cautiously toward the exhibit. He killed the barrier and climbed the railing on to a concrete pavement. A few curious visitors blinked, as the small, oddly dressed man crept among the authentic replicas of the twentieth century that made up the exhibit and disappeared within.

Breathing hard, Miller advanced up the pavement and on to a carefully tended gravel path. Maybe it was one of the other theorists, a minion of the Board, snooping around looking for something with which to discredit him. An inaccuracy here — a trifling error of no consequence there. Sweat came out of his forehead; anger became terror. To his right was a flower bed. Paul Scarlet roses and low-growing pansies. Then the moist green lawn. The gleaming white garage, with its door half up. The sleek rear of a 1954 Buick — and then the house itself.

He'd have to be careful. If is *was* somebody from the Board he'd be up against official hierarchy. Maybe it was somebody big. Maybe even Edwin Carnap, President of the Board, the highest ranking official in the N'York branch of the World Directorate. Shakily, Miller climbed the three cement steps. Now he was on the porch of the twentieth-century house that made up the center of the exhibit.

It was a nice little house; if he had lived back in those days he would have wanted one of his own. Three bedrooms, a ranch style California bungalow. He pushed open the front door and entered the living room. Fireplace at one end. Dark wine-colored carpets. Modern couch and easy chair. Low hardwood glass-topped coffee table. Copper ashtrays. A cigarette lighter and a stack of magazines. Sleek plastic and steel floor lamps. A bookcase. Television set. Picture window overlooking the front garden. He crossed the room to the hall.

The house was amazingly complete. Below his feet the floor furnace radiated a faint aura of warmth. He peered into the first bedroom. A woman's boudoir. Silk bedcover. White starched sheets. Heavy drapes. A vanity table. Bottles and jars. Huge round mirror. Clothes visible within the closet. A dressing gown thrown over the back of a chair. Slippers. Nylon hose carefully placed at the foot of the bed.

Miller moved down the hall and peered into the next room. Brightly painted wallpaper: clowns and elephants and tight-rope walkers. The children's room. Two little beds for the two boys. Model airplanes. A dresser with a radio on it, pair of combs, school books, pennants, a No Parking sign, snapshots stuck in the mirror. A postage stamp album.

Nobody there, either.

Miller peered in the modern bathroom, even in the yellow-tiled shower. He passed through the dining room, glanced down the basement stairs where the washing machine and dryer were. Then he opened the back door and examined the back yard. A lawn, and the incinerator. A couple of small trees and then the three-dimensional projected backdrop of other houses receding off into incredibly convincing blue hills. And still no one. The yard was empty — deserted. He closed the door and started back.

From the kitchen came laughter.

A woman's laugh. The clink of spoons and dishes. And smells. It took him a moment to identify them, scholar that he was. Bacon and coffee. And hot cakes. Somebody was eating breakfast. A twentieth-century breakfast.

He made his way down the hall, past a man's bedroom, shoes and clothing strewn about, to the entrance of the kitchen.

A handsome late-thirtyish woman and two teenage boys were sitting around the little chrome and plastic breakfast table. They had finished eating; the two boys were fidgeting impatiently. Sunlight filtered through the window over the sink. The electric clock read half past eight. The radio was chirping merrily in the corner. A big pot of black coffee rested in the center of the table, surrounded by empty plates and milk glasses and silverware.

The woman had on a white blouse and checkered tweed skirt. Both boys wore faded blue jeans, sweatshirts, and tennis shoes. As yet they hadn't noticed him. Miller stood frozen at the doorway, while laughter and small talk bubbled around him.

"You'll have to ask your father," the woman was saying, with mock sternness. "Wait until he comes back."

"He already said we could," one of the boys protested.

"Well, ask him again."

"He's always grouchy in the morning."

"Not today. He had a good night's sleep. His hay fever didn't bother him. The new anti-hist the doctor gave him." She glanced up at the clock. "Go see what's keeping him, Don. He'll be late for work."

"He was looking for the newspaper." One of the boys pushed back his chair and got up. "It missed the porch again and fell in the flowers." He turned towards the door, and Miller found himself confronting him face to face. Briefly, the observation flashed through his mind that the boy looked familiar. Damn familiar — like somebody he knew, only younger. He tensed himself for the impact, as the boy abruptly halted.

"Gee," the boy said. "You scared me."

The woman glanced quickly up at Miller. "What are you doing out there, George?" she demanded. "Come on back in here and finish you coffee."

Miller came slowly into the kitchen. The woman was finishing her coffee; both boys were on their feet and beginning to press around him.

"Didn't you tell me I could go camping over the weekend up at Russian River with the group from school?" Don demanded. "You said I could borrow a sleeping bag from the gym because the one I had you gave to the Salvation Army because you were allergic to the kapok in it."

"Yeah," Miller muttered uncertainly. Don. That was the boy's name. And his brother, Ted. But how did he know that? At the table the woman had got up and was collecting the dirty dishes to carry over to the sink. "They said you already promised them," she said over her shoulder. The dishes clattered into the sink and she began sprinkling soap flakes over them. "But you remember that time they wanted to drive the car and the way they said it, you'd think they had got your okay. And they hadn't, of course."

Miller sank weakly down at the table. Aimlessly, he fooled with his pipe. He set it down in the copper ashtray and examined the cuff of his coat. What was happening? His head spun. He got up abruptly and hurried to the window, over the sink.

Houses, streets. The distant hills beyond the town. The sights and sounds of people. The three dimensional projected backdrop was utterly convincing; or was it the projected backdrop? How could he be sure. *What was happening?*

"George, what's the matter?" Marjorie asked, as she tied a pink plastic apron around her waist and began running hot water in the sink. "You better get the car out and get started to work. Weren't you saying last night old man Davidson was shouting about employees being late for work and standing around the water cooler talking and having a good time on company time?"

Davidson. The word stuck in Miller's mind. He knew it, of course. A clear picture leaped up; a tall, white-haired old man, thin and stern. Vest and pocket watch. And the whole office, United Electronic Supply. The twelve-story building in downtown San Francisco. The newspaper and cigar stand in the lobby. The honking cars. Jammed parking lots. The elevator, packed with bright-eyed secretaries, tight sweaters and perfume.

He wandered out of the kitchen, through the hall, past his own bedroom, his wife's, and into the living room. The front door was open and he stepped out on to the porch.

The air was cool and sweet. It was a bright April morning. The lawns were still wet. Cars moved down Virginia Street, towards Shattuck Avenue. Early morning commuting traffic, businessmen on their way to work. Across the street Earl Kelly cheerfully waved his Oakland Tribune as he hurried down the pavement towards the bus stop.

A long way off Miller could see the Bay Bridge, Yerba Buena Island, and Treasure Island. Beyond that was San Francisco itself. In a few minutes he'd be shooting across the bridge in his Buick, on his way to the office. Along with thousands of other businessmen in blue pinstripe suits.

Ted pushed past him and out on the porch. "Then it's okay? You don't care if we go camping?"

Miller licked his dry lips. "Ted, listen to me. There's something strange."

"Like what?"

"I don't know." Miller wandered nervously around on the porch. "This is Friday, isn't it?"

"Sure."

"I thought it was." But how did he know it was Friday? How did he know anything? But of course it was Friday. A long hard week — old man Davidson breathing down his neck. Wednesday, especially, when the General Electric order was slowed down because of a strike.

"Let me ask you something," Miller said to his son. "This morning — I left the kitchen to get the newspaper."

Ted nodded. "Yeah. So?"

"I got up and went out of the room. *How long was I gone?* Not long, was I?" He searched for words, but his mind was a maze of disjointed thoughts. "I was sitting at the breakfast table with you all, and then I got up and went to look for the paper. Right? And then I came back in. Right?" His voice rose desperately. "I got up and shaved and dressed this morning. I ate breakfast. Hot cakes and coffee. Bacon. *Right?*"

"Right," Ted agreed. "So?"

"Like I always do."

"We only have hot cakes on Friday."

Miller nodded slowly. "That's right. Hot cakes on Friday. Because your uncle Frank eats with us Saturday and Sunday and he can't stand hot cakes, so we stopped having them on weekends. Frank is Marjorie's brother. He was in the Marines in the First World War. He was a corporal."

"Good-bye," Ted said, as Don came out to join him. "We'll see you this evening."

School books clutched, the boys sauntered off towards the big modern high school in the center of Berkeley.

Miller re-entered the house and automatically began searching the closet for his briefcase. Where was it? Damn it, he needed it. The whole Throckmorton account was in it; Davidson would be yelling his head off if he left it anywhere, like in the True Blue Cafeteria that time they were all celebrating the Yankees' winning the series. Where the hell was it?

He straightened up slowly, as memory came. Of course. He had left it by his work desk, where he had tossed it after taking out the research tapes. While Fleming was talking to him. Back at the History Agency.

He joined his wife in the kitchen. "Look," he said huskily. "Marjorie, I think maybe I won't go down to the office this morning."

Marjorie spun in alarm. "George, is anything wrong?"

"I'm — completely confused."

"Your hay fever again?"

"No. My mind. What's the name of that psychiatrist the PTA recommended when Mrs. Bentley's kid had that fit?" He searched his disorganized brain. "Grunberg, I think. In the Medical-Dental building." He moved towards the door. "I'll drop by and see him. Something's wrong — really wrong. And I don't know what it is."

Adam Grunberg was a large heavy-set man in his late forties, with curly brown hair and horn-rimmed glasses. After Miller had finished, Grunberg cleared his throat, brushed at the sleeve of his Brooks Bros. suit, and asked thoughtfully, "Did anything happen while you were out looking for the newspaper? Any sort of accident? You might try going over that part in detail. You got up from the breakfast table, went out on the porch, and started looking around in the bushes. And then what?"

Miller rubbed his forehead vaguely. "I don't know. It's all confused. I don't remember looking for any newspaper. I remember coming back in the house. Then it gets clear. But before that it's all tied up with the History Agency and my quarrel with Fleming."

"What was that again about your briefcase? Go over that."

"Fleming said it looked like a squashed Jurassic lizard. And I said — "

"No. I mean, about looking for it in the closet and not finding it."

"I looked in the closet and it wasn't there, of course. It's sitting beside my desk at the History Agency. On the Twentieth Century level. By my exhibits." A strange expression crossed Miller's face. "Good God, Grunberg. You realize this may be nothing but an *exhibit*? You and everybody else — maybe you're not real. Just pieces of this exhibit."

"That wouldn't be very pleasant for us, would it?" Grunberg said, with a faint smile.

"People in dreams are always secure until the dreamer wakes up," Miller retorted.

"So you're dreaming me," Grunberg laughed tolerantly. "I suppose I should thank you."

"I'm not here because I especially like you. I'm here because I can't stand Fleming and the whole History Agency."

Grunberg protested. "This Fleming. Are you aware of thinking about him before you went out looking for the newspaper?"

Miller got to his feet and paced around the luxurious office, between the leather-covered chairs and the huge mahogany desk. "I want to face this thing. I'm an exhibit. An artificial replica of the past. Fleming said something like this would happen to me."

"Sit down, Mr. Miller," Grunberg said, in a gentle but commanding voice.

When Miller had taken his chair again, Grunberg continued, "I understand what you say. You have a general feeling that everything around you is unreal. A sort of stage."

"An exhibit."

"Yes, an exhibit in a museum."

"In the N'York History Agency. Level R, the Twentieth Century level."

"And in addition to this general feeling of — insubstantiality, there are specific projected memories of persons and places beyond this world. Another realm in which this one is contained. Perhaps I should say, the reality within which this is only a sort of shadow world."

"This world doesn't look shadowy to me." Miller struck the leather arm of the chair savagely. "This world is completely real. That's what's wrong. I came in to investigate the noises and now I can't get back out. Good God, do I have to wander around this replica the rest of my life?"

"You know, of course, that your feeling is common to most of mankind. Especially during periods of great tension. Where — by the way — was the newspaper? Did you find it?"

"As far as I'm concerned — "

"Is that a source of irritation with you? I see you react strongly to a mention of the newspaper."

Miller shook his head wearily. "Forget it."

"Yes, a trifle. The paperboy carelessly throws the newspaper in the bushes, not on the porch. It makes you angry. It happens again and again. Early in the day, just as you're starting to work. It seems to symbolize in a small way the whole petty frustrations and defeats of your job. Your whole life."

"Personally, I don't give a damn about the newspaper." Miller examined his wristwatch. "I'm going — it's almost noon. Old man Davidson will be yelling his head off if I'm not at the office by — " He broke off. "There it is again."

"There what is?"

"All this!" Miller gestured impatiently out the window. "This whole place. This damn world. This *exhibition*."

"I have a thought," Doctor Grunberg said slowly. "I'll put it to you for what it's worth. Feel free to reject it if it doesn't fit." He raised his shrewd, professional eyes. "Ever see kids playing with rocket ships?"

"Lord," Miller said wretchedly. "I've seen commercial rocket freighters hauling cargo between Earth and Jupiter, landing at La Guardia Spaceport."

Grunberg smiled slightly. "Follow me through on this. A question. Is it job tension?"

"What do you mean?"

"It would be nice," Grunberg said blandly, "to live in the world of tomorrow. With robots and rocket ships to do all the work. You could just sit back and take it easy. No worries, no cares. No frustrations."

"My position in the History Agency has plenty of cares and frustrations." Miller rose abruptly. "Look, Grunberg. Either this is an exhibit on R level of the History Agency, or I'm a middle-class businessman with an escape fantasy. Right now I can't decide which. One minute I think this is real, and the next minute — "

"We can decide easily," Grunberg said.

"How?"

"You were looking for the newspaper. Down the path, on to the lawn. *Where did it happen?* Was it on the path? On the porch? Try to remember."

"I don't have to try. I was still on the pavement. I had just jumped over the rail past the safety screens."

"On the pavement. Then go back there. Find the exact place."

"Why?"

"So you can prove to yourself there's nothing on the other side."

Miller took a deep slow breath. "Suppose there is?"

"There can't be. You said yourself: only one of the worlds can be real. This world is real — " Grunberg thumped his massive mahogany desk. "Ergo, you won't find anything on the other side."

"Yes," Miller said, after a moment's silence. A peculiar expression cut across his face and stayed there. "You've found the mistake."

"What mistake?" Grunberg was puzzled. "What — "

Miller moved towards the door of the office. "I'm beginning to get it. I've been putting up a false question. Trying to decide which world is real." He grinned humorlessly back at Doctor Grunberg. "They're both real, of course."

He grabbed a taxi and headed back to the house. No one was home. The boys were in school and Marjorie had gone downtown to shop. He waited indoors until he was sure nobody was watching along the street, and then started down the path to the pavement.

He found the spot without any trouble. There was a faint shimmer in the air, a weak place just at the edge of the parking strip. Through it he could see faint shapes.

He was right. There it was — complete and real. As real as the pavement under him.

A long metallic bar was cut off by the edges of the circle. He recognized it; the safety railing he had leaped over to enter the exhibit. Beyond it was the safety screen system. Turned off, of course. And beyond that, the rest of the level and the far walls of the History building.

He took a cautious step into the weak haze. It shimmered around him, misty and oblique. The shapes beyond became clearer. A moving figure in a dark blue robe. Some curious person examining the exhibits. The figure moved on and was lost. He could see his own work desk now. His tape scanner and heaps of study spools. Beside the desk was his briefcase, exactly where he had expected it.

While he was considering stepping over the railing to get the briefcase, Fleming appeared.

Some inner instinct made Miller step back through the weak spot, as Fleming approached. Maybe it was the expression on Fleming's face. In any case, Miller was back and standing firmly on the concrete pavement, when Fleming halted just beyond the juncture, face red, lips twisted with indignation.

"Miller," he said thickly. "Come out of there."

Miller laughed. "Be a good fellow, Fleming. Toss me my briefcase. It's that strange looking thing over by the desk. I showed it to you — remember?"

"Stop playing games and listen to me!" Fleming snapped. "This is serious. *Carnap knows.* I had to inform him."

"Good for you. The loyal bureaucrat."

Miller bent over to light his pipe. He inhaled and puffed a great cloud of gray tobacco smoke through the weak spot, out into the R level. Fleming coughed and retreated.

"What's that stuff?" he demanded.

"Tobacco. One of the things they have around here. Very common substance in the twentieth century. You wouldn't know about that — your period is the second century, B.C. The Hellenistic world. I don't know how well you'd like that. They didn't have very good plumbing back there. Life expectancy was damn short."

"What are you talking about?"

"In comparison, the life expectancy of *my* research period is quite high. And you should see the bathroom I've got. Yellow tile. And a shower. We don't have anything like that at the Agency leisure-quarters."

Fleming grunted sourly. "In other words, you're going to stay in there."

"It's a pleasant place," Miller said easily. "Of course, my position is better than average. Let me describe it for you. I have an attractive wife: marriage is permitted, even sanctioned in this era. I have two fine kids — both boys — who are going up to the Russian River this weekend. They live with me and my wife — we have complete custody of them. The State has no power of that, yet. I have a brand new Buick — "

"Illusions," Fleming spat. "Psychotic delusions."

"Are you sure?"

"You damn fool! I always knew you were too ego-recessive to face reality. You and your anachronistic retreats. Sometimes I'm ashamed I'm a theoretician. I wish I had gone into engineering." Fleming's lips twitched. "You're insane, you know. You're standing in the middle of an artificial exhibit, which is owned by the History Agency, a bundle of plastic and wire and struts. A replica of a past age. An imitation. And you'd rather be there than in the real world."

"Strange," Miller said thoughtfully. "Seems to me I've heard the same thing very recently. You don't know a Doctor Grunberg, do you? A psychiatrist."

Without formality, Director Carnap arrived with his company of assistants and experts. Fleming quickly retreated. Miller found himself facing one of the most powerful figures of the twenty-second century. He grinned and held out his hand.

"You insane imbecile," Carnap rumbled. "Get out of there before we drag you out. If we have to do that, you're through. You know what they do with advanced psychotics. It'll be euthanasia for you. I'll give you one last chance to come out of that fake exhibit — "

"Sorry," Miller said. "It's not an exhibit."

Carnap's heavy face registered sudden surprise. For a brief instant his massive pose vanished. "You still try to maintain — "

"This is a time gate," Miller said quietly. "You can't get me out, Carnap. You can't reach me. I'm in the past, two hundred years back. I've crossed back to a previous existence-coordinate. I found a bridge and escaped from your continuum to this. And there's nothing you can do about it."

Carnap and his experts huddled together in a quick technical conference. Miller waited patiently. He had plenty of time; he had decided not to show up at the office until Monday.

After a while Carnap approached the juncture again, being careful not to step over the safety rail. "An interesting theory, Miller. That's the strange part about psychotics. They rationalize their delusions into a logical system. *A priori*, your concept stands up well. It's internally consistent. Only — "

"Only what?"

"Only it doesn't happen to be true." Carnap had regained his confidence; he seemed to be enjoying the interchange. "You think you're really back in the past. Yes, this exhibit is extremely accurate. Your work has always been good. The authenticity of detail is unequalled by any of the other exhibits."

"I tried to do my work well," Miller murmured.

"You wore archaic clothing and affected archaic speech mannerisms. You did everything possible to throw yourself back. You devoted yourself to your work." Carnap tapped the safety railing with his fingernail. "It would be a shame, Miller. A terrible shame to demolish such an authentic replica."

"I see your point," Miller said, after a time. "I agree with you, certainly. I've been very proud of my work — I'd hate to see it all torn down. But that really won't do you any good. All you'll succeed in doing is closing the time gate."

"You're sure?"

"Of course. The exhibit is only a bridge, a link with the past. I passed *through* the exhibit, but I'm not there now. I'm beyond the exhibit." He grinned tightly. "Your demolition can't reach me. But seal me off, if you want. I don't think I'll be wanting to come back. I wish you could see this side, Carnap. It's a nice place here. Freedom, opportunity. Limited government, responsible to the people. If you don't like a job here you quit. There's no euthanasia, here. Come on over. I'll introduce you to my wife."

"We'll get you," Carnap said. "And all your psychotic figments along with you."

"I doubt if any of my 'psychotic figments' are worried. Grunberg wasn't. I don't think Marjorie is — "

"We've already begun demolition preparations," Carnap said calmly. "We'll do it piece by piece, not all at once. So you may have the opportunity to appreciate the scientific and — *artistic* way we take your imaginary world apart."

"You're wasting your time," Miller said. He turned and walked off, down the pavement, to the gravel path and up on to the front porch of the house.

In the living room he threw himself down in the easy chair and snapped on the television set. Then he went to the kitchen and got a can of ice cold beer. He carried it happily back into the safe, comfortable living room.

As he was seating himself in front of the television set he noticed something rolled up on the low coffee table.

He grinned wryly. It was the morning newspaper, which he had looked so hard for. Marjorie had brought it in with the milk, as usual. And of course forgotten to tell him. He yawned contentedly and reached over to pick it up. Confidently, he unfolded it — and read the big black headlines.

RUSSIA REVEALS COBALT BOMB
TOTAL WORLD DESTRUCTION AHEAD

The Crawlers

He built, and the more he built the more he enjoyed building. Hot sunlight filtered down; summer breezes stirred around him as he toiled joyfully. When he ran out of material he paused awhile and rested. His edifice wasn't large; it was more a practice model than the real thing. One part of his brain told him that, and another part thrilled with excitement and pride. It was at least large enough to enter. He crawled down the entrance tunnel and curled up inside in a contented heap.

Through a rent in the roof a few bits of dirt rained down. He oozed binder fluid and reinforced the weak place. In his edifice the air was clean and cool, almost dust-free. He crawled over the inner walls one last time, leaving a quick-drying coat of binder over everything. What else was needed? He was beginning to feel drowsy; in a moment he'd be asleep.

He thought about it, and then he extended a part of himself up through the still-open entrance. That part watched and listened warily, as the rest of him dozed off in a grateful slumber. He was peaceful and content, conscious that from a distance all that was visible was a light mound of dark clay. No one would notice it: no one would guess what lay beneath.

And if they did notice, he had methods of taking care of them.

The farmer halted his ancient Ford truck with a grinding shriek of brakes. He cursed and backed up a few yards. "There's one. Hop down and take a look at it. Watch the cars — they go pretty fast along here."

Ernest Gretry pushed the cabin door open and stepped down gingerly onto the hot mid-morning pavement. The air smelled of sun and drying grass. Insects buzzed around him as he advanced cautiously up the highway, hands in his trouser pockets, lean body bent forward. He stopped and peered down.

The thing was well mashed. Wheel marks crossed it in four places and its internal organs had ruptured and burst through. The whole thing was snail-like, a gummy elongated tube with sense organs at one end and a confusing mass of protoplasmic extensions at the other.

What got him most was the face. For a time he couldn't look directly at it: he had to contemplate the road, the hills, the big cedar trees, anything else. There was something in the little dead eyes, a glint that was rapidly fading. They weren't the lusterless eyes of a fish, stupid and vacant. The life he had seen haunted him, and he had got only a brief glimpse, as the truck bore down on it and crushed it flat.

"They crawl across here every once in a while," the farmer said quietly. "Sometimes they get as far as town. The first one I saw was heading down the middle of Grant Street, about fifty yards an hour. They go pretty slow. Some of the teenage kids like to run them down. Personally I avoid them, if I see them."

Gretry kicked aimlessly at the thing. He wondered vaguely how many more there were in the bushes and hills. He could see farmhouses set back from the road, white gleaming squares in the hot Tennessee sun. Horses and sleeping cattle. Dirty chickens scratching. A sleepy, peaceful countryside, basking in the late-summer sun.

"Where's the radiation lab from here?" he asked.

The farmer indicated. "Over there, on the the side of those hills. You want to collect the remains? They have one down at the Standard Oil Station in a big tank. Dead, of course. They filled the tank with kerosene to try to preserve it. That one's in pretty good shape, compared to this. Joe Jackson cracked its head with a two-by-four. He found it crawling across his property one night."

Gretry got shakily back into the truck. His stomach turned over and he had to take some long deep breaths. "I didn't realize there were so many. When they sent me out from Washington they just said a few had been seen."

"There's been quite a lot." The farmer started up the truck and carefully skirted the remains on the pavement. "We're trying to get used to them, but we can't. It's not nice stuff. A lot of people are moving away. You can feel it in the air, a sort of heaviness. We've got this problem and we have to meet it." He increased speed, leathery hands tight around the wheel. "It seems like there's more of *them* born all the time, and almost no normal children."

Back in town, Gretry called Freeman long distance from the booth in the shabby hotel lobby. "We'll have to do something. They're all around here. I'm going out at three to see a colony of them. The fellow who runs the taxi stand knows where they are. He says there must be eleven or twelve of them together."

"How do the people around there feel?"

"How the hell do you expect? They think it's God's Judgment. Maybe they're right."

"We should have made them move earlier. We should have cleaned out the whole area for miles around. Then we wouldn't have this problem." Freeman paused. "What do you suggest?"

"That island we took over for the H-bomb tests."

"It's a damn big island. There was a whole group of natives we moved off and resettled." Freeman choked. "Good God, are there *that* many of them?"

"The staunch citizens exaggerate, of course. But I get the impression there must be at least a hundred."

Freeman was silent a long time. "I didn't realize," he said finally. "I'll have to put it through channels, of course. We were going to make further tests on that island. But I see your point."

"I'd like it," Gretry said. "This is a bad business. We can't have things like this. People can't live with this sort of thing. You ought to drop out here and take a look. It's something to remember."

"I'll — see what I can do. I'll talk to Gordon. Give me a ring tomorrow."

Gretry hung up and wandered out of the drab, dirty lobby onto the blazing sidewalk. Dingy stores and parked cars. A few old men hunched over on steps and sagging cane-bottom chairs. He lit a cigarette and shakily examined his watch. It was almost three. He moved slowly toward the taxi stand.

The town was dead. Nothing stirred. Only the motionless old men in their chairs and the out-of-town cars zipping along the highway. Dust and silence lay over everything. Age, like a gray spider web, covered all the houses and stores. No laughter. No sounds of any kind.

No children playing games.

A dirty blue taxicab pulled up silently beside him. "Okay, mister," the driver said, a rat-faced man in his thirties, toothpick hanging between his crooked teeth. He kicked the bent door open. "Here we go."

"How far is it?" Gretry asked, as he climbed in.

"Just outside town." The cab picked up speed and hurtled noisily along, bouncing and bucking. "You from the FBI?"

"No."

"I thought from your suit and hat you was." The driver eyed him curiously. "How'd you hear about the crawlers?"

"From the radiation lab."

"Yeah, it's that hot stuff they got there." The driver turned off the highway and onto a dirt side-road. "It's up here on the Higgins farm. The crazy damn things picked the bottom of old lady Higgins' place to build their houses."

"*Houses?*"

"They've got some sort of city, down under the ground. You'll see it — the entrances, at least. They work together, building and fussing." He twisted the cab off the dirt road, between two huge cedars, over a bumpy field, and finally brought it to rest at the edge of a rocky gully. "This is it."

It was the first time Gretry had seen one alive.

He got out of the cab awkwardly, his legs numb and unresponding. The things were moving slowly between the woods and the entrance tunnels in the center of the clearing. They were bringing building material, clay and weeds. Smearing it with some kind of ooze and plastering it in rough forms which were carefully carried beneath the ground. The crawlers were two or three feet long; some were older than others, darker and heavier. All of them moved with agonizing slowness, a silent flowing motion across the sun-baked ground. They were soft, shell-less, and looked harmless.

Again, he was fascinated and hypnotized by their faces. The weird parody of human faces. Wizened little baby features, tiny shoebutton eyes, slit of a mouth, twisted ears, and a few wisps of damp hair. What should have been arms were elongated pseudopods that grew and receded like soft dough. The crawlers seemed incredibly flexible; they extended themselves, then snapped their bodies back, as their feelers made contact with obstructions. They paid no attention to the two men; they didn't even seem to be aware of them.

"How dangerous are they?" Gretry asked finally.

"Well, they have some sort of stinger. They stung a dog, I know. Stung him pretty hard. He swelled up and his tongue turned black. He had fits and got hard. He died." The driver added half-apologetically, "He was nosing around. Interrupting their building. They work all the time. Keep busy."

"Is this most of them?"

"I guess so. They sort of congregate here. I see them crawling this way." The driver gestured. "See, they're born in different places. One or two at each farmhouse, near the radiation lab."

"Which way is Mrs. Higgins' farmhouse?" Gretry asked.

"Up there. See it through the trees? You want to — "

"I'll be right back," Gretry said, and started abruptly off. "Wait here."

The old woman was watering the dark red geraniums that grew around her front porch, when Gretry approached. She looked up quickly, her ancient wrinkled face shrewd and suspicious, the sprinkling can poised like a blunt instrument.

"Afternoon," Gretry said. He tipped his hat and showed her his credentials. "I'm investigating the — crawlers. At the edge of your land."

"Why?" Her voice was empty, bleak, cold. Like her withered face and body.

"We're trying to find a solution." Gretry felt awkward and uncertain. "It's been suggested we transport them away from here, out to an island in the Gulf of Mexico. They shouldn't be here. It's too hard on people. It isn't right," he finished lamely.

"No. It isn't right."

"And we've already begun moving everybody away from the radiation lab. I guess we should have done that a long time ago."

The old woman's eyes flashed. "You people and your machines. See what you've done!" She jabbed a bony finger at him excitedly. "Now you have to fix it. You have to do something."

"We're taking them away to an island as soon as possible. But there's one problem. We have to be sure about the parents. They have complete custody of them. We can't just — " He broke off futilely. "How do they feel? Would they let us cart up their — children, and haul them away?"

Mrs. Higgins turned and headed into the house. Uncertainly, Gretry followed her through the dim, dusty interior rooms. Musty chambers full of oil lamps and faded pictures, ancient sofas and tables. She led him through a great kitchen of immense cast iron pots and pans down a flight of wooden stairs to a painted white door. She knocked sharply.

Flurry and movement on the other side. The sound of people whispering and moving things hurriedly.

"Open the door," Mrs. Higgins commanded. After an agonized pause the door opened slowly. Mrs. Higgins pushed it wide and motioned Gretry to follow her.

In the room stood a young man and woman. They backed away as Gretry came in. The woman hugged a long pasteboard carton which the man had suddenly passed to her.

"Who are you?" the man demanded. He abruptly grabbed the carton back; his wife's small hands were trembling under the shifting weight.

Gretry was seeing the parents of one of them. The young woman, brown-haired, not more than nineteen. Slender and small in a cheap green dress, a full-breasted girl with dark frightened eyes. The man was bigger and stronger, a handsome dark youth with massive arms and competent hands gripping the pasteboard carton tight.

Gretry couldn't stop looking at the carton. Holes had been punched in the top; the carton moved slightly in the man's arms, and there was a faint shudder that rocked it back and forth.

"This man," Mrs. Higgins said to the husband, "has come to take it away."

The couple accepted the information in silence. The husband made no move except to get a better grip on the box.

"He's going to take all of them to an island," Mrs. Higgins said. "It's all arranged. Nobody'll harm them. They'll be safe and they can do what they want. Build and crawl around where nobody has to look at them."

The young woman nodded blankly.

"Give it to him," Mrs. Higgins ordered impatiently. "Give him the box and let's get it over with once and for all."

After a moment the husband carried the box over to a table and put it down. "You know anything about them?" he demanded. "You know what they eat?"

"We — " Gretry began helplessly.

"They eat leaves. Nothing but leaves and grass. We've been bringing in the smallest leaves we could find."

"It's only a month old," the young woman said huskily. "It already wants to go down with the others, but we keep it here. We don't want it to go down here. Not yet. Later, maybe, we thought. We didn't know what to do. We weren't sure." Her large dark eyes flashed briefly in mute appeal, then faded out again. "It's a hard thing to know."

The husband untied the heavy brown twine and took the lid from the carton. "Here. You can see it."

It was the smallest Gretry had seen. Pale and soft, less than a foot long. It had crawled in a corner of the box and was curled up in a messy web of chewed leaves and some kind of wax. A translucent covering spun clumsily around it, behind which it lay asleep. It paid no attention to them; they were out of its scope. Gretry felt a strange helpless horror rise up in him. He moved away, and the young man replaced the lid.

"We knew what it was," he said hoarsely. "Right away, as soon as it was born. Up the road, there was one we saw. One of the first. Bob Douglas made us come over and look at it. It was his and Julie's. That was before they started coming down and collecting together by the gully."

"Tell him what happened," Mrs. Higgins said.

"Douglas mashed its head with a rock. Then he poured gasoline on it and burned it up. Last week he and Julie packed and left."

"Have many of them been destroyed?" Gretry managed to ask.

"A few. A lot of men, they see something like that and they go sort of wild. You can't blame them." The man's dark eyes darted hopelessly. "I guess I almost did the same thing."

"Maybe we should have," his wife murmured. "Maybe I should have let you."

Gretry picked up the pasteboard carton and moved toward the door. "We'll get this done as quickly as we can. The trucks are on the way. It should be over in a day."

"Thank God for that," Mrs. Higgins exclaimed in a clipped, emotionless voice. She held the door open, and Gretry carried the carton through the dim, musty house, down the sagging front steps and out into the blazing mid-afternoon sun.

Mrs. Higgins stopped at the red geraniums and picked up her sprinkling can. "When you take them, take them all. Don't leave any behind. Understand?"

"Yes," Gretry muttered.

"Keep some of your men and trucks here. Keep checking. Don't let any stay where we have to look at them."

"When we get the people near the radiation lab moved away there shouldn't be any more of — "

He broke off. Mrs. Higgins had turned her back and was watering the geraniums. Bees buzzed around her. The flowers swayed dully with the hot wind. The old woman passed on around the side of the house, still watering and stooping over. In a few moments she was gone and Gretry was alone with his carton.

Embarrassed and ashamed, he carried the carton slowly down the hill and across the field to the ravine. The taxi driver was standing by his cab, smoking a cigarette and waiting patiently for him. The colony of crawlers was working steadily on its city. There were streets and passages. On some of the entrance-mounds he noticed intricate scratches that might have been words. Some of the crawlers were grouped together, setting up involved things he couldn't make out.

"Let's go," he said wearily to the driver.

The driver grinned and yanked the back door. "I left the meter running," he said, his ratty face bright with craft. "You guys all have a swindle sheet — you don't care."

He built, and the more he built the more he enjoyed building. By now the city was over eighty miles deep and five miles in diameter. The whole island had been converted into a single vast city that honeycombed and interlaced farther each day. Eventually it would reach the land beyond the ocean; then the work would begin in earnest.

To his right, a thousand methodically moving companions toiled silently on the structural support that was to reinforce the main breeding chamber. As soon as it was in place everyone would feel better; the mothers were just now beginning to bring forth their young.

That was what worried him. It took some of the joy out of building. He had seen one of the first born — before it was quickly hidden and the thing hushed up. A brief glimpse of a bulbous head, foreshortened body, incredibly rigid extensions. It shrieked and wailed and turned red in the face. Gurgled and plucked aimlessly and kicked its *feet*.

In horror, somebody had finally mashed the throwback with a rock. And hoped there wouldn't be any more.

SALES PITCH

COMMUTE SHIPS roared on all sides, as Ed Morris made his way wearily home to Earth at the end of a long hard day at the office. The Ganymede-Terra lanes were choked with exhausted, grim-faced businessmen; Jupiter was in opposition to Earth and the trip was a good two hours. Every few million miles the great flow slowed to a grinding, agonized halt; signal-lights flashed as streams from Mars and Saturn fed into the main traffic-arteries.

"Lord," Morris muttered. "How tired can you *get?*" He locked the auto-pilot and momentarily turned from the control-board to light a much-needed cigarette. His hands shook. His head swam. It was past six; Sally would be fuming; dinner would be spoiled. The same old thing. Nerve-wracking driving, honking horns and irate drivers zooming past his little ship, furious gesturing, shouting, cursing...

And the ads. That was what really did it. He could have stood everything else — but the ads, the whole long way from Ganymede to Earth. And on Earth, the swarms of sales robots; it was too much. And they were everywhere.

He slowed to avoid a fifty-ship smashup. Repair-ships were scurrying around trying to get the debris out of the lane. His audio-speaker wailed as police rockets hurried up. Expertly, Morris raised his ship, cut between two slow-moving commercial transports, zipped momentarily into the unused left lane, and then sped on, the wreck left behind. Horns honked furiously at him; he ignored them.

"Trans-Solar Products greets you!" an immense voice boomed in his ear. Morris groaned and hunched down in his seat. He was getting near Terra; the barrage was increasing. "Is your tension-index pushed over the safety-margin by the ordinary frustrations of the day? Then you need an Id-Persona Unit. So small it can be worn behind the ear, close to the frontal lobe — "

Thank God, he was past it. The ad dimmed and receded behind, as his fast-moving ship hurtled forward. But another was right ahead.

"Drivers! Thousands of unnecessary deaths each year from inter-planet driving. Hypno-Motor Control from an expert source-point insures your safety. Surrender your body and save your life!" The voice roared louder. "Industrial experts say — "

Both audio ads, the easiest to ignore. But now a visual ad was forming; he winced, closed his eyes, but it did no good.

"Men!" an unctuous voice thundered on all sides of him. "Banish internally-caused obnoxious odors *forever.* Removal by modern painless methods of the gastrointestinal tract and substitution system will relieve you of the most acute cause of social rejection." The visual image locked; a vast nude girl, blonde hair disarranged, blue eyes half shut, lips parted, head tilted back in sleep-drugged ecstasy. The features ballooned as the lips approached his own. Abruptly the orgiastic expression on the girl's face vanished. Disgust and revulsion swept across, and then the image faded out.

"Does this happen to you?" the voice boomed. "During erotic sex-play do you offend your love-partner by the presence of gastric processes which — "

The voice died, and he was past. His mind his own again, Morris kicked savagely at the throttle and sent the little ship leaping. The pressure, applied directly to the audio-visual regions of his brain, had faded below spark point. He groaned and shook his head to clear it. All around him the vague half-defined echoes of ads glittered and gibbered, like ghosts of distant video-stations. Ads waited on all sides; he steered a careful course, dexterity born of animal desperation, but not all could be avoided. Despair seized him. The outline of a new visual-audio ad was already coming into being.

"You, mister wage-earner!" it shouted into the eyes and ears, noses and throats, of a thousand weary commuters. "Tired of the same old job? Wonder Circuits Inc. has perfected a marvelous long-range thoughtwave scanner. Know what others are thinking and saying. Get the edge on fellow employees. Learn facts, figures about your employer's personal existence. Banish uncertainty!"

Morris' despair swept up wildly. He threw the throttle on full blast; the little ship bucked and rolled as it climbed from the traffic-lane into the dead zone beyond. A shrieking roar, as his fender whipped through the protective wall — and then the ad faded behind him.

He slowed down, trembling with misery and fatigue. Earth lay ahead. He'd be home, soon. Maybe he could get a good night's sleep. He shakily dropped the nose of the ship and prepared to hook onto the tractor beam of the Chicago commute field.

"The best metabolism adjuster on the market," the salesrobot shrilled. "Guaranteed to maintain a perfect endocrine-balance, or your money refunded in full."

Morris pushed wearily past the salesrobot, up the sidewalk toward the residential-block that contained his living-unit. The robot followed a few steps, then forgot him and hurried after another grim-faced commuter.

"All the news while it's news," a metallic voice dinned at him. "Have a retinal vidscreen installed in your least-used eye. Keep in touch with the world; don't wait for out-of-date hourly summaries."

"Get out of the way," Morris muttered. The robot stepped aside for him and he crossed the street with a pack of hunched-over men and women.

Robot-salesmen were everywhere, gesturing, pleading, shrilling. One started after him and he quickened his pace. It scurried along, chanting its pitch and trying to attract his attention, all the way up the hill to his living-unit. It didn't give up until he stooped over, snatched up a rock, and hurled it futilely. He scrambled in the house and slammed the doorlock after him. The robot hesitated, then turned and raced after a woman with an armload of packages toiling up the hill. She tried vainly to elude it, without success.

"Darling!" Sally cried. She hurried from the kitchen, drying her hands on her plastic shorts, bright-eyed and excited. "Oh, you poor thing! You look so tired!"

Morris peeled off his hat and coat and kissed his wife briefly on her bare shoulder. "What's for dinner?"

Sally gave his hat and coat to the closet. "We're having Uranian wild pheasant; your favorite dish."

Morris' mouth watered, and a tiny surge of energy crawled back into his exhausted body. "No kidding? What the hell's the occasion?"

His wife's brown eyes moistened with compassion. "Darling, it's your birthday; you're thirty-seven years old today. Had you forgotten?"

"Yeah," Morris grinned a little. "I sure had." He wandered into the kitchen. The table was set; coffee was steaming in the cups and there was butter and white bread, mashed potatoes and green peas. "My golly. A real occasion."

Sally punched the stove controls and the container of smoking pheasant was slid onto the table and neatly sliced open. "Go wash your hands and we're ready to eat. Hurry — before it gets cold."

Morris presented his hands to the wash slot and then sat down gratefully at the table. Sally served the tender, fragrant pheasant, and the two of them began eating.

"Sally," Morris said, when his plate was empty and he was leaning back and sipping slowly at his coffee. "I can't go on like this. Something's got to be done."

"You mean the drive? I wish you could get a position on Mars like Bob Young. Maybe if you talked to the Employment Commission and explained to them how all the strain — "

"It's not just the drive. *They're right out front.* Everywhere. Waiting for me. All day and night."

"Who are, dear?"

"Robots selling things. As soon as I set down the ship. Robots and visual-audio ads. They dig right into a man's brain. They follow people around until they die."

"I know." Sally patted his hand sympathetically. "When I go shopping they follow me in clusters. All talking at once. It's really a panic — you can't understand half what they're saying."

"We've got to break out."

"Break out?" Sally faltered. "What do you mean?"

"We've got to get away from them. They're destroying us."

Morris fumbled in his pocket and carefully got out a tiny fragment of metal-foil. He unrolled it with painstaking care and smoothed it out on the table. "Look at this. It was circulated in the office, among the men; it got to me and I kept it."

"What does it mean?" Sally's brow wrinkled as she made out the words. "Dear, I don't think you got all of it. There must be more than this."

"A new world," Morris said softly. "Where they haven't got to, yet. It's a long way off, out beyond the solar system. Out in the stars."

"Proxima?"

"Twenty planets. Half of them habitable. Only a few thousand people out there. Families, workmen, scientists, some industrial survey teams. Land free for the asking."

"But it's so — " Sally made a face. "Dear, isn't it sort of under-developed? They say it's like living back in the twentieth century. Flush toilets, bathtubs, gasoline driven cars — "

"That's right." Morris rolled up the bit of crumpled metal, his face grim and dead-serious. "It's a hundred years behind times. None of this." He indicated the stove and the furnishings in the living room. "We'll have to do without. We'll have to get used to a simpler life. The way our ancestors lived." He tried to smile but his face wouldn't cooperate. "You think you'd like it? No ads, no salesrobots, traffic moving at sixty miles an hour instead of sixty million. We could raise passage on one of the big trans-system liners. I could sell my commute rocket . . . "

There was a hesitant, doubtful silence.

"Ed," Sally began. "I think we should think it over more. What about your job? What would you do out there?"

"I'd find something."

"But *what*? Haven't you got that part figured out?" A shrill tinge of annoyance crept into her voice. "It seems to me we should consider that part just a little more before we throw away everything and just — take off."

"If we don't go," Morris said slowly, trying to keep his voice steady, "they'll get us. There isn't much time left. I don't know how much longer I can hold them off."

"Really, Ed! You make it sound so melodramatic. If you feel that bad why don't you take some time off and have complete inhibition check? I was watching a vidprogram and I saw them going over a man whose psychosomatic system was much worse than yours. A much older man."

She leaped to her feet. "Let's go out tonight and celebrate. Okay?" Her slim fingers fumbled at the zipper of her shorts. "I'll put on my new plasti-robe, the one I've never had nerve enough to wear."

Her eyes sparkled with excitement as she hurried into the bedroom. "You know the one I mean? When you're up close it's translucent but as you get farther off it becomes more and more sheer until — "

"I know the one," Morris said wearily. "I've seen them advertised on my way home from work." He got slowly to his feet and wandered into the living room. At the door of the bedroom he halted. "Sally — "

"Yes?"

Morris opened his mouth to speak. He was going to ask her again, talk to her about the metal-foil fragment he had carefully wadded up and carried home. He was going to talk to her about the frontier. About Proxima Centauri. Going away and never coming back. But he never had a chance.

The doorchimes sounded.

"Somebody's at the door!" Sally cried excitedly. "Hurry up and see who it is!"

In the evening darkness the robot was a silent, unmoving figure. A cold wind blew around it and into the house. Morris shivered and moved back from the door. "What do you want?" he demanded. A strange fear licked at him. "What is it?"

The robot was larger than any he had seen. Tall and broad, with heavy metallic grippers and elongated eye-lenses. Its upper trunk was a square tank instead of the usual cone. It rested on four treads, not the customary two. It towered over Morris, almost seven feet high. Massive and solid.

"Good evening," it said calmly. Its voice was whipped around by the night wind; it mixed with the dismal noises of evening, the echoes of traffic and the clang of distant street signals. A few vague shapes hurried through the gloom. The world was black and hostile.

"Evening," Morris responded automatically. He found himself trembling. "What are you selling?"

"I would like to show you a fasrad," the robot said.

Morris' mind was numb; it refused to respond. What was a *fasrad?* There was something dreamlike and nightmarish going on. He struggled to get his mind and body together. "A what?" he croaked.

"A fasrad." The robot made no effort to explain. It regarded him without emotion, as if it was not its responsibility to explain anything. "It will take only a moment."

"I — " Morris began. He moved back, out of the wind. And the robot, without change of expression, glided past him and into the house.

"Thank you," it said. It halted in the middle of the living room. "Would you call your wife, please? I would like to show her the fasrad, also."

"Sally," Morris muttered helplessly. "Come here."

Sally swept breathlessly into the living room, her breasts quivering with excitement. "What is it? Oh!" She saw the robot and halted uncertainly. "Ed, did you order something? Are we buying something?"

"Good evening," the robot said to her. "I am going to show you the fasrad. Please be seated. On the couch, if you will. Both together."

Sally sat down expectantly, her cheeks flushed, eyes bright with wonder and bewilderment. Numbly, Ed seated himself beside her. "Look," he muttered thickly. "What the hell is a fasrad? *What's going on?* I don't want to buy anything!"

"What is your name?" the robot asked him.

"Morris." He almost choked. "Ed Morris."

The robot turned to Sally. "Mrs. Morris." It bowed slightly. "I'm glad to meet you, Mr. and Mrs. Morris. You are the first persons in your neighborhood to see the fasrad. This is the initial demonstration in this area." Its cold eyes swept the room. "Mr. Morris, you are employed, I assume. Where are you employed?"

"He works on Ganymede," Sally said dutifully, like a little girl in school. "For the Terran Metals Development Co."

The robot digested this information. "A fasrad will be of value to you." It eyed Sally. "What do you do?"

"I'm a tape transcriber at Histo-Research."

"A fasrad will be of no value in your professional work, but it will be helpful here in the home." It picked up a table in its powerful steel grippers. "For example, sometimes an attractive piece of furniture is damaged by a clumsy guest." The robot smashed the table to bits; fragments of wood and plastic rained down. "A fasrad is needed."

Morris leaped helplessly to his feet. He was powerless to halt events; a numbing weight hung over him, as the robot tossed the fragments of table away and selected a heavy floor lamp.

"Oh dear," Sally gasped. "That's my best lamp."

"When a fasrad is possessed, there is nothing to fear." The robot seized the lamp and twisted it grotesquely. It ripped the shade, smashed the bulbs, then threw away the remnants. "A situation of this kind can occur from some violent explosion, such as an H-Bomb."

"For God's sake," Morris muttered. "We — "

"An H-Bomb attack may never occur," the robot continued, "but in such an event a fasrad is indispensable." It knelt down and pulled an intricate tube from its waist. Aiming the tube at the floor it atomized a hole five feet in diameter. It stepped back from the yawning pocket. "I have not extended this tunnel, but you can see a fasrad would save your life in case of attack."

The word *attack* seemed to set off a new train of reactions in its metal brain.

"Sometimes a thug or hood will attack a person at night," it continued. Without warning it whirled and drove its fist through the wall. A section of the wall collapsed in a heap of powder and debris. "That takes care of the thug." The robot straightened out and peered around the room. "Often you are too tired in the evening to manipulate the buttons on the stove." It strode into the kitchen and began punching the stove controls; immense quantities of food spilled in all directions.

"Stop!" Sally cried. "Get away from my stove!"

"You may be too weary to run water for your bath." The robot tripped the controls of the tub and water poured down. "Or you may wish to go right to bed." It yanked the bed from its concealment and threw it flat. Sally retreated in fright as the robot advanced toward her. "Sometimes after a hard day at work you are too tired to remove your clothing. In that event — "

"Get out of here!" Morris shouted at it. "Sally, run and get the cops. The thing's gone crazy. *Hurry.*"

"The fasrad is a necessity in all modern homes," the robot continued. "For example, an appliance may break down. The fasrad repairs it instantly." It seized the automatic humidity control and tore the wiring and replaced it on the wall. "Sometimes you would prefer not to go to work. The fasrad is permitted by law to occupy your position for a consecutive period not to exceed ten days. If, after that period — "

"Good God," Morris said, as understanding finally came. "You're the fasrad."

"That's right," the robot agreed. "Fully Automatic Self-Regulating Android (Domestic). There is also the fasrac (Construction), the fasram (Managerial), the fasras (Soldier), and the fasrab (Bureaucrat). I am designed for home use."

"You — " Sally gasped. "You're for sale. You're selling yourself."

"I am demonstrating myself," the fasrad, the robot, answered. Its impassive metal eyes were fixed intently on Morris as it continued, "I am sure, Mr. Morris, you would like to own me. I am reasonably priced and fully guaranteed. A full book of instructions is included. I cannot conceive of taking *no* for an answer."

At half past twelve, Ed Morris still sat at the foot of the bed, one shoe on, the other in his hand. He gazed vacantly ahead. He said nothing.

"For heaven's sake," Sally complained. "Finish untying that knot and get into bed; you have to be up at five-thirty."

Morris fooled aimlessly with the shoelace. After a while he dropped the shoe and tugged at the other one. The house was cold and silent. Outside, the dismal night-wind whipped and lashed at the cedars that grew along the side of the building. Sally lay curled up beneath the radiant-lens, a cigarette between her lips, enjoying the warmth and half-dozing.

In the living room stood the fasrad. It hadn't left. It was still there, was waiting for Morris to buy it.

"Come on!" Sally said sharply. "What's wrong with you? It fixed all the things it broke; it was just demonstrating itself." She sighed drowsily. "It certainly gave me a scare. I thought something had gone wrong with it. They certainly had an inspiration, sending it around to sell itself to people."

Morris said nothing.

Sally rolled over on her stomach and languidly stubbed out her cigarette. "That's not so much, is it? Ten thousand gold units, and if we get our friends to buy one we get a five per cent commission. All we have to do is show it. It isn't as if we had to *sell* it. It sells itself." She giggled. "They always wanted a product that sold itself, didn't they?"

Morris untied the knot in his shoelace. He slid his shoe back on and tied it tight.

"What are you doing?" Sally demanded angrily. "You come to bed!" She sat up furiously, as Morris left the room and moved slowly down the hall. "Where are you going?"

In the living room, Morris switched on the light and sat down facing the fasrad. "Can you hear me?" he said.

"Certainly," the fasrad answered. "I'm never inoperative. Sometimes an emergency occurs at night: a child is sick or an accident takes place. You have no children as yet, but in the event — "

"Shut up," Morris said, "I don't want to hear you."

"You asked me a question. Self-regulating androids are plugged in to a central information exchange. Sometimes a person wishes immediate information; the fasrad is always ready to answer any theoretical or factual inquiry. Anything not metaphysical."

Morris picked up the book of instructions and thumbed it. The fasrad did thousands of things; it never wore out; it was never at a loss; it couldn't make a mistake. He threw the book away. "I'm not going to buy you," he said to it. "Never. Not in a million years."

"Oh, yes you are," the fasrad corrected. "This is an opportunity you can't afford to miss." There was calm, metallic confidence in its voice. "You can't turn me down, Mr. Morris. A fasrad is an indispensable necessity in the modern home."

"Get out of here," Morris said evenly. "Get out of my house and don't come back."

"I'm not your fasrad to order around. Until you've purchased me at the regular list price, I'm responsible only to Self-Regulating Android Inc. Their instructions were to the contrary; I'm to remain with you until you buy me."

"Suppose I never buy you?" Morris demanded, but in his heart ice formed even as he asked. Already he felt the cold terror of the answer that was coming; there could be no other.

"I'll continue to remain with you," the fasrad said; "eventually you'll buy me." It plucked some withered roses from a vase on the mantel and dropped them into its disposal slot. "You will see more and more situations in which a fasrad is indispensable. Eventually you'll wonder how you ever existed without one."

"Is there anything you can't do?"

"Oh, yes; there's a great deal I can't do. But I can do anything *you* can do — and considerably better."

Morris let out his breath slowly. "I'd be insane to buy you."

"You've got to buy me," the impassive voice answered. The fasrad extended a hollow pipe and began cleaning the carpet. "I am useful in all situations. Notice how fluffy and free of dust this rug is." It withdrew the pipe and extended another. Morris coughed and staggered quickly away; clouds of white particles billowed out and filled every part of the room.

"I am spraying for moths," the fasrad explained.

The white cloud turned to an ugly blue-black. The room faded into ominous darkness; the fasrad was a dim shape moving methodically about in the center. Presently the cloud lifted and the furniture emerged.

"I sprayed for harmful bacteria," the fasrad said.

It painted the walls of the room and constructed new furniture to go with them. It reinforced the ceiling in the bathroom. It increased the number of heat-vents from the furnace. It put in new electrical wiring. It tore out all the fixtures in the kitchen and assembled more modern ones. It examined Morris' financial accounts and computed his income tax for the following year. It sharpened all the pencils; it caught hold of his wrist and quickly diagnosed his high blood-pressure as psychosomatic.

"You'll feel better after you've turned responsibility over to me," it explained. It threw out some old soup Sally had been saving. "Danger of botulism," it told him. "Your wife is sexually attractive, but not capable of a high order of intellectualization."

Morris went to the closet and got his coat.

"Where are you going?" the fasrad asked.

"To the office."

"At this time of night?"

Morris glanced briefly into the bedroom. Sally was sound asleep under the soothing radiant-lens. Her slim body was rosy pink and healthy, her face free of worry. He closed the front door and hurried down the steps into the darkness. Cold night wind slashed at him as he approached the parking lot. His little commute ship was parked with hundreds of others; a quarter sent the attendant robot obediently after it.

In ten minutes he was on his way to Ganymede.

The fasrad boarded his ship when he stopped at Mars to refuel.

"Apparently you don't understand," the fasrad said. "My instructions are to demonstrate myself until you're satisfied. As yet, you're not wholly convinced; further demonstration is necessary." It passed an intricate web over the controls of the ship until all the dials and meters were in adjustment. "You should have more frequent servicing."

It retired to the rear to examine the drive jets. Morris numbly signalled the attendant, and the ship was released from the fuel pumps. He gained speed and the small sandy planet fell behind. Ahead, Jupiter loomed.

"Your jets aren't in good repair," the fasrad said, emerging from the rear. "I don't like that knock to the main brake drive. As soon as you land I'll make extensive repair."

"The Company doesn't mind your doing favors for me?" Morris asked, with bitter sarcasm.

"The Company considers me your fasrad. An invoice will be mailed to you at the end of the month." The robot whipped out a pen and a pad of forms. "I'll explain the four easy-payment plans. Ten thousand gold units cash means a three per cent discount. In addition, a number of household items may be traded in — items you won't have further need for. If you wish to divide the purchase in four parts, the first is due at once, and the last in ninety days."

"I always pay cash," Morris muttered. He was carefully resetting the route positions on the control board.

"There's no carrying charge for the ninety day plan. For the six month plan there's a six per cent annum charge which will amount to approximately — " It broke off. "We've changed course."

"That's right."

"We've left the official traffic lane." The fasrad stuck its pen and pad away and hurried to the control board. "What are you doing? There's a two unit fine for this."

Morris ignored it. He hung on grimly to the controls and kept his eyes on the viewscreen. The ship was gaining speed rapidly. Warning buoys sounded angrily as he shot past them and into the bleak darkness of space beyond. In a few seconds they had left all traffic behind. They were alone, shooting rapidly away from Jupiter, out into deep space.

The fasrad computed the trajectory. "We're moving out of the solar system. Toward Centaurus."

"You guessed it."

"Hadn't you better call your wife?"

Morris grunted and notched the drive bar farther up. The ship bucked and pitched, then managed to right itself. The jets began to whine ominously. Indicators showed the main turbines were beginning to heat. He ignored them and threw on the emergency fuel supply.

"I'll call Mrs. Morris," the fasrad offered. "We'll be beyond range in a short while."

"Don't bother."

"She'll worry." The fasrad hurried to the back and examined the jets again. It popped back into the cabin buzzing with alarm. "Mr. Morris, this ship is not equipped for inter-system travel. It's a Class D four-shaft domestic model for home consumption only. It was never made to stand this velocity."

"To get to Proxima," Morris answered, "we need this velocity."

The fasrad connected its power cables to the control board. "I can take some of the strain off the wiring system. But unless you rev her back to normal I can't be responsible for the deterioration of the jets."

"The hell with the jets."

The fasrad was silent. It was listening intently to the growing whine under them. The whole ship shuddered violently. Bits of paint drifted down. The floor was hot from the grinding shafts. Morris' foot stayed on the throttle. The ship gained more velocity as Sol fell behind. They were out of the charted area. Sol receded rapidly.

"It's too late to vid your wife," the fasrad said. "There are three emergency-rockets in the stern; if you want, I'll fire them off in the hope of attracting a passing military transport."

"Why?"

"They can take us in tow and return us to the Sol system. There's a six hundred gold unit fine, but under the circumstances it seems to me the best policy."

Morris turned his back to the fasrad and jammed down the throttle with all his weight. The whine had grown to a violent roar. Instruments smashed and cracked. Fuses blew up and down the board. The lights dimmed, faded, then reluctantly came back.

"Mr. Morris," the fasrad said, "you must prepare for death. The statistical probabilities of turbine explosion are seventy-thirty. I'll do what I can, but the danger-point has already passed."

Morris returned to the viewscreen. For a time he gazed hungrily up at the growing dot that was the twin star Centaurus. "They look all right, don't they? Prox is the important one. Twenty planets." He examined the wildly fluttering instruments. "How are the jets holding up? I can't tell from these; most of them are burned out."

The fasrad hesitated. It started to speak, then changed his mind. "I'll go back and examine them," it said. It moved to the rear of the ship and disappeared down the short ramp into the thundering, vibrating engine chamber.

Morris leaned over and put out his cigarette. He waited a moment longer, then reached out and yanked the drives full up, the last possible notch on the board.

The explosion tore the ship in half. Sections of hull hurtled around him. He was lifted weightless and slammed into the control board. Metal and plastic rained down on him. Flashing incandescent points winked, faded, and finally died into silence, and there was nothing but cold ash.

The dull *swish-swish* of emergency air-pumps brought consciousness back. He was pinned under the wreckage of the control board; one arm was broken and bent under him. He tried to move his legs but there was no sensation below his waist.

The splintered debris that had been his ship was still hurling toward Centaurus. Hull-sealing equipment was feebly trying to patch the gaping holes. Automatic temperature and grav feeds were thumping spasmodically from self-contained batteries. In the viewscreen the vast flaming bulk of the twin suns grew quietly, inexorably.

He was glad. In the silence of the ruined ship he lay buried beneath the debris, gratefully watching the growing bulk. It was a beautiful sight. He had wanted to see it for a long time. There it was, coming closer each moment. In a day or two the ship would plunge into the fiery mass and be consumed. But he could enjoy this interval; there was nothing to disturb his happiness..

He thought about Sally, sound asleep under the radiant-lens. Would Sally have liked Proxima? Probably not. Probably she would have wanted to go back home as soon as possible. This was something he had to enjoy alone. This was for him only. A vast peace descended over him. He could lie here without stirring, and the flaming magnificence would come nearer and nearer ...

A sound. From the heaps of fused wreckage something was rising. A twisted, dented shape dimly visible in the flickering glare of the viewscreen. Morris managed to turn his head.

The fasrad staggered to a standing position. Most of its trunk was gone, smashed and broken away. It tottered, then pitched forward on its face with a grinding crash. Slowly it inched its way toward him, then settled to a dismal halt a few feet off. Gears whirred creakily. Relays popped open and shut. Vague, aimless life animated its devastated hulk.

"Good evening," its shrill, metallic voice grated.

Morris screamed. He tried to move his body but the ruined beams held him tight. He shrieked and shouted and tried to crawl away from it. He spat and wailed and wept.

"I would like to show you a fasrad," the metallic voice continued. "Would you call your wife, please? I would like to show her a fasrad, too."

"Get away!" Morris screamed. "Get away from me!"

"Good evening," the fasrad continued, like a broken tape. "Good evening. Please be seated. I am happy to meet you. What is your name? Thank you. You are the first persons in your neighborhood to see the fasrad. Where are you employed?"

Its dead eye-lenses gaped at him empty and vacant.

"Please be seated," it said again. "This will take only a second. Only a second. This demonstration will take only a — "

Shell Game

A SOUND awoke O'Keefe instantly. He threw back his covers, slid from the cot, grabbed his B-pistol from the wall and, with his foot, smashed the alarm box. High frequency waves tripped emergency bells throughout the camp. As O'Keefe burst from his house, lights already flickered on every side.

"Where?" Fisher demanded shrilly. He appeared beside O'Keefe, still in his pajamas, grubby-faced with sleep.

"Over to the right." O'Keefe leaped aside for a massive cannon being rolled from its underground storage-chambers. Soldiers were appearing among the night-clad figures. To the right lay the black bog of mists and obese foliage, ferns and pulpy onions, sunk in the half-liquid ooze that made up the surface of Betelgeuse II. Nocturnal phosphorescence danced and flitted over the bog, ghostly yellow lights snapped in the thick darkness.

"I figure," Horstokowski said, "they came in close to the road, but not actually on it. There's a shoulder fifty feet on each side, where the bog has piled up. That's why our radar's silent."

An immense mechanical fusing "bug" was eating its way into the mud and shifting water of the bog, leaving behind a trail of hard, smoked surface. The vegetation and the rotting roots and dead leaves were sucked up and efficiently cleared away.

"What did you see?" Portbane asked O'Keefe.

"I didn't see anything. I was sound asleep. But I *heard* them."

"Doing what?"

"They were getting ready to pump nerve gas into my house. I heard them unreeling the hose from portable drums and uncapping the pressure tanks. But, by God, I was out of the house before they could get the joints leak-tight!"

Daniels hurried up. "You say it's a gas attack?" He fumbled for the gas mask at his belt. "Don't stand there — get your masks on!"

"They didn't get their equipment going," Silberman said. "O'Keefe gave the alarm in time. They retreated back to the bog."

"You're sure?" Daniels demanded.

"You don't smell anything, do you?"

"No," Daniels admitted. "But the odorless type is the most deadly. And you don't know you've been gassed till it's too late." He put on his gas mask, just to be sure.

A few women appeared by the rows of houses — slim, large-eyed shapes in the flickering glare of the emergency searchlights. Some children crept cautiously after them.

Silberman and Horstokowski moved over in the shadows by the heavy cannon.

"Interesting," Horstokowski said. "Third gas attack this month. Plus two tries to wire bomb terminals within the camp site. They're stepping it up."

"You have it all figured out, don't you?"

"I don't have to wait for the composite to see we're getting it heavier all the time." Horstokowski peered warily around, then pulled Silberman close. "Maybe there's a reason why the radar screen didn't react. It's supposed to get everything, even knocker-bats."

"But if they came in along the shoulder, like you said — "

"I just said that as a plant. *There's somebody waving them in, setting up interference for the radar.*"

"You mean one of us?"

Horstokowski was intently watching Fisher through the moist night gloom. Fisher had moved carefully to the edge of the road, where the hard surface ended and the slimy, scorched bog began. He was squatting down and rooting in the ooze.

"What's he doing?" Horstokowski demanded.

"Picking up something," Silberman said indifferently. "Why not? He's supposed to be looking around, isn't he?"

"Watch," Horstokowski warned. "When he comes back, he's going to pretend nothing happened."

Presently, Fisher returned, walking rapidly and rubbing the muck from his hands.

Horstokowski intercepted him. "What'd you find?"

"Me?" Fisher blinked. "I didn't find anything."

"Don't kid me! You were down on your hands and knees, grubbing in the bog."

"I — thought I saw something metal, that's all."

A vast inner excitement radiated through Horstokowski. He had been right.

"Come on!" he shouted. "What'd you find?"

"I thought it was a gas pipe," Fisher muttered. "But it was only a root. A big, wet root."

There was a tense silence.

"Search him," Portbane ordered.

Two soldiers grabbed Fisher. Silberman and Daniels quickly searched him.

They spilled out his belt pistol, knife, emergency whistle, automatic relay checker, Geiger counter, pulse tab, medical kit and identification papers. There was nothing else.

The soldiers let him go, disappointed, and Fisher sullenly collected his things.

"No, he didn't find anything," Portbane stated. "Sorry, Fisher. We have to be careful. We have to watch all the time, as long as they're out there, plotting and conspiring against us."

Silberman and Horstokowski exchanged glances, then moved quietly away.

"I think I get it," Silberman said softly.

"Sure," Horstokowski answered. "He *hid* something. We'll dig up that section of bog he was poking around in. I think maybe we'll find something interesting." He hunched his shoulders combatively. "I knew somebody was working for them, here in the camp. A spy for Terra."

Silberman started. "Terra? Is that who's attacking us?"

"Of course that's who."

There was a puzzled look on Silberman's face.

"Seemed to me we're fighting somebody else."

Horstokowski was outraged.

"For instance?"

Silberman shook his head. "I don't know. I didn't think about who so much as what to do about it. I guess I just took it for granted they were aliens."

"And what do you think those Terran monkey men are?" Horstokowski challenged.

The weekly Pattern Conference brought together the nine leaders of the camp in their reinforced underground conference chamber. Armed guards protected the entrance, which was sealed tight as soon as the last leader had been examined, checked over and finally passed.

Domgraf-Schwach, the conference chairman, sat attentively in his deep chair, one hand on the Pattern composite, the other on the switch that could instantly catapult him from the room and into a special compartment, safe from attack. Portbane was making his routine inspection of the chamber, examining each chair and desk for scanning eyes. Daniels sat with eyes fixed on his Geiger counter. Silberman was completely encased in an elaborate steel and plastic suit, configured with wiring, from which continual whirrings came.

"What in God's name is that suit of armor?" Domgraf-Schwach asked angrily. "Take it off so we can see you."

"Nuts to you," Silberman snapped, his voice muted by his intricate hull. "I'm wearing this from now on. Last night, somebody tried to jab me with bacteria-impregnated needles."

Lanoir, who was half-dozing at his place, came alive. "Bacteria-impregnated needles?" He leaped up and hurried over to Silberman. "Let me ask you if — "

"*Keep away from me*!" Silberman shouted. "If you come any closer, I'll electrocute you!"

"The attempt I reported last week," Lanoir panted excitedly, "when they tried to poison the water supply with metallic salts. It occurred to me their next method would be bacterial wastes, filterable virus we couldn't detect until actual outbreak of disease." From his pocket, he yanked a bottle and shook out a handful of white capsules. One after another, he popped the capsules into his mouth.

Every man in the room was protected in some fashion. Each chose whatever apparatus conformed to his individual experience. But the totality of defense-systems was integrated in the general Pattern planning. The only man who didn't seem busy with a device was Tate. He sat pale and tense, but otherwise unoccupied. Domgraf-Schwach made a mental note — Tate's confidence-level was unusually high. It suggested he somehow felt safe from attack.

"No talking," Domgraf-Schwach said. "Time to start."

He had been chosen as chairman by the turn of a wheel. There was no possibility of subversion under such a system. In an isolated, autonomous colony of sixty men and fifty women, such a random method was necessary.

"Daniels will read the week's Pattern composite," Domgraf-Schwach ordered.

"Why?" Portbane demanded bluntly. "We were the ones who put it together. We all know what's in it."

"For the same reason it's always read," Silberman answered. "So we'll know it wasn't tampered with."

"Just the summation!" Horstokowski said loudly. "I don't want to stay down here in this vault any longer than I have to."

"Afraid somebody'll fill up the passage?" Daniels jeered. "There are half a dozen emergency escape exits. You ought to know — you insisted on every one of them."

"Read the summation," Lanoir demanded.

Daniels cleared his throat. "During the last seven days, there were eleven overt attacks in all. The main attack was on our new class-A bridge network, which was sabotaged and wrecked. The struts were weakened and the plastic mix that served as base material was diluted, so that when the very first convoy of trucks passed over it, the whole thing collapsed."

"We know that," Portbane said gloomily.

"Loss consisted of six lives and considerable equipment. Troops scoured the area for a whole day, but the saboteurs managed to escape. Shortly after this attack, it was discovered that the water supply was poisoned with metallic salts. The wells were therefore filled and new ones drilled. Now all our water passes through filter and analysis systems."

"I boil mine," Lanoir added feelingly.

"It's agreed by everyone that the frequency and severity of attacks have been stepped up." Daniels indicated the massive wall charts and graphs. "Without our bomb-proof screen and our constant direction network, we'd be overwhelmed tonight. The real question is — *who are our attackers*?"

"Terrans," Horstokowski said.

Tate shook his head. "Terrans, hell! What would monkey men be doing out this far?"

"We're out this far, aren't we?" Lanoir retorted. "And we were Terrans once."

"Never!" Fisher shouted. "Maybe we lived on Terra, but we aren't Terrans. We're a superior mutant race."

"Then who are they?" Horstokowski insisted.

"They're other survivors from the ship," Tate said.

"How do you know?" asked Silberman. "Have you ever seen them?"

"*We salvaged no lifeboats, remember*? They must have blasted off in them."

"If they were isolated survivors," O'Keefe objected, "they wouldn't have the equipment and weapons and machines they're using. They're a trained, integrated force. We haven't been able to defeat them or even *kill* any of them in five years. That certainly shows their strength."

"We haven't tried to defeat them," Fisher said. "We've only tried to defend ourselves."

A sudden tense silence fell over the nine men.

"You mean the ship," Horstokowski said.

"It'll be up out of the bog soon," Tate replied. "And then we'll have something to show them — something they'll remember."

"Good God!" Lanoir exclaimed, disgusted. "The ship's a wreck — the meteor completely smashed it. What happens when we do get it up? We can't operate it unless we can completely rebuild it."

"If the monkey men could build the thing," Portbane said, "we can repair it. We have the tools and machinery."

"And we've finally located the control cabin," O'Keefe pointed out. "I see no reason why we can't raise it."

There was an abrupt change of expression on Lanoir's face. "All right, I withdraw my objections. Let's get it up."

"What's your motive?" Daniels yelled excitedly. "You're trying to put something over on us!"

"He's planning something," Fisher furiously agreed. "Don't listen to him. Leave the damn thing down there!"

"Too late for that," O'Keefe said. "It's been rising for weeks."

"You're in with him!" Daniels screeched. "Something's being put over on us."

The ship was a dripping, corroded ruin. Slime poured from it as the magnetic grapples dragged it from the bog and onto the hard surface that the fusing bugs had laid down.

The bugs burned a hard track through the bog, out to the control cabin. While the lift suspended the cabin, heavy reinforced plastic beams were slid under it. Tangled weeds, matted like ancient hair, covered the globular cabin in the midday sun, the first light that had struck it in five years.

"In you go," Domgraf-Schwach said eagerly.

Portbane and Lanoir advanced over the fused surface to the moored control cabin. Their handlights flashed ominously yellow around the steaming walls and encrusted controls. Livid eels twisted and convulsed in the thick pools underfoot. The cabin was a smashed, twisted ruin. Lanoir, who was first, motioned Portbane impatiently after him.

"*You* look at these controls — you're the engineer."

Portbane set down his light on a sloping heap of rusted metal and sloshed through the knee-deep rubbish to the demolished control panel. It was a maze of fused, buckled machinery. He squatted down in front of it and began tearing away the pitted guard-plates.

Lanoir pushed open a supply closet and brought down metal-packed audio and video tapes. He eagerly spilled open a can of the video and held a handful of frames to the flickering light. "Here's the ship's data. Now I'll be able to prove there was nobody but us aboard."

O'Keefe appeared at the jagged doorway. "How's it coming?"

Lanoir elbowed past him and out on the support boards. He deposited a load of tape-cans and returned to the drenched cabin. "Find anything on the controls?" he asked Portbane.

"Strange," Portbane murmured.

"What's the matter?" Tate demanded. "Too badly wrecked?"

"There are lots of wires and relays. Plenty of meters and power circuits and switches. But no controls to operate them."

Lanoir hurried over. "There must be!"

"For repairs, you have to remove all these plates — practically dismantle the works to even see them. Nobody could sit here and control the ship. There's nothing but a smooth, sealed shell."

"Maybe this wasn't the control cabin," Fisher offered.

"This is the steering mechanism — no doubt about that." Portbane pulled out a heap of charred wiring. "But all this was self-contained. They're robot controls. Automatic."

They looked at each other.

"Then we were prisoners," Tate said, dazed.

"Whose?" Fisher asked baffledly.

"The Terrans!" Lanoir said.

"I don't get it," Fisher muttered vaguely. "*We* planned the whole flight — didn't we? We broke out of Ganymede and got away."

"Get the tapes going," Portbane said to Lanoir. "Let's see what's in them."

Daniels snapped the vidtape scanner off and raised the light.

"Well," he said, "you saw for yourselves this was a hospital ship. It carried no crew. It was directed from a central guide-beam at Jupiter. The beam carried it from the Sol System here, where, because of a mechanical error, a meteor penetrated the protection screen and the ship crashed."

"And if it hadn't crashed?" Domgraf-Schwach asked faintly.

"Then we would have been taken to the main hospital at Fomalhaut IV."

"Play the last tape again," Tate urged.

The wall-seaker spluttered and then said smoothly: "The distinction between paranoids and paranoiac syndromes in other psychotic personality disorders must be borne in mind when dealing with these patients. The paranoid retains his general personality structure unimpaired. Outside of the region of his complex, he is logical, rational, even brilliant. He can be talked to — he can discuss himself — he is aware of his surroundings.

"The paranoid differs from other psychotics in that he remains actively oriented to the outside world. He differs from so-called normal personality types in that he has a set of fixed ideas, false postulates from which he has relentlessly constructed an elaborate system of beliefs, logical and consistent with these false postulates."

Shakily, Daniels interrupted the tape. "These tapes were for the hospital authorities on Fomalhaut IV. Locked in a supply closet in the control cabin. The control cabin itself was sealed off from the rest of the ship. None of us was able to enter it."

"The paranoid is totally rigid," the calm voice of the Terran doctor continued. "His fixed ideas cannot be shaken. They dominate his life. He logically weaves all events, all persons, all chance remarks and happenings, into his system. He is convinced the world is plotting against him — that he is a person of unusual importance and ability against whom endless machinations are directed. To thwart these plots, the paranoid goes to infinite lengths to protect himself. He repeatedly vidtapes the authorities, constantly moves from place to place and, in the dangerous final phases, may even become — "

Silberman snapped it off savagely and the chamber was silent. The nine leaders of the camp sat unmoving in their places.

"We're a bunch of nuts," Tate said finally. "A shipload of psychos who got wrecked by a chance meteor."

"Don't kid yourself," Horstokowski snapped. "There wasn't anything chance about that meteor."

Fisher giggled hysterically. "More paranoid talk. Good God, all these attacks — hallucinations — all in our minds!"

Lanoir poked vaguely at the pile of tape. "What are we to believe? *Are there any attackers?*"

"We've been defending ourselves against them for five years!" Portbane retorted. "Isn't that proof enough?"

"Have you ever seen them?" Fisher asked slyly.

"We're up against the best agents in the Galaxy. Terran shock troops and military spies, carefully trained in subversion and sabotage. They're too clever to show themselves."

"They wrecked the bridge-system," O'Keefe said. "It's true we didn't see them, but the bridge is sure as hell in ruins."

"Maybe it was badly built," Fisher pointed out. "Maybe it just collapsed."

"Things don't 'just collapse'! There's a reason for all these things that have been happening."

"Like what?" Tate demanded.

"Weekly poison gas attacks," Portbane said. "Metallic wastes in the water supply, to name only two."

"And bacteriological crystals," Daniels added.

"Maybe none of these things exist," Lanoir argued. "But how are we to prove it? If we're all insane, *how would we know*?"

"There are over a hundred of us," Domgraf-Schwach said. "We've all experienced these attacks. Isn't that proof enough?"

"A myth can be picked up by a whole society, believed and taught to the next generation. Gods, fairies, witches — believing a thing doesn't make it true. For centuries, Terrans believed the Earth was flat."

"If all foot-rulers grow to thirteen inches," Fisher asked, "how would anybody know? One of them would have to stay twelve inches long, a nonvariable, a constant. We're a bunch of inaccurate rulers, each thirteen inches long. We need one nonparanoid for comparison."

"Or maybe this is all part of their strategy," Silberman said. "Maybe they rigged up that control cabin and planted those tapes there."

"This ought to be no different from trying to test any belief," Portbane explained. "What's the characteristic of a scientific test?"

"It can be duplicated," Fisher said promptly. "Look, we're going around in circles. *We're trying to measure ourselves.* You can't take your ruler, either twelve inches or thirteen inches long, and ask it to measure itself. No instrument can test its own accuracy."

"Wrong," Portbane answered calmly. "I can put together a valid, objective test."

"There's no such test!" Tate shouted excitedly.

"There sure as hell is. And inside of a week, I'll have it set up."

"Gas!" the soldier shouted. On all sides, sirens wailed into life. Women and children scrambled for their masks. Heavy-duty cannon rumbled up from subsurface chambers and took up positions. Along the perimeter of the bog, the fusing bugs were searing away a ribbon of muck. Searchlights played out into the fern-thick darkness.

Portbane snapped off the cock of the steel tank and signaled the workmen. The tank was rolled quickly away from the sea of mud and seared weeds.

"All right," Portbane gasped. "Get it below."

He emerged in the subsurface chamber as the cylinder was being rolled into position.

"That cylinder," Portbane said, "should contain hydrocyanic vapor. It's a sampling made at the site of the attack."

"This is useless," Fisher complained. "They're attacking and here we stand!"

Portbane signaled the workmen and they began laying out the test apparatus. "There will be two samples, precipitates of different vapors, each clearly marked and labeled A and B. One comes from the cylinder filled at the scene of the attack. The other is condensed from air taken out of this room."

"Suppose we describe both as negative?" Silberman asked worriedly. "Won't that throw your test off?"

"Then we'll take more tests. After a couple of months, if we still haven't got anything but negative findings, then the attack hypothesis is destroyed."

"We may see both as positive," Tate said, perplexed.

"In that case, we're dead right now. If we see both samples as positive, I think the case for the paranoid hypothesis has been proved."

After a moment, Domgraf-Schwach reluctantly agreed. "One is the control. If we maintain that it isn't possible to get a control sample that is free of hydrocyanic acid ... "

"Pretty damn slick," O'Keefe admitted. "You start from the one known factor — our own existence. We can't very well doubt *that*."

"Here are all the choices," Portbane said. "Both positive means we're psychotic. Both negative means either the attack was a false alarm or there are no attackers. One positive and one negative would indicate there are real attackers, that we're fully sane and rational." He glanced around at the camp leads. "*But we'll all have to agree which sample is which*."

"Our reactions will be recorded secretly?" Tate asked.

"Tabulated and punched by the mechanical eye. Tallied by machinery. Each of us will make an individual discrimination."

After a pause, Fisher said, "I'll try it." He came forward, leaned over the colorimeter and studied the two samples intently. He alternated them for a time and then firmly grabbed the check-stylus.

"You're sure?" Domgraf-Schwach asked. "You really know which is the negative control sample?"

"I know." Fisher noted his findings on the punch sheet and moved away.

"I'm next," Tate said, impatiently pushing up. "Let's get this over with."

One by one, the men examined the two samples, recorded their findings, and then moved off to stand waiting uneasily.

"All right," Portbane said finally. "I'm the last one." He peered down briefly, scribbled his results, then pushed the equipment away. "Give me the readings," he told the workmen by the scanner.

A moment later, the findings were flashed up for everyone to see.

Fisher	A
Tate	A
O'Keefe	B
Horstokowski	B
Silberman	B
Daniels	B
Portbane	A
Domgraf-Schwach	B
Lanoir	A

"I'll be damned," Silberman said softly. "As simple as that. We're paranoids."

"You cluck!" Tate shouted at Horstokowski. "It was A, not B! How the hell could you get it wrong?"

"B was as bright as a searchlight!" Domgraf-Schwach answered furiously. "A was completely colorless!"

O'Keefe pushed forward. "Which was it, Portbane? Which was the positive sample?"

"I don't know," Portbane confessed. "How could any of us be sure?"

The buzzer on Domgraf-Schwach's desk clicked and he snapped on the vidscreen.

The face of a soldier-operator appeared. "The attack's over, sir. We drove them away."

Domgraf-Schwach smiled ironically. "Catch any of them?"

"No, sir. They slipped back into the bog. I think we hit a couple, though. We'll go out tomorrow and try to find the corpses."

"You think you'll find them?"

"Well, the bog usually swallows them up. But maybe this time — "

"All right," Domgraf-Schwach interrupted. "If this turns out to be an exception, let me know." He broke the circuit.

"Now what?" Daniels inquired icily.

"There's no point in continuing work on the ship," O'Keefe said. "Why waste our time bombing empty bogs?"

"I suggest we keep working on the ship," Tate contradicted.

"Why?" O'Keefe asked.

"So we can head for Fomalhaut and give ourselves up to the hospital station."

Silberman stared at him incredulously. "Turn ourselves in? Why not stay here? We're not harming anybody."

"No, not yet. It's the future I'm thinking of, centuries from now."

"We'll be dead."

"Those of us in this room, sure, but what about our descendants?"

"He's right," Lanoir conceded. "Eventually our descendants will fill this whole solar system. Sooner or later, our ships might spread over the Galaxy." He tried to smile, but his muscles would not respond. "The tapes point out how tenacious paranoids are. They cling fanatically to their fixed beliefs. If our descendants expand into Terran regions, there'll be a fight and we might win because we're more one-track. We would never deviate."

"Fanatics," Daniels whispered.

"We'll have to keep this information from the rest of the camp," O'Keefe said.

"Absolutely," Fisher agreed. "We'll have to keep them thinking the ship is for H-bomb attacks. Otherwise, we'll have one hell of a situation on our hands."

They began moving numbly toward the sealed door.

"Wait a minute," Domgraf-Schwach said urgently. "The two workmen." He started back, while some of them went out into the corridor, the rest back toward their seats.

And then it happened.

Silberman fired first. Fisher screamed as half of him vanished in swirling particles of radioactive ash. Silberman dropped to one knee and fired up at Tate. Tate leaped back and brought out his own B-pistol. Daniels stepped from the path of Lenoir's beam. It missed him and struck the first row of seats.

Lanoir calmly crept along the wall through the billowing clouds of smoke. A figure loomed ahead; he raised his gun and fired. The figure fell to one side and fired back. Lanoir staggered and collapsed like a deflated balloon and Silberman hurried on.

At his desk, Domgraf-Schwach was groping wildly for his escape button. His fingers touched it, but as he depressed the stud, a blast from Portbane's pistol removed the top of his head. The lifeless corpse stood momentarily, then was whisked to "safety" by the intricate apparatus beneath the desk.

"This way!" Portbane shouted, above the sizzle of the B-blasts. "Come on, Tate!"

Various beams were turned in his direction. Half the chamber burst apart and thundered down, disintegrating into rubble and flaming debris. He and Tate scrambled for one of the emergency exits. Behind them, the others hurried, firing savagely.

Horstokowski found the exit and slid past the jammed lock. He fired as the two figures raced up the passage ahead of him. One of them stumbled, but the other grabbed at him and they hobbled off together. Daniels was a better shot. As Tate and Portbane emerged on the surface, one of Daniels' blasts undercut the taller of the two.

Portbane continued running a little way, and then silently pitched face-forward against the side of a plastic house, a gloomy square of opaque blackness against the night sky.

"Where'd they go?" Silberman demanded hoarsely, as he appeared at the mouth of the passage. His right arm had been torn away by Lanoir's blast. The stump was seared hard.

"I got one of them." Daniels and O'Keefe approached the inert figure warily. "It's Portbane. That leaves Tate. We got three of the four. Not bad, on such short notice."

"Tate's damn smart," Silberman panted. "I think he suspected."

He scanned the darkness around them. Soldiers, returning from the gas attack, came hurrying up. Searchlights rumbled toward the scene of the shooting. Off in the distance, sirens wailed.

"Which way did he go?" Daniels asked.

"Over toward the bog."

O'Keefe moved cautiously along the narrow street. The others came slowly behind.

"You were the first to realize," Horstokowski said to Silberman. "For a while, I believed the test. Then I realized we were being tricked — the four of them were plotting in unison."

"I didn't expect four of them," Silberman admitted. "I knew there was at least one Terran spy among us. But Lanoir ... "

"I always knew Lanoir was a Terran agent," O'Keefe declared flatly. "I wasn't surprised at the test results. They gave themselves away by faking their findings."

Silberman waved over a group of soldiers. "Have Tate picked up and brought here. He's somewhere at the periphery of the camp."

The soldiers hurried away, dazed and muttering. Alarm bells dinned shrilly on all sides. Figures scampered back and forth. Like a disturbed ant colony, the whole camp was alive with excitement.

"In other words," Daniels said, "the four of them really saw the same as we. They saw B as the positive sample, but they put down A instead."

"They knew we'd put down B," O'Keefe said, "since B was the positive sample taken from the attack site. All they had to do was record the opposite. The results seemed to substantiate Lanoir's paranoid theory, which was why Portbane set up the test in the first place. It was planned a long time ago — part of their overall job."

"Lanoir dug up the tapes in the first place!" Daniels exclaimed. "Fisher and he planted them down in the ruins of the ship. Portbane got us to accept his testing device."

"What were they trying to do?" Silberman asked suddenly. "Why were they trying to convince us we're paranoids?"

"Isn't it obvious?" O'Keefe replied. "They wanted us to turn ourselves in. The Terran monkey men naturally are trying to choke off the race that's going to supplant them. We won't surrender, of course. The four of them were clever — they almost had me convinced. When the results flashed up five to four, I had a momentary doubt. But then I realized what an intricate strategy they had worked out."

Horstokowski examined his B-pistol. "I'd like to get hold of Tate and wring the whole story from him, the whole damn account of their planning, so we'd have it in black and white."

"You're still not convinced?" Daniels inquired.

"Of course. But I'd like to hear him admit it."

"I doubt if we'll see Tate again," O'Keefe said. "He must have reached the Terran lines by now. He's probably sitting in a big inter-system military transport, giving his story to gold-braid Terran officials. I'll bet they're moving up heavy guns and shock troops while we stand here."

"We'd better get busy," Daniels said sharply. "We'll repair the ship and load it with H-bombs. After we wipe out their bases here, we'll carry the war to them. A few raids on the Sol System ought to teach them to leave us alone."

Horstokowski grinned. "It'll be an uphill fight — we're alone against a whole galaxy. But I think we'll take care of them. One of us is worth a million Terran monkey men."

Tate lay trembling in the dark tangle of weeds. Dripping black stalks of nocturnal vegetables clutched and stirred around him. Poisonous night insects slithered across the surface of the fetid bog.

He was covered with slime. His clothing was torn and ripped. Somewhere along the way, he had lost his B-pistol. His right shoulder ached; he could hardly move his arm. Bones broken, probably. He was too numb and dazed to care. He lay facedown in the sticky muck and closed his eyes.

He didn't have a chance. Nobody survived in the bogs. He feebly smashed an insect oozing across his neck. It squirmed in his hand and then, reluctantly, died. For a long time, its dead legs kicked.

The probing stalk of a stinging snail began tracing webs across Tate's inert body. As the sticky pressure of the snail crept heavily onto him, he heard the first faint far-off sounds of the camp going into action. For a time, it meant nothing to him. Then he understood — and shuddered miserably, helplessly.

The first phase of the big offensive against Earth was already moving into high gear.

UPON THE DULL EARTH

SILVIA RAN LAUGHING through the night brightness, between the roses and cosmos and Shasta daisies, down the gravel path and beyond the heaps of sweet-tasting grass swept from the lawns. Stars, caught in pools of water, glittered everywhere, as she brushed through them to the slope beyond the brick wall. Cedars supported the sky and ignored the slim shape squeezing past, her brown hair flying, her eyes flashing.

"Wait for me," Rick complained, as he cautiously threaded his way after her, along the half familiar path. Silvia danced on without stopping. "Slow down!" he shouted angrily.

"Can't — we're late." Without warning, Silvia appeared in front of him, blocking the path. "Empty your pockets," she gasped, her gray eyes sparkling. "Throw away all metal. You know they can't stand metal."

Rick searched his pockets. In his overcoat were two dimes and a fifty-cent piece. "Do these count?"

"*Yes!*" Silvia snatched the coins and threw them into the dark heaps of calla lilies. The bits of metal hissed into the moist depths and were gone. "Anything else?" She caught hold of his arm anxiously. "They're already on their way. Anything else, Rick?"

"Just my watch." Rick pulled his wrist away as Silvia's wild fingers snatched for the watch. "*That's* not going in the bushes."

"Then lay it on the sundial — or the wall. Or in a hollow tree." Silvia raced off again. Her excited, rapturous voice danced back to him. "Throw away your cigarette case. And your keys, your belt buckle — everything metal. You know how they hate metal. Hurry, we're late!"

Rick followed sullenly after her. "All right, *witch*."

Silvia snapped at him furiously from the darkness. "Don't *say* that! It isn't true. You've been listening to my sisters and my mother and — "

Her words were drowned out by the sound. Distant flapping, a long way off, like vast leaves rustling in a winter storm. The night sky was alive with the frantic poundings; they were coming very quickly this time. They were too greedy, too desperately eager to wait. Flickers of fear touched the man and he ran to catch up with Silvia.

Silvia was a tiny column of green skirt and blouse in the center of the thrashing mass. She was pushing them away with one arm and trying to manage the faucet with the other. The churning activity of wings and bodies twisted her like a reed. For a time she was lost from sight.

"Rick!" she called faintly. "Come here and help!" She pushed them away and struggled up. "They're suffocating me!"

Rick fought his way through the wall of flashing white to the edge of the trough. They were drinking greedily at the blood that spilled from the wooden faucet. He pulled Silvia close against him; she was terrified and trembling. He held her tight until some of the violence and fury around them had died down.

"They're hungry," Silvia gasped feebly.

"You're a little cretin for coming ahead. They can sear you to ash!"

"I know. They can do anything." She shuddered, excited and frightened. "Look at them," she whispered, her voice husky with awe. "Look at the size of them — their wing-spread. And they're *white*, Rick. Spotless — perfect. There's nothing in our world as spotless as that. Great and clean and wonderful."

"They certainly wanted the lamb's blood."

Silvia's soft hair blew against his face as the wings fluttered on all sides. They were leaving now, roaring up into the sky. Not up, really — away. Back to their own world whence they had scented the blood. But it was not only the blood — they had come because of Silvia. *She* had attracted them.

The girl's gray eyes were wide. She reached up towards the rising white creatures. One of them swooped close. Grass and flowers sizzled as blinding white flames roared in a brief fountain. Rick scrambled away. The flaming figure hovered momentarily over Silvia and then there was a hollow *pop*. The last of the white-winged giants was gone. The air, the ground, gradually cooled into darkness and silence.

"I'm sorry," Silvia whispered.

"Don't do it again," Rick managed. He was numb with shock. "It isn't safe."

"Sometimes I forget. I'm sorry, Rick. I didn't mean to draw them so close." She tried to smile. "I haven't been that careless in months. Not since that other time, when I first brought you out here." The avid, wild look slid across her face. "Did you *see* him? Power and flames! And he didn't even touch us. He just — looked at us. That was all. And everything's burned up, all around."

Rick grabbed hold of her. "Listen," he grated. "You mustn't call them again. It's wrong. This isn't their world."

"It's not wrong — it's beautiful."

"It's not safe!" His fingers dug into her flesh until she gasped. "Stop tempting them down here!"

Silvia laughed hysterically. She pulled away from him, out into the blasted circle that the horde of angels had seared behind them as they rose into the sky. "I can't *help* it," she cried. "I belong with them. They're my family, my people. Generations of them, back into the past."

"What do you mean?"

"They're my ancestors. And some day I'll join them."

"You are a little witch!" Rick shouted furiously.

"No," Silvia answered. "Not a witch, Rick. Don't you see? I'm a saint."

The kitchen was warm and bright. Silvia plugged in the Silex and got a big red can of coffee down from the cupboards over the sink. "You mustn't listen to them," she said, as she set out plates and cups and got cream from the refrigerator. "You know they don't understand. Look at them in there."

Silvia's mother and her sisters, Betty Lou and Jean, stood huddled together in the living room, fearful and alert, watching the young couple in the kitchen. Walter Everett was standing by the fireplace, his face blank, remote.

"Listen to *me*," Rick said. "You have this power to attract them. You mean you're not — isn't Walter your real father?"

"Oh, yes — of course he is. I'm completely human. Don't I look human?"

"But you're the only one who has the power."

"I'm not physically different," Silvia said thoughtfully. "I have the ability to see, that's all. Others have had it before me — saints, martyrs. When I was a child, my mother read to me about St. Bernadette. Remember where her cave was? Near a hospital. They were hovering there and she saw one of them."

"But the blood! It's grotesque. There never was anything like that."

"Oh, yes. The blood draws them, lamb's blood especially. They hover over battlefields. Valkyries — carrying off the dead to Valhalla. That's why saints and martyrs cut and mutilate themselves. You know where I got the idea?"

Silvia fastened a little apron around her waist and filled the Silex with coffee. "When I was nine years old, I read of it in Homer, in the Odyssey. Ulysses dug a trench in the ground and filled it with blood to attract the spirits. The shades from the nether world."

"That's right," Rick admitted reluctantly. "I remember."

"The ghosts of people who died. They had lived once. Everybody lives here, then dies and goes there." Her face glowed. "We're all going to have wings! We're all going to fly. We'll all be filled with fire and power. We won't be worms any more."

"Worms! That's what you always call me."

"Of course you're a worm. We're all worms — grubby worms creeping over the crust of the Earth, through dust and dirt."

"Why should blood bring them?"

"Because it's life and they're attracted by life. Blood is *uisge beatha* — the water of life."

"Blood means death! A trough of spilled blood ... "

"It's *not* death. When you see a caterpillar crawl into its cocoon, do you think it's dying?"

Walter Everett was standing in the doorway. He stood listening to his daughter, his face dark. "One day," he said hoarsely, "they're going to grab her and carry her off. She wants to go with them. She's waiting for that day."

"You see?" Silvia said to Rick. "He doesn't understand either." She shut off the Silex and poured coffee. "Coffee for you?" she asked her father.

"No," Everett said.

"Silvia," Rick said, as if speaking to a child, "if you went away with them, you know you couldn't come back to us."

"We all have to cross sooner or later. It's all part of our life."

"But you're only nineteen," Rick pleaded. "You're young and healthy and beautiful. And our marriage — what about our marriage?" He half rose from the table. "Silvia, you've got to stop this!"

"I *can't* stop it. I was seven when I saw them first." Silvia stood by the sink, gripping the Silex, a faraway look in her eyes. "Remember, Daddy? We were living back in Chicago. It was winter. I fell, walking home from school." She held up a slim arm. "See the scar? I fell and cut myself on the gravel and slush. I came home crying — it was sleeting and the wind was howling around me. My arm was bleeding and my mitten was soaked with blood. And then I looked up and saw them."

There was silence.

"They want you," Everett said wretchedly. "They're flies — bluebottles, hovering around, waiting for you. Calling you to come along with them."

"Why not?" Silvia's gray eyes were shining and her cheeks radiated joy and anticipation. "You've seen them, Daddy. You know what it means. Transfiguration — from clay into gods!"

Rick left the kitchen. In the living-room, the two sisters stood together, curious and uneasy. Mrs. Everett stood by herself, her face granite-hard, eyes bleak behind her steel-rimmed glasses. She turned away as Rick passed them.

"What happened out there?" Betty Lou asked him in a taut whisper. She was fifteen, skinny and plain, hollow cheeked, with mousy, sand-colored hair. "Silvia never lets us come out with her."

"Nothing happened," Rick answered.

Anger stirred the girl's barren face. "That's not true. You were both out in the garden, in the dark, and — "

"Don't talk to him!" her mother snapped. She yanked the two girls away and shot Rick a glare of hatred and misery. Then she turned quickly from him.

Rick opened the door to the basement and switched on the light. He descended slowly into the cold, damp room of concrete and dirt, with its unwinking yellow light hanging from the dust-covered wires overhead.

In one corner loomed the big floor furnace with its mammoth hot air pipes. Beside it stood the water heater and discarded bundles, boxes of books, newspapers and old furniture, thick with dust, encrusted with strings of spider webs.

At the far end were the washing machine and spin dryer. And Silvia's pump and refrigeration system.

From the work bench Rick selected a hammer and two heavy pipe wrenches. He was moving towards the elaborate tanks and pipes when Silvia appeared abruptly at the top of the stairs, her coffee cup in one hand.

She hurried quickly down to him. "What are you doing down here?" she asked, studying him intently. "Why that hammer and those two wrenches?"

Rick dropped the tools back onto the bench. "I thought maybe this could be solved on the spot."

Silvia moved between him and the tanks. "I thought you understood. They've always been a part of my life. When I brought you with me the first time, you seemed to see what — "

"I don't want to lose you," Rick said harshly, "to anybody or anything — in this world or any other. *I'm not going to give you up.*"

"It's not giving me up!" Her eyes narrowed. "You came down here to destroy and break everything. The moment I'm not looking you'll smash all this, won't you?"

"That's right."

Fear replaced anger on the girl's face. "Do you want me to be chained here? I have to go on — I'm through with this part of the journey. I've stayed here long enough."

"Can't you wait?" Rick demanded furiously. He couldn't keep the ragged edge of despair out of his voice. "Doesn't it come soon enough anyhow?"

Silvia shrugged and turned away, her arms folded, her red lips tight together. "You want to be a worm always. A fuzzy, little creeping caterpillar."

"I want *you*."

"You can't *have* me!" She whirled angrily. "I don't have any time to waste with this."

"You have higher things in mind," Rick said savagely.

"Of course." She softened a little. "I'm sorry, Rick. Remember Icarus? You want to fly, too. I know it."

"In my time."

"Why not now? Why wait? You're afraid." She slid lithely away from him, cunning twisting her red lips. "Rick, I want to show you something. Promise me first — you won't tell anybody."

"What is it?"

"Promise?" She put her hand to his mouth. "I have to be careful. It cost a lot of money. Nobody knows about it. It's what they do in China — everything goes towards it."

"I'm curious," Rick said. Uneasiness flicked at him. "Show it to me."

Trembling with excitement, Silvia disappeared behind the huge lumbering refrigerator, back into the darkness behind the web of frost-hard freezing coils. He could hear her tugging and pulling at something. Scraping sounds, sounds of something large being dragged out.

"See?" Silvia gasped. "Give me a hand, Rick. It's heavy. Hardwood and brass — and metal lined. It's hand-stained and polished. And the carving — see the carving! Isn't it beautiful?"

"What is it?" Rick demanded huskily.

"It's my cocoon," Silvia said simply. She settled down in a contented heap on the floor, and rested her head happily against the polished oak coffin.

Rick grabbed her by the arm and dragged her to her feet. "You can't sit with that coffin, down here in the basement with — " He broke off. "What's the matter?"

Silvia's face was twisting with pain. She backed away from him and put her finger quickly to her mouth. "I cut myself — when you pulled me up — on a nail or something." A thin trickle of blood oozed down her fingers. She groped in her pocket for a handkerchief.

"Let me see it." He moved towards her, but she avoided him. "Is it bad?" he demanded.

"Stay away from me," Silvia whispered.

"What's wrong? Let me see it!"

"Rick," Silvia said in a low intense voice, "get some water and adhesive tape. As quickly as possible!" She was trying to keep down her rising terror. "I have to stop the bleeding."

"Upstairs?" He moved awkwardly away. "It doesn't look too bad. Why don't you … "

"Hurry." The girl's voice was suddenly bleak with fear. "Rick, *hurry!*"

Confused, he ran a few steps.

Silvia's terror poured after him. "No, it's too late," she called thinly. "Don't come back — keep away from me. It's my own fault. I trained them to come. *Keep away!* I'm sorry, Rick. *Oh* — " Her voice was lost to him, as the wall of the basement burst and shattered. A cloud of luminous white forced its way through and blazed out into the basement.

It was Silvia they were after. She ran a few hesitant steps towards Rick, halted uncertainly, then the white mass of bodies and wings settled around her. She shrieked once. Then a violent explosion blasted the basement into a shimmering dance of furnace heat.

He was thrown to the floor. The cement was hot and dry — the whole basement crackled with heat. Windows shattered as pulsing white shapes pushed out again. Smoke and flames licked up the walls. The ceiling sagged and rained plaster down.

Rick struggled to his feet. The furious activity was dying away. The basement was a littered chaos. All surfaces were scorched black, seared and crusted with smoking ash. Splintered wood, torn cloth and broken concrete were strewn everywhere. The furnace and washing machine were in ruins. The elaborate pumping and refrigeration system — now were a glittering mass of slag. One whole wall had been twisted aside. Plaster was rubbled over everything.

Silvia was a twisted heap, arms and legs doubled grotesquely. Shriveled, carbonized remains of fire-scorched ash, settling in a vague mound. What had been left were charred fragments, a brittle burned-out husk.

It was a dark night, cold and intense. A few stars glittered like ice from above his head. A faint, dank wind stirred through the dripping calla lilies and whipped gravel up in a frigid mist along the path between the black roses.

He crouched for a long time, listening and watching. Behind the cedars, the big house loomed against the sky. At the bottom of the slope a few cars slithered along the highway. Otherwise, there was no sound. Ahead of him jutted the squat outline of the porcelain trough and the pipe that had carried blood from the refrigerator in the basement. The trough was empty and dry, except for a few leaves that had fallen in it.

Rick took a deep breath of thin night air and held it. Then he got stiffly to his feet. He scanned the sky, but saw no movement. They were there, though, watching and waiting — dim shadows, echoing into the legendary past, a line of god-figures.

He picked up the heavy gallon drums, dragged them to the trough and poured blood from a New Jersey abattoir, cheap-grade steer refuse, thick and clotted. It splashed against his clothes and he backed away nervously. But nothing stirred in the air above. The garden was silent, drenched with night fog and darkness.

He stood beside the trough, waiting and wondering if they were coming. They had come for Silvia, not merely for the blood. Without her there was no attraction but the raw food. He carried the empty metal cans over to the bushes and kicked them down the slope. He searched his pockets carefully, to make sure there was no metal in them.

Over the years, Silvia had nourished their habit of coming. Now she was on the other side. Did that mean they wouldn't come? Somewhere in the damp bushes something rustled. An animal or a bird?

In the trough the blood glistened, heavy and dull, like old lead. It was their time to come, but nothing stirred the great trees above. He picked out the rows of nodding black roses, the gravel path down which he and Silvia had run — violently he shut out the recent memory of her flashing eyes and deep red lips. The highway beyond the slope — the empty, deserted garden — the silent house in which her family huddled and waited. After a time, there was a dull, swishing sound. He tensed, but it was only a diesel truck lumbering along the highway, headlights blazing.

He stood grimly, his feet apart, his heels dug into the soft black ground. He wasn't leaving. He was staying there until they came. He wanted her back — at any cost.

Overhead, foggy webs of moisture drifted across the moon. The sky was a vast barren plain, without life or warmth. The deathly cold of deep space, away from suns and living things. He gazed up until his neck ached. Cold stars, sliding in and out of the matted layer of fog. Was there anything else? Didn't they want to come, or weren't they interested in him? It had been Silvia who had interested them — now they had her.

Behind him there was a movement without sound. He sensed it and started to turn, but suddenly, on all sides, the trees and undergrowth shifted. Like cardboard props they wavered and ran together, blending dully in the night shadows. Something moved through them, rapidly, silently, then was gone.

They had come. He could feel them. They had shut off their power and flame. Cold, indifferent statues, rising among the trees, dwarfing the cedars — remote from him and his world, attracted by curiosity and mild habit.

"Silvia," he said clearly. "Which are you?"

There was no response. Perhaps she wasn't among them. He felt foolish. A vague flicker of white drifted past the trough, hovered momentarily and then went on without stopping. The air above the trough vibrated, then died into immobility, as another giant inspected briefly and withdrew.

Panic breathed through him. They were leaving again, receding back into their own world. The trough had been rejected; they weren't interested.

"Wait," he muttered thickly.

Some of the white shadows lingered. He approached them slowly, wary of their flickering immensity. If one of them touched him, he would sizzle briefly and puff into a dark heap of ash. A few feet away he halted.

"You know what I want," he said. "I want her back. She shouldn't have been taken yet."

Silence.

"You were too greedy," he said. "You did the wrong thing. She was going to come over to you, eventually. She had it all worked out."

The dark fog rustled. Among the trees the flickering shapes stirred and pulsed, responsive to his voice. "*True*," came a detached impersonal sound. The sound drifted around him, from tree to tree, without location or direction. It was swept off by the night wind to die into dim echoes.

Relief settled over him. They had paused — they were aware of him — listening to what he had to say.

"You think it's right?" he demanded. "She had a long life here. We were to marry, have children."

There was no answer, but he was conscious of a growing tension. He listened intently, but he couldn't make out anything. Presently he realized a struggle was taking place, a conflict among them. The tension grew — more shapes flickered — the clouds, the icy stars, were obscured by the vast presence swelling around him.

"Rick!" A voice spoke close by. Wavering, drifting back into the dim regions of the trees and dripping plants. He could hardly hear it — the words were gone as soon as they were spoken. "Rick — help me get back."

"Where are you?" He couldn't locate her. "What can I do?"

"I don't know." Her voice was wild with bewilderment and pain. "I don't understand. Something went wrong. They must have thought I — wanted to come right away. I *didn't*!"

"I know," Rick said. "It was an accident."

"They were waiting. The cocoon, the trough — but it was too soon." Her terror came across to him, from the vague distances of another universe. "Rick, I've changed my mind. I want to come back."

"It's not as simple as that."

"I know. Rick, time is different on this side. I've been gone so long — your world seems to creep along. It's been years, hasn't it?"

"One week," Rick said.

"It was their fault. You don't blame me, do you? They know they did the wrong thing. Those who did it have been punished, but that doesn't help me." Misery and panic distorted her voice so he could hardly understand her. "How can I come back?"

"Don't they know?"

"They say it can't be done." Her voice trembled. "They say they destroyed the clay part — it was incinerated. There's nothing for me to go back to."

Rick took a deep breath. "Make them find some other way. It's up to them. Don't they have the power? They took you over too soon — they must send you back. It's *their* responsibility."

The white shapes shifted uneasily. The conflict rose sharply; they couldn't agree. Rick warily moved back a few paces.

"They say it's dangerous," Silvia's voice came from no particular spot. "They say it was attempted once." She tried to control her voice. "The nexus between this world and yours is unstable. There are vast amounts of free-floating energy. The power we — on this side — have isn't really our own. It's a universal energy, tapped and controlled."

"Why can't they ... "

"This is a higher continuum. There's a natural process of energy from lower to higher regions. But the reverse process is risky. The blood — it's a sort of guide to follow — a bright marker."

"Like moths around a light bulb," Rick said bitterly.

"If they send me back and something goes wrong — " She broke off and then continued, "If they make a mistake, I might be lost between the two regions. I might be absorbed by the free energy. It seems to be partly alive. It's not understood. Remember Prometheus and the fire ... "

"I see," Rick said, as calmly as he could.

"Darling, if they try to send me back, I'll have to find some shape to enter. You see, I don't exactly have a shape any more. There's no real material form on this side. What you see, the wings and the whiteness, are not really there. If I succeeded in making the trip back to your side ... "

"You'd have to mold something," Rick said.

"I'd have to take something there — something of clay. I'd have to enter it and reshape it. As He did a long time ago, when the original form was put on your world."

"If they did it once, they can do it again."

"The One who did that is gone. He passed on upward." There was unhappy irony in her voice. "There are regions beyond this. The ladder doesn't stop here. Nobody knows where it ends, it just seems to keep on going up and up. World after world."

"Who decides about you?" Rick demanded.

"It's up to me," Silvia said faintly. "They say, if I want to take the chance, they'll try it."

"What do you think you'll do?" he asked.

"I'm afraid. What if something goes wrong? You haven't seen it, the region between. The possibilities there are incredible — they terrify me. He was the only one with enough courage. Everyone else has been afraid."

"It was their fault. They have to take responsibility."

"They know that." Silvia hesitated miserably. "Rick, darling, please tell me what to do."

"Come back!"

Silence. Then her voice, thin and pathetic. "All right, Rick. If you think that's the right thing."

"It is," he said firmly. He forced his mind not to think, not to picture or imagine anything. *He had to have her back.* "Tell them to get started now. Tell them — "

A deafening crack of heat burst in front of him. He was lifted up and tossed into a flaming sea of pure energy. They were leaving and the scalding lake of sheer power bellowed and thundered around him. For a split second he thought he glimpsed Silvia, her hands reaching imploringly towards him.

Then the fire cooled and he lay blinded in dripping, night-moistened darkness. Alone in the silence.

Walter Everett was helping him up. "You damn fool!" he was saying, again and again. "You shouldn't have brought them back. They've got enough from us."

Then he was in the big, warm living room. Mrs. Everett stood silently in front of him, her face hard and expressionless. The two daughters hovered anxiously around him, fluttering and curious, eyes wide with morbid fascination.

"I'll be all right," Rick muttered. His clothing was charred and blacked. He rubbed black ash from his face. Bits of dried grass stuck to his hair — they had seared a circle around him as they'd ascended. He lay back against the couch and closed his eyes. When he opened them, Betty Lou Everett was forcing a glass of water into his hands.

"Thanks," he muttered.

"You should never have gone out there," Walter Everett repeated. "Why? Why'd you do it? You know what happened to her. You want the same thing to happen to you?"

"I want her back," Rick said quietly.

"Are you mad? You can't get her back. She's gone." His lips twitched convulsively. "You saw her."

Betty Lou was gazing at Rick intently. "What happened out there?" she demanded. "You saw her."

Rick got heavily to his feet and left the living room. In the kitchen he emptied the water in the sink and poured himself a drink. While he was leaning wearily against the sink, Betty Lou appeared in the doorway.

"What do you want?" Rick demanded.

The girl's face was flushed an unhealthy red. "I know something happened out there. You were feeding them, weren't you?" She advanced towards him. "You're trying to get her back?"

"That's right," Rick said.

Betty Lou giggled nervously. "But you can't. She's dead — her body's been cremated — I saw it." Her face worked excitedly. "Daddy always said that something bad would happen to her, and it did." She leaned close to Rick. "She was a witch! She got what she deserved!"

"She's coming back," Rick said.

"*No!*" Panic stirred the girl's drab features. "She *can't* come back. She's dead — like she always said — worm into butterfly — she's a butterfly!"

"Go inside," Rick said.

"You can't order me around," Betty Lou answered. Her voice rose hysterically. "This is *my* house. We don't want you around here any more. Daddy's going to tell you. He doesn't want you and I don't want you and my mother and sister . . . "

The change came without warning. Like a film gone dead, Betty Lou froze, her mouth half open, one arm raised, her words dead on her tongue. She was suspended, an instantly lifeless thing raised off the floor, as if caught between two slides of glass. A vacant insect, without speech or sound, inert and hollow. Not dead, but abruptly thinned back to primordial inanimacy.

Into the captured shell filtered new potency and being. It settled over her, a rainbow of life that poured into place eagerly — like hot fluid — into every part of her. The girl stumbled and moaned; her body jerked violently and pitched against the wall. A china teacup tumbled from an overhead shelf and smashed on the floor. The girl retreated numbly, one hand to her mouth, her eyes wide with pain and shock.

"Oh!" she gasped. "I cut myself." She shook her head and gazed up mutely at him, appealing to him. "On a nail or something."

"*Silvia!*" He caught hold of her and dragged her to her feet, away from the wall. It was *her* arm he gripped, warm and full and mature. Stunned gray eyes, brown hair, quivering breasts — she was now as she had been those last moments in the basement.

"Let's see it," he said. He tore her hand from her mouth and shakily examined her finger. There was no cut, only a thin white line rapidly dimming. "It's all right, honey. You're all right. There's nothing wrong with you!"

"Rick, I was over *there*." Her voice was husky and faint. "They came and dragged me across with them." She shuddered violently. "Rick, am I actually *back?*"

He crushed her tight. "Completely back."

"It was so long. I was over there a century. Endless ages. I thought — " Suddenly she pulled away. "Rick . . . "

"What is it?"

Silvia's face was wild with fear. "There's something wrong."

"There's nothing wrong. You've come back home and that's all that matters."

Silvia retreated from him. "But they took a living form, didn't they? Not discarded clay. They don't have the power, Rick. They altered His work instead." Her voice rose in panic. "A mistake — they should have known better than to alter the balance. It's unstable and none of them can control the . . . "

Rick blocked the doorway. "Stop talking like that!" he said fiercely. "It's worth it — *anything's* worth it. If they set things out of balance, it's their own fault."

"We can't turn it back!" Her voice rose shrilly, thin and hard, like drawn wire. "We've set it in motion, started the waves lapping out. The balance He set up is *altered*."

"Come on, darling," Rick said. "Let's go and sit in the living room with your family. You'll feel better. You'll have to try to recover from this."

They approached the three seated figures, two on the couch, one in the straight chair by the fireplace. The figures sat motionless, their faces blank, their bodies limp and waxen, dulled forms that did not respond as the couple entered the room.

Rick halted, uncomprehending. Walter Everett was slumped forward, newspaper in one hand, slippers on his feet; his pipe was still smoking in the deep ashtray on the arm of his chair. Mrs. Everett sat with a lapful of sewing, her face grim and stern, but strangely vague. An unformed face, as if the material were melting and running together. Jean sat huddled in a shapeless heap, a ball of clay wadded up, more formless each moment.

Abruptly Jean collapsed. Her arms fell loose beside her. Her head sagged. Her body, her arms and legs filled out. Her features altered rapidly. Her clothing changed. Colors flowed in her hair, her eyes, her skin. The waxen pallor was gone.

Pressing her fingers to her lips she gazed up at Rick mutely. She blinked and her eyes focused. "Oh," she gasped. Her lips moved awkwardly; the voice was faint and uneven, like a poor soundtrack. She struggled up jerkily, with uncoordinated movements that propelled her stiffly to her feet and towards him — one awkward step at a time — like a wire dummy.

"Rick, I cut myself," she said. "On a nail or something."

What had been Mrs. Everett stirred. Shapeless and vague, it made dull sounds and flopped grotesquely. Gradually it hardened and shaped itself. "My finger," its voice gasped feebly. Like mirror echoes dimming off into darkness, the third figure in the easy chair took up the words. Soon, they were all of them repeating the phrase, four fingers, their lips moving in unison.

"My finger. I cut myself, Rick."

Parrot reflections, receding mimicries of words and movement. And the settling shapes were familiar in every detail. Again and again, repeated around him, twice on the couch, in the easy chair, close beside him — so close he could hear her breath and see her trembling lips.

"What is it?" the Silvia beside him asked.

On the couch one Silvia resumed its sewing — she was sewing methodically, absorbed in her work. In the deep chair another took up its newspapers, its pipe and continued reading. One huddled, nervous and afraid. The one beside him followed as he retreated to the door. She was panting with uncertainty, her gray eyes wide, her nostrils flaring.

"Rick ... "

He pulled the door open and made his way out onto the dark porch. Machine-like, he felt his way down the steps, through the pools of night collected everywhere, toward the driveway. In the yellow square of light behind him, Silvia was outlined, peering unhappily after him. And behind her, the other figures, identical, pure repetitions, nodding over their tasks.

He found his coupe and pulled out onto the road.

Gloomy trees and houses flashed past. He wondered how far it would go. Lapping waves spreading out — a widening circle as the imbalance spread.

He turned onto the main highway; there were soon more cars around him. He tried to see into them, but they moved too swiftly. The car ahead was a red Plymouth. A heavyset man in a blue business suit was driving, laughing merrily with the woman beside him. He pulled his own coupe up close behind the Plymouth and followed it. The man flashed gold teeth, grinned, waved his plump hands. The girl was dark-haired, pretty. She smiled at the man, adjusted her white gloves, smoothed down her hair, then rolled up the window on her side.

He lost the Plymouth. A heavy diesel truck cut in between them. Desperately he swerved around the truck and nosed in beyond the swift-moving red sedan. Presently it passed him and, for a moment, the two occupants were clearly framed. The girl resembled Silvia. The same delicate line of her small chin — the same deep lips, parting slightly when she smiled — the same slender arms and hands. It was Silvia. The Plymouth turned off and there was no other car ahead of him.

He drove for hours through the heavy night darkness. The gas gauge dropped lower and lower. Ahead of him dismal rolling countryside spread out, blank fields between towns and unwinking stars suspended in the bleak sky. Once, a cluster of red and yellow lights gleamed. An intersection — filling stations and a big neon sign. He drove on past it.

At a single-pump stand, he pulled the car off the highway, onto the oil-soaked gravel. He climbed out, his shoes crunching the stone underfoot, as he grabbed the gas hose and unscrewed the cap of his car's tank. He had the tank almost full when the door of the drab station building opened and a slim woman in white overalls and navy shirt, with a little cap lost in her brown curls, stepped out.

"Good evening, Rick," she said quietly.

He put back the gas hose. Then he was driving out onto the highway. Had he screwed the cap back on again? He didn't remember. He gained speed. He had gone over a hundred miles. He was nearing the state line.

At a little roadside cafe, warm, yellow light glowed in the chill gloom of early morning. He slowed the car down and parked at the edge of the highway in the deserted parking lot. Bleary-eyed he pushed the door open and entered.

Hot, thick smells of cooking ham and black coffee surrounded him, the comfortable sight of people eating. A jukebox blared in the corner. He threw himself onto a stool and hunched over, his head in his hands. A thin farmer next to him glanced at him curiously and then returned to his newspaper. Two hard-faced women across from him gazed at him momentarily. A handsome youth in denim jacket and jeans was eating red beans and rice, washing it down with steaming coffee from a heavy mug.

"What'll it be?" the pert blonde waitress asked, a pencil behind her ear, her hair tied back in a tight bun. "Looks like you've got some hangover, mister."

He ordered coffee and vegetable soup. Soon he was eating, his hands working automatically. He found himself devouring a ham and cheese sandwich; had he ordered it? The jukebox blared and people came and went. There was a little town sprawled beside the road, set back in some gradual hills. Gray sunlight, cold and sterile, filtered down as morning came. He ate hot apple pie and sat wiping dully at his mouth with a napkin.

The cafe was silent. Outside nothing stirred. An uneasy calm hung over everything. The jukebox had ceased. None of the people at the counter stirred or spoke. An occasional truck roared past, damp and lumbering, windows rolled up tight.

When he looked up, Silvia was standing in front of him. Her arms were folded and she gazed vacantly past him. A bright yellow pencil was behind her ear. Her brown hair was tied back in a hard bun. At the corner others were sitting, other Silvias, dishes in front of them, half dozing or eating, some of them reading. Each the same as the next, except for their clothing.

He made his way back to his parked car. In half an hour he had crossed the state line. Cold, bright sunlight sparkled off dew-moist roofs and pavements as he sped through tiny unfamiliar towns.

Along the shiny morning streets he saw them moving — early risers, on their way to work. In twos and threes they walked, their heels echoing in sharp silence. At bus stops he saw groups of them collected together. In the houses, rising from their beds, eating breakfast, bathing, dressing, were more of them — hundreds of them, legions without number. A town of them preparing for the day, resuming their regular tasks, as the circle widened and spread.

He left the town behind. The car slowed under him as his foot slid heavily from the gas pedal. Two of them walked across a level field together. They carried books — children on their way to school. Repetition, unvarying and identical. A dog circled excitedly after them, unconcerned, his joy untainted.

He drove on. Ahead a city loomed, its stern columns of office buildings sharply outlined against the sky. The streets swarmed with noise and activity as he passed through the main business section. Somewhere, near the center of the city, he overtook the expanding periphery of the circle and emerged beyond. Diversity took the place of the endless figures of Silvia. Gray eyes and brown hair gave way to countless varieties of men and women, children and adults, of all ages and appearances. He increased his speed and raced out on the far side, onto the wide four-lane highway.

He finally slowed down. He was exhausted. He had driven for hours; his body was shaking with fatigue.

Ahead of him a carrot-haired youth was cheerfully thumbing a ride, a thin bean-pole in brown slacks and light camel's-hair sweater. Rick pulled to a halt and opened the front door. "Hop in," he said.

"Thanks, buddy." The youth hurried to the car and climbed in as Rick gathered speed. He slammed the door and settled gratefully back against the seat. "It was getting hot, standing there."

"How far are you going?" Rick demanded.

"All the way to Chicago." The youth grinned shyly. "Of course, I don't expect you to drive me that far. Anything at all is appreciated." He eyed Rick curiously. "Which way you going?"

"Anywhere," Rick said. "I'll drive you to Chicago."

"It's two hundred miles!"

"Fine," Rick said. He steered over into the left lane and gained speed. "If you want to go to New York, I'll drive you there."

"You feel all right?" The youth moved away uneasily. "I sure appreciate a lift, but ... " He hesitated. "I mean, I don't want to take you out of your way."

Rick concentrated on the road ahead, his hands gripping hard around the rim of the wheel. "I'm going fast. I'm not slowing down or stopping."

"You better be careful," the youth warned, in a troubled voice. "I don't want to get in an accident."

"I'll do the worrying."

"But it's dangerous. What if something happens? It's too risky."

"You're wrong," Rick muttered grimly, eyes on the road. "It's worth the risk."

"But if something goes wrong — " The voice broke off uncertainly and then continued, "I might be lost. It would be so easy. It's all so unstable." The voice trembled with worry and fear. "Rick, please ... "

Rick whirled. "How do you know my name?"

The youth was crouched in a heap against the door. His face had a soft, molten look, as if it were losing its shape and sliding together in an unformed mass. "I want to come back," he was saying, from within himself, "but I'm afraid. You haven't seen it — the region between. It's nothing but energy, Rick. He tapped it a long time ago, but nobody else knows how."

The voice lightened, became clear and treble. The hair faded to a rich brown. Gray, frightened eyes flickered up at Rick. Hands frozen, he hunched over the wheel and forced himself not to move. Gradually he decreased speed and brought the car over into the right-hand lane.

"Are we stopping?" the shape beside him asked. It was Silvia's voice now. Like a new insect, drying in the sun, the shape hardened and locked into firm reality. Silvia struggled up on the seat and peered out. "Where are we? We're between towns."

He jammed on the brakes, reached past her and threw open the door. "Get out!"

Silvia gazed at him uncomprehendingly. "What do you mean?" she faltered. "Rick, what is it? What's wrong?"

"*Get out!*"

"Rick, I don't understand." She slid over a little. Her toes touched the pavement. "Is there something wrong with the car? I thought everything was all right."

He gently shoved her out and slammed the door. The car leaped ahead, out into the stream of mid-morning traffic. Behind him the small, dazed figure was pulling itself up, bewildered and injured. He forced his eyes from the rearview mirror and crushed down the gas pedal with all his weight.

The radio buzzed and clicked in vague static when he snapped it briefly on. He turned the dial and, after a time, a big network station came in. A faint, puzzled voice, a woman's voice. For a time he couldn't make out the words. Then he recognized it and, with a pang of panic, switched the thing off.

Her voice. Murmuring plaintively. Where was the station? Chicago. The circle had already spread that far.

He slowed down. There was no point hurrying. It had already passed him by and gone on. Kansas farms — sagging stores in little old Mississippi towns — along the bleak streets of New England manufacturing cities swarms of brown-haired gray-eyed women would be hurrying.

It would cross the ocean. Soon it would take in the whole world. Africa would be strange — kraals of white-skinned young women, all exactly alike, going about the primitive chores of hunting and fruit-gathering, mashing grain, skinning animals. Building fires and weaving cloth and carefully shaping razor-sharp knives.

In China ... he grinned inanely. She'd look strange there, too. In the austere high-collar suit, the almost monastic robe of the young communist cadres. Parade marching up the main streets of Peiping. Row after row of slim-legged full-breasted girls, with heavy Russian-made rifles. Carrying spades, picks, shovels. Columns of cloth-booted soldiers. Fast-moving workers with their precious tools. Reviewed by an identical figure on the elaborate stand overlooking the street, one slender arm raised, her gentle, pretty face expressionless and wooden.

He turned off the highway onto a side road. A moment later he was on his way back, driving slowly, listlessly, the way he had come.

At an intersection a traffic cop waded out through traffic to his car. He sat rigid, hands on the wheel, waiting numbly.

"Rick" she whispered pleadingly as she reached the window. "Isn't everything all right?"

"Sure," he answered dully.

She reached in through the open window and touched him imploringly on the arm. Familiar fingers, red nails, the hand he knew so well. "I want to be with you so badly. Aren't we together again? Aren't I back?"

"Sure."

She shook her head miserably. "I don't understand," she repeated. "I thought it was all right again."

Savagely he put the car into motion and hurtled ahead. The intersection was left behind.

It was afternoon. He was exhausted, riddled with fatigue. He guided the car towards his own town automatically. Along the streets she hurried everywhere, on all sides. She was omnipresent. He came to his apartment building and parked.

The janitor greeted him in the empty hall. Rick identified him by the greasy rag clutched in one hand, the big push-broom, the bucket of wood shavings. "Please," she implored, "tell me what it is, Rick. Please tell me."

He pushed past her, but she caught at him desperately. "Rick, *I'm back.* Don't you understand? They took me too soon and then they sent me back again. It was a mistake. I won't ever call them again — that's all in the past." She followed after him, down the hall to the stairs. "I'm never going to call them again."

He climbed the stairs. Silvia hesitated, then settled down on the bottom step in a wretched, unhappy heap, a tiny figure in thick workman's clothing and huge cleated boots.

He unlocked his apartment door and entered.

The late afternoon sky was a deep blue beyond the windows. The roofs of nearby apartment buildings sparkled white in the sun.

His body ached. He wandered clumsily into the bathroom — it seemed alien and unfamiliar, a difficult place to find. He filled the bowl with hot water, rolled up his sleeves and washed his face and hands in the swirling hot stream. Briefly, he glanced up.

It was a terrified reflection that showed out of the mirror above the bowl, a face, tear-stained and frantic. The face was difficult to catch — it seemed to waver and slide. Gray eyes, bright with terror. Trembling red mouth, pulse-fluttering throat, soft brown hair. The face gazed out pathetically — and then the girl at the bowl bent to dry herself.

She turned and moved wearily out of the bathroom into the living room.

Confused, she hesitated, then threw herself onto a chair and closed her eyes, sick with misery and fatigue.

"Rick," she murmured pleadingly. "Try to help me. I'm back, aren't I?" She shook her head, bewildered. "Please, Rick, I thought everything was all right."

FOSTER, YOU'RE DEAD

SCHOOL WAS AGONY, as always. Only today it was worse. Mike Foster finished weaving his two watertight baskets and sat rigid, while all around him the other children worked. Outside the concrete-and-steel building the late-afternoon sun shone cool. The hills sparkled green and brown in the crisp autumn air. In the overhead sky a few NATS circled lazily above the town.

The vast, ominous shape of Mrs. Cummings, the teacher, silently approached his desk. "Foster, are you finished?"

"Yes, ma'am," he answered eagerly. He pushed the baskets up. "Can I leave now?"

Mrs. Cummings examined his baskets critically. "What about your trap-making?" she demanded.

He fumbled in his desk and brought out his intricate small-animal trap. "All finished, Mrs. Cummings. And my knife, it's done, too." He showed her the razor-edged blade of his knife, glittering metal he had shaped from a discarded gasoline drum. She picked up the knife and ran her expert finger doubtfully along the blade.

"Not strong enough," she stated. "You've oversharpened it. It'll lose its edge the first time you use it. Go down to the main weapons-lab and examine the knives they've got there. Then hone it back some and get a thicker blade."

"Mrs. Cummings," Mike Foster pleased, "could I fix it *tomorrow*? Could I leave right now, please?"

Everybody in the classroom was watching with interest. Mike Foster flushed; he hated to be singled out and made conspicuous, but he *had* to get away. He couldn't stay in school one minute more.

Inexorable, Mrs. Cummings rumbled, "Tomorrow is digging day. You won't have time to work on your knife."

"I will," he assured her quickly. "After the digging."

"No, you're not too good at digging." The old woman was measuring the boy's spindly arms and legs. "I think you better get your knife finished today. And spend all day tomorrow down at the field."

"What's the use of digging?" Mike Foster demanded, in despair.

"Everybody has to know how to dig," Mrs. Cummings answered patiently. Children were snickering on all sides; she shushed them with a hostile glare. "You all know the importance of digging. When the war begins the whole surface will be littered with debris and rubble. If we hope to survive we'll have to dig down, won't we? Have any of you ever watched a gopher digging around the roots of plants? The gopher knows he'll find something valuable down there under the surface of the ground. We're all going to be little brown gophers. We'll all have to learn to dig down in the rubble and find the good things, because that's where they'll be."

Mike Foster sat miserably plucking his knife, as Mrs. Cummings moved away from his desk and up the aisle. A few children grinned contemptuously at him, but nothing penetrated his haze of wretchedness. Digging wouldn't do him any good. When the bombs came he'd be killed instantly. All the vaccination shots up and down his arms, on his thighs and buttocks, would be of no use. He had wasted his allowance money: Mike Foster wouldn't be alive to catch any of the bacterial plagues. Not unless —

He sprang up and followed Mrs. Cummings to her desk. In an agony of desperation he blurted, "Please, I have to leave. I have to do something."

Mrs. Cumming's tired lips twisted angrily. But the boy's fearful eyes stopped her. "What's wrong?" she demanded. "Don't you feel well?"

The boy stood frozen, unable to answer her. Pleased by the tableau, the class murmured and giggled until Mrs. Cummings rapped angrily on her desk with a writer. "Be quiet," she snapped. Her voice softened a shade. "Michael, if you're not functioning properly, go downstairs to the psyche clinic. There's no point trying to work when your reactions are conflicted. Miss Groves will be glad to optimum you."

"No," Foster said.

"Then what is it?"

The class stirred. Voices answered for Foster; his tongue was stuck with misery and humiliation. "His father's an anti-P," the voices explained. "They don't have a shelter and he isn't registered in Civic Defense. His father hasn't even contributed to the NATS. They haven't done anything."

Mrs. Cummings gazed up in amazement at the mute boy. "You don't have a shelter?"

He shook his head.

A strange feeling filled the woman. "But — " She had started to say, *But you'll die up here.* She changed it to "But where'll you go?"

"Nowhere," the mild voices answered for him. "Everybody else'll be down in their shelters and he'll be up here. He even doesn't have a permit for the school shelter."

Mrs. Cummings was shocked. In her dull, scholastic way she had assumed every child in the school had a permit to the elaborate subsurface chambers under the building. But of course not. Only children whose parents were part of CD, who contributed to arming the community. And if Foster's father was an anti-P . . .

"He's afraid to sit here," the voices chimed in calmly. "He's afraid it'll come while he's sitting here, and everybody else will be safe down in the shelter."

He wandered slowly along, hands deep in his pockets, kicking at dark stones on the sidewalk. The sun was setting. Snub-nosed commute rockets were unloading tired people, glad to be home from the factory strip a hundred miles to the west. On the distant hills something flashed: a radar tower revolving silently in the evening gloom. The circling NATS had increased in number. The twilight hours were the most dangerous; visual observers couldn't spot high-speed missiles coming in close to the ground. Assuming the missiles came.

A mechanical news-machine shouted at him excitedly as he passed. War, death, amazing new weapons developed at home and abroad. He hunched his shoulders and continued on, past the little concrete shells that served as houses, each exactly alike, sturdy reinforced pillboxes. Ahead of him bright neon signs glowed in the settling gloom: the business district, alive with traffic and milling people.

Half a block from the bright cluster of neons he halted. To his right was a public shelter, a dark tunnel-like entrance with a mechanical turnstile glowing dully. Fifty cents admission. If he was here, on the street, and he had fifty cents, he'd be all right. He had pushed down into public shelters many times, during the practice raids. But other times, hideous, nightmare times that never left his mind, he hadn't had the fifty cents. He had stood mute and terrified, while people pushed excitedly past him; and the shrill shrieks of the sirens thundered everywhere.

He continued slowly, until he came to the brightest blotch of light, the great, gleaming showrooms of General Electronics, two blocks long, illuminated on all sides, a vast square of pure color and radiation. He halted and examined for the millionth time the fascinating shapes, the display that always drew him to a hypnotized stop whenever he passed.

In the center of the vast room was a single object. An elaborate pulsing blob of machinery and support struts, beams and walls and sealed locks. All spotlights were turned on it; huge signs announced its hundred and one advantages — as if there could be any doubt.

THE NEW 1972 BOMBPROOF RADIATION-SEALED
SUBSURFACE SHELTER IS HERE! CHECK THESE
STAR-STUDDED FEATURES:
* automatic descent-lift — jam-proof, self-powered, e-z locking
* triple-layer hull guaranteed to withstand 5*g* pressure without buckling
* A-powered heating and refrigeration system — self-servicing air-purification network
* three decontamination stages for food and water
* four hygienic stages for pre-burn exposure
* complete antibiotic processing
* e-z payment plan

He gazed at the shelter a long time. It was mostly a big tank, with a neck at one end that was the descent tube, and an emergency escape-hatch at the other. It was completely self-contained: a miniature world that supplied its own light, heat, air, water, medicines, and almost inexhaustible food. When fully stocked there were visual and audio tapes, entertainment, beds, chairs, vidscreen, everything that made up the above-surface home. It was, actually, a home below the ground. Nothing was missing that might be needed or enjoyed. A family would be safe, even comfortable, during the most severe H-bomb and bacterial-spray attack.

It cost twenty thousand dollars.

While he was gazing silently at the massive display, one of the salesmen stepped out onto the dark sidewalk, on his way to the cafeteria. "Hi, sonny," he said automatically, as he passed Mike Foster. "Not bad, is it?"

"Can I go inside?" Foster asked quickly. "Can I go down in it?"

The salesman stopped, as he recognized the boy. "You're that kid," he said slowly, "that damn kid who's always pestering us."

"I'd like to go down in it. Just for a couple minutes. I won't bust anything — I promise. I won't even touch anything."

The salesman was young and blond, a good-looking man in his early twenties. He hesitated, his reactions divided. The kid was a pest. But he had a family, and that meant a reasonable prospect. Business was bad; it was late September and the seasonal slump was still on. There was no profit in telling the boy to go peddle his newstapes; but on the other hand it was bad business encouraging small fry to crawl around the merchandise. They wasted time; they broke things; they pilfered small stuff when nobody was looking.

"No dice," the salesman said. "Look, send your old man down here. Has he seen what we've got?"

"Yes," Mike Foster said tightly.

"What's holding him back?" The salesman waved expansively up at the great gleaming display. "We'll give him a good trade-in on his old one, allowing for depreciation and obsolescence. What model has he got?"

"We don't have any," Mike Foster said.

The salesman blinked. "Come again?"

"My father says it's a waste of money. He says they're trying to scare people into buying things they don't need. He says — "

"Your father's an anti-P?"

"Yes," Mike Foster answered unhappily.

The salesman let out his breath. "Okay, kid. Sorry we can't do business. It's not your fault." He lingered. "What the hell's wrong with him? Does he put on the NATS?"

"No."

The salesman swore under his breath. A coaster, sliding along, safe because the rest of the community was putting up thirty per cent of its income to keep a constant-defense system going. There were always a few of them, in every town. "How's your mother feel?" the salesman demanded. "She go along with him?"

"She says — " Mike Foster broke off. "Couldn't I go down in it for a little while? I won't bust anything. Just *once*."

"How'd we ever sell it if we let kids run through it? We're not marking it down as a demonstration model — we've got roped into that too often." The salesman's curiosity was aroused. "How's a guy get to be anti-P? He always feel this way, or did he get stung with something?"

"He says they sold people as many cars and washing machines and television sets as they could use. He says NATS and bomb shelters aren't good for anything, so people never get all they can use. He says factories can keep turning out guns and gas masks forever, and as long as people are afraid they'll keep paying for them because they think if they don't they might get killed, and maybe a man gets tired of paying for a new car every year and stops, but he's never going to stop buying shelters to protect his children."

"You believe that?" the salesman asked.

"I wish we had that shelter," Mike Foster answered. "If we had a shelter like that I'd go down and sleep in it every night. It'd be there when we needed it."

"Maybe there won't be a war," the salesman said. He sensed the boy's misery and fear, and he grinned good-naturedly down at him. "Don't worry all the time. You probably watch too many vidtapes — get out and play, for a change."

"Nobody's safe on the surface," Mike Foster said. "We have to be down below. And there's no place I can go."

"Send your old man around," the salesman muttered uneasily. "Maybe we can talk him into it. We've got a lot of time-payment plans. Tell him to ask for Bill O'Neill. Okay?"

Mike Foster wandered away, down the black evening street. He knew he was supposed to be home, but his feet dragged and his body was heavy and dull. His fatigue made him remember what the athletic coach had said the day before, during exercises. They were practicing breath suspension, holding a lungful of air and running. He hadn't done well; the others were still redfaced and racing when he halted, expelled his air, and stood gasping frantically for breath.

"Foster," the coach said angrily, "you're dead. You know that? If this had been a gas attack — " He shook his head wearily. "Go over there and practice by yourself. You've got to do better, if you expect to survive."

But he didn't expect to survive.

When he stepped up onto the porch of his home, he found the living room lights already on. He could hear his father's voice, and more faintly his mother's from the kitchen. He closed the door after him and began unpeeling his coat.

"Is that you?" his father demanded. Bob Foster sat sprawled out in his chair, his lap full of tapes and report sheets from his retail furniture store. "Where have you been? Dinner's been ready half an hour." He had taken off his coat and rolled up his sleeves. His arms were pale and thin, but muscular. He was tired; his eyes were large and dark, his hair thinning. Restlessly, he moved the tapes around, from one stack to another.

"I'm sorry," Mike Foster said.

His father examined his pocket watch; he was surely the only man who still carried a watch. "Go wash our hands. What have you been doing?" He scrutinized his son. "You look odd. Do you feel all right?"

"I was downtown," Mike Foster said.

"What were you doing?"

"Looking at the shelters."

Wordless, his father grabbed up a handful of reports and stuffed them into a folder. His thin lips set; hard lines wrinkled his forehead. He snorted furiously as tapes spilled everywhere; he bent stiffly to pick them up. Mike Foster made no move to help him. He crossed to the closet and gave his coat to the hanger. When he turned away his mother was directing the table of food into the dining room.

They ate without speaking, intent on their food and not looking at each other. Finally his father said, "What'd you see? Same old dogs, I suppose."

"There's the new '72 models," Mike Foster answered.

"They're the same as the '71 models." His father threw down his fork savagely; the table caught and absorbed it. "A few new gadgets, some more chrome. That's all." Suddenly he was facing his son defiantly. "Right?"

Mike Foster toyed wretchedly with his creamed chicken. "The new ones have a jam-proof descent lift. You can't get stuck halfway down. All you have to do is get in it, and it does the rest."

"There'll be one next year that'll pick you up and carry you down. This one'll be obsolete as soon as people buy it. That's what they want — they want you to keep buying. They keep putting out new ones as fast as they can. This isn't 1972, it's still 1971. What's that thing doing out already? Can't they wait?"

Mike Foster didn't answer. He had heard it all before, many times. There was never anything new, only chrome and gadgets; yet the old ones became obsolete, anyhow. His father's argument was loud, impassioned, almost frenzied, but it made no sense. "Let's get an old one, then," he blurted out. "I don't care, any one'll do. Even a secondhand one."

"No, you want the *new* one. Shiny and glittery to impress the neighbors. Lots of dials and knobs and machinery. How much do they want for it?"

"Twenty thousand dollars."

His father let his breath out. "Just like that."

"They've easy time-payment plans."

"Sure. You pay for it the rest of your life. Interest, carrying charges, and how long is it guaranteed for?"

"Three months."

"What happens when it breaks down? It'll stop purifying and decontaminating. It'll fall apart as soon as the three months are over."

Mike Foster shook his head. "No. It's big and sturdy."

His father flushed. He was a small man, slender and light, brittle-boned. He thought suddenly of his lifetime of lost battles, struggling up the hard way, carefully collecting and holding on to something, a job, money, his retail store, bookkeeper to manager, finally owner. "They're scaring us to keep the wheels going," he yelled desperately at his wife and son. "They don't want another depression."

"Bob," his wife said, slowly and quietly, "you have to stop this. I can't stand any more."

Bob Foster blinked. "What're you talking about?" he muttered. "I'm tired. These goddamn taxes. It isn't possible for a little store to keep open, not with the big chains. There ought to be a law." His voice trailed off. "I guess I'm through eating." He pushed away from the table and got to his feet. "I'm going to lie down on the couch and take a nap."

His wife's thin face blazed. "You have to get one! I can't stand the way they talk about us. All the neighbors and the merchants, everybody who knows. I can't go anywhere or do anything without hearing about it. Ever since that day they put up the flag. *Anti-P.* The last in the whole town. Those things circling around up there, and everybody paying for them but us."

"No," Bob Foster said. "I can't get one."

"Why not?"

"Because," he answered simply, "I can't afford it."

There was silence.

"You've put everything in that store," Ruth said finally. "And it's failing anyhow. You're just like a pack-rat, hoarding everything down at that ratty little hole-in-the-wall. Nobody wants wood furniture anymore. You're a relic — a curiosity." She slammed at the table and it leaped wildly to gather the empty dishes, like a startled animal. It dashed furiously from the room and back into the kitchen, the dishes churning in its washtank as it raced.

Bob Foster sighed wearily. "Let's not fight. I'll be in the living room. Let me take a nap for an hour or so. Maybe we can talk about it later."

"Always later," Ruth said bitterly.

Her husband disappeared into the living room, a small, hunched-over figure, hair scraggly and gray, shoulder blades like broken wings.

Mike got to his feet. "I'll go study my homework," he said. He followed after his father, a strange look on his face.

The living room was quiet; the vidset was off and the lamp was down low. Ruth was in the kitchen setting the controls on the stove for the next month's meals. Bob Foster lay stretched out on the couch, his shoes off, his head on a pillow. His face was gray with fatigue. Mike hesitated for a moment and then said, "Can I ask you something?"

His father grunted and stirred, opened his eyes. "What?"

Mike sat down facing him. "Tell me again how you gave advice to the President."

His father pulled himself up. "I didn't give any advice to the President. I just talked to him."

"Tell me about it."

"I've told you a million times. Every once in a while, since you were a baby. You were with me." His voice softened, as he remembered. "You were just a toddler — we had to carry you."

"What did he look like?"

"Well," his father began, slipping into a routine he had worked out and petrified over the years, "he looked about like he does in the vidscreen. Smaller, though."

"Why was he here?" Mike demanded avidly, although he knew every detail. The President was his hero, the man he most admired in all the world. "Why'd he come all the way out here to *our* town?"

"He was on a tour." Bitterness crept into his father's voice. "He happened to be passing through."

"What kind of a tour?"

"Visiting towns all over the country." The harshness increased. "Seeing how we were getting along. Seeing if we had bought enough NATS and bomb shelters and plague shots and gas masks and radar networks to repel attack. The General Electronics Corporation was just beginning to put up its big showrooms and displays — everything bright and glittering and expensive. The first defense equipment available for home purchase." His lips twisted.

"All on easy-payment plans. Ads, posters, searchlights, free gardenias and dishes for the ladies."

Mike Foster's breath panted in his throat. "That was the day we got our Preparedness Flag," he said hungrily. "That was the day he came to give us our flag. And they ran it up on the flagpole in the middle of the town, and everybody was there yelling and cheering."

"You remember that?"

"I — think so. I remember people and sounds. And it was hot. It was June, wasn't it?"

"June 10, 1965. Quite an occasion. Not many towns had the big green flag, then. People were still buying cars and TV sets. They hadn't discovered those days were over. TV sets and cars are good for something — you can only manufacture and sell so many of them."

"He gave *you* the flag, didn't he?"

"Well, he gave it to all us merchants. The Chamber of Commerce had it arranged. Competition between towns, see who can buy the most the soonest. Improve our town and at the same time stimulate business. Of course, the way they put it, the idea was if we had to *buy* our gas masks and bomb shelters we'd take better care of them. As if we ever damaged telephones and sidewalks. Or highways, because the whole state provided them. Or armies. Haven't there always been armies? Hasn't the government always organized its people for defense? I guess defense costs too much. I guess they save a lot of money, cut down the national debt by this."

"Tell me what he said," Mike Foster whispered.

His father fumbled for his pipe and lit it with trembling hands. "He said, '*Here's your flag, boys. You've done a good job.*' " Bob Foster choked, as acrid pipe fumes guzzled up. "He was red-faced, sunburned, not embarrassed. Perspiring and grinning. He knew how to handle himself. He knew a lot of first names. Told a funny joke."

The boy's eyes were wide with awe. "He came all the way out here, and you talked to him."

"Yeah," his father said. "I talked to him. They were all yelling and cheering. The flag was going up, the big green Preparedness Flag."

"You said — "

"I said to him, '*Is that all you brought us? A strip of green cloth?*' " Bob Foster dragged tensely on his pipe. "That was when I became an anti-P. Only I didn't know it at the time. All I knew was we were on our own, except for a strip of green cloth. We should have been a country, a whole nation, one hundred and seventy million people working together to defend ourselves. And instead, we're a lot of separate little towns, little walled forts. Sliding and slipping back to the Middle Ages. Raising our separate armies — "

"Will the President ever come back?" Mike asked.

"I doubt it. He was — just passing through."

"If he comes back," Mike whispered, tense and not daring to hope, "can we go *see* him? Can we *look* at him?"

Bob Foster pulled himself up to a sitting position. His bony arms were bare and white; his lean face was drab with weariness. And resignation. "How much was the damn thing you saw?" he demanded hoarsely. "That bomb shelter?"

Mike's heart stopped beating. "Twenty thousand dollars."

"This is Thursday. I'll go down with you and your mother next Saturday." Bob Foster knocked out his smoldering, half-lit pipe. "I'll get it on the easy-payment plan. The fall buying season is coming up soon. I usually do good — people buy wood furniture for Christmas gifts." He got up abruptly from the couch. "Is it a deal?"

Mike couldn't answer; he could only nod.

"Fine," his father said, with desperate cheerfulness. "Now you won't have to go down and look at it in the window."

The shelter was installed — for an additional two hundred dollars — by a fast-working team of laborers in brown coats with the words GENERAL ELECTRONICS stitched across their backs. The back yard was quickly restored, dirt and shrubs spaded in place, the surface smoothed over, and the bill respectfully slipped under the front door. The lumbering delivery truck, now empty, clattered off down the street and the neighborhood was again silent.

Mike Foster stood with his mother and a small group of admiring neighbors on the back porch of the house. "Well," Mrs. Carlyle said finally, "now you've got a shelter. The best there is."

"That's right," Ruth Foster agreed. She was conscious of the people around her; it had been some time since so many had shown up at once. Grim satisfaction filled her gaunt frame, almost resentment. "It certainly makes a difference," she said harshly.

"Yes," Mr. Douglas from down the street agreed. "Now you have some place to go." He had picked up the thick book of instructions the laborers had left. "It says here you can stock it for a whole year. Live down there twelve months without coming up once." He shook his head admiringly. "Mine's an old '69 model. Good for only six months. I guess maybe — "

"It's still good enough for us," his wife cut in, but there was a longing wistfulness in her voice. "Can we go down and peek at it, Ruth? It's all ready, isn't it?"

Mike made a strangled noise and moved jerkily forward. His mother smiled understandingly. "He has to go down there first. He gets first look at it — it's really for him, you know."

Their arms folded against the chill September wind, the group of men and women stood waiting and watching, as the boy approached the neck of the shelter and halted a few steps in front of it.

He entered the shelter carefully, almost afraid to touch anything. The neck was big for him; it was built to admit a full grown man. As soon as his weight was on the descent lift it dropped beneath him. With a breathless *whoosh* it plummeted down the pitch-black tube to the body of the shelter. The lift slammed hard against its shock absorbers and the boy stumbled from it. The lift shot back to the surface, simultaneously sealing off the subsurface shelter, an impassable steel-and-plastic cork in the narrow neck.

Lights had come on around him automatically. The shelter was bare and empty; no supplies had yet been carried down. It smelled of varnish and motor grease: below him the generators were throbbing dully. His presence activated the purifying and decontamination systems; on the blank concrete wall meters and dials moved into sudden activity.

He sat down on the floor, knees drawn up, face solemn, eyes wide. There was no sound but that of the generators; the world above was completely cut off. He was in a little self-contained cosmos; everything needed was here — or would be here, soon: food, water, air, things to do. Nothing else was wanted. He could reach out and touch — whatever he needed. He could stay here forever, through all time, without stirring. Complete and entire. Not lacking, not fearing, with only the sound of the generators purring below him, and the sheer, ascetic walls around and above him on all sides, faintly warm, completely friendly, like a living container.

Suddenly he shouted, a loud jubilant shout that echoed and bounced from wall to wall. He was deafened by the reverberation. He shut his eyes tight and clenched his fists. Joy filled him. He shouted again — and let the roar of sound lap over him, his own voice reinforced by the near walls, close and hard and incredibly powerful.

The kids in school knew even before he showed up, the next morning. They greeted him as he approached, all of them grinning and nudging each other. "Is it true your folks got a new General Electronics Model S-72ft?" Earl Peters demanded.

"That's right," Mike answered. His heart swelled with a peaceful confidence he had never known. "Drop around," he said, as casually as he could. "I'll show it to you."

He passed on, conscious of their envious faces.

"Well, Mike," Mrs. Cummings said, as he was leaving the classroom at the end of the day. "How does it feel?"

He halted by her desk, shy and full of quiet pride. "It feels good," he admitted.

"Is your father contributing to the NATS?"

"Yes."

"And you've got a permit for our school shelter?"

He happily showed her the small blue seal clamped around his wrist. "He mailed a check to the city for everything. He said, 'As long as I've gone this far I might as well go the rest of the way.' "

"Now you have everything everybody else has." The elderly woman smiled across at him. "I'm glad of that. You're now a pro-P, except there's no such term. You're just — like everyone else."

The next day the news-machines shrilled out the news. The first revelation of the new Soviet bore-pellets.

Bob Foster stood in the middle of the living room, the newstape in his hands, his thin face flushed with fury and despair. "Goddamn it, it's a plot!" His voice rose in baffled frenzy. "We just bought the thing and now look. *Look!*" He shoved the tape at his wife. "You see? I told you!"

"I've seen it," Ruth said wildly. "I suppose you think the whole world was just waiting with you in mind. They're always improving weapons, Bob. Last week it was those grain-impregnation flakes. This week it's bore-pellets. You don't expect them to stop the wheels of progress because you finally broke down and bought a shelter, do you?"

The man and woman faced each other. "What the hell are we going to do?" Bob Foster asked quietly.

Ruth paced back into the kitchen. "I heard they were going to turn out adaptors."

"Adaptors! What do you mean?"

"So people won't have to buy new shelters. There was a commercial on the vidscreen. They're going to put some kind of metal grill on the market, as soon as the government approves it. They spread it over the ground and it intercepts the bore-pellets. It screens them, makes them explode on the surface, so they can't burrow down to the shelter."

"How much?"

"They didn't say."

Mike Foster sat crouched on the sofa, listening. He had heard the news at school. They were taking their test on berry-identification, examining encased samples of wild berries to distinguish the harmless ones from the toxic, when the bell had announced a general assembly. The principal read them the news about the bore-pellets and then gave a routine lecture on emergency treatment of a new variant of typhus, recently developed.

His parents were still arguing. "We'll have to get one," Ruth Foster said calmly. "Otherwise it won't make any difference whether we've got a shelter or not. The bore-pellets were specifically designed to penetrate the surface and seek out warmth. As soon as the Russians have them in production — "

"I'll get one," Bob Foster said. "I'll get an anti-pellet grill and whatever else they have. I'll buy everything they put on the market. I'll never stop buying."

"It's not as bad as that."

"You know, this game has one real advantage over selling people cars and TV sets. With something like this we *have* to buy. It isn't a luxury, something big and flashy to impress the neighbors, something we could do without. If we don't buy this we die. They always said the way to sell something was create anxiety in people. Create a sense of insecurity — tell them they smell bad or look funny. But this makes a joke out of deodorant and hair oil. You can't escape this. If you don't buy, *they'll kill you.* The perfect sales-pitch. Buy or die — new slogan. Have a shiny new General Electronics H-bomb shelter in your back yard or be slaughtered."

"Stop talking like that!" Ruth snapped.

Bob Foster threw himself down at the kitchen table. "All right. I give up. I'll go along with it."

"You'll get one? I think they'll be on the market by Christmas."

"Oh, yes," Foster said. "They'll be out by Christmas." There was a strange look on his face. "I'll buy one of the damn things for Christmas, and so will everybody else."

The GEC grill-screen adaptors were a sensation.

Mike Foster walked slowly along the crowd-packed December street, through the late-afternoon twilight. Adaptors glittered in every store window All shapes and sizes, for every kind of shelter. All prices, for every pocketbook. The crowds of people were gay and excited, typical Christmas crowds, shoving good-naturedly, loaded down with packages and heavy overcoats. The air was white with gusts of sweeping snow. Cars nosed cautiously along the jammed streets. Lights and neon displays, immense glowing store windows gleamed on all sides.

His own house was dark and silent. His parents weren't home yet. Both of them were down at the store working; business had been bad and his mother was taking the place of one of the clerks. Mike held his hand up to the code-key, and the front door let him in. The automatic furnace had kept the house warm and pleasant. He removed his coat and put away his schoolbooks.

He didn't stay in the house long. His heart pounding with excitement, he felt his way out the back door and started onto the back porch.

He forced himself to stop, turn around, and reenter the house. It was better if he didn't hurry things. He had worked out every moment of the process, from the first instant he saw the low hinge of the neck reared up hard and firm against the evening sky. He had made a fine art of it; there was no wasted motion. His procedure had been shaped, molded until it was a beautiful thing. The first overwhelming sense of *presence* as the neck of the shelter came around him. Then the blood-freezing rush of air as the descent-lift hurtled down all the way to the bottom.

And the grandeur of the shelter itself.

Every afternoon, as soon as he was home, he made his way down into it, below the surface, concealed and protected in its steel silence, as he had done since the first day. Now the chamber was full, not empty. Filled with endless cans of food, pillows, books, vidtapes, audio-tapes, prints on the walls, bright fabrics, textures and colors, even vases of flowers. The shelter was his place, where he crouched curled up, surrounded by everything he needed.

Delaying things as long as possible, he hurried back through the house and rummaged in the audio-tape file. He'd sit down in the shelter until dinner, listening to *Wind in the Willows*. His parents knew where to find him; he was always down there. Two hours of uninterrupted happiness, alone by himself in the shelter. And then when dinner was over he would hurry back down, to stay until time for bed. Sometimes late at night, when his parents were sound asleep, he got quietly up and made his way outside, to the shelter-neck, and down into its silent depths. To hide until morning.

He found the audio-tape and hurried through the house, out onto the back porch and into the yard. The sky was a bleak gray, shot with streamers of ugly black clouds. The lights of the town were coming on here and there. The yard was cold and hostile. He made his way uncertainly down the steps — and froze.

A vast yawning cavity loomed. A gaping mouth, vacant and toothless, fixed open to the night sky. There was nothing else. The shelter was gone.

He stood for an endless time, the tape clutched in one hand, the other hand on the porch railing. Night came on; the dead hole dissolved in darkness. The whole world gradually collapsed into silence and abysmal gloom. Weak stars came out; lights in nearby houses came on fitfully, cold and faint. The boy saw nothing. He stood unmoving, his body rigid as stone, still facing the great pit where the shelter had been.

Then his father was standing beside him. "How long have you been here?" his father was saying. "How long, Mike? Answer me!"

With a violent effort Mike managed to drag himself back. "You're home early," he muttered.

"I left the store early on purpose. I wanted to be here when you — got home."

"It's gone."

"Yes." His father's voice was cold, without emotion. "The shelter's gone. I'm sorry, Mike. I called them and told them to take it back."

"Why?"

"I couldn't pay for it. Not this Christmas, with those grills everyone's getting. I can't compete with them." He broke off and then continued wretchedly, "They were damn decent. They gave me back half the money I put in." His voice twisted ironically. "I knew if I made a deal with them before Christmas I'd come out better. They can resell it to somebody else."

Mike said nothing.

"Try to understand," his father went on harshly. "I had to throw what capital I could scrape together into the store. I have to keep it running. It was either give up the shelter or the store. And if I gave up the store — "

"Then we wouldn't have anything."

His father caught hold of his arm. "Then we'd have to give up the shelter, too." His thin, strong fingers dug in spasmodically. "You're growing up — you're old enough to understand. We'll get one later, maybe not the biggest, the most expensive, but something. It was a mistake, Mike. I couldn't swing it, not with the goddamn adaptor things to buck. I'm keeping up the NAT payments, though. And your school tab. I'm keeping that going. This isn't a matter of principle," he finished desperately. "I can't help it. Do you understand, Mike? *I had to do it.*"

Mike pulled away.

"Where are you going?" His father hurried after him. "Come back here!" He grabbed for his son frantically, but in the gloom he stumbled and fell. Stars blinded him as his head smashed into the edge of the house; he pulled himself up painfully and groped for some support.

When he could see again, the yard was empty. His son was gone.

"Mike!" he yelled. "Where are you?"

There was no answer. The night wind blew clouds of snow around him, a think bitter gust of chilled air. Wind and darkness, nothing else.

Bill O'Neill wearily examined the clock on the wall. It was nine thirty: he could finally close the doors and lock up the big dazzling store. Push the milling, murmuring throngs of people outside and on their way home.

"Thank God," he breathed, as he held the door open for the last old lady, loaded down with packages and presents. He threw the code bolt in place and pulled down the shade. "What a mob. I never saw so many people."

"All done," Al Conners said, from the cash register. "I'll count the money — you go around and check everything. Make sure we got all of them out."

O'Neill pushed his blond hair back and loosened his tie. He lit a cigarette gratefully, then moved around the store, checking light switches, turning off the massive GEC displays and appliances. Finally he approached the huge bomb shelter that took up the center of the floor.

He climbed the ladder to the neck and stepped onto the lift. The lift dropped with a *whoosh* and a second later he stepped out in the cavelike interior of the shelter.

In one corner Mike Foster sat curled up in a tight heap, his knees drawn up against his chin, his skinny arms wrapped around his ankles. His face was pushed down; only his ragged brown hair showed. He didn't move as the salesman approached him, astounded.

"Jesus!" O'Neill exclaimed. "It's that kid."

Mike said nothing. He hugged his legs tighter and buried his head as far down as possible.

"What the hell are you doing down here?" O'Neill demanded, surprised and angry. His outrage increased. "I thought your folks got one of these." Then he remembered. "That's right. We had to repossess it."

Al Conners appeared from the descent-lift. "What's holding you up? Let's get out of here and — " He saw Mike and broke off. "What's he doing down here? Get him out and let's go."

"Come on, kid," O'Neill said gently. "Time to go home."

Mike didn't move.

The two men looked at each other. "I guess we're going to have to drag him out," Conners said grimly. He took off his coat and tossed it over a decontamination fixture. "Come on. Let's get it over with."

It took both of them. The boy fought desperatley, without sound, clawing and struggling and tearing at them with his fingernails, kicking them, slashing at them, biting them when they grabbed him. They half-dragged, half-carried him to the descent-lift and pushed him into it long enough to activate the mechanism. O'Neill rode up with him; Conners came immediately after. Grimly, efficiently, they bundled the boy to the front door, threw him out, and locked the bolts after him.

"Wow," Conners gasped, sinking down against the counter. His sleeve was torn and his cheek was cut and gashed. His glasses hung from one ear; his hair was rumpled and he was exhausted. "Think we ought to call the cops? There's something wrong with that kid."

O'Neill stood by the door, panting for breath and gazing out into the darkness. He could see the boy sitting on the pavement. "He's still out there," he muttered. People pushed by the boy on both sides. Finally one of them stopped and got him up. The boy struggled away, and then disappeared into the darkness. The larger figure picked up its packages, hesitated a moment, and then went on. O'Neill turned away. "What a hell of a thing." He wiped his face with his handkerchief. "He sure put up a fight."

"What was the matter with him? He never said anything, not a goddamn word."

"Christmas is a hell of a time to repossess something," O'Neill said. He reached shakily for his coat. "It's too bad. I wish they could have kept it."

Conners shrugged. "No tickie, no laundry."

"Why the hell can't we give them a deal? Maybe — " O'Neill struggled to get the word out. "Maybe sell the shelter wholesale, to people like that."

Conners glared at him angrily. "*Wholesale*? And then everybody wants it wholesale. It wouldn't be fair — and how long would we stay in business? How long would GEC last that way?"

"I guess not very long," O'Neill admitted moodily.

"Use your head." Conners laughed sharply. "What you need is a good stiff drink. Come on in the back closet — I've got a fifty of Haig and Haig in a drawer back there. A little something to warm you up, before you go home. That's what you need."

Mike Foster wandered aimlessly along the dark street, among the crowds of shoppers hurrying home. He saw nothing; people pushed against him but he was unaware of them. Lights, laughing people, the honking of car horns, the clang of signals. He was blank, his mind empty and dead. He walked automatically, without consciousness or feeling.

To his right a garish neon sign winked and glowed in the deepening night shadows. A huge sign, bright and colorful.

PEACE ON EARTH   GOOD WILL TO MEN
PUBLIC SHELTER   ADMISSION 50¢

Pay for the Printer

Ash, black and desolate, stretched out on both sides of the road. Uneven heaps extended as far as the eye could see — the dim ruins of buildings, cities, a civilization — a corroded planet of debris, wind-whipped black particles of bone and steel and concrete mixed together in an aimless mortar.

Allen Fergesson yawned, lit a Lucky Strike, and settled back drowsily against the shiny leather seat of his '57 Buick. "Depressing damn sight," he commented. "The monotony — nothing but mutilated trash. It gets you down."

"Don't look at it," the girl beside him said indifferently.

The sleek, powerful car glided silently over the rubble that made up the road. His hand barely touching the power-driven wheel, Fergesson relaxed comfortably to the soothing music of a Brahms Piano Quintet filtering from the radio, a transmission of the Detroit settlement. Ash blew up against the windows — a thick coat of black had already formed, though he had gone no more than a few miles. But it didn't matter. In the basement of her apartment, Charlotte had a green-plastic garden hose, a zinc bucket and a DuPont sponge.

"And you have a refrigerator full of good Scotch," he added aloud. "As I recall — unless that fast crowd of yours has finished it off."

Charlotte stirred beside him. She had drifted into half-sleep, lulled by the purr of the motor and the heavy warmth of the air. "Scotch?" she murmured. "Well, I have a fifth of Lord Calvert." She sat up and shook back her cloud of blonde hair. "But it's a little puddinged."

In the back seat, their thin-faced passenger responded. They had picked him up along the way, a bony, gaunt man in coarse gray work-pants and shirt. "How puddinged?" he asked tautly.

"About as much as everything else," she said.

Charlotte wasn't listening. She was gazing vacantly through the ash-darkened window at the scene outside. To the right of the road, the jagged, yellowed remains of a town jutted up like broken teeth against the sooty midday sky. A bathtub here, a couple of upright telephone poles, bones and bleak fragments, lost amid miles of pocked debris. A forlorn, dismal sight. Somewhere in the moldy cave-like cellars a few mangy dogs huddled against the chill. The thick fog of ash kept real sunlight from reaching the surface.

"Look there," Fergesson said to the man in the back.

A mock-rabbit had bounded across the ribbon of road. He slowed the car to avoid it. Blind, deformed, the rabbit hurtled itself with sickening force against a broken concrete slab and bounced off, stunned. It crawled feebly a few paces, then one of the cellar dogs rose and crunched it.

"*Ugh*!" said Charlotte, revolted. She shuddered and reached to turn up the car heater. Slim legs tucked under her, she was an attractive little figure in her pink wool sweater and embroidered skirt. "I'll be glad when we get back to my settlement. It's not *nice* out here. . . . "

Fergesson tapped the steel box on the seat between them. The firm metal felt good under his fingers. "They'll be glad to get hold of these," he said, "if things are as bad as you say."

"Oh, yes," Charlotte agreed. "Things are terrible. I don't know if this will help — he's just about useless." Her small smooth face wrinkled with concern. "I guess it's worth trying. But I can't see much hope."

"We'll fix up your settlement," Fergesson reassured her easily. The first item was to put the girl's mind to rest. Panic of this kind could get out of hand — *had* got out of hand, more than once. "But it'll take a while," he added, glancing at her. "You should have told us sooner."

"We thought it was just laziness. But he's really going, Allen." Fear flicked in her blue eyes. "We can't get anything good out of him anymore. He just sits there like a big lump, as if he's sick or dead."

"He's old," Fergesson said gently. "As I recall, your Biltong dates back a hundred and fifty years."

"But they're supposed to go on for centuries!"

"It's a terrible drain on them," the man in the back seat pointed out. He licked his dry lips, leaned forward tensely, his dirt-cracked hands clenched. "You're forgetting this isn't natural to them. On Proxima they worked together. Now they've broken up into separate units — and gravity is greater here."

Charlotte nodded, but she wasn't convinced. "Gosh!" she said plaintively. "It's just terrible — look at this!" She fumbled in her sweater pocket and brought out a small bright object the size of a dime. "Everything he prints is like this, now — or worse."

Fergesson took the watch and examined it, one eye on the road. The strap broke like a dried leaf between his fingers into small brittle fragments of dark fiber without tensile strength. The face of the watch looked all right — but the hands weren't moving.

"It doesn't run," Charlotte explained. She grabbed it back and opened it. "See?" She held it up in front of his face, her crimson lips tight with displeasure. "I stood in line half an hour for this, and it's just a blob!"

The works of the tiny Swiss watch were a fused, unformed mass of shiny steel. No separate wheels or jewels or springs, just a glitter of pudding.

"What did he have to go on?" the man in back asked. "An original?"

"A print — but a good print. One he did thirty-five years ago — my mother's, in fact. How do you think I felt when I saw it? I can't use it." Charlotte took the puddinged watch back and restored it to her sweater pocket. "I was so mad I — " She broke off and sat up straight. "Oh, we're here. See the red neon sign? That's the beginning of the settlement."

The sign read STANDARD STATIONS INC. Its colors were blue, red, and white — a spotlessly clean structure at the edge of the road. Spotless? Fergesson slowed the car as he came abreast of the station. All three of them peered out intently, stiffening for the shock they knew was coming.

"You see?" said Charlotte in a thin, clipped voice.

The gas station was crumbling away. The small white building was *old* — old and worn, a corroded, uncertain thing that sagged and buckled like an ancient relic. The bright red neon sign sputtered fitfully. The pumps were rusted and bent. The gas station was beginning to settle back into the ash, back into black, drifting particles, back to the dust from which it had come.

As Fergesson gazed at the sinking station, the chill of death touched him. In his settlement, there was no decay — yet. As fast as prints wore out, they were replaced by the Pittsburgh Biltong. New prints were made from the original objects preserved from the War. But here, the prints that made up the settlement were not being replaced.

It was useless to blame anyone. The Biltong were limited, like any race. They had done the best they could — and they were working in an alien environment.

Probably they were indigenous to the Centaurus system. They had appeared in the closing days of the War, attracted by the H-bomb flashes — and found the remnants of the human race creeping miserably through radioactive black ash, trying to salvage what they could of their destroyed culture.

After a period of analysis, the Biltong had separated into individual units, begun the process of duplicating surviving artifacts humans brought to them. That was their mode of survival — on their own planet, they had created an enclosing membrane of satisfactory environment in an otherwise hostile world.

At one of the gasoline pumps a man was trying to fill the tank of his '66 Ford. Cursing in futility, he tore the rotting hose away. Dull amber fluid poured on the ground and soaked into the grease-encrusted gravel. The pump itself spouted leaks in a dozen places. Abruptly, one of the pumps tottered and crashed in a heap.

Charlotte rolled down the car window. "The Shell station is in better shape, Ben!" she called. "At the other end of the settlement."

The heavyset man clumped over, red-faced and perspiring. "*Damn*!" he muttered. "I can't get a damn thing out of it. Give me a lift across town, and I'll fill me a bucket there."

Fergesson shakily pushed open the car door. "It's all like this here?"

"Worse." Ben Untermeyer settled back gratefully with their other passenger as the Buick purred ahead. "Look over there."

A grocery store had collapsed in a twisted heap of concrete and steel supports. The windows had fallen in. Stacks of goods lay strewn everywhere. People were picking their way around, gathering up armloads, trying to clear some of the debris aside. Their faces were grim and angry.

The street itself was in bad repair, full of cracks, deep pits and eroded shoulders. A broken water main oozed slimy water in a growing pool. The stores and cars on both sides were dirty and run-down. Everything had a senile look. A shoe-shine parlor was boarded up, its broken windows stuffed with rags, its sign peeling and shabby. A filthy cafe next door had only a couple of patrons, miserable men in rumpled business suits, trying to read their newspapers and drink the mud-like coffee from cups that cracked and dribbled ugly brown fluid as they lifted them from the worm-eaten counter.

"It can't last much longer," Untermeyer muttered, as he mopped his forehead. "Not at this rate. People are even scared to go into the theatre. Anyhow, the film breaks and half the time it's upside-down." He glanced curiously at the lean-jawed man sitting silently beside him. "My name's Untermeyer," he grunted.

They shook. "John Dawes," the gray-wrapped man answered. He volunteered no more information. Since Fergesson and Charlotte had picked him up along the road, he hadn't said fifty words.

Untermeyer got a rolled-up newspaper from his coat pocket and tossed it onto the front seat beside Fergesson. "This is what I found on the porch, this morning."

The newspaper was a jumble of meaningless words. A vague blur of broken type, watery ink that still hadn't dried, faint, streaked and uneven. Fergesson briefly scanned the text, but it was useless. Confused stories wandered off aimlessly, bold headlines proclaimed nonsense.

"Allen has some originals for us," Charlotte said. "In the box there."

"They won't help," Untermeyer answered gloomily. "He didn't stir all morning. I waited in line with a pop-up toaster I wanted a print of. No dice. I was driving back home when my car began to break down. I looked under the hood, but who knows anything about motors? That's not *our* business. I poked around and got it to run as far as the Standard station ... the damn metal's so weak I put my thumb through it."

Fergesson pulled his Buick to a halt in front of the big white apartment building where Charlotte lived. It took him a moment to recognize it; there had been changes since he last saw it, a month before. A wooden scaffolding, clumsy and amateur, had been erected around it. A few workmen were poking uncertainly at the foundations; the whole building was sinking slowly to one side. Vast cracks yawned up and down the walls. Bits of plaster were strewn everywhere. The littered sidewalk in front of the building was roped off.

"There isn't anything we can do on our own," Untermeyer complained angrily. "All we can do is just sit and watch everything fall apart. If he doesn't come to life soon ... "

"Everything he printed for us in the old days is beginning to wear out," Charlotte said, as she opened the car door and slid onto the pavement. "And everything he prints for us now is a pudding. So what are we going to do?" She shivered in the chill midday cold. "I guess we're going to wind up like the Chicago settlement."

The word froze all four of them. Chicago, the settlement that had collapsed! The Biltong printing there had grown old and died. Exhausted, he had settled into a silent, unmoving mound of inert matter. The buildings and streets around him, all the things he had printed, had gradually worn out and returned to black ash.

"He didn't spawn," Charlotte whispered fearfully. "He used himself up printing, and then he just — *died*."

After a time, Fergesson said huskily, "But the others noticed. They sent a replacement as soon as they could."

"It was too late!" Untermeyer grunted. "The settlement had already gone back. All that was left were maybe a couple of survivors wandering around with nothing on, freezing and starving, and the dogs devouring them. The damn dogs, flocking from everywhere, having a regular feast!"

They stood together on the corroded sidewalk, frightened and apprehensive. Even John Dawes' lean face had a look of bleak horror on it, a fear that cut to the bone. Fergesson thought yearningly of his own settlement, a dozen miles to the East. Thriving and virile — the Pittsburgh Biltong was in his prime, still young and rich with the creative powers of his race. Nothing like this!

The buildings in the Pittsburgh settlement were strong and spotless. The sidewalks were clean and firm underfoot. In the store windows, the television sets and mixers and toasters and autos and pianos and clothing and whiskey and frozen peaches were perfect prints of the originals — authentic, detailed reproductions that couldn't be told from the actual articles preserved in the vacuum-sealed subsurface shelters.

"If this settlement goes out," Fergesson said awkwardly, "maybe a few of you can come over with us."

"Can your Biltong print for more than a hundred people?" John Dawes asked softly.

"Right now he can," Fergesson answered. He proudly indicated his Buick. "You rode in it — you know how good it is. Almost as good as the original it was printed from. You'd have to have them side by side to tell the difference." He grinned and made an old joke. "Maybe I got away with the original."

"We don't have to decide now," Charlotte said curtly. "We still have *some* time, at least." She picked up the steel box from the seat of the Buick and moved toward the steps of the apartment building. "Come on up with us, Ben." She nodded toward Dawes. "You, too. Have a shot of whiskey. It's not too bad — tastes a little like anti-freeze, and the label isn't legible, but other than that it's not too puddinged."

A workman caught her as she put a foot on the bottom step. "You can't go up, miss."

Charlotte pulled away angrily, her face pale with dismay. "My apartment's up there! All my things — this is where I *live*!"

"The building isn't safe," the workman repeated. He wasn't a real workman. He was one of the citizens of the settlement, who had volunteered to guard the buildings that were deteriorating. "Look at the cracks, miss."

"They've been there for weeks." Impatiently, Charlotte waved Fergesson after her. "Come on." She stepped nimbly up onto the porch and reached to open the big glass-and-chrome front door.

The door fell from its hinges and burst. Glass shattered everywhere, a cloud of lethal shards flying in all directions. Charlotte screamed and stumbled back. The concrete crumbled under her heels; with a groan the whole porch settled down in a heap of white powder, a shapeless mound of billowing particles.

Fergesson and the workman caught hold of the struggling girl. In the swirling clouds of concrete dust, Untermeyer searched frantically for the steel box; his fingers closed over it and he dragged it to the sidewalk.

Fergesson and the workman fought back through the ruins of the porch, Charlotte gripped between them. She was trying to speak, but her face jerked hysterically.

"My things!" she managed to whisper.

Fergesson brushed her off unsteadily. "Where are you hurt? Are you all right?"

"I'm not hurt." Charlotte wiped a trickle of blood and white powder from her face. Her cheek was cut, and her blonde hair was a sodden mass. Her pink wool sweater was torn and ragged. Her clothes were totally ruined. "The box — have you got it?"

"It's fine," John Dawes said impassively. He hadn't moved an inch from his position by the car.

Charlotte hung on tight to Fergesson — against him, her body shuddered with fear and despair. "*Look*!" she whispered. "Look at my hands." She held up her white-stained hands. "It's beginning to turn black."

The thick powder streaking her hands and arms had begun to darken. Even as they watched, the powder became gray, then black as soot. The girl's shredded clothing withered and shriveled up. Like a shrunken husk, her clothing cracked and fell away from her body.

"Get in the car," Fergesson ordered. "There's a blanket in there — from my settlement."

Together, he and Untermeyer wrapped the trembling girl in the heavy wool blanket. Charlotte crouched against the seat, her eyes wide with terror, drops of bright blood sliding down her cheek onto the blue and yellow stripes of the blanket. Fergesson lit a cigarette and put it between her quivering lips.

"Thanks." She managed a grateful half-whimper. She took hold of the cigarette shakily. "Allen, what the hell are we going to do?"

Fergesson softly brushed the darkening powder from the girl's blonde hair. "We'll drive over and show him the originals I brought. Maybe he can do something. They're always stimulated by the sight of new things to print from. Maybe this'll arouse some life in him."

"He's not just asleep," Charlotte said in a stricken voice. "He's dead, Allen. I *know* it!"

"Not yet," Untermeyer protested thickly. But the realization was in the minds of all of them.

"Has he spawned?" Dawes asked.

The look on Charlotte's face told them the answer. "He tried to. There were a few that hatched, but none of them lived. I've seen eggs back there, but ... "

She was silent. They all knew. The Biltong had become sterile in their struggle to keep the human race alive. Dead eggs, progeny hatched without life ...

Fergesson slid in behind the wheel and harshly slammed the door. The door didn't close properly. The metal was sprung — or perhaps it was mis-shapen. His hackles rose. Here, too, was an imperfect print — a trifle, a microscopic element botched in the printing. Even his sleek, luxurious Buick was puddinged. The Biltong at his settlement was wearing out, too.

Sooner or later, what had happened to the Chicago settlement would happen to them all. ...

Around the park, rows of automobiles were lined up, silent and unmoving. The park was full of people. Most of the settlement was there. Everybody had something that desperately needed printing. Fergesson snapped off the motor and pocketed the keys.

"Can you make it?" he asked Charlotte. "Maybe you'd better stay here."

"I'll be all right," Charlotte said, and tried to smile.

She had put on a sports shirt and slacks that Fergesson had picked up for her in the ruins of a decaying clothing store. He felt no qualms — a number of men and women were picking listlessly through the scattered stock that littered the sidewalk. The clothing would be good for perhaps a few days.

Fergesson had taken his time picking Charlotte's wardrobe. He had found a heap of sturdy-fibered shirts and slacks in the back storeroom, material still a long way from the dread black pulverization. Recent prints? Or, perhaps — incredible but possible — originals the store owners had used for printing. At a shoe store still in business, he found her a pair of low-heeled slippers. It was his own belt she wore — the one he had picked up in the clothing store rotted away in his hands while he was buckling it around her.

Untermeyer gripped the steel box with both hands as the four of them approached the center of the park. The people around them were silent and grim-faced. No one spoke. They all carried some article, originals carefully preserved through the centuries or good prints with only minor imperfections. On their faces were desperate hope and fear fused, in a taut mask.

"Here they are," said Dawes, lagging behind. "The dead eggs."

In a grove of trees at the edge of the park was a circle of gray-brown pellets, the size of basketballs. They were hard, calcified. Some were broken. Fragments of shell were littered everywhere.

Untermeyer kicked at one egg; it fell apart, brittle and empty. "Sucked dry by some animal," he stated. "We're seeing the end, Fergesson. I think dogs sneak in here at night, now, and get at them. He's too weak to protect them."

A dull undercurrent of outrage throbbed through the waiting men and women. Their eyes were red-rimmed with anger as they stood clutching their objects, jammed in together in a solid mass, a circle of impatient, indignant humanity ringing the center of the park. They had been waiting a long time. They were getting tired of waiting.

"What the hell is this?" Untermeyer squatted down in front of a vague shape discarded under a tree. He ran his fingers over the indistinct blur of metal. The object seemed melted together like wax — nothing was distinguishable. "I can't identify it."

"That's a power lawnmower," a man nearby said sullenly.

"How long ago did he print it?" Fergesson asked.

"Four days ago." The man knocked at it in hostility. "You can't even tell what it is — it could be anything. My old one's worn out. I wheeled the settlement's original up from the vault and stood in line all day — and look what I got." He spat contemptuously. "It isn't worth a damn. I left it sitting here — no point taking it home."

His wife spoke up in a shrill, harsh wail. "What are we going to do? We can't use the old one. It's crumbling away like everything else around here. If the new prints aren't any good, then what — "

"Shut up," her husband snapped. His face was ugly and strained. His long-fingered hands gripped a length of pipe. "We'll wait a little longer. Maybe he'll snap out of it."

A murmur of hope rippled around them. Charlotte shivered and pushed on. "I don't blame him," she said to Fergesson. "But ... " She shook her head wearily. "What good would it do? If he won't print copies for us that are any good ... "

"He can't," John Dawes said. "Look at him!" He halted and held the rest of them back. "Look at him and tell me how he could do better."

The Biltong was dying. Huge and old, it squatted in the center of the settlement park, a lump of ancient yellow protoplasm, thick, gummy, opaque. Its pseudopodia were dried up, shriveled to blackened snakes that lay inert on the brown grass. The center of the mass looked oddly sunken. The Biltong was gradually settling, as the moisture was burned from its veins by the weak overhead sun.

"Oh, dear!" Charlotte whispered. "How *awful* he looks!"

The Biltong's central lump undulated faintly. Sickly, restless heavings were noticeable as it struggled to hold onto its dwindling life. Flies clustered around it in dense swarms of black and shiny blue. A thick odor hung over the Biltong, a fetid stench of decaying organic matter. A pool of brackish waste liquid had oozed from it.

Within the yellow protoplasm of the creature, its solid core of nervous tissue pulsed in agony, with quick, jerky movements that sent widening waves across the sluggish flesh. Filaments were almost visibly degenerating into calcified granules. Age and decay — and suffering.

On the concrete platform, in front of the dying Biltong, lay a heap of originals to be duplicated. Beside them, a few prints had been commenced, unformed balls of black ash mixed with the moisture of the Biltong's body, the juice from which it laboriously constructed its prints. It had halted the work, pulled its still-functioning pseudopodia painfully back into itself. It was resting — and trying not to die.

"The poor damn thing!" Fergesson heard himself say. "It can't keep on."

"He's been sitting like that for six solid hours," a woman snapped sharply in Fergesson's ear. "Just sitting there! What does he expect us to do, get down on our hands and knees and *beg* him?"

Dawes turned furiously on her. "Can't you see it's dying? For God's sake, *leave it alone*!"

An ominous rumble stirred through the ring of people. Faces turned toward Dawes — he icily ignored them. Beside him, Charlotte had stiffened to a frightened ramrod. Her eyes were pale with fear.

"Be careful," Untermeyer warned Dawes softly. "Some of these boys need things pretty bad. Some of them are waiting here for food."

Time was running out. Fergesson grabbed the steel box from Untermeyer and tore it open. Bending down, he removed the originals and laid them on the grass in front of him.

At the sight, a murmur went up around him, a murmur blended of awe and amazement. Grim satisfaction knifed through Fergesson. These were originals lacking in this settlement. Only imperfect prints existed here. Printing had been done from defective duplicates. One by one, he gathered up the precious originals and moved toward the concrete platform in front of the Biltong. Men angrily blocked his way — until they saw the originals he carried.

He laid down a silver Ronson cigarette lighter. Then a Bausch and Lomb binocular microscope, still black and pebbled in its original leather. A high-fidelity Pickering phonograph cartridge. And a shimmering Steuben crystal cup.

"Those are fine-looking originals," a man nearby said enviously. "Where'd you get them?"

Fergesson didn't reply. He was watching the dying Biltong.

The Biltong hadn't moved. But it had seen the new originals added to the others. Inside the yellow mass, the hard fibers raced and blurred together. The front orifice shuddered and then split open. A violent wave lashed the whole lump of protoplasm. Then from the opening, rancid bubbles oozed. A pseudopodium twitched briefly, struggled forward across the slimy grass, hesitated, touched the Steuben glass.

It pushed together a heap of black ash, wadded it with fluid from the front orifice. A dull globe formed, a grotesque parody of the Steuben cup. The Biltong wavered and drew back to gather more strength. Presently it tried once more to form the blob. Abruptly, without warning, the whole mass shuddered violently, and the pseudopodium dropped, exhausted. It twitched, hesitated pathetically, and then withdrew, back into the central bulk.

"No use," Untermeyer said hoarsely. "He can't do it. It's too late."

With stiff, awkward fingers, Fergesson gathered the originals together and shakily stuffed them back in the steel box. "I guess I was wrong," he muttered, climbing to his feet. "I thought this might do it. I didn't realize how far it had gone."

Charlotte, stricken and mute, moved blindly away from the platform. Untermeyer followed her through the coagulation of angry men and women, clustered around the concrete platform.

"Wait a minute," Dawes said. "I have something for him to try."

Fergesson waited wearily, as Dawes groped inside his coarse gray shirt. He fumbled and brought out something wrapped in old newspaper. It was a cup, a wooden drinking cup, crude and ill-shaped. There was a strange wry smile on his face as he squatted down and placed the cup in front of the Biltong.

Charlotte watched, vaguely puzzled. "What's the use? Suppose he does make a print of it." She poked listlessly at the rough wooden object with the toe of her slipper. "It's so simple you could duplicate it yourself."

Fergesson started. Dawes caught his eye — for an instant the two men gazed at each other, Dawes smiling faintly, Fergesson rigid with burgeoning understanding.

"That's right," Dawes said. "I made it."

Fergesson grabbed the cup. Trembling, he turned it over and over. "You made it with *what*? I don't see how! What did you make it *out* of?"

"We knocked down some trees." From his belt, Dawes slid something that gleamed metallically, dully, in the weak sunlight. "Here — be careful you don't cut yourself."

The knife was as crude as the cup — hammered, bent, tied together with wire. "You made this knife?" Fergesson asked, dazed. "I can't believe it. *Where do you start*? You have to have tools to make this. It's a paradox!" His voice rose with hysteria. "It isn't *possible*!"

Charlotte turned despondently away. "It's no good — you couldn't cut anything with that." Wistfully, pathetically, she added, "In my kitchen I had that whole set of stainless steel carving knives — the best Swedish steel. And now they're nothing but black ash."

There were a million questions bursting in Fergesson's mind. "This cup, this knife — there's a group of you? And that material you're wearing — you wove that?"

"Come on," Dawes said brusquely. He retrieved the knife and cup, moved urgently away. "We'd better get out of here. I think the end has about come."

People were beginning to drift out of the park. They were giving up, shambling wretchedly off to forage in the decaying stores for food remnants. A few cars muttered into life and rolled hesitantly away.

Untermeyer licked his flabby lips nervously. His doughy flesh was mottled and grainy with fear. "They're getting wild," he muttered to Fergesson. "This whole settlement's collapsing — in a few hours there won't be anything. No food, no place to stay!" His eyes darted toward the car, then faded to opaqueness.

He wasn't the only one who had noticed the car.

A group of men were slowly forming around the massive dusty Buick, their faces dark. Like hostile, greedy children, they poked at it intently, examining its fenders, hood, touching its headlights, its firm tires. The men had clumsy weapons — pipes, rocks, sections of twisted steel ripped from collapsing buildings.

"They know it isn't from this settlement," Dawes said. "They know it's going back."

"I can take you to the Pittsburgh settlement," Fergesson said to Charlotte. He headed toward the car. "I'll register you as my wife. You can decide later on whether you want to go through with the legalities."

"What about Ben?" Charlotte asked faintly.

"I can't marry him, too." Fergesson increased his pace. "I can take him there, but they won't let him stay. They have their quota system. Later on, when they realize the emergency ... "

"Get out of the way," Untermeyer said to the cordon of men. He lumbered toward them vengefully. After a moment, the men uncertainly retreated and finally gave way. Untermeyer stood by the door, his huge body drawn up and alert.

"Bring her through — and watch it!" he told Fergesson.

Fergesson and Dawes, with Charlotte between them, made their way through the line of men to Untermeyer. Fergesson gave the fat man the keys, and Untermeyer yanked the front door open. He pushed Charlotte in, then motioned Fergesson to hurry around to the other side.

The group of men came alive.

With his great fist, Untermeyer smashed the leader into those behind him. He struggled past Charlotte and got his bulk wedged behind the wheel of the car. The motor came on with a whirr. Untermeyer threw it into low gear and jammed savagely down on the accelerator. The car edged forward. Men clawed at it crazily, groping at the open door for the man and woman inside.

Untermeyer slammed the doors and locked them. As the car gained speed, Fergesson caught a final glimpse of the fat man's sweating, fear-distorted face.

Men grabbed vainly for the slippery sides of the car. As it gathered momentum, they slid away one by one. One huge red-haired man clung maniacally to the hood, pawing at the shattered windshield for the driver's face beyond. Untermeyer sent the car spinning into a sharp curve; the red-haired man hung on for a moment, then lost his grip and tumbled silently, face-forward, onto the pavement.

The car wove, careened, at last disappeared from view beyond a row of sagging buildings. The sound of its screaming tires faded. Untermeyer and Charlotte were on their way to safety at the Pittsburgh settlement.

Fergesson stared after the car until the pressure of Dawes' thin hand on his shoulder aroused him. "Well," he muttered, "there goes the car. Anyhow, Charlotte got away."

"Come on," Dawes said tightly in his ear. "I hope you have good shoes — we've got a long way to walk."

Fergesson blinked. "Walk? Where ... ?"

"The nearest of our camps is thirty miles from here. We can make it, I think." He moved away, and after a moment Fergesson followed him. "I've done it before. I can do it again."

Behind them, the crowd was collecting again, centering its interest upon the inert mass that was the dying Biltong. The hum of wrath sounded—frustration and impotence at the loss of the car pitched the ugly cacophony to a gathering peak of violence. Gradually, like water seeking its level, the ominous, boiling mass surged toward the concrete platform.

On the platform, the ancient dying Biltong waited helplessly. It was aware of them. Its pseudopodia were twisted in one last decrepit action, a final shudder of effort.

Then Fergesson saw a terrible thing—a thing that made shame rise inside him until his humiliated fingers released the metal box he carried, let it fall, splintering, to the ground. He retrieved it numbly, stood gripping it helplessly. He wanted to run off blindly, aimlessly, anywhere but here. Out into the silence and darkness and driving shadows beyond the settlement. Out in the dead acres of ash.

The Biltong was trying to print himself a defensive shield, a protective wall of ash, as the mob descended on him....

When they had walked a couple of hours, Dawes came to a halt and threw himself down in the black ash that extended everywhere. "We'll rest awhile," he grunted to Fergesson. "I've got some food we can cook. We'll use that Ronson lighter you have there, if it's got any fluid in it."

Fergesson opened the metal box and passed him the lighter. A cold, fetid wind blew around them, whipping ash into dismal clouds across the barren surface of the planet. Off in the distance, a few jagged walls of buildings jutted upward like splinters of bones. Here and there dark, ominous stalks of weeds grew.

"It's not as dead as it looks," Dawes commented, as he gathered bits of dried wood and paper from the ash around them. "You know about the dogs and the rabbits. And there's lots of plant seeds—all you have to do is water the ash, and up they spring."

"Water? But it doesn't—rain. Whatever the word used to be."

"We have to dig ditches. There's still water, but you have to dig for it." Dawes got a feeble fire going—there was fluid in the lighter. He tossed it back and turned his attention to feeding the fire.

Fergesson sat examining the lighter. "How can you build a thing like this?" he demanded bluntly.

"We can't." Dawes reached into his coat and brought out a flat packet of food—dried, salted meat and parched corn. "You can't start out building complex stuff. You have to work your way up slowly."

"A healthy Biltong could print from this. The one in Pittsburgh could make a perfect print of this lighter."

"I know," Dawes said. "That's what's held us back. We have to wait until they give up. They will, you know. They'll have to go back to their own star-system — it's genocide for them to stay here."

Fergesson clutched convulsively at the lighter. "Then our civilization goes with them."

"That lighter?" Dawes grinned. "Yes, that's going — for a long time, at least. But I don't think you've got the right slant. We're going to have to re-educate ourselves, every damn one of us. It's hard for me, too."

"Where did you come from?"

Dawes said quietly, "I'm one of the survivors from Chicago. After it collapsed, I wandered around — killed with a stone, slept in cellars, fought off the dogs with my hands and feet. Finally, I found my way to one of the camps. There were a few before me — you don't know it, my friend, but Chicago wasn't the first to fall."

"And you're printing tools? Like that knife?"

Dawes laughed long and loud. "The word isn't print — the word is *build*. We're building tools, making things." He pulled out the crude wooden cup and laid it down on the ash. "Printing means merely copying. I can't explain to you what building is; you'll have to try it yourself to find out. Building and printing are two totally different things."

Dawes arranged three objects on the ash. The exquisite Steuben glassware, his own crude wooden drinking cup and the blob, the botched print the dying Biltong had attempted.

"This is the way is was," he said, indicating the Steuben cup. "Someday it'll be that way again ... but we're going up the right way — the hard way — step by step, until we get back there." He carefully replaced the glassware back in its metal box. "We'll keep it — not to copy, but as a model, as a goal. You can't grasp the difference now, but you will."

He indicated the crude wooden cup. "That's where we are right now. Don't laugh at it. Don't say it's not civilization. It is — it's simple and crude, but it's the real thing. We'll go up from here."

He picked up the blob, the print the Biltong had left behind. After a moment's reflection, he drew back and hurled it away from him. The blob struck, bounced once, then broke into fragments.

"That's nothing," Dawes said fiercely. "Better this cup. This wooden cup is closer to that Steuben glass than any print."

"You're certainly proud of your little wooden cup," Fergesson observed.

"I sure as hell am," Dawes agreed, as he placed the cup in the metal box beside the Steuben glassware. "You'll understand that, too, one of these days. It'll take awhile, but you'll get it." He began closing the box, then halted a moment and touched the Ronson lighter.

He shook his head regretfully. "Not in our time," he said, and closed the box. "Too many steps in between." His lean face glowed suddenly, a flicker of joyful anticipation. "But by God, we're moving that way!"

WAR VETERAN

THE OLD MAN sat on the park bench in the bright hot sunlight and watched the people moving back and forth.

The park was neat and clean; the lawns glittered wetly in the spray piped from a hundred shiny copper tubes. A polished robot gardener crawled here and there, weeding and plucking and gathering waste debris in its disposal slot. Children scampered and shouted. Young couples sat basking sleepily and holding hands. Groups of handsome soldiers strolled lazily along, hands in their pockets, admiring the tanned, naked girls sunbathing around the pool. Beyond the park the roaring cars and towering needle-spires of New York sparkled and gleamed.

The old man cleared his throat and spat sullenly into the bushes. The bright hot sun annoyed him; it was too yellow and it made perspiration stream through his seedy, ragged coat. It made him conscious of his grizzled chin and missing left eye. And the deep ugly burn-scar that had seared away the flesh of one cheek. He pawed fretfully at the h-loop around his scrawny neck. He unbottoned his coat and pulled himself upright against the glowing metal slats of the bench. Bored, lonely, bitter, he twisted around and tried to interest himself in the pastoral scene of trees and grass and happily playing children.

Three blond-faced young soldiers sat down on the bench opposite him and began unrolling picnic lunch-cartons.

The old man's thin rancid breath caught in his throat. Painfully, his ancient heart thudded, and for the first time in hours he came fully alive. He struggled up from his lethargy and focused his dim sight on the soldiers. The old man got out his handkerchief, mopped his sweat-oozing face, and then spoke to them.

"Nice afternoon."

The soldiers glanced up briefly. "Yeah," one said.

"They done a good job." The old man indicated the yellow sun and the spires of the city. "Looks perfect."

The soldiers said nothing. They concentrated on their cups of boiling black coffee and apple pie.

"Almost fools you," the old man went on plaintively. "You boys with the seed teams?" he hazarded.

"No," one of them said. "We're rocketeers."

The old man gripped his aluminum cane and said, "I was in demolition. Back in the old Ba-3 Squad."

None of the soldiers responded. They were whispering among themselves. The girls on a bench farther down had noticed them.

The old man reached into his coat pocket and brought out something wrapped in gray torn tissue-paper. He unfolded it with shaking fingers and then go to his feet. Unsteadily, he crossed the gravel path to the soldiers. "See this?" He held out the object, a small square of glittering metal. "I won that back in '87. That was before your time, I guess."

A flicker of interest momentarily roused the young soldiers. "Hey," one whistled appreciatively. "That's a Crystal Disc — first class." He raised his eyes questioningly. "You won that?"

The old man cackled proudly, as he wrapped up the medal and restored it to his coat pocket. "I served under Nathan West, in the *Wind Giant*. It wasn't until the final jump they took against us I got mine. But I was out there with my d-squad. You probably remember the day we set off our network, rigged all the way from — "

"Sorry," one of the soldiers said vaguely. "We don't go back that far. That must have been before our time."

"Sure," the old man agreed eagerly. "That was more than sixty years ago. You heard of Major Perati, haven't you? How he rammed their covering fleet into a meteor cloud as they were converging for their final attack? And how the Ba-3 was able to hold them back months before they finally slammed us?" He swore bitterly. "We held them off. Until there wasn't more'n a couple of us left. And then they came in like vultures. And what they found they — "

"Sorry, Pop." The soldiers had got lithely up, collected their lunches, and were moving toward the bench of girls. The girls glanced at them shyly and giggled in anticipation. "We'll see you some other time."

The old man turned and hobbled furiously back to his own bench. Disappointed, muttering under his breath and spitting into the wet bushes, he tried to make himself comfortable. But the sun irritated him; and the noises of people and cars made him sick.

He sat on the park bench, eye half shut, wasted lips twisted in a snarl of bitterness and defeat. Nobody was interested in a decrepit half-blind old man. Nobody wanted to hear his garbled, rambling tales of the battles he had fought and strategies he had witnessed. Nobody seemed to remember the war that still burned like a twisting, corroding fire in the decaying old man's brain. A war he longed to speak of, if he could only find listeners.

Vachel Patterson jerked his car to a halt and slammed on the emergency brake. "That's that," he said over his shoulder. "Make yourselves comfortable. We're going to have a short wait."

The scene was familiar. A thousand Earthmen in gray caps and armbands streamed along the street, chanting slogans, waving immense crude banners that were visible for blocks.

NO NEGOTIATION! TALK IS FOR TRAITORS!
ACTION IS FOR MEN!
DON'T TELL THEM SHOW THEM!
A STRONG EARTH IS THE BEST GUARANTEE OF PEACE!

In the back seat of the car Edwin LeMarr put aside his report tapes with a grunt of near-sighted surprise. "Why have we stopped? What is it?"

"Another demonstration," Evelyn Cutter said distantly. She leaned back and disgustedly lit a cigarette. "Same as all of them."

The demonstration was in full swing. Men, women, youths out of school for the afternoon, marched wild-faced, excited and intense, some with signs, some with crude weapons and in partial uniform. Along the sidewalks more and more watching spectators were being tugged along. Blue-clad policemen had halted surface traffic; they stood watching indifferently, waiting for somebody to try to interfere. Nobody did, of course. Nobody was that foolish.

"Why doesn't the Directorate put a stop to this?" LeMarr demanded. "A couple of armored columns would finish this once and for all."

Beside him, John V-Stephens laughed coldly. "The Directorate finances it, organizes it, gives it free time on the vidnet, even beats up people who complain. Look at those cops standing over there. Waiting for somebody to beat up."

LeMarr blinked. "Patterson, is that true?"

Rage-distorted faces loomed up beyond the hood of the sleek '64 Buick. The tramp of feet made the chrome dashboard rattle; Doctor LeMarr tugged his tapes nervously into their metal case and peered around like a frightened turtle.

"What are you worried about?" V-Stephens said harshly. "They wouldn't touch you — you're an Earthman. I'm the one who should be sweating."

"They're crazy," LeMarr muttered. "All those morons chanting and marching — "

"They're not morons," Patterson answered mildly. "They're just too trusting. They believe what they're told, like the rest of us. The only trouble is, what *they're* told isn't true."

He indicated one of the gigantic banners, a vast 3-D photograph that twisted and turned as it was carried forward. "Blame *him*. He's the one who thinks up the lies. He's the one who puts the pressure on the Directorate, fabricates the hate and violence — and has the funds to sell it."

The banner showed a stern-browed white-haired gentleman, clean-shaven and dignified. A scholarly man, heavy-set, in his late fifties. Kindly blue eyes, firm jawline, an impressive and respected dignitary. Under his handsome portrait was his personal slogan, coined in a moment of inspiration.

ONLY TRAITORS COMPROMISE!

"That's Francis Gannet," V-Stephens said to LeMarr. "Fine figure of a man, isn't he?" He corrected himself. "Of an *Earth*man."

"He looks so genteel," Evelyn Cutter protested. "How could an intelligent-looking man like that have anything to do with this?"

V-Stephens bellowed with taut laughter. "His nice clean white hands are a lot filthier than any of those plumbers and carpenters marching out there."

"But why — "

"Gannet and his group own Transplan Industries, a holding company that controls most of the export-import business of the inner worlds. If my people and the Martian people are given their independence they'll start cutting into his trade. They'll be competition. But as it stands, they're bottled up in a cold-decked mercantile system."

The demonstrators had reached an intersection. A group of them dropped their banners and sprouted clubs and rocks. They shouted orders, waved the others on, and then headed grimly for a small modern building that blinked the word COLOR-AD in neon lights.

"Oh, God," Patterson said. "They're after the Color-Ad office." He grabbed at the door handle, but V-Stephens stopped him.

"You can't do anything," V-Stephens said. "Anyhow, nobody's in there. They usually get advance warning."

The rioters smashed the plate-plastic windows and poured into the swank little store. The police sauntered over, arms folded, enjoying the spectacle. From the ruined front office, smashed furniture was tossed out onto the sidewalks. Files, desks, chairs, vidscreens, ashtrays, even gay posters of happy life on the inner worlds. Acrid black fingers of smoke curled up as the store room was ignited by a hot-beam. Presently the rioters came streaming back out, satiated and happy.

Along the sidewalk, people watched with a variety of emotions. Some showed delight. Some a vague curiosity. But most showed fear and dismay.

They backed hurriedly away as the wild-faced rioters pushed brutally past them, loaded down with stolen goods.

"See?" Patterson said. "This stuff is done by a few thousand, a Committee Gannet's financing. Those in front are employees of Gannet's factories, goon squads on extracurricular duty. They try to sound like Mankind, but they aren't. They're a noisy minority, a small bunch of hard-working fanatics."

The demonstration was breaking up. The Color-Ad office was a dismal fire-gutted ruin; traffic had been stopped; most of downtown New York had seen the lurid slogans and heard the tramp of feet and shouted hate. People began drifting back into offices and shops, back to their daily routine.

And then the rioters saw the Venusian girl, crouched in the locked and bolted doorway.

Patterson gunned the car forward. Bucking and grinding savagely, it hurtled across the street and up on the sidewalk, toward the running knot of dark-faced hoods. The nose of the car caught the first wave of them and tossed them like leaves. The rest collided with the metal hull and tumbled down in a shapeless mass of struggling arms and legs.

The Venusian girl saw the car sliding toward her — and the Earth-people in the front seat. For a moment she crouched in paralyzed terror. Then she turned and scurried off in panic, down the sidewalk and into the milling throng that filled up the street. The rioters regrouped themselves and in an instant were after her in full cry.

"Get the webfoot!"

"Webfoots back to their own planet!"

"Earth for Earthmen!"

And beneath the chanted slogans, the ugly undercurrent of unverbalized lust and hate.

Patterson backed the car up and onto the street. His fist clamped savagely over the horn, he gunned the car after the girl, abreast with the loping rioters and then past them. A rock crashed off the rear-view window and for an instant a hail of rubbish banged and clattered. Ahead, the crowd separated aimlessly, leaving an open path for the car and the rioters. No hand was lifted against the desperately running girl as she raced sobbing and panting between parked cars and groups of people. And nobody made a move to help her. Everybody watched dull-eyed and detached. Remote spectators viewing an event in which they had no part.

"I'll get her," V-Stephens said. "Pull up in front of her and I'll head her off."

Patterson passed the girl and jammed on the brakes. The girl doubled off the street like a terrified hare. V-Stephens was out of the car in a single bound. He sprinted after her as she darted mindlessly back toward the rioters. He swept her up and then plunged back to the car. LeMarr and Evelyn Cutter dragged the two of them in; and Patterson sent the car bucking ahead.

A moment later he turned a corner, snapped a police rope, and passed beyond the danger zone. The roar of people, the flap-flap of feet against the pavement, died down behind them.

"It's all right," V-Stephens was saying gently and repeatedly to the girl. "We're friends. Look, I'm a webfoot, too."

The girl was huddled against the door of the car, green eyes wide with terror, thin face convulsed, knees pulled up against her stomach. She was perhaps seventeen years old. Her webbed fingers scrabbled aimlessly with the torn collar of her blouse. One shoe was missing. Her face was scratched, dark hair disheveled. From her trembling mouth only vague sounds came.

LeMarr took her pulse. "Her heart's about to pop out of her," he muttered. From his coat he took an emergency capsule and shot a narcotic into the girl's trembling forearm. "That'll relax her. She's not harmed — they didn't get to her."

"It's all right," V-Stephens murmured. "We're doctors from the City Hospital, all but Miss Cutter, who manages the files and records. Dr. LeMarr is a neurologist, Dr. Patterson is a cancer specialist, I'm a surgeon — see my hand?" He traced the girl's forehead with his surgeon's hand. "And I'm a Venusian, like you. We'll take you to the hospital and keep you there for a while."

"Did you see them?" LeMarr sputtered. "Nobody lifted a finger to help her. They just stood there."

"They were afraid," Patterson said. "They want to avoid trouble."

"They can't," Evelyn Cutter said flatly. "Nobody can avoid this kind of trouble. They can't keep standing on the sidelines watching. This isn't a football game."

"What's going to happen?" the girl quavered.

"You better get off Earth," V-Stephens said gently. "No Venusian is safe here. Get back to your own planet and stay there until this thing dies down."

"Will it?" the girl gasped.

"Eventually." V-Stephens reached down and passed her Evelyn's cigarette. "It can't go on like this. We have to be free."

"Take it easy," Evelyn said in a dangerous voice. Her eyes faded to hostile coals. "I thought you were above all this."

V-Stephens' dark green face flushed. "You think I can stand idly by while my people are killed and insulted, and our interests passed over, ignored so paste-faces like Gannet can get rich on blood squeezed from — "

"Paste-face," LeMarr echoed wonderingly. "What's that mean, Vachel?"

"That's their word for Earthmen," Patterson answered. "Can it, V-Stephens. As far as we're concerned it's not your people and our people. We're all the same race. Your ancestors were Earthmen who settled Venus back in the late twentieth century."

"The changes are only minor adaptive alterations," LeMarr assured V-Stephens. "We can still interbreed — that proves we're the same race."

"We can," Evelyn Cutter said thinly. "But who wants to marry a webfoot or a crow?"

Nobody said anything for a while. The air in the car was tense with hostility as Patterson sped toward the hospital. The Venusian girl sat crouched, smoking silently, her terrified eyes on the vibrating floor.

Patterson slowed down at the check-point and showed his i.d. tab. The hospital guard signaled the car ahead and he picked up speed. As he put his tab away his fingers touched something clipped to the inside of his pocket. Sudden memory returned.

"Here's something to take your mind off your troubles," he said to V-Stephens. He tossed the sealed tube back to the webfoot. "Military fired it back this morning. Clerical error. When you're through with it hand it over to Evelyn. It's supposed to go to her, but I got interested."

V-Stephens slit open the tube and spilled out the contents. It was a routine application for admission to a Government hospital, stamped with the number of a war-veteran. Old sweat-grimed tapes, papers torn and mutilated throughout the years. Greasy bits of metal foil that had been folded and refolded, stuffed in a shirt pocket, carried next to some filthy, hair-matted chest. "Is this important?" V-Stephens asked impatiently. "Do we have to worry over clerical trifles?"

Patterson halted the car in the hospital parking lot and turned off the motor. "Look at the number of the application," he said, as he pushed open the car door. "When you have time to examine it you'll find something unusual. The applicant is carrying around an old veteran's i.d. card — with a number that hasn't been issued yet."

LeMarr, hopelessly baffled, looked from Evelyn Cutter to V-Stephens, but got no explanation.

The old man's h-loop awoke him from a fitful slumber. "David Unger," the tinny female voice repeated. "You are wanted back at the hospital. It is requested that you return to the hospital immediately."

The old man grunted and pulled himself up with an effort. Grabbing his aluminum cane he hobbled away from his sweat-shiny bench, toward the escape ramp of the park. Just when he was getting to sleep, shutting out the too-bright sun and the shrill laughter of children and girls and young soldiers . . .

At the edge of the park two shapes crept furtively into the bushes. David Unger halted and stood in disbelief, as the shapes glided past him along the path.

His voice surprised him. He was screaming at the top of his lungs, shrieks of rage and revulsion that echoed through the park, among the quiet trees and lawns. "*Webfoots*!" he wailed. He began to run clumsily after them. "Webfoots and crows! Help! Somebody help!"

Waving his aluminum cane, he hobbled after the Martian and Venusian, panting wildly. People appeared, blank-faced with astonishment. A crowd formed, as the old man hurried after the terrified pair. Exhausted, he stumbled against a drinking fountain and half-fell, his cane sliding from his fingers. His shrunken face was livid; the burn-scar stood out sick and ugly against the mottled skin. His good eye was red with hate and fury. From his wasted lips saliva drooled. He waved his skinny claw-like hands futilely, as the two altereds crept into the grove of cedars toward the far end of the park.

"Stop them!" David Unger slobbered. "Don't let them get away! What's the matter with you? You bunch of lily-white cowards. What kind of men are you?"

"Take it easy, Pop," a young soldier said good-naturedly. "They're not hurting anybody."

Unger retrieved his cane and whooshed it past the soldier's head. "You — *talker*," he snapped. "What kind of a soldier are you?" A fit of coughing choked off his words; he bent double, struggling to breathe. "In my day," he managed to gasp, "we poured rocket fuel on them and strung them up. We mutilated them. We cut up the dirty webfoots and crows. We showed them."

A looming cop had stopped the pair of altereds. "Get going," he ordered ominously. "You things got no right here."

The two altereds scuttled past him. The cop leisurely raised his stick and cracked the Martian across the eyes. The brittle, thin-shelled head splintered, and the Martian careened on, blinded and in agony.

"That's more like it," David Unger gasped, in weak satisfaction.

"You evil dirty old man," a woman muttered at him, face white with horror. "It's people like you that make all this trouble."

"What are you?" Unger snapped. "A crow-lover?"

The crowd melted and broke. Unger, grasping his cane, stumbled toward the exit ramp, muttering curses and abuse, spitting violently into the bushes and shaking his head.

He arrived at the hospital grounds still trembling with rage and resentment. "What do you want?" he demanded, as he came up to the big receiving desk in the center of the main lobby. "I don't know what's going on around here. First you wake me out of the first real sleep I've had since I got here, and then what do I see but two webfoots walking around in broad daylight, sassy as — "

"Doctor Patterson wants you," the nurse said patiently. "Room 301." She nodded to a robot. "Take Mr. Unger down to 301."

The old man hobbled sullenly after the smoothly-gliding robot. "I thought all you tinmen were used up in the Europa battle of '88," he complained. "It don't make sense, all these lily-white boys in uniforms. Everybody wandering around having a good time, laughing and diddling girls with nothing better to do than lie around on the grass naked. Something's the matter. Something must be — "

"In here, sir," the robot said, and the door of 301 slid away.

Vachel Patterson rose slightly as the old man entered and stood fuming and gripping his aluminum cane in front of the work-desk. It was the first time he had seen David Unger face to face. Each of them sized the other up intently; the thin hawk-faced old soldier and the well-dressed young doctor, black thinning hair, horn-rimmed glasses and good-natured face. Beside his desk Evelyn Cutter stood watching and listening impassively, a cigarette between her red lips, blond hair swept back.

"I'm Doctor Patterson, and this is Miss Cutter." Patterson toyed with the dog-eared, eroded tape strewn across his desk. "Sit down, Mr. Unger. I want to ask you a couple of questions. Some uncertainty has come up regarding one of your papers. A routine error, probably, but they've come back to me."

Unger seated himself warily. "Questions and red tape. I've been here a week and every day it's something. Maybe I should have just laid there in the street and died."

"You've been here eight days, according to this."

"I suppose so. If it says so there, must be true." The old man's thin sarcasm boiled out viciously. "Couldn't put it down if it wasn't true."

"You were admitted as a war veteran. All costs of care and maintenance are covered by the Directorate."

Unger bristled. "What's wrong with that? I earned a little care." He leaned toward Patterson and jabbed a crabbed finger at him. "I was in the Service when I was sixteen. Fought and worked for Earth all my life. Would be there yet, if I hadn't been half killed by that dirty mop-up attack of theirs. Lucky to be alive at all." He self-consciously rubbed the livid ruin of his face. "Looks like you weren't even in it. Didn't know there *was* any place got by."

Patterson and Evelyn Cutter looked at each other. "How old are you?" Evelyn asked suddenly.

"Don't it say?" Unger muttered furiously. "Eighty-nine."

"And the year of your birth?"

"2154. Can't you figure that?"

Patterson made a faint notation on the metal foil reports. "And your unit?"

At that, Unger broke loose. "The Ba-3, if maybe you've heard of it. Although the way things are around here, I wonder if you know there was ever a war."

"The Ba-3," Patterson repeated. "And you served with them how long?"

"Fifty years. Then I retired. The first time, I mean. I was sixty-six years old. Usual age. Got my pension and bit of land."

"And they called you back?"

"Of course they called me back! Don't you remember how the Ba-3 went back into the line, all us old guys, and damn near stopped them, the last time? You must have been just a kid, but everybody knows what we did." Unger fumbled out his Crystal Disc first class and slammed it on the desk. "I got *that*. All us survivors did. All ten of us, out of thirty thousand." He gathered the medal up with shaking fingers. "I was hurt bad. You see my face. Burned, when Nathan West's battleship blew up. I was in the military hospital for a couple years. That was when they cracked Earth wide open." The ancient hands clenched into futile fists. "We had to sit there, watching them turn Earth into a smoking ruin. Nothing but slag and ash, miles of death. No towns, no cities. We sat there, while their C-missiles whizzed by. Finally they got finished — and got us on Luna, too."

Evelyn Cutter tried to speak, but no words came. At his work-desk Patterson's face had turned chalk-white. "Continue," he managed to mutter. "Go on talking."

"We hung on there, subsurface, down under the Copernicus crater, while they slammed their C-missiles into us. We held out maybe five years. Then they started landing. Me and those still left took off in high-speed attack torpedoes, set up pirate bases among the outer planets." Unger twitched restlessly. "I hate to talk about that part. Defeat, the end of everything. Why do you ask me? I helped build 3-4-9-5, the best artibase of the lot. Between Uranus and Neptune. Then I retired again. Until the dirty rats slid in and *leisurely* blew it to bits. Fifty thousand men, women, kids. The whole colony."

"You escaped?" Evelyn Cutter whispered.

"Of course I escaped! I was on patrol. I got one of those webfoot ships. Shot it down and watched them die. It made me feel a little better. I moved over to 3-6-7-7 for a few years. Until it was attacked. That was early this month. I was fighting with my back to the wall." The dirty yellow teeth glinted in agony. "No place to escape to, that time. None that I knew of." The red-rimmed eye surveyed the luxurious office. "Didn't know about this. You people sure done a good job fixing up your artibase. Looks almost like I remember the real Earth. A little too fast and bright; not so peaceful as Earth really was. But you even got the smell of the air the same."

There was silence.

"Then you came here after — that colony was destroyed?" Patterson asked hoarsely.

"I guess so." Unger shrugged wearily. "Last I remember was the bubble shattering and the air and heat and grav leaking out. Crow and webfoot ships landing everywhere. Men dying around me. I was knocked out by the concussion. The next thing I knew I was lying out in the street here, and some people were getting me to my feet. A tinman and one of your doctors took me here."

Patterson let out a deep shuddering breath. "I see." His fingers plucked aimlessly at the eroded, sweat-grimed i.d. papers. "Well, that explains this irregularity."

"Ain't it all there? Is something missing?"

"All your papers are here. Your tube was hanging around your wrist when they brought you in."

"Naturally." Unger's bird-like chest swelled with pride. "I learned that when I was sixteen. Even when you're dead you have to have that tube with you. Important to keep the records straight."

"The records are straight," Patterson admitted thickly. "You can go back to your room. Or the park. Anywhere." He waved and the robot calmly escorted the withered old man from the office and out into the hall.

As the door slid shut Evelyn Cutter began swearing slowly and monotonously. She crushed out her cigarette with her sharp heel and paced wildly back and forth. "Good God what have we got ourselves into?"

Patterson snatched up the intervid, dialed outside, and said to the supraplan monitor, "Get me military headquarters. Right away."

"At Luna, sir?"

"That's right," Patterson said. "At the main base on Luna."

On the wall of the office, past the taut, pacing figure of Evelyn Cutter, the calendar read August 4, 2169. If David Unger was born in 2154 he would be a boy of fifteen. And he *had* been born in 2154. It said so on his battered, yellowed, sweat-stained cards. On the i.d. papers carried through a war that hadn't yet happened.

"He's a veteran, all right," Patterson said to V-Stephens. "Of a war that won't begin for another month. No wonder his application was turned back by the IBM machines."

V-Stephens licked his dark green lips. "This war will be between Earth and the two colony planets. And Earth will lose?"

"Unger fought through the whole war. He saw it from the start to finish — to the total destruction of Earth." Patterson paced over to the window and gazed out. "Earth lost the war and the race of Earthmen was wiped out."

From the window of V-Stephens' office, Patterson could see the city spread out. Miles of buildings, white and gleaming in the late afternoon sun. Eleven million people. A gigantic center of commerce and industry, the economic hub of the system. And beyond it, a world of cities and farms and highways, three billion men and women. A thriving, healthy planet, the mother world from which the altereds had originally sprung, the ambitious settlers of Venus and Mars. Endless cargo carriers lumbered between Earth and the colonies, weighed down with minerals and ores and produce. And already, survey teams were poking around the outer planets, laying claim in the Directorate's name to new sources of raw-materials.

"He saw all this go up in radioactive dust," Patterson said. "He saw the final attack on Earth that broke our defenses. And then they wiped out the Lunar base."

"You say some brass hats are on their way here from Luna?"

"I gave them enough of the story to start them moving. It usually takes weeks to stir up those fellows."

"I'd like to see this Unger," V-Stephens said thoughtfully. "Is there some way I can — "

"You've seen him. You revived him, remember? When he was originally found and brought in."

"Oh," V-Stephens said softly. "That filthy old man?" His dark eyes flickered. "So that's Unger ... the veteran of the war we're going to fight."

"The war you're going to win. The war Earth is going to lose." Patterson abruptly left the window. "Unger thinks this is an artificial satellite someplace between Uranus and Neptune. A reconstruction of a small part of New York — a few thousand people and machines under a plastic dome. He has no conception of what's actually happened to him. Somehow, he must have been hurled back along his time-track."

"I suppose the release of energy ... and maybe his frantic desire to escape. But even so, the whole thing is fantastic. It has a sort of — " V-Stephens groped for the word. " — a sort of mystic ring to it. What the hell is this, a visitation? A prophet from heaven?"

The door opened and V-Rafia slid in. "Oh," she said, as she saw Patterson. "I didn't know — "

"That's all right." V-Stephens nodded her inside his office. "You remember Patterson. He was with us in the car when we picked you up."

V-Rafia looked much better than she had a few hours before. Her face was no longer scratched, her hair was back in place, and she had changed to a crisp gray sweater and skirt. Her green skin sparkled as she moved over beside V-Stephens, still nervous and apprehensive. "I'm staying here," she said defensively to Patterson. "I can't go back out there, not for a while." She darted a quick glance of appeal at V-Stephens.

"She has no family on Earth," V-Stephens explained. "She came here as a Class-2 biochemist. She's been working over at a Westinghouse lab outside Chicago. She came to New York on a shopping trip, which was a mistake."

"Can't she join the V-colony at Denver?" Patterson asked.

V-Stephens flushed. "You don't want another webfoot around here?"

"What can she do? We're not an embattled fortress. There's no reason why we can't shoot her to Denver in a fast freight rocket. Nobody'll interfere with that."

"We can discuss it later," V-Stephens said irritably. "We've got more important things to talk about. You've made a check of Unger's papers? You're certain they're not forgeries? I suppose it's possible this is on the level, but we have to be certain."

"This has to be kept quiet," Patterson said urgently, with a glance at V-Rafia. "Nobody on the outside should be brought in."

"You mean me?" V-Rafia asked hesitantly. "I guess I better leave."

"Don't leave," V-Stephens said, grabbing hold of her arm roughly. "Patterson, you can't keep this quiet. Unger's probably told it to fifty people; he sits out there on his park bench all day, buttonholing everybody who passes."

"What is this?" V-Rafia asked curiously.

"Nothing important," Patterson said warningly.

"Nothing important?" V-Stephens echoed. "Just a little war. Programs for sale in advance." Across his face a spasm of emotion passed, excitement and yearning hunger pouring up from inside him. "Place your bets *now*. Don't take chances. Bet on a sure thing, sweetheart. After all, it's history. Isn't that right?" He turned toward Patterson, his expression demanding confirmation. "What do you say? I can't stop it — you can't stop it. Right?"

Patterson nodded slowly. "I guess you're right," he said unhappily. And swung with all his strength.

He caught V-Stephens slightly to one side, as the Venusian scrambled away. V-Stephens' cold-beam came out; he aimed with shaky fingers. Patterson kicked it from his hands and dragged him to his feet. "It was a mistake, John," he panted. "I shouldn't have showed you Unger's i.d. tube. I shouldn't have let you know."

"That's right," V-Stephens managed to whisper. His eyes were blank with sorrow as he focused on Patterson. "Now I know. Now we both know. *You're going to lose the war.* Even if you lock Unger up in a box and sink him to the center of the Earth, it's too late. Color-Ad will know as soon as I'm out of here."

"They burned down the Color-Ad office in New York."

"Then I'll find the one in Chicago. Or Baltimore. I'll fly back to Venus, if I have to. I'm going to spread the good news. It'll be hard and long, but we'll win. And you can't do anything about it."

"I can kill you," Patterson said. His mind was racing frantically. It wasn't too late. If V-Stephens were contained, and David Unger turned over to the Military —

"I know what you're thinking," V-Stephens gasped. "If Earth doesn't fight, if you avoid war, you may still have a chance." His green lips twisted savagely. "You think we'd *let* you avoid war? Not now! Only traitors compromise, according to you. Now it's too late!"

"Only too late," Patterson said, "if you get out of here." His hand groped on the desk and found a steel paper weight. He drew it to him — and felt the smooth tip of the cold-beam in his ribs.

"I'm not sure how this thing words," V-Rafia said slowly, "but I guess there's only this one button to press."

"That's right," V-Stephens said, with relief. "But don't press it yet. I want to talk to him a few minutes more. Maybe he can be brought around to rationality." He pulled himself gratefully out of Patterson's grip and moved back a few paces, exploring his cut lip and broken front teeth. "You brought this on yourself, Vachel."

"This is insane," Patterson snapped, his eyes on the snout of the cold-beam as it wavered in V-Rafia's uncertain fingers. "You expect us to fight a war we know we're going to lose?"

"You won't have a choice." V-Stephens' eyes gleamed. "We'll make you fight. When we attack your cities you'll come back at us. It's — human nature."

The first blast of the cold-beam missed Patterson. He floundered to one side and grabbed for the girl's slim wrist. His fingers caught air, and then he was down, as the beam hissed again. V-Rafia retreated, eyes wide with fright and dismay, aiming blindly for his rising body. He leaped up, hands extended for the terrified girl. He saw her fingers twist, saw the snout of the tube darken as the field clicked on. And that was all.

From the kicked-open door, the blue-clad soldiers caught V-Rafia in a crossfire of death. A chill breath mushroomed in Patterson's face. He collapsed back, arms up frantically, as the frigid whisper glided past him.

V-Rafia's trembling body danced briefly, as the cloud of absolute cold glowed around her. Then abruptly she halted as rigid as if the tape-track of her life had stopped in the projector. All color drained from her body. The bizarre imitation of a still-standing human figure stood silently, one arm raised, caught in the act of futile defense.

Then the frozen pillar burst. The expanded cells ruptured in a shower of crystalline particles that were hurled sickeningly into every part of the office.

Francis Gannet moved cautiously in behind the troops, red-faced and perspiring. "You're Patterson?" he demanded. He held out his heavy hand, but Patterson didn't take it. "The Military people notified me as a matter of course. Where's this old man?"

"Somewhere around," Patterson muttered. "Under guard." He turned toward V-Stephens and briefly their eyes met. "You see?" he said huskily. "This is what happens. Is this what you really want?"

"Come on, Mr. Patterson," Francis Gannet boomed impatiently. "I don't have much time to waste. From your description this sounds like something important."

"It is," V-Stephens answered calmly. He wiped at the trickle of mouth-blood with his pocket handkerchief. "It's worth the trip from Luna. Take my word for it — I *know*."

The man who sat on Gannet's right was a lieutenant. He gazed in mute awe at the vidscreen. His young, handsome blond face was alive with amazement as from the bank of gray haze a huge battleship lumbered, one reactor smashed, its forward turrets crumpled, hull twisted open.

"Good God," Lieutenant Nathan West said faintly. "That's the *Wind Giant*. The biggest battleship we have. Look at it — it's out of commission. Totally disabled."

"That will be your ship," Patterson said. "You'll be commander of it in '87 when it's destroyed by the combined Venusian and Martian fleets. David Unger will be serving under you. You'll be killed, but Unger will escape. The few survivors of your ship will watch from Luna as Earth is systematically demolished by C-missiles from Venus and Mars."

On the screen, the figures leaped and swirled like fish in the bottom of a dirt-saturated tank. A violent maelstrom surged in the center, a vortex of energy that lashed the ships on vast spasms of motion. The silver Earth ships hesitated, then broke. Flashing black Mars battleships swept through the wide breach — and the Earth flank was turned simultaneously by the waiting Venusians. Together, they caught the remnants of the Earth ships in a steel pincers and crunched them out of existence. Brief puffs of light, as the ships winked out of being. In the distance, the solemn blue and green orb that was Earth slowly and majestically revolved.

Already, it showed ugly pocks. Bomb craters from the C-missiles that had penetrated the defense network.

LeMarr snapped off the projector and the screen died. "That ends that brain-sequence. All we can get are visual fragments like this, brief instants that left strong impressions on him. We can't get continuity. The next one takes up years later, on one of the artificial satellites."

The lights came on, and the group of spectators moved stiffly to their feet. Gannet's face was a sickly putty-gray. "Doctor LeMarr, I want to see that shot again. The one of Earth." He gestured helplessly. "You know which one I mean."

The lights dimmed and again the screen came to life. This time it showed only Earth, a receding orb that fell behind as the high-velocity torpedo on which David Unger rode hurtled toward outer space. Unger had placed himself so his dead world would be visible to the last.

Earth was a ruin. Involuntarily, a gasp rose from the group of watching officers. Nothing lived. Nothing moved. Only dead clouds of radioactive ash billowed aimlessly over the crater-pocked surface. What had been a living planet of three billion people was a charred cinder of ash. Nothing remained but heaps of debris, dispersed and blown dismally across vacant seas by the howling, ceaseless wind.

"I suppose some kind of vegetable life will take over," Evelyn Cutter said harshly, as the screen faded and the overhead lights returned. She shuddered violently and turned away.

"Weeds, maybe," LeMarr said. "Dark dry weeds poking up through the slag. Maybe some insects, later on. Bacteria, of course. I suppose in time bacterial action will transform the ash into usable soil. And it'll rain for a billion years."

"Let's face it," Gannet said. "The webfoots and crows will resettle it. They'll be living here on Earth after we're all dead."

"Sleeping in our beds?" LeMarr inquired mildly. "Using our bathrooms and sitting rooms and transports?"

"I don't understand you," Gannet answered impatiently. He waved Patterson over. "You're sure nobody knows but we here in this room?"

"V-Stephens knows," Patterson said. "But he's locked up in the psychotic ward. V-Rafia knew. She's dead."

Lieutenant West came over to Patterson. "Could we interview him?"

"Yes, where's Unger?" Gannet demanded. "My staff is eager to meet him face to face."

"You have all the essential facts," Patterson answered. "You know how the war is going to come out. You know what's going to happen to Earth."

"What do you suggest?" Gannet asked warily.

"Avoid the war."

Gannet shrugged his plump well-fed body. "After all, you can't change history. And this is future history. We have no choice but to go ahead and fight."

"At least we'll get our share of them," Evelyn Cutter said icily.

"What are you talking about?" LeMarr stuttered excitedly. "You work in a hospital and you talk like that?"

The woman's eyes blazed. "You saw what they did to Earth. You saw them cut us to ribbons."

"We have to stand above this," LeMarr protested. "If we allow ourselves to get dragged into this hate and violence — " He appealed to Patterson. "Why is V-Stephens locked up? He's no crazier than she is."

"True," Patterson agreed. "But she's crazy on *our* side. We don't lock up that kind of lunatic."

LeMarr moved away from him. "Are you going out and fight, too? Alongside Gannet and his soldiers?"

"I want to avoid the war," Patterson said dully.

"Can it be done?" Gannet demanded. An avid glow winked briefly behind his pale, blue eyes and then faded out.

"Maybe it can be done. Why not? Unger coming back here adds a new element."

"If the future can be changed," Gannet said slowly, "then maybe we have a choice of various possibilities. If there's two possible futures there may be an infinite number. Each branching off at a different point." A granite mask slid over his face. "We can use Unger's knowledge of the battles."

"Let me talk to him," Lieutenant West interrupted excitedly. "Maybe we can get a clear idea of the webfoot battle-strategy. He's probably gone over the battles in his mind a thousand times."

"He'd recognize you," Gannet said. "After all, he served under your command."

Patterson was deep in thought. "I don't think so," he said to West. "You're a lot older than David Unger."

West blinked. "What do you mean? He's a broken-down old man and I'm still in my twenties."

"David Unger is fifteen," Patterson answered. "At this point you're almost twice his age. You're already a commissioned officer on the Lunar policy-level staff. Unger isn't even in the Military Service. He'll volunteer when war breaks out, as a buck private without experience or training. When you're an old man, commanding the *Wind Giant*, David Unger will be a middle-aged nonentity working one of the gun turrets, a name you won't even know."

"Then Unger is already alive?" Gannet said, puzzled.

"Unger is someplace around, waiting to step onto the stage." Patterson filed the thought away for future study; it might have valuable possibilities. "I don't think he'll recognize you, West. He may never even have seen you. The *Wind Giant* is a big ship."

West quickly agreed. "Put a bug-system on me, Gannet. So the command staff can have the aud and vid images of what Unger says."

In the bright mid-morning sunlight, David Unger sat moodily on his park bench, gnarled fingers gripping his aluminum cane, gazing dully at the passers-by.

To his right a robot gardener worked over the same patch of grass again and again, its metallic eye-lenses intently fastened on the wizened, hunched-over figure of the old man. Down the gravel path a group of loitering men sent random comments to the various monitors scattered through the park, keeping the relay system open. A bare-bosomed young woman sunbathing by the pool nodded faintly to a pair of soldiers pacing around the park, within constant sight of David Unger.

That morning there were a hundred people in the park. All were integrated elements of the screen surrounding the half-dozing, resentful old man.

"All right," Patterson said. His car was parked at the edge of the plot of green trees and lawns. "Remember not to overexcite him. V-Stephens revived him originally. If something goes wrong with his heart we can't get V-Stephens to pump him back."

The blond young lieutenant nodded, straightened his immaculate blue tunic and slid onto the sidewalk. He pushed his helmet back and briskly strode down the gravel path, toward the center of the park. As he approached, the lounging figures moved imperceptibly. One by one they took up positions on the lawns, on the benches, in groups here and there around the pool.

Lieutenant West stopped at a drinking-fountain and allowed the robot water-brain to find his mouth with a jet of ice-cold spray. He wandered slowly away and stood for a moment, arms loose at his sides, vacantly watching a young woman as she removed her clothes and stretched out languidly on a multi-colored blanket. Her eyes shut, red lips parted, the woman relaxed with a grateful sigh.

"Let him speak to you first," she said faintly, to the lieutenant standing a few feet from her, one black boot on the edge of a bench. "Don't start the conversation."

Lieutenant West watched her a moment longer and then continued along the path. A passing heavy-set man said swiftly in his ear. "Not so fast. Take your time and don't appear to hurry."

"You want to give the impression you have all day," a hatchet-faced nurse greeted, as she passed him wheeling a baby carriage.

Lieutenant West slowed almost to a halt. He aimlessly kicked a bit of gravel from the path into the wet bushes. Hands deep in his pockets he wandered over to the central pool and stood gazing absently into its depths. He lit a cigarette, then bought an ice cream bar from a passing robot salesman.

"Spill some on your tunic, sir," the robot's speaker instructed faintly. "Swear and start dabbing at it."

Lieutenant West let the ice cream melt in the warm summer sun. When some had dripped down his wrist onto his starched blue tunic he scowled, dug out his handkerchief, dipped it in the pool, and began clumsily to wipe the ice cream away.

On his bench, the scar-faced old man watched with his one good eye, gripping his aluminum cane and cackling happily. "Watch out," he wheezed. "Look out there!"

Lieutenant West glanced up in annoyance.

"You're dripping more," the old man cackled, and lay back in weak amusement, toothless mouth slack with pleasure.

Lieutenant West grinned good-naturedly. "I guess so," he admitted. He dropped the melting half-eaten ice cream bar into a disposal slot and finished cleaning his tunic. "Sure is warm," he observed, wandering vaguely over.

"They do a good job," Unger agreed, nodding his bird-like head. He peered and craned his neck, trying to make out the insignia markings on the young soldier's shoulder. "You with the rocketeers?"

"Demolition," Lieutenant West said. As of that morning his insignia had been changed. "Ba-3."

The old man shuddered. He hawked and spat feverishly into the nearby bushes. "That so?" He half-rose, excited and fearful, as the lieutenant started to move away. "Say, you know, I was in the Ba-3 years ago." He tried to make his voice sound calm and casual. "Long before your time."

Amazement and disbelief slid over Lieutenant West's handsome blond face. "Don't kid me. Only a couple guys from the old group are still alive. You're pulling my leg."

"I was, I was," Unger wheezed, fumbling with trembling haste at his coat pocket. "Say, look at this. Stop a minute and I'll show you something." Reverent and awed, he held out his Crystal Disc. "See? You know what this is?"

Lieutenant West gazed down at the metal a long time. Real emotion welled up inside him; he didn't have to counterfeit it. "Can I examine it?" he asked finally.

Unger hesitated. "Sure," he said. "Take it."

Lieutenant West took the medal and held it for a long moment, weighing it and feeling its cold surface against his smooth skin. Finally he returned it. "You got that back in '87?"

"That's right," Unger said. "You remember?" He returned it to his pocket. "No, you weren't even alive, then. But you heard about it, haven't you?"

"Yes," West said. "I've heard about it many times."

"And you haven't forgotten? A lot of people forgot that, what we did there."

"I guess we took a beating that day," West said. He sat down slowly on the bench beside the old man. "That was a bad day for Earth."

"We lost," Unger agreed. "Only a few of us got out of there. I got to Luna. I saw Earth go, piece by piece, until there was nothing left. It broke my heart. I cried until I lay like a dead thing. We were all weeping, soldiers, workmen, standing there helpless. And then they turned their missiles on us."

The lieutenant licked his dry lips. "Your Commander didn't get out, did he?"

"Nathan West died on his ship," Unger said. "He was the finest commander in the line. They didn't give him the *Wind Giant* for nothing." His ancient, withered features dimmed in recollection. "There'll never be another man like West. I saw him, once. Big stern-faced man, wide-shouldered. A giant himself. He was a great old man. Nobody could have done better."

West hesitated. "You think if somebody else had been in command — "

"*No*!" Unger shrieked. "Nobody could have done better! I've heard it said — I know what some of those fat-bottomed armchair strategists say. But they're wrong! Nobody could have won that battle. We didn't have a chance. We were outnumbered five to one — two huge fleets, one straight at our middle and the other waiting to chew us up and swallow us."

"I see," West said thickly. Reluctantly he continued, in an agony of turmoil, "These armchair men, what the hell is it they say? I never listen to the brass." He tried to grin but his face refused to respond. "I know they're always saying we could have won the battle and maybe even saved the *Wind Giant*, but I — "

"Look here," Unger said fervently, his sunken eye wild and glittering.

With the point of his aluminum cane he began gouging harsh, violent ditches in the gravel by his feet. "This line is our fleet. Remember how West had it drawn up? It was a mastermind arranged our fleet, that day. A genius. We held them off for twelve hours before they busted through. Nobody thought we'd have a chance of even doing that." Savagely, Unger gouged another line. "That's the crow fleet."

"I see," West muttered. He leaned over so his chest-lens would vid the rough lines in the gravel back to the scanning center in the mobile unit circling lazily overhead. And from there to main headquarters on Luna. "And the webfoot fleet?"

Unger glanced cagily at him, suddenly shy. "I'm not boring you, am I? I guess an old man likes to talk. Sometimes I bother people, trying to take up their time."

"Go on," West answered. He meant what he said. "Keep drawing — I'm watching."

Evelyn Cutter paced restlessly around her softly-lit apartment, arms folded, red lips tight with anger. "I don't understand you!" She paused to lower the heavy drapes. "You were willing to kill V-Stephens a little while ago. Now you won't even help block LeMarr. You know LeMarr doesn't grasp what's happening. He dislikes Gannet and he prattles about the interplan community of scientists, our duty to all mankind and that sort of stuff. Can't you see if V-Stephens gets hold of him — "

"Maybe LeMarr is right," Patterson said. "I don't like Gannet either."

Evelyn exploded. "They'll destroy us! We can't fight a war with them — we don't have a chance." She halted in front of him, eyes blazing. "But they don't know that yet. We've got to neutralize LeMarr, at least for a while. Every minute he's walking around free puts our world in jeopardy. Three billion lives depend on keeping this suppressed."

Patterson was brooding. "I suppose Gannet briefed you on the initial exploration West conducted today."

"No results so far. The old man knows every battle by heart, and we lost them all." She rubbed her forehead wearily. "I mean, we *will* lose them all." With numb fingers she gathered up the empty coffee cups. "Want some more coffee?"

Patterson didn't hear her; he was intent on his own thoughts. He crossed over to the window and stood gazing out until she returned with fresh coffee, hot and black and steaming.

"You didn't see Gannet kill that girl," Patterson said.

"What girl? That webfoot?" Evelyn stirred sugar and cream into her coffee. "She was going to kill you. V-Stephens would have lit out for Color-Ad and the war would begin." Impatiently, she pushed his coffee cup to him. "Anyhow, that was the girl we saved."

"I know," Patterson said. "That's why it bothers me." He took the coffee automatically and sipped without tasting. "What was the point of dragging her from the mob? Gannet's work. We're employees of Gannet."

"So?"

"You know what kind of game he's playing!"

Evelyn shrugged. "I'm just being practical. I don't want Earth destroyed. Neither does Gannet — he wants to avoid the war."

"He wanted war a few days ago. When he expected to win."

Evelyn laughed sharply. "Of course! Who'd fight a war they knew they'd lose? That's irrational."

"Now Gannet will hold off the war," Patterson admitted slowly. "He'll let the colony planets have their independence. He'll recognize Color-Ad. He'll destroy David Unger and everybody who knows. He'll pose as a benevolent peacemaker."

"Of course. He's already making plans for a dramatic trip to Venus. A last minute conference with Color-Ad officials, to prevent war. He'll put pressure on the Directorate to back down and let Mars and Venus sever. He'll be the idol of the system. But isn't that better than Earth destroyed and our race wiped out?"

"Now the big machine turns around and roars *against* war." Patterson's lips twisted ironically. "Peace and compromise instead of hate and destructive violence."

Evelyn perched on the arm of a chair and made rapid calculations. "How old was David Unger when he joined the Military?"

"Fifteen or sixteen."

"When a man joins the Service he gets his i.d. number, doesn't he?"

"That's right. So?"

"Maybe I'm wrong, but according to my figures — " She glanced up. "Unger should appear and claim his number, soon. That number will be coming up any day, according to how fast the enlistments pour in."

A strange expression crossed Patterson's face. "Unger is already alive ... a fifteen year old kid. Unger the youth and Unger the senile old war veteran. Both alive at once."

Evelyn shuddered. "It's weird. Suppose they ran into each other? There'd be a lot of difference between them."

In Patterson's mind a picture of a bright-eyed youth of fifteen formed. Eager to get into the fight. Ready to leap in and kill webfoots and crows with idealistic enthusiasm. At this moment, Unger was moving inexorably toward the recruiting office ... and the half-blind, crippled old relic of eighty-nine wretched years was creeping hesitantly from his hospital room to his park bench, hugging his aluminum cane, whispering in his raspy, pathetic voice to anyone who would listen.

"We'll have to keep our eyes open," Patterson said. "You better have somebody at Military notify you when that number comes up. When Unger appears to claim it."

Evelyn nodded. "It might be a good idea. Maybe we should request the Census Department to make a check for us. Maybe we can locate — "

She broke off. The door of the apartment had swung silently open. Edwin LeMarr stood gripping the knob, blinking red-eyed in the half-light. Breathing harshly, he came into the room. "Vachel, I have to talk to you."

"What is it?" Patterson demanded. "What's going on?"

LeMarr shot Evelyn a look of pure hate. "He found it. I knew he would. As soon as he can get it analyzed and the whole thing down on tape — "

"Gannet?" Cold fear knifed down Patterson's spine. "Gannet found what?"

"The moment of crisis. The old man's babbling about a five-ship convoy. Fuel for the crow warfleet. Unescorted and moving toward the battle line. Unger says our scouts will miss it." LeMarr's breathing was hoarse and frenzied. "He says if we knew in advance — " He pulled himself together with a violent effort. "Then we could destroy it."

"I see," Patterson said. "And throw the balance in Earth's favor."

"If West can plot the convoy route," LeMarr finished, "Earth will win the war. That means Gannet will fight — as soon as he gets the exact information."

V-Stephens sat crouched on the single-piece bench that served as chair and table and bed for the psychotic ward. A cigarette dangled between his dark green lips. The cube-like room was ascetic, barren. The walls glittered dully. From time to time V-Stephens examined his wristwatch and then turned his attention back to the object crawling up and down the sealed edges of the entrance-lock.

The object moved slowly and cautiously. It had been exploring the lock for twenty-nine hours straight; it had traced down the power leads that kept the heavy plate fused in place. It had located the terminals at which the leads joined the magnetic rind of the door. During the last hour it had cut its way through the rexeroid surface to within an inch of the terminals. The crawling, exploring object was V-Stephens' surgeon-hand, a self-contained robot of precision quality usually joined to his right wrist.

It wasn't joined there now. He had detached it and sent it up the face of the cube to find a way out. The metal fingers clung precariously to the smooth dull surface, as the cutting-thumb laboriously dug its way in. It was a big job for the surgeon-hand; after this it wouldn't be of much use at the operating table. But V-Stephens could easily get another — they were for sale at any medical supply house on Venus.

The forefinger of the surgeon-hand reached the anode terminal and paused questioningly. All four fingers rose erect and waved like insect antennae. One by one they fitted themselves into the cut slot and probed for the nearby cathode lead.

Abruptly there was a blinding flash. A white acrid cloud billowed out, and then came a sharp *pop*. The entrance-lock remained motionless as the hand dropped to the floor, its work done. V-Stephens put out his cigarette, got leisurely to his feet, and crossed the cube to collect it.

With the hand in place and acting as part of his own neuromuscular system again, V-Stephens gingerly grasped the lock by its perimeter and after a moment pulled inward. The lock came without resistance and he found himself facing a deserted corridor. There was no sound or motion. No guards. No check-system on the psych patients. V-Stephens loped quickly ahead, around a turn, and through a series of connecting passages.

In a moment he was at a wide view-window, overlooking the street, the surrounding buildings, and the hospital grounds.

He assembled his wristwatch, cigarette lighter, fountain pen, keys and coins. From them his agile flesh and metal fingers rapidly formed an intricate gestalt of wiring and plates. He snapped off the cutting-thumb and screwed a heat-element in its place. In a brief flurry he had fused the mechanism to the underside of the window ledge, invisible from the hall, too far from ground level to be noticed.

He was starting back down the corridor when a sound stopped him rigid. Voices, a routine hospital guard and somebody else. A familiar somebody else.

He raced back to the psych ward and into his sealed cube. The magnetic lock fitted reluctantly in place; the heat generated by the short had sprung its clamps. He got it shut as footsteps halted outside. The magnetic field of the lock was dead, but of course the visitors didn't know that. V-Stephens listened with amusement as the visitor carefully negated the supposed magnetic field and then pushed the lock open.

"Come in," V-Stephens said.

Doctor LeMarr entered, briefcase in one hand, cold-beam in the other. "Come along with me. I have everything arranged. Money, fake identification, passport, tickets and clearance. You'll go as a webfoot commercial agent. By the time Gannet finds out you'll be past the Military monitor and out of Earth jurisdiction."

V-Stephens was astounded. "But — "

"Hurry up!" LeMarr waved him into the corridor with his cold-beam. "As a staff member of the hospital I have authority over psych prisoners. Technically, you're listed as a mental patient. As far as I'm concerned you're no more crazy than the rest of them. If not less. That's why I'm here."

V-Stephens eyed him doubtfully. "You sure you know what you're doing?" He followed LeMarr down the corridor, past the blank-faced guard and into the elevator. "They'll destroy you as a traitor, if they catch you. That guard saw you — how are you going to keep this quiet?"

"I don't expect to keep this quiet. Gannet is here, you know. He and his staff have been working over the old man."

"Why are you telling me this?" The two of them strode down the descent ramp to the subsurface garage. An attendant rolled out LeMarr's car and they climbed into it, LeMarr behind the wheel. "You know why I was thrown in the psych-cube in the first place."

"Take this." LeMarr tossed V-Stephens the cold-beam and steered up the tunnel to the surface, into the bright mid-day New York traffic. "You were going to contact Color-Ad and inform them Earth will absolutely lose the war." He spun the car from the mainstream of traffic and onto a side lane, toward the interplan spacefield. "Tell them to stop working for compromise and strike hard — immediately. Full scale war. Right?"

"Right," V-Stephens said. "After all, if we're certain to win — "

"You're not certain."

V-Stephens raised a green eyebrow. "Oh? I thought Unger was a veteran of total defeat."

"Gannet is going to change the course of the war. He's found a critical point. As soon as he gets the exact information he'll pressure the Directorate into an all-out attack on Venus and Mars. War can't be avoided, not now." LeMarr slammed his car to a halt at the edge of the interplan field. "If there has to be war at least nobody's going to be taken by a sneak attack. You can tell your Colonial Organization and Administration our warfleet is on its way. Tell them to get ready. Tell them — "

LeMarr's voice trailed off. Like an unwound toy he sagged against the seat, slid silently down, and lay quietly with his head against the steering wheel. His glasses dropped from his nose onto the floor and after a moment V-Stephens replaced them. "I'm sorry," he said softly. "You meant well, but you sure fouled everything up."

He briefly examined the surface of LeMarr's skull. The impulse from the cold-beam had not penetrated into brain tissue; LeMarr would regain consciousness in a few hours with nothing worse than a severe headache. V-Stephens pocketed the cold-beam, grabbed up the briefcase, and pushed the limp body of LeMarr away from the wheel. A moment later he was turning on the motor and backing the car around.

As he sped back to the hospital he examined his watch. It wasn't too late. He leaned forward and dropped a quarter in the pay vidphone mounted on the dashboard. After a mechanical dialing process the Color-Ad receptionist flickered into view.

"This is V-Stephens," he said. "Something went wrong. I was taken out of the hospital building. I'm heading back there now. I can make it in time, I think."

"Is the vibrator-pack assembled?"

"Assembled, yes. But not with me. I had already fused it into polarization with the magnetic flux. It's ready to go — if I can get back there and at it."

"There's a hitch at this end," the green-skinned girl said. "Is this a closed circuit?"

"It's open," V-Stephens admitted. "But it's public and probably random. They couldn't very well have a bug on it." He checked the power meter on the guarantee seal fastened to the unit. "It shows no drain. Go ahead."

"The ship won't be able to pick you up in the city."

"Hell," V-Stephens said.

"You'll have to get out of New York on your own power; we can't help you there. Mobs destroyed our New York port facilities. You'll have to go by surface car to Denver. That's the nearest place the ship can land. That's our last protected spot on Earth."

V-Stephens groaned. "Just my luck. You know what'll happen if they catch me?"

The girl smiled faintly. "All webfoots look alike to Earthmen. They'll be stringing us up indiscriminately. We're in this together. Good luck; we'll be waiting for you."

V-Stephens angrily broke the circuit and slowed the car. He parked in a public parking lot on a dingy side street and got quickly out. He was at the edge of the green expanse of park. Beyond it, the hospital buildings rose. Gripping the briefcase tightly he ran toward the main entrance.

David Unger wiped his mouth on his sleeve, then lay back weakly against his chair. "I don't know," he repeated, his voice faint and dry. "I told you I don't remember any more. It was so long ago."

Gannet signaled, and the officers moved away from the old man. "It's coming," he said wearily. He mopped his perspiring forehead. "Slowly and surely. We should have what we want inside another half hour."

One side of the therapy house had been turned into a Military table-map. Counters had been laid out across the surface to represent units of the webfoot and crow fleets. White luminous chips represented Earth ships lined up against them in a tight ring around the third planet.

"It's someplace near here," Lieutenant West said to Patterson. Red-eyed, stubble-chinned, hands shaking with fatigue and tension, he indicated a section of the map. "Unger remembers hearing officers talking about this convoy. The convoy took off from a supply base on Ganymede. It disappeared on some kind of deliberate random course." His hands swept the area. "At the time, nobody on Earth paid any attention to it. Later, they realized what they'd lost. Some military expert charted the thing in retrospect and it was taped and passed around. Officers got together and analyzed the incident. Unger *thinks* the convoy route took it close to Europa. But maybe it was Callisto."

"That's not good enough," Gannet snapped. "So far we don't have any more route data than Earth tacticians had at that time. We need to add exact knowledge, material released after the event."

David Unger fumbled with a glass of water. "Thanks," he muttered gratefully, as one of the young officers handed it to him. "I sure wish I could help you fellows out better," he said plaintively. "I'm trying to remember. But I don't seem able to think clear, like I used to." His wizened face twisted with futile concentration. "You know, it seems to me that convoy was stopped near Mars by some kind of meteor swarm."

Gannet moved forward. "Go on."

Unger appealed to him pathetically. "I want to help you all I can, mister. Most people go to write a book about a war, they just scan stuff from other books." There was a pitiful gratitude on the eroded face. "I guess you'll mention my name in your book, someplace."

"Sure," Gannet said expansively. "Your name'll be on the first page. Maybe we could even get in a picture of you."

"I know all about the war," Unger muttered. "Give me time and I'll have it straight. *Just give me time.* I'm trying as best I can."

The old man was deteriorating rapidly. His wrinkled face was an unhealthy gray. Like drying putty, his flesh clung to his brittle, yellowed bones. His breath rattled in his throat. It was obvious to everyone present that David Unger was going to die — and soon.

"If he croaks before he remembers," Gannet said softly to Lieutenant West, "I'll — "

"What's that?" Unger asked sharply. His one good eye was suddenly keen and wary. "I can't hear so good."

"Just fill in the missing elements,"Gannet said wearily. He jerked his head. "Get him over to the map where he can see the setup. Maybe that'll help."

The old man was yanked to his feet and propelled to the table. Technicians and brass hats closed in around him and the dim-eyed stumbling figure was lost from sight.

"He won't last long," Patterson said savagely. "If you don't let him rest his heart's going to give out."

"We must have the information," Gannet retorted. He eyed Patterson. "Where's the other doctor? LeMarr, I think he's called."

Patterson glanced briefly around. "I don't see him. He probably couldn't stand it."

"LeMarr never came," Gannet said, without emotion. "I wonder if we should have somebody round him up." He indicated Evelyn Cutter, who had just arrived, white-faced, her black eyes wide, breathing quickly. "She suggests — "

"It doesn't matter now," Evelyn said frigidly. She shot a quick, urgent glance at Patterson. "I want nothing to do with you and your war."

Gannet shrugged. "I'll send out a routine net, in any case. Just to be on the safe side." He moved off, leaving Evelyn and Patterson standing alone together.

"Listen to me," Evelyn said harshly, her lips hot and close to his ear. "*Unger's number has come up.*"

"When did they notify you?" Patterson demanded.

"I was on my way here. I did what you said — I fixed it up with a clerk at Military."

"How long ago?"

"Just now." Evelyn's face trembled. "Vachel, *he's here.*"

It was a moment before Patterson understood. "You mean they sent him over here? To the hospital?"

"I told them to. I told them when he came to volunteer, when his number came to the top — "

Patterson grabbed her and hurried her from the therapy house, outside into the bright sunlight. He pushed her onto an ascent ramp and crowded in after her. "Where are they holding him?"

"In the public reception room. They told him it was a routine physical check. A minor test of some kind." Evelyn was terrified. "What are we going to do? *Can* we do something?"

"Gannet thinks so."

"Suppose we — stopped him? Maybe we could turn him aside?" She shook her head, dazed. "What would happen? What would the future be like if we stopped him here? You could keep him out of the Service — you're a doctor. A little red check on his health card." She began to laugh wildly. "I see them all the time. A little red check, and no more David Unger. Gannet never sees him, Gannet never knows Earth can't win and then Earth will win, and V-Stephens doesn't get locked up as a psychotic and that webfoot girl — "

Patterson's open hand smashed across the woman's face. "Shut up and snap out of it! We don't have time for that!"

Evelyn shuddered; he caught hold of her and held on tight to her until finally she raised her face. A red welt was rising slowly on her cheek. "I'm sorry," she managed to murmur. "Thanks. I'll be all right."

The lift had reached the main floor. The door slid back and Patterson led her out into the hall. "You haven't seen him?"

"No. When they told me the number had come up and he was on his way" — Evelyn hurried breathlessly after Patterson — "I came as quickly as I could. Maybe it's too late. Maybe he got tired of waiting and left. He's a fifteen year old boy. He wants to get into the fight. Maybe he's gone!"

Patterson halted a robot attendant. "Are you busy?"

"No sir," the robot answered.

Patterson gave the robot David Unger's i.d. number. "Get this man from the main reception room. Send him out here and then close off this hall. Seal it at both ends so nobody can enter or leave."

The robot clicked uncertainly. "Will there be further orders? This syndrome doesn't complete a — "

"I'll instruct you later. Make sure nobody comes out with him. I want to meet him here alone."

The robot scanned the number and then disappeared into the reception room.

Patterson gripped Evelyn's arm. "Scared?"

"I'm terrified."

"I'll handle it. You just stand there." He passed her his cigarettes. "Light one for both of us."

"Three, maybe. One for Unger."

Patterson grinned. "He's too young, remember? He's not old enough to smoke."

The robot returned. With it was a blond boy, plump and blue-eyed, his face wrinkled with perplexity. "You wanted me, Doc?" He came uncertainly up to Patterson. "Is there something wrong with me? They told me to come here, but they didn't say what for." His anxiety increased with a tidal rush. "There's nothing to keep me out of the Service is there?"

Patterson grabbed the boy's newly stamped i.d. card, glanced at it, and then passed it to Evelyn. She accepted it with paralyzed fingers, her eyes on the blond youth.

He was not David Unger.

"What's your name?" Patterson demanded.

The boy stammered out his name shyly. "Bert Robinson. Doesn't it say there on my card?"

Patterson turned to Evelyn. "It's the right number. But this isn't Unger. Something's happened."

"Say, Doc," Robinson asked plaintively, "is there something going to keep me out of the Service or not? Give me the word."

Patterson signaled the robot. "Open up the hall. It's all over with. You can go back to what you were doing."

"I don't understand," Evelyn murmured. "It doesn't make sense."

"You're all right," Patterson said to the youth. "You can report for induction."

The boy's face sagged with relief. "Thanks a lot, Doc." He edged toward the descent ramp. "I sure appreciate it. I'm dying to get a crack at those webfoots."

"Now what?" Evelyn said tightly, when the youth's broad back had disappeared. "Where do we go from here?"

Patterson shook himself alive. "We'll get the Census Department to make their check. *We've got to locate Unger.*"

The transmission room was a humming blur of vid and aud reports. Patterson elbowed his way to an open circuit and placed the call.

"That information will take a short time, sir," the girl at Census told him. "Will you wait, or shall we return your call?"

Patterson grabbed up an h-loop and clipped it around his neck. "As soon as you have any information on Unger let me know. Break into this loop immediately."

"Yes, sir," the girl said dutifully, and broke the circuit.

Patterson headed out of the room and down the corridor. Evelyn hurried after him. "Where are we going?" she asked.

"To the therapy house. I want to talk to the old man. I want to ask him some things."

"Gannet's doing that," Evelyn gasped, as they descended to the ground level. "Why do you — "

"I want to ask him about the present, not the future." They emerged in the blinding afternoon sunlight. "I want to ask him about things going on right now."

Evelyn stopped him. "Can't you explain it to me?"

"I have a theory," Patterson pushed urgently past her. "Come on, before it's too late."

They entered the therapy house. Technicians and officers were standing around the huge map table, examining the counters and indicator lines. "Where's Unger?" Patterson demanded.

"He's gone," one of the officers answered. "Gannet gave up for today."

"Gone where?" Patterson began to swear savagely. "What happened?"

"Gannet and West took him back to the main building. He was too worn out to continue. We almost had it. Gannet's ready to burst a blood vessel, but we'll have to wait."

Patterson grabbed Evelyn Cutter. "I want you to set off a general emergency alarm. Have the building surrounded. And *hurry*!"

Evelyn gaped at him. "But — "

Patterson ignored her and raced out of the therapy house, toward the main hospital building. Ahead of him were three slowly moving figures. Lieutenant West and Gannet walked on each side of the old man, supporting him as he crept forward.

"Get away!" Patterson shouted at them.

Gannet turned. "What's going on?"

"Get him away!" Patterson dived for the old man — but it was too late.

The burst of energy seared past him; an ignited circle of blinding white flame lapped everywhere. The hunched-over figure of the old man wavered, then charred. The aluminum cane fused and ran down in a molten mass.

What had been the old man began to smoke. The body cracked open and shriveled. Then very slowly, the dried, dehydrated fragment of ash crumpled in a weightless heap. Gradually the circle of energy faded out.

Gannet kicked aimlessly at it, his heavy face numb with shock and disbelief. "He's dead. And we didn't get it."

Lieutenant West stared at the still-smoking ash. His lips twisted into words. "We'll never find out. We can't change it. We can't win." Suddenly his fingers grabbed at his coat. He tore the insignia from it and hurled the square of cloth savagely away. "I'll be damned if I'm going to give up my life so you can corner the system. I'm not getting into that death trap. Count me out!"

The wail of the general emergency alarm dinned from the hospital building. Scampering figures raced toward Gannet, soldiers and hospital guards scurrying in confusion. Patterson paid no attention to them; his eyes were on the window directly above.

Someone was standing there. A man, his hands deftly at work removing an object that flashed in the afternoon sun. The man was V-Stephens. He got the object of metal and plastic loose and disappeared with it, away from the window.

Evelyn hurried up beside Patterson. "What — " She saw the remains and screamed. "Oh, God. Who did it? *Who*?"

"V-Stephens."

"LeMarr must have let him out. I knew it would happen." Tears filled her eyes and her voice rose in shrill hysteria. "I told you he'd do it! I warned you!"

Gannet appealed childishly to Patterson. "What are we going to do? He's been murdered." Rage suddenly swept away the big man's fear. "I'll kill every webfoot on the planet. I'll burn down their homes and string them up. I'll — " He broke off raggedly. "But it's too late, isn't it? There's nothing we can do. We've lost. We're beaten, and the war hasn't even begun."

"That's right," Patterson said. "It's too late. Your chance is gone."

"If we could have got him to talk — " Gannet snarled helplessly.

"You couldn't. It wasn't possible."

Gannet blinked. "Why not?" Some of his innate animal cunning filtered back. "Why do you say that?"

Around Patterson's neck his h-loop buzzed loudly. "Doctor Patterson," the monitor's voice came, "there is a rush call for you from Census."

"Put it through," Patterson said.

The voice of the Census clerk came tinnily in his ears. "Doctor Patterson, I have the information you requested."

"What is it?" Patterson demanded. But he already knew the answer.

"We have cross-checked our results to be certain. There is no person such as you described. There is no individual at this time or in our past records named David L. Unger with the identifying characteristics you outlined. The brain, teeth, and fingerprints do not refer to anything extant in our files. Do you wish us to — "

"No," Patterson said. "That answers my question. Let it go." He cut off the h-loop switch.

Gannet was listening dully. "This is completely over my head, Patterson. Explain it to me."

Patterson ignored him. He squatted down and poked at the ash that had been David Unger. After a moment he snapped the h-loop on again. "I want this taken upstairs to the analytical labs," he ordered quietly. "Get a team out here at once." He got slowly to his feet and added even more softly, "Then I'm going to find V-Stephens — if I can."

"He's undoubtedly on his way to Venus by now," Evelyn Cutter said bitterly. "Well, that's that. There's nothing we can do about it."

"We're going to have war," Gannet admitted. He came slowly back to reality. With a violent effort he focused on the people around him. He smoothed down his mane of white hair and adjusted his coat. A semblance of dignity was restored to his once-impressive frame. "We might as well meet it like men. There's no use trying to escape it."

Patterson moved aside as a group of hospital robots approached the charred remains and began gingerly to collect them in a single heap. "Make a complete analysis," he said to the technician in charge of the work-detail. "Break down the basic cell-units, especially the neurological apparatus. Report what you find to me as soon as you possibly can."

It took just about an hour.

"Look for yourself," the lab technician said. "Here, take hold of some of the material. It doesn't even *feel* right."

Patterson accepted a sample of dry, brittle organic matter. It might have been the smoked skin of some sea creature. It broke apart easily in his hands; as he put it down among the test equipment it crumbled into powdery fragments. "I see," he said slowly.

"It's good, considering. But it's weak. Probably it wouldn't have stood up another couple of days. It was deteriorating rapidly; sun, air, everything was breaking it down. There was no innate repair-system involved. Our cells are constantly reprocessed, cleaned and maintained. This thing was set up and then pushed into motion. Obviously, somebody's a long way ahead of us in biosynthetics. This is a masterpiece."

"Yes, it's a good job," Patterson admitted. He took another sample of what had been the body of David Unger and thoughtfully broke it into small dry pieces. "It fooled us completely."

"You knew, didn't you?"

"Not at first."

"As you can see we're reconstructing the whole system, getting the ash back into one piece. Parts are missing, of course, but we can get the general outlines. I'd like to meet the manufacturers of this thing. This really worked. This was no machine."

Patterson located the charred ash that had been reconstructed into the android's face. Withered, blackened paper-thin flesh. The dead eye gazed out lusterless and blind. Census had been right. There was never a David Unger. Such a person had never lived on Earth or anywhere else. What they had called "David Unger" was a man-made synthetic.

"We were really taken in," Patterson admitted. "How many people know, besides the two of us?"

"Nobody else." The lab technician indicated his squad of work-robots. "I'm the only human on this detail."

"Can you keep it quiet?"

"Sure. You're my boss, you know."

"Thanks," Patterson said. "But if you want, this information would get you another boss any time."

"Gannet?" The lab technician laughed. "I don't think I'd like to work for him."

"He'd pay you pretty well."

"True," said the lab technician. "But one of these days I'd be in the front lines. I like it better here in the hospital."

Patterson started toward the door. "If anybody asks, tell them there wasn't enough left to analyze. Can you dispose of these remains?"

"I'd hate to, but I guess I can." The technician eyed him curiously. "You have any idea who put this thing together? I'd like to shake hands with them."

"I'm interested in only one thing right now," Patterson said obliquely. "V-Stephens has to be found."

LeMarr blinked, as dull late-afternoon sunlight filtered into his brain. He pulled himself upright — and banged his head sharply on the dashboard of the car. Pain swirled around him and for a time he sank back down into agonized darkness. Then slowly, gradually, he emerged. And peered around him.

His car was parked in the rear of a small, dilapidated public lot. It was about five-thirty. Traffic swarmed noisily along the narrow street onto which the lot fed. LeMarr reached up and gingerly explored the side of his skull. There was a numb spot the size of a silver dollar, an area totally without sensation. The spot radiated a chill breath, the utter absence of heat, as if somehow he had bumped against a nexus of outer space.

He was still trying to collect himself and recollect the events that had preceded his period of unconsciousness, when the swift-moving form of Doctor V-Stephens appeared.

V-Stephens ran lithely between the parked surface cars, one hand in his coat pocket, eyes alert and wary. There was something strange about him, a difference that LeMarr in his befuddled state couldn't pin down. V-Stephens had almost reached the car before he realized what it was — and at the same time was lashed by the full surge of memory. He sank down and lay against the door, as limp and inert as possible. In spite of himself he started slightly, as V-Stephens yanked the door open and slid behind the wheel.

V-Stephens was no longer green.

The Venusian slammed the door, jabbed the car key in the lock, and started up the motor. He lit a cigarette, examined his pair of heavy gloves, glanced briefly at LeMarr, and pulled out of the lot into the early-evening traffic. For a moment he drove with one gloved hand on the wheel, the other still inside his coat. Then, as he gained full speed, he slid his cold-beam out, gripped it briefly, and dropped it on the seat beside him.

LeMarr pounced on it. From the corner of his eye, V-Stephens saw the limp body swing into life. He slammed on the emergency brake and forgot the wheel; the two of them struggled silently, furiously. The car shrieked to a halt and immediately became the center of an angry mass of honking car-horns. The two men fought with desperate intensity, neither of them breathing, locked almost immobile as momentarily all forces balanced. Then LeMarr yanked away, the cold-beam aimed at V-Stephens' colorless face.

"What happened?" he croaked hoarsely. "I'm missing five hours. *What did you do?*"

V-Stephens said nothing. He released the brake and began driving slowly with the swirl of traffic. Gray cigarette smoke dribbled from between his lips; his eyes were half-closed, filmed over and opaque.

"You're an Earthman," LeMarr said, wonderingly. "You're not a webfoot after all."

"I'm a Venusian," V-Stephens answered indifferently. He showed his webbed fingers, then replaced his heavy driving gloves.

"But how — "

"You think we can't pass over the color line when we want to?" V-Stephens shrugged. "Dyes, chemical hormones, a few minor surgical operations. A half hour in the men's room with a hypodermic and salve ... This is no planet for a man with green skin."

Across the street a hasty barricade had been erected. A group of sullen-faced men stood around with guns and crude hand-clubs, some of them wearing gray Home Guard caps. They were flagging down cars one by one and searching them. A beefy-faced man waved V-Stephens to a halt. He strolled over and gestured for the window to be rolled down.

"What's going on?" LeMarr demanded nervously.

"Looking for webfoots," the man growled, a thick odor of garlic and perspiration steaming from his heavy canvas shirt. He darted quick, suspicious glances into the car. "Seen any around?"

"No," V-Stephens said.

The man ripped open the luggage compartment and peered in. "We caught one a couple minutes ago." He jerked his thick thumb. "See him up there?"

The Venusian had been strung up to a street lamp. His green body dangled and swayed with the early-evening wind. His face was a mottled, ugly mass of pain. A crowd of people stood around the pole, grim, mean-looking. Waiting.

"There'll be more," the man said, as he slammed the luggage compartment. "Plenty more."

"What happened?" LeMarr managed to ask. He was nauseated and horrified; his voice came out almost inaudible. "Why all this?"

"A webfoot killed a man. An *Earth*man." The man pulled back and slapped the car. "Okay — you can go."

V-Stephens moved the car forward. Some of the loitering people had whole uniforms, combinations of the Home Guard gray and Terran blue. Boots, heavy belt-buckles, caps, pistols, and armbands. The armbands read D.C. in bold black letters against a red background.

"What's that?" LeMarr asked faintly.

"Defense Committee," V-Stephens answered. "Gannet's front outfit. To defend Earth against the webfoots and crows."

"But — " LeMarr gestured helplessly. "Is Earth being attacked?"

"Not that I know of."

"Turn the car around. Head back to the hospital."

V-Stephens hesitated, then did as he was told. In a moment the car was speeding back toward the center of New York. "What's this for?" V-Stephens asked. "Why do you want to go back?"

LeMarr didn't hear him; he was gazing with fixed horror at the people along the street. Men and women prowling like animals, looking for something to kill. "They've gone crazy," LeMarr muttered. "They're beasts."

"No," V-Stephens said. "This'll die down, soon. When the Committee gets its financial support jerked out from under it. It's still going full blast, but pretty soon the gears will change around and the big engine will start grinding in reverse."

"Why?"

"Because Gannet doesn't want war, now. It takes a while for the new line to trickle down. Gannet will probably finance a movement called P.C. Peace Committee."

The hospital was surrounded by a wall of tanks and trucks and heavy mobile guns. V-Stephens slowed the car to a halt and stubbed out his cigarette. No cars were being passed. Soldiers moved among the tanks with gleaming heavy-duty weapons that were still shiny with packing grease.

"Well?" V-Stephens said. "What now? You have the gun. It's your hot potato."

LeMarr dropped a coin in the vidphone mounted on the dashboard. He gave the hospital number, and when the monitor appeared, asked hoarsely for Vachel Patterson.

"Where are you?" Patterson demanded. He saw the cold-beam in LeMarr's hand, and then his eyes fastened on V-Stephens. "I see you got him."

"Yes," LeMarr agreed, "but I don't understand what's happening." He appealed helplessly to Patterson's miniature vidimage. "What'll I do? What is all this?"

"Give me your location," Patterson said tensely.

LeMarr did so. "You want me to bring him to the hospital? Maybe I should — "

"Just hold onto that cold-beam. I'll be right there." Patterson broke the connection and the screen died.

LeMarr shook his head in bewilderment. "I was trying to get you away," he said to V-Stephens. "Then you cold-beamed me. *Why*?" Suddenly LeMarr shuddered violently. Full understanding came to him. "You killed David Unger!"

"That's right," V-Stephens answered.

The cold beam trembled in LeMarr's hand. "Maybe I ought to kill you right now. Maybe I ought to roll down the window and yell to those madmen to come and get you. I don't know."

"Do whatever you think best," V-Stephens said.

LeMarr was still trying to decide, when Patterson appeared beside the car. He rapped on the window and LeMarr unlocked the door. Patterson climbed quickly in, and slammed the door after him.

"Start up the car," he said to V-Stephens. "Keep moving, away from downtown."

V-Stephens glanced briefly at him, and then slowly started up the motor. "You might as well do it here," he said to Patterson. "Nobody'll interfere."

"I want to get out of the city," Patterson answered. He added in explanation, "My lab staff analyzed the remains of David Unger. They were able to reconstruct most of the synthetic."

V-Stephens' face registered a surge of frantic emotion. "Oh?"

Patterson reached out his hand. "Shake," he said grimly.

"Why?" V-Stephens asked, puzzled.

"Somebody told me to do this. Somebody who agrees you Venusians did one hell of a good job when you made that android."

The car purred along the highway, through the evening gloom. "Denver is the last place left," V-Stephens explained to the two Earthmen. "There're too many of us, there. Color-Ad says a few Committee men started shelling our offices, but the Directorate put a sudden stop to it. Gannet's pressure, probably."

"I want to hear more," Patterson said. "Not about Gannet; I know where he stands. I want to know what you people are up to."

"Color-Ad engineered the synthetic," V-Stephens admitted. "We don't know any more about the future than you do — which is absolutely nothing. There never was a David Unger. We forged the i.d. papers, built up a whole false personality, history of a non-existent war — everything."

"Why?" LeMarr demanded.

"To scare Gannet into calling off the dogs. To terrify him into letting Venus and Mars become independent. To keep him from fanning up a war to preserve his economic strangle-hold. The fake history we constructed in Unger's mind has Gannet's nine-world empire broken and destroyed. Gannet's a realist. He'd take a risk when he had odds — but our history put the odds one hundred percent against him."

"So Gannet pulls out," Patterson said slowly. "And you?"

"We were always out," V-Stephens said quietly. "We were never in this war game. All we want is our freedom and independence. I don't now what the war would really be like, but I can guess. Not very pleasant. Not worth it for either of us. And as things were going, war was in the cards."

"I want to get a few things straight," Patterson said. "You're a Color-Ad agent?"

"Right."

"And V-Rafia?"

"She was also Color-Ad. Actually, all Venusians and Martians are Color-Ad agents as soon as they hit Earth. We wanted to get V-Rafia into the hospital to help me out. There was a chance I'd be prevented from destroying the synthetic at the proper time. If I hadn't been able to do it, V-Rafia would have. But Gannet killed her."

"Why didn't you simply cold-beam Unger?"

"For one thing we wanted the synthetic body completely destroyed. That isn't possible, of course. Reduced to ash was the next best thing. Broken down small enough so a cursory examination wouldn't show anything." He glanced up at Patterson. "Why'd you order such a radical examination?"

"Unger's i.d. number had come up. And Unger didn't appear to claim it."

"Oh," V-Stephens said uneasily. "That's bad. We had no way to tell when it would appear. We tried to pick a number due in a few months — but enlistment rose sharply the last couple of weeks."

"Suppose you hadn't been able to destroy Unger?"

"We had the demolition machinery phased in such a way that the synthetic didn't have a chance. It was tuned to his body; all I had to do was activate it with Unger in the general area. If I had been killed, or I hadn't been able to set off the mechanism, the synthetic would have died naturally before Gannet got the information he wanted. Preferably, I was to destroy it in plain view of Gannet and his staff. It was important they think we knew about the war. The psychological shock-value of seeing Unger murdered outweighs the risk of my capture."

"What happens next?" Patterson asked presently.

"I'm supposed to join with Color-Ad. Originally, I was to grab a ship at the New York office, but Gannet's mobs took care of that. Of course, this is assuming you won't stop me."

LeMarr had begun to sweat. "Suppose Gannet finds out he was tricked? If he discovers there never was a David Unger — "

"We're patching that up," V-Stephens said. "By the time Gannet checks, there will be a David Unger. Meanwhile — " He shrugged. "It's up to you two. You've got the gun."

"Let him go," LeMarr said fervently.

"That's not very patriotic," Patterson pointed out. "We're helping the webfoots put over something. Maybe we ought to call in one of those Committee men."

"The devil with them," LeMarr grated. "I wouldn't turn anybody over to those lynch-happy lunatics. Even a — "

"Even a webfoot?" V-Stephens asked.

Patterson was gazing up at the black, star-pocked sky. "What's finally going to happen?" he asked V-Stephens. "You think this stuff will end?"

"Sure," V-Stephens said promptly. "One of these days we'll be moving out into the stars. Into other systems. We'll bump into other races — and I mean *real* other races. Non-human in the true sense of the word. Then people will see we're all of the same stem. It'll be obvious, when we've got something to compare ourselves to."

"Okay," Patterson said. He took the cold-beam and handed it to V-Stephens. "That was all that worried me. I'd hate to think this stuff might keep on going."

"It won't," V-Stephens answered quietly. "Some of those non-human races ought to be pretty hideous. After a look at them, Earthmen will be *glad* to have their daughters marry men with green skin." He grinned briefly. "Some of the non-human races may not have any skin at all. . . . "

THE CHROMIUM FENCE

EARTH TILTED toward six o'clock, the work-day almost over. Commute discs rose in dense swarms and billowed away from the industrial zone toward the surrounding residential rings. Like nocturnal moths, the thick clouds of discs darkened the evening sky. Silent, weightless, they whisked their passengers toward home and waiting families, hot meals and bed.

Don Walsh was the third man on his disc; he completed the load. As he dropped the coin in the slot the carpet rose impatiently. Walsh settled gratefully against the invisible safety-rail and unrolled the evening newspaper. Across from him the other two commuters were doing the same.

HORNEY AMENDMENT STIRS UP FIGHT

Walsh reflected on the significance of the headline. He lowered the paper from the steady windcurrents and perused the next column.

HUGE TURNOUT EXPECTED MONDAY
ENTIRE PLANET TO GO TO POLLS

On the back of the single sheet was the day's scandal.

WIFE MURDERS HUSBAND OVER POLITICAL TIFF

And an item that made strange chills up and down his spine. He had seen it crop up repeatedly, but it always made him feel uncomfortable.

PURIST MOB LYNCHES NATURALIST IN BOSTON
WINDOWS SMASHED — GREAT DAMAGE DONE

And in the next column:

NATURALIST MOB LYNCHES PURIST IN CHICAGO
BUILDINGS BURNED — GREAT DAMAGE DONE

Across from Walsh, one of his companions was beginning to mumble aloud. He was a big heavy-set man, middle-aged, with red hair and beer-swollen features. Suddenly he waded up his newspaper and hurled it from the disc. "They'll never pass it!" he shouted. "They won't get away with it!"

Walsh buried his nose in his paper and desperately ignored the man. It was happening again, the thing he dreaded every hour of the day. A political argument. The other commuter had lowered his newspaper; briefly, he eyed the red-haired man and then continued reading.

The red-haired man addressed Walsh. "You signed the Butte Petition?" He yanked a mentalfoil tablet from his pocket and pushed it in Walsh's face. "Don't be afraid to put down your name for liberty."

Walsh clutched his newspaper and peered frantically over the side of the disc. The Detroit residential units were spinning by; he was almost home. "Sorry," he muttered. "Thanks, no thanks."

"Leave him alone," the other commuter said to the red-haired man. "Can't you see he doesn't want to sign it?"

"Mind your own business." The red-haired man moved close to Walsh, the tablet extended belligerently. "Look, friend. You know what it'll mean to you and yours if this thing gets passed? You think you'll be safe? Wake up, friend. When the Horney Amendment comes in, freedom and liberty go out."

The other commuter quietly put his newspaper away. He was slim, well-dressed, a gray-haired cosmopolitan. He removed his glasses and said, "You smell like a Naturalist, to me."

The red-haired man studied his opponent. He noticed the wide plutonium ring on the slender man's hand; a jaw-breaking band of heavy metal. "What are you?" the red-haired man muttered, "a sissy-kissing Purist? Agh." He made a disgusting spitting motion and returned to Walsh. "Look, friend, you know what these Purists are after. They want to make us degenerates. They'll turn us into a race of women. If God made the universe the way it is, it's good enough for me. They're going against God when they go against nature. This planet was built up by red-blooded *men*, who were proud of their bodies, proud of the way they looked and smelled." He tapped his own heavy chest. "By God, I'm proud of the way *I* smell!"

Walsh stalled desperately. "I — " he muttered. "No, I can't sign it."

"You already signed?"

"No."

Suspicion settled over the red-haired man's beefy features. "You mean you're *for* the Horney Amendment?" His thick voice rose wrathfully. "You want to see an end to the natural order of — "

"This is where I get off," Walsh interrupted; he hurriedly yanked the stop-cord of the disc. It swept down toward the magnetic grapple at the end of his unit-section, a row of white squares set across the green and brown hill-side.

"Wait a minute, friend." The red-haired man reached ominously for Walsh's sleeve, as the disc slid to a halt on the flat surface of the grapple.

Surface cars were parked in rows; wives waiting to cart their husbands home. "I don't like your attitude. You afraid to stand up and be counted? You ashamed to be a part of your race? By God, if you're not man enough to — "

The lean, gray-haired man smashed him with his plutonium ring, and the grip on Walsh's sleeve loosened. The petition clattered to the ground and the two of them fought furiously, silently.

Walsh pushed aside the safety-rail and jumped from the disc, down the three steps of the grapple and onto the ashes and cinders of the parking lot. In the gloom of early evening he could make out his wife's car; Betty sat watching the dashboard tv, oblivious of him and the silent struggle between the red-haired Naturalist and the gray-haired Purist.

"Beast," the gray-haired man gasped, as he straightened up. "Stinking animal!"

The red-haired man lay semi-conscious against the safety-rail. "God damn — lily!" he grunted.

The gray-haired man pressed the release, and the disc rose above Walsh and on its way. Walsh waved gratefully. "Thanks," he called up. "I appreciate that."

"Not at all," the gray-haired man answered, cheerfully examining a broken tooth. His voice dwindled, as the disc gained altitude. "Always glad to help out a fellow ... " The final words came drifting to Walsh's ears. " ... A fellow Purist."

"I'm not!" Walsh shouted futilely "I'm not a Purist and I'm not a Naturalist! You hear me?"

Nobody heard him.

"I'm not," Walsh repeated monotonously, as he sat at the dinner table spooning up creamed corn, potatoes, and rib steak. "I'm not a Purist and I'm not a Naturalist. Why do I have to be one or the other? Isn't there any place for a man who has his *own* opinion?"

"Eat your food, dear," Betty murmured.

Through the thin walls of the bright little dining room came the echoing clink of other families eating, other conversations in progress. The tinny blare of tv sets. The purr of stoves and freezers and air conditioners and wall-heaters. Across from Walsh his brother-in-law Carl was gulping down a second plateful of steaming food. Beside him, Walsh's fifteen year old son Jimmy was scanning a paper-bound edition of *Finnegans Wake* he had bought in the downramp store that supplied the self-contained housing unit.

"Don't read at the table," Walsh said angrily to his son.

Jimmy glanced up. "Don't kid me. I know the unit rules; that one sure as hell isn't listed. And anyhow, I have to get this read before I leave."

"Where are you going tonight, dear?" Betty asked.

"Official party business," Jimmy answered obliquely. "I can't tell you any more than that."

Walsh concentrated on his food and tried to brake the tirade of thoughts screaming through his mind. "On the way home from work," he said, "there was a fight."

Jimmy was interested. "Who won?"

"The Purist."

A glow of pride slowly covered the boy's face; he was a sergeant in the Purist Youth League. "Dad, you ought to get moving. Sign up now and you'll be eligible to vote next Monday."

"I'm going to vote."

"Not unless you're a member of one of the two parties."

It was true. Walsh gazed unhappily past his son, into the days that lay ahead. He saw himself involved in endless wretched situations like the one today; sometimes it would be Naturalists who attacked him, and other times (like last week) it would be enraged Purists.

"You know," his brother-in-law said, "you're helping the Purists by just sitting around here doing nothing." He belched contentedly and pushed his empty plate away. "You're what *we* class as unconsciously pro-Purist." He glared at Jimmy. "You little squirt! If you were legal age I'd take you out and whale the tar out of you."

"Please," Betty sighed. "No quarreling about politics at the table. Let's have peace and quiet, for a change. I'll certainly be glad when the election is over."

Carl and Jimmy glared at each other and continued eating warily. "You should eat in the kitchen — " Jimmy said to him. "Under the stove. That's where you belong. Look at you — there's sweat all over you." A nasty sneer interrupted his eating. "When we get the Amendment passed, you better get rid of that, if you don't want to get hauled off to jail."

Carl flushed. "You creeps won't get it passed." But his gruff voice lacked conviction. The Naturalists were scared; Purists had control of the Federal Council. If the election moved in their favor it was really possible the legislation to compel forced observation of the five-point Purist code might get on the books. "Nobody is going to remove my sweat glands," Carl muttered. "Nobody is going to make me submit to breath-control and teeth-whitening and hair-restorer. It's part of life to get dirty and bald and fat and old."

"Is it true?" Betty asked her husband. "Are you really unconsciously pro-Purist?"

Don Walsh savagely speared a remnant of rib steak. "Because I don't join either party I'm called unconsciously pro-Purist and unconsciously pro-Naturalist. I claim they balance. If I'm everybody's enemy that I'm nobody's enemy." He added, "Or friend."

"You Naturalists have nothing to offer the future," Jimmy said to Carl. "What can you give the youth of the planet — like me? Caves and raw meat and a bestial existence. You're anti-civilization."

"Slogans," Carl retorted.

"You want to carry us back to a primitive existence, away from social integration." Jimmy waved an excited skinny finger in his uncle's face. "You're thalamically oriented!"

"I'll break your head," Carl snarled, half out of his chair. "You Purist squirts have no respect for your elders."

Jimmy giggled shrilly. "I'd like to see you try. It's five years in prison for striking a minor. Go ahead — hit me."

Don Walsh got heavily to his feet and left the dining room.

"Where are you going?" Betty called peevishly after him. "You're not through eating."

"The future belongs to youth," Jimmy was informing Carl. "And the youth of the planet is firmly Purist. You don't have a chance; the Purist revolution is coming."

Don Walsh left the apartment and wandered down the common corridor toward the ramp. Closed doors extended in rows on both sides of him. Noise and light and activity radiated around him, the close presence of families and domestic interaction. He pushed past a boy and girl making love in the dark shadows and reached the ramp. For a moment he halted, then abruptly he moved forward and descended to the lowest level of the unit.

The level was deserted and cool and slightly moist. Above him the sounds of people had faded to dull echoes against the concrete ceiling. Conscious of his sudden plunge into isolation and silence he advanced thoughtfully between the dark grocery and dry goods stores, past the beauty shop and the liquor store, past the laundry and medical supply store, past the dentist and physical doctor, to the ante-room of the unit analyst.

He could see the analyst within the inner chamber. It sat immobile and silent, in the dark shadows of evening. Nobody was consulting it; the analyst was turned off. Walsh hesitated, then crossed the check-frame of the ante-room and knocked on the transparent inner door. The presence of his body closed relays and switches; abruptly the lights of the inner office winked on and the analyst itself sat up, smiled and half-rose to its feet.

"Don," it called heartily. "Come on in and sit down."

He entered and wearily seated himself. "I thought maybe I could talk to you, Charley," he said.

"Sure, Don." The robot leaned forward to see the clock on its wide mahogany desk. "But, isn't it dinner time?"

"Yes," Walsh admitted. "I'm not hungry. Charley, you know what we were talking about last time ... you remember what I was saying. You remember what's been bothering me."

"Sure, Don." The robot settled back in its swivel chair, rested its almost-convincing elbows on the desk, and regarded its patient kindly. "How's it been going, the last couple of days?"

"Not so good. Charley, I've go to do something. You can help me; you're not biased." He appealed to the quasi-human face of metal and plastic. "You can see this undistorted, Charley. *How can I join one of the parties?* All their slogans and propaganda, it seems so damn — silly. How the hell can I get excited about clean teeth and underarm odor? People kill each other over these trifles ... it doesn't make sense. There's going to be suicidal civil war, if that Amendment passes, and I'm supposed to join one side or the other."

Charley nodded. "I have the picture, Don."

"Am I supposed to go out and knock some fellow over the head because he does or doesn't smell? Some man I never saw before? I won't do it. I refuse. Why can't they let me alone? Why can't I have my own opinions? Why do I have to get in on this — insanity?"

The analyst smiled tolerantly. "That's a little harsh, Don. You're out of phase with your society, you know. So the cultural climate and mores seem a trifle unconvincing to you. But this is your society; you have to live in it. You can't withdraw."

Walsh forced his hands to relax. "Here's what I think. Any man who wants to smell should be allowed to smell. Any man who doesn't want to smell should go and get his glands removed. What's the matter with that?"

"Don, you're avoiding the issue." The robot's voice was calm, dispassionate. "What you're saying is that neither side is right. And that's foolish, isn't it? One side must be right."

"Why?'

"Because the two sides exhaust the practical possibilities. Your position isn't really a position ... it's a sort of description. You see, Don, you have a psychological inability to come to grips with an issue. You don't want to commit yourself for fear you'll lose your freedom and individuality. You're sort of an intellectual virgin; you want to stay pure."

Walsh reflected. "I want," he said, "to keep my integrity."

"You're not an isolated individual, Don. You're a part of society ... ideas don't exist in a vacuum."

"I have a right to hold my own ideas."

"No, Don," the robot answered gently. "They're not your ideas; you didn't create them. You can't turn them on and off when you feel like it. They operate through you ... they're conditionings deposited by your environment. What you believe is a reflection of certain social forces and pressures. In your case the two mutually-exclusive social trends have produced a sort of stalemate. You're at war with yourself ... you can't decide which side to join because elements of both exist in you." The robot nodded wisely. "But you've got to make a decision. You've got to resolve this conflict and act. You can't remain a spectator . . . you've got to be a participant. Nobody can be a spectator to life . . . and this is life."

"You mean there's no other world but this business about sweat and teeth and hair?"

"Logically, there are other societies. But this is the one you were born into. This is your society . . . the only one you will ever have. You either live in it, or you don't live."

Walsh got to his feet. "In other words, *I* have to make the adjustment. Something has to give, and it's got to be me."

"Afraid so, Don. It would be silly to expect everybody else to adjust to you, wouldn't it? Three and a half billion people would have to change just to please Don Walsh. You see, Don, you're not quite out of your infantile-selfish stage. You haven't quite got to the point of facing reality." The robot smiled. "But you will."

Walsh started moodily from the office. "I'll think it over."

"It's for your own good, Don."

At the door, Walsh turned to say something more. But the robot had clicked off; it was fading into darkness and silence, elbows still resting on the desk. The dimming overhead lights caught something he hadn't noticed before. The powercord that was the robot's umbilicus had a white-plastic tag wired to it. In the semi-gloom he could make out the printed words.

PROPERTY OF THE FEDERAL COUNCIL
FOR PUBLIC USE ONLY

The robot, like everything else in the multi-family unit, was supplied by the controlling institutions of society. The analyst was a creature of the state, a bureaucrat with a desk and job. Its function was to equate people like Don Walsh with the world as it was.

But if he didn't listen to the unit analyst, who was he supposed to listen to? Where else could he go?

Three days later the election took place. The glaring headline told him nothing he didn't already know; his office had buzzed with the news all day. He put the paper away in his coat pocket and didn't examine it until he got home.

PURISTS WIN BY LANDSLIDE
HORNEY AMENDMENT CERTAIN TO PASS

Walsh lay back wearily in his chair. In the kitchen Betty was briskly preparing dinner. The pleasant clink of dishes and the warm odor of cooking food drifted through the bright little apartment.

"The Purists won," Walsh said, when Betty appeared with an armload of silver and cups. "It's all over."

"Jimmy will be happy," Betty answered vaguely. "I wonder if Carl will be home in time for dinner." She calculated silently. "Maybe I ought to run downramp for some more coffee."

"Don't you understand?" Walsh demanded. "It's happened! The Purists have complete power!"

"I understand," Betty answered peevishly. "You don't have to shout. Did you sign that petition thing? That Butte Petition the Naturalists have been circulating?"

"No."

"Thank God. I didn't think so; you never sign anything anybody brings around." She lingered at the kitchen door. "I hope Carl has sense enough to do something. I never did like him sitting around guzzling beer and smelling like a pig in summer."

The door of the apartment opened and Carl hurried in, flushed and scowling. "Don't fix dinner for me, Betty. I'll be at an emergency meeting." He glanced briefly at Walsh. "Now are you satisfied? If you'd put your back to the wheel, maybe this wouldn't have happened."

"How soon will they get the Amendment passed?" Walsh asked.

Carl bellowed with nervous laughter. "They've already passed it." He grabbed up an armload of papers from his desk and stuffed them in a waste-disposal slot. "We've got informants at Purist headquarters. As soon as the new councilmen were sworn in they rammed the Amendment through. They want to catch us unawares." He grinned starkly. "But they won't."

The door slammed and Carl's hurried footsteps diminished down the public hall.

"I've never seen him move so fast," Betty remarked wonderingly.

Horror rose in Don Walsh as he listened to the rapid, lumbering footsteps of his brother-in-law. Outside the unit, Carl was climbing quickly into his surface car. The motor gunned, and Carl drove off. "He's afraid," Walsh said. "He's in danger."

"I guess he can take care of himself. He's pretty big."

Walsh shakily lit a cigarette. "Even your brother isn't that big. It doesn't seem possible they really mean this. Putting over an Amendment like this, forcing everybody to conform to their idea of what's right. But it's been in the cards for years . . . this is the last step on a large road."

"I wish they'd get it over with, once and for all," Betty complained. "Was it always this way? I don't remember always hearing about politics when I was a child."

"They didn't call it politics, back in those days. The industrialists hammered away at the people to buy and consume. It centered around this hair-sweat-teeth purity; the city people got it and developed an ideology around it."

Betty set the table and brought in the dishes of food. "You mean the Purist political movement was deliberately started?"

"They didn't realize what a hold it was getting on them. They didn't know their children were growing up to take such things as underarm perspiration and white teeth and nice-looking hair as the most important things in the world. Things worth fighting and dying for. Things important enough to kill those who didn't agree."

"The Naturalists were country people?"

"People who lived outside the cities and weren't conditioned by the stimuli." Walsh shook his head irritably. "Incredible, that one man will kill another over trivialities. All through history men murdering each other over verbal nonsense, meaningless slogans instilled in them by somebody else — who sits back and benefits."

"It isn't meaningless if they believe in it."

"It's meaningless to kill another man because he has halitosis! It's meaningless to beat up somebody because he hasn't had his sweat glands removed and artificial waste-excretion tubes installed. There's going to be senseless warfare; the Naturalists have weapons stored up at party headquarters. Men'll be just as dead as if they died for something real."

"Time to eat, dear," Betty said, indicating the table.

"I'm not hungry."

"Stop sulking and eat. Or you'll have indigestion, and you know what that means."

He knew what it meant, all right. It meant his life was in danger. One belch in the presence of a Purist and it was a life and death struggle. There was no room in the same world for men who belched and men who wouldn't tolerate men who belched. Something had to give ... and it had already given. The Amendment had been passed: the Naturalists' days were numbered.

"Jimmy will be late tonight," Betty said, as she helped herself to lamb chops, green peas, and creamed corn. "There's some sort of Purist celebration. Speeches, parades, torch-light rallies." She added wistfully, "I guess we can't go down and watch, can we? It'll be pretty, all the lights and voices, and marching."

"Go ahead." Listlessly, Walsh spooned up his food. He ate without tasting. "Enjoy yourself."

They were still eating, when the door burst open and Carl entered briskly. "Anything left for me?" he demanded.

Betty half-rose, astonished. "Carl! You don't — smell any more."

Carl seated himself and grabbed for the plate of lamb chops. Then he recollected, and daintily selected a small one, and a tiny portion of peas. "I'm hungry," he admitted, "but not too hungry." He ate carefully, quietly.

Walsh gazed at him dumbfounded. "What the hell happened?" he demanded. "Your hair — and your teeth and breath. *What did you do?*"

Without looking up, Carl answered, "Party tactics. We're beating a strategical retreat. In the face of this Amendment, there's no point in doing something foolhardy. Hell, we don't intend to get slaughtered." He sipped some luke-warm coffee. "As a matter of fact, we've gone underground."

Walsh slowly lowered his fork. "You mean you're not going to fight?"

"Hell, no. It's suicide." Carl glanced furtively around. "Now listen to me. I'm completely in conformity with the provisions of the Horney Amendment; nobody can pin a thing on me. When the cops come snooping around, keep your mouths shut. The Amendment gives the right to recant, and that's technically what we've done. We're clean; they can't touch us. But let's just not say anything." He displayed a small blue card. "A Purist membership card. Backdated; we planned for any eventuality."

"Oh, Carl!" Betty cried delightedly. "I'm so glad. You look just—*wonderful!*"

Walsh said nothing.

"What's the matter?" Betty demanded. "Isn't this what you wanted? You didn't want them to fight and kill each other—" Her voice rose shrilly. "Won't anything satisfy you? This is what you wanted and you're still dissatisfied. What on earth more do you want?"

There was noise below the unit. Carl sat up straight, and for an instant color left his face. He would have begun sweating if it were still possible. "That's the conformity police," he said thickly. "Just sit tight; they'll make a routine check and keep on going."

"Oh, dear," Betty gasped. "I hope they don't break anything. Maybe I better go and freshen up."

"Just sit still," Carl grated. "There's no reason for them to suspect anything."

When the door opened, Jimmy stood dwarfed by the green-tinted conformity police.

"There he is!" Jimmy shrilled, indicating Carl. "He's a Naturalist official! *Smell* him!"

The police spread efficiently into the room. Standing around the immobile Carl, they examined him briefly, then moved away. "No body odor," the police sergeant disagreed. "No halitosis. Hair thick and well-groomed." He signalled, and Carl obediently opened his mouth. "Teeth white, totally brushed. Nothing nonacceptable. No, this man is all right."

Jimmy glared furiously at Carl. "Pretty smart."

Carl picked stoically at his plate of food and ignored the boy and the police.

"Apparently we've broken the core of Naturalist resistance," the sergeant said into his neck-phone. "At lease in this area there's no organized opposition."

"Good," the phone answered. "Your area was a stronghold. We'll go ahead and set up the compulsory purification machinery, though. It should be implemented as soon as possible."

One of the cops turned his attention to Don Walsh. His nostrils twitched and then a harsh, oblique expression settled over his face. "What's your name?" he demanded.

Walsh gave his name.

The police came cautiously around him. "Body odor," one noted. "But hair fully restored and groomed. Open your mouth."

Walsh opened his mouth.

"Teeth clean and white. But— " The cop sniffed. "Faint halitosis... stomach variety. I don't get it. Is he a Naturalist or isn't he?'

"He's not a Purist," the sergeant said. "No Purist would have body odor. So he must be a Naturalist."

Jimmy pushed forward. "This man," he explained, "is only a fellow hiker. He's not a party member."

"You know him?"

"He's — related to me," Jimmy admitted.

The police took notes. "He's been playing around with Naturalists, but he hasn't gone the whole way?"

"He's on the fence," Jimmy agreed. "A quasi-Naturalist. He can be salvaged; this shouldn't be a criminal case."

"Remedial action," the sergeant noted. "All right, Walsh," he addressed Walsh. "Get your things and let's go. The Amendment provides compulsory purification for your type of person; let's not waste time."

Walsh hit the sergeant in the jaw.

The sergeant sprawled foolishly, arms flapping, dazed with disbelief. The cops drew their guns hysterically and milled around the room shouting and knocking into each other. Betty began to scream wildly. Jimmy's shrill voice was lost in the general uproar.

Walsh grabbed up a table lamp and smashed it over a cop's head. The lights in the apartment flickered and died out; the room was a chaos of yelling blackness. Walsh encountered a body; he kicked with his knee and with a groan of pain the body settled down. For a moment he was lost in the seething din; then his fingers found the door. He pried it open and scrambled out into the public corridor.

One shape followed, as Walsh reached the descent lift. "*Why?*" Jimmy wailed unhappily. "I had it all fixed — you didn't have to worry!"

His thin, metallic voice faded as the lift plunged down the well to the ground floor. Behind Walsh, the police were coming cautiously out into the hall; the sound of their boots echoed dismally after him.

He examined his watch. Probably, he had fifteen or twenty minutes. They'd get him, then; it was inevitable. Taking a deep breath, he stepped from the lift and as calmly as possible walked down the dark, deserted commercial corridor, between the rows of black store-entrances.

* * *

Charley was lit up and animate, when Walsh entered the ante-chamber. Two men were waiting, and a third was being interviewed. But at the sight of the expression on Walsh's face the robot waved him instantly in.

"What is it, Don?" it asked seriously, indicating a chair. "Sit down and tell me what's on your mind."

Walsh told it.

When he was finished, the analyst sat back and gave a low, soundless whistle. "That's a felony, Don. They'll freeze you for that; it's a provision of the new Amendment."

"I know," Walsh agreed. He felt no emotion. For the first time in years the ceaseless swirl of feelings and thoughts had been purged from his mind. He was a little tired and that was all.

The robot shook its head. "Well, Don, you're finally off the fence. That's something, at least; you're finally moving." It reached thoughtfully into the top drawer of its desk and got out a pad. "Is the police pick-up van here, yet?"

"I heard sirens as I came in the ante-room. It's on its way."

The robot's metal fingers drummed restlessly on the surface of the big mahogany desk. "Your sudden release of inhibition marks the moment of psychological integration. You're not undecided anymore, are you?"

"No," Walsh said.

"Good. Well, it had to come sooner or later. I'm sorry it had to come this way, though."

"I'm not," Walsh said. "This was the only way possible. It's clear to me, now. Being undecided isn't necessarily a negative thing. Not seeing anything in slogans and organized parties and beliefs and dying can be a belief worth dying for, in itself. I thought I was without a creed ... now I realize I have a very strong creed."

The robot wasn't listening. It scribbled something on its pad, signed it, and then expertly tore it off. "Here." It handed the paper briskly to Walsh.

"What's this?" Walsh demanded.

"I don't want anything to interfere with your therapy. You're finally coming around — and we want to keep moving." The robot got quickly to its feet. "Good luck, Don. Show that to the police; if there's any trouble have them call me."

The slip was a voucher from the Federal Psychiatric Board. Walsh turned it over numbly. "You mean this'll get me off?"

"You were acting compulsively; you weren't responsible. There'll be a cursory examination, of course, but nothing to worry about." The robot slapped him good-naturedly on the back. "It was your final neurotic act ... now you're free. That was the pent-up stuff; strictly a symbolic assertion of libido — with no political significance."

"I see," Walsh said.

The robot propelled him firmly toward the external exit. "Now go on out there and give the slip to them." From its metal chest the robot popped a small bottle. "And take one of these capsules before you go to sleep. Nothing serious, just a mild sedative to quiet your nerves. Everything will be all right; I'll expect to see you again, soon. And keep this in mind: we're finally making some real progress."

Walsh found himself outside in the night darkness. A police van was pulled up at the entrance of the unit, a vast ominous black shape against the dead sky. A crowd of curious people had collected at a safe distance, trying to make out what was going on.

Walsh automatically put the bottle of pills away in his coat pocket. He stood for a time breathing the chill night air, the cold clear smell of darkness and evening. Above his head a few bright pale stars glittered remotely.

"Hey," one of the policemen shouted. He flashed his light suspiciously in Walsh's face. "Come over here."

"That looks like him," another said. "Come on, buddy. Make it snappy."

Walsh brought out the voucher Charley had given him. "I'm coming," he answered. As he walked up to the policeman he carefully tore the paper to shreds and tossed the shreds to the night wind. The wind picked the shreds up and scattered them away.

"What the hell did you do?" one of the cops demanded.

"Nothing," Walsh answered. "I just threw away some waste paper. Something I won't be needing."

"What a strange one this one is," a cop muttered, as they froze Walsh with their cold beams. "He gives me the creeps."

"Be glad we don't get more like him," another said. "Except for a few guys like this, everything's going fine."

Walsh's inert body was tossed in the van and the doors slammed shut. Disposal machinery immediately began consuming his body and reducing it to basic mineral elements. A moment later, the van was on its way to the next call.

MISADJUSTMENT

WHEN RICHARDS GOT HOME from work he had a secret little routine he went through, a pleasant series of actions that brought him more satisfaction than his ten-hour workday at the Commerce Institute. He tossed his briefcase into a chair, rolled up his sleeves, grabbed a squirt-tank of liquid fertilizer, and kicked open the back door. Cool late-evening sunlight filtered down on him as he stepped gingerly across the moist black soil to the center of the garden. His heart thudded excitedly; how was it coming?

Fine. Growing bigger every day.

He watered it, tore off a few old leaves, spaded up the soil, killed a weed that had edged in, squirted fertilizer at random, and then stepped back to survey it. There was no satisfaction like that of creative activity. On the job he was a high-paid cog in the niplan economic system; he worked with verbal signs, and somebody else's signs at that. Here, he dealt directly with reality.

Richards squatted on his haunches and surveyed what he had accomplished. It was a good sight; almost ready, almost fully grown. He leaned forward to poke cautiously at the firm sides.

In the dwindling light of day the high-velocity transport glittered dully. Its windows had already formed: four pale squares in the tapered metal hull. The control bubble was just starting to burgeon from the center of the chassis. The jet flanges were full and developed. The input hatch and emergency locks hadn't grown into existence, yet; but it wouldn't be long.

Richards' satisfaction rose to fever-pitch. No doubt about it: the transport was almost ripe. Any day now he could pick it . . . and start flying it around.

At nine the waiting room had been full of people and cigarette smoke; now, at three-thirty, it was almost empty. One by one the visitors had given up and departed. Discarded tapes, bulging ashtrays, empty chairs surrounded the robot desk industriously grinding out its mechanical business. But in one corner, sitting bolt upright, her small hands clasped around her purse, remained a last young woman the desk hadn't been able to discourage.

The desk tried once more. It was getting close to four; Eggerton would soon be leaving. The gross irrationality of waiting for a man about to put on his hat and coat and go home grated against the desk's sensitive nerves. And the girl had been sitting there since nine, eyes large and wide, gazing at nothing, not smoking or examining tapes, only sitting and waiting.

"Look, lady," the desk said aloud, "there's nobody going to see Mr. Eggerton today."

The girl smiled slightly. "It'll only take a minute."

The desk sighed. "You're persistent. What do you want? Your firm must do a spectacular business with jobbers like you — but as I said, Mr. Eggerton never buys anything. That's how he got where he is, by throwing people like you out. I suppose you think that figure of yours is going to get you a big order." The desk added peevishly, "You ought to be ashamed, wearing a dress like that. A nice girl like you."

"He'll see me," the girl answered faintly.

The desk whizzed forms through its scanner and searched for a double-entendre on the word *see*. "Yes, I suppose with a dress like that," it began, but at that moment the inner door lifted and John Eggerton appeared.

"Turn yourself off," he ordered the desk; "I'm going home. Set yourself for ten; I'll be late tomorrow. The id bloc is holding a policy level conference in Pittsburgh, and I have a few things to say to them while they're together."

The girl slid to her feet. John Eggerton was a huge, ape-shouldered man, shaggy and unkempt, his jacket hanging open and food-stained, sleeves rolled up, eyes deep-set and dark with industrial cunning. He peered at her warily as she approached.

"Mr. Eggerton," she said, "do you have a moment? There's something I want to discuss with you."

"I'm not buying and I'm not hiring." Eggerton's voice was gruff with fatigue. "Young lady, go back to your employer and tell them if they want to show me something to send around an experienced representative, not a kid just out of . . . "

Eggerton was nearsighted. It wasn't until the girl was almost to him that he saw the card between her fingers. For a man of his size he moved with astonishing agility; with one leap he knocked the girl aside, dashed around the robot desk, and disappeared through a side exit from the office. The girl's purse clattered to the floor, its contents spilling wildly. She hesitated between them and the door, then with an exasperated hiss, rushed from the office and out into the hall. The express elevator to the roof showed red; it was already on its way up fifty stories to the building's private field.

"Damn," the girl said. She turned and reentered the office, seething with disgust.

The desk had begun to recover. "Why didn't you tell me you're an Immune?" it demanded. Its outrage grew — the indignation of a bureaucrat. "I gave you form s045 to fill out and line six distinctly asked for specific information on your occupation. You — *deceived* me!"

The girl ignored the desk and knelt down to collect her things. Gun, magnetic bracelet, intercom neck-mike, lipstick, keys, mirror, small change, handkerchief, the twenty-four hour notice intended for John Eggerton ... she was going to get hell when she appeared back at the Agency. Eggerton had even manage to avoid oral acknowledgement: the spool of recording tape spilled from her purse was blank and useless.

"You've got a clever boss," she said to the desk, in a burst of wrath. "All day sitting here in this reeking office with all these salesmen for nothing."

"I wondered why you were so persistent," the desk said. "I never saw a saleswoman so persistent; I should have known something was wrong. You almost got him."

"We'll get him," the girl said, on her way out of the office. "Tell him that tomorrow, when he shows up."

"He won't show up," the desk answered; to itself, since the girl was gone. "He won't ever come back here, not now. Not with you Immunes hanging around. A man's life is worth more than his business, even a business this size."

The girl entered a public vid booth and dialed the Agency. "He skipped," she said to the grim-faced woman who was her immediate superior. "He didn't touch the summons-card; I guess I'm not much of a server."

"Did he see the card?"

"Of course; that's why he bolted."

The older woman scratched a few tentative lines on a note pad. "Technically, we have him. I'll let our lawyers battle it out with his heirs; I'm going ahead with the twenty-four hour notice, just as if he accepted it. If he was wary before, he'll be impossible from now on; we'll never get closer than this. It's too bad you muffed this ... " The woman decided. "Call his home and give his personal staff the notice of culpability. Tomorrow morning we'll release it over the regular newsmachines."

Doris broke the circuit, held her hand over the screen to clear it, and then dialed Eggerton's personal number. To the attendant she gave the formal notice that Eggerton was legal prey for any niplan citizen. The attendant — mechanical — dutifully took the information as if it had been an order for so many dozen yards of cloth. Somehow, the machine's calmness made her more discouraged than ever. She left the booth and wandered gloomily downramp to the cocktail bar to wait for her husband.

* * *

John Eggerton didn't seem like a parakineticist. Doris's mind imagined small wan-faced youths, withdrawn and agonized, buried in out-of-the-way towns and farms, hidden away from urban areas. Eggerton was prominent... but of course that didn't affect his chance of being picked up in the random check-net. As she sipped her Tom Collins, she tried to think of other reasons why John Eggerton would ignore his initial check notice, then his warning — fine and possible imprisonment — and now this, his last notice.

Was Eggerton really P-K?

Her face in the dark mirror behind the bar wavered, rings of half-shadows, nebulous succubi, a gloom of fog like that which lay over the niplan system. Her reflection might have been that of a young female parakineticist: black circles for eyes, moist lashes, dank hair around her thin shoulders, fingers too tapered and too sharp. But it was only the mirror; there were no distaff parakineticists. At least, none reported *yet*.

Unnoticed, her husband came up behind her, tossed his coat over a stool, and seated himself. "How did it come off?" Harvey asked sympathetically.

Doris started in surprise. "You scared me!"

Harvey lit a cigarette and attracted the attention of the bartender. "Bourbon and water." He turned mildly to his wife. "Cheer up — there're other mutants to track down." He tossed her the foil from the afternoon newsmachines. "You probably know already, but your San Francisco office picked up four in a row. All of them unique; there was one party who had a sweet little talent of speeding up metabolic processes in those he didn't care for."

Doris nodded absently. "We heard through the Agency memos. And one could walk through walls, without falling through floors. And one animated stones."

"Eggerton got away?"

"Like lightning — I wouldn't think a man that big would react that fast. But maybe he isn't a man." She spun her tall cold glass between her fingers. "The Agency is going to give the public twenty-four hour notice. I've already called his home ... that gives his personal staff a head start."

"They ought to have it. After all, they've been working for him; they ought to have first crack at the bounty." Harvey was trying to be funny, but his wife didn't respond. "You think a man that big can hide out?"

Doris shrugged. The problem was simple with the ones who hid; they gave themselves away by departing more and more from the behavior norm. It was the ones unaware of their innate difference, those who kept on functioning until discovered by accident... the so-called *unconscious* P-K's had forced into existence the random check system and its Agency of female Immunes. In Doris's mind, the weird thought crept that a man might not be P-K and think he was — the timeless neurotic fear that one was somehow different, oddball, when in fact one was quite normal. Eggerton, for all his industrial power and influence, might be an ordinary human being suffering from a gnawing phobia that he was P-K. Such had happened ... and there were genuine P-K's wandering around blithely unaware of their alienness.

"We need a sure-fire test," Doris said aloud. "Something an individual can apply on himself. So he can be *certain*."

"Don't you have it? Can't you be positive when you get hold of them in your net?"

"*If* we get hold of them. One out of ten thousand. Too damn small a number come up in the nets." Abruptly she pushed away her drink and got to her feet. "Let's go home. I'm hungry and tired; I want to go to bed."

Harvey gathered up his coat as he paid the tab. "Sorry, honey, we're going out for dinner tonight. A fellow in the Commerce Institute, a man named Jay Richards. I met him at luncheon ... as a matter of fact, you were along. We're all invited over to celebrate something."

"Celebrate what?" Doris demanded irritably. "What do we have to celebrate?"

"Something secret of his," Harvey answered, as he pushed open the wide street door. "He's going to spring it on us after dinner. Cheer up — it may be good for an evening's entertainment."

Eggerton did not fly directly home. At high velocity he circled aimlessly near the first ring of residential syndromes at the edge of New York, his mind ebbing first with terror, then with outrage. His natural impulse was to head for his own lands and houses, but fear of running into more Agency servers paralyzed his will. While he was trying to make up his mind, his neck-mike came on with the relay of the Agency's call.

He was lucky. The girl had given the twenty-four hour notice to one of his robots; and robots weren't interested in bounty.

He landed on a randomly-selected roof field within the industrial area of Pittsburgh. No one saw him: lucky again. He was trembling as he entered the descent elevator, and began the trip down to the street level. With him were crowded a blank-faced clerk, two elderly woman, a serious young man, and the pretty daughter of some minor official. A harmless clump of people, but he wasn't fooled; at the end of twenty-four hours any and all of them would be panting for his hide. And he couldn't blame them: ten million dollars was a lot of money.

Theoretically, he had a one-day grace period; but final notices were badly-kept secrets. Most higher-ups were undoubtedly in on it; he'd approach an old friend, be welcomed, wined and dined, given a cabin-shelter on Ganymede and plenty of supplies — and be shot between the eyes as soon as the day was up.

He had remote units of his own industrial combine, of course; but they'd be checked off systematically. He had a variety of holding companies, dummy corporations, but the Agency would run through them if they considered it worth their time. The intuitive realization that he could easily become an object lesson to the niplan system, manipulated and exploited by the Agency, drove him to a frenzy. The female Immunes had always tripped deep-buried complexes built up in his mind from early infancy; the thought of a matriarchal culture was vitally abhorrent to him. And to pick off Eggerton was to unfasten a basic pivot of the bloc: now it occurred to him that his number on the random check might not really be random after all.

Clever — compile the identifying serial numbers of the id bloc leaders, revolve them in the check-nets from time to time, gradually eliminate them one by one.

He reached the street level and stood undecided, as urban traffic flowed around him noisily. Suppose the id bloc leaders simply cooperated with the check-nets? Compliance with the initial notice meant only a routine mind-probe by the protected corps of mutants society sanctioned, the telepathic *castrati* tolerated because of their usefulness against other mutants. Pulled at random or by design, the victim could simply permit the probe, lay his mind bare to the Agency, let the battleaxes claw and peck over the contents of his psyche, and then return to his office, cleared and safe. But this posited one item: that the industrial leader could pass the probe, that he was not P-K.

Sweat stood out on Eggerton's heavy forehead. Wasn't he, in a roundabout way, telling himself that he *was* P-K? No, that wasn't it. The issue was a principle; the Agency had no moral right to probe the half-dozen men whose industrial bloc was the mainstay of the niplan system. On that point every id bloc leader agreed with him ... an attack on Eggerton was an assault on the bloc itself.

Fervently, he prayed they *would* see it that way. He hailed a robot taxi and ordered: "Get me over to the id bloc hall. And if anybody tries to halt you, fifty dollars says keep going."

The vast, echoing hall was dark and gloomy when he reached it. The meeting wouldn't begin for several days, yet; Eggerton wandered aimlessly up and down the aisles, between the rows of seats where the technological and clerical staffs of the various industrial units would be placed, past the steel and plastic benches where the leaders themselves sat, up finally to the vacant speaker's stand. Faint lights glowed for him as he halted vaguely before the marble stand. The futility of his position came to him with a rush: standing here in this empty hall, he momentarily comprehended how completely he had made himself an outcast. He could yell and shout and nobody would appear. He could summon up nobody and nothing; the Agency was the legal government of the niplan system. In tilting with it he had placed himself against all organized society — powerful as he was he couldn't hope to defeat society itself.

He left the hall hurriedly, located an expensive restaurant, and enjoyed a lavish dinner. Almost feverishly, he downed immense quantities of scarce imported delicacies; at least he could enjoy his last twenty-four hours. As he ate he gazed apprehensively at the waiters and the other diners. Bland, indifferent faces — but very soon they would see his number and image in every newsmachine. The great hunt would be on; billions of hunters after one quarry. Abruptly, he finished his meal, examined his watch, and left the restaurant. It was six in the evening.

For an hour he squandered himself furiously in a swank bed girl mart, going from one apartment to the next, only half-seeing the occupants. He left behind a chaos — for which he paid and then abandoned the frenetic turmoil for the fresh air of the evening streets. Until eleven he wandered through the dark star-lit parks that surrounded the residential area of the city, among other dim shadows, his hands stuffed miserably in his pockets, hunched over, wretched. Somewhere far off a city clock-tower radiated an audio time signal. The twenty-four hours were leaking out and no one could stop them.

At eleven-thirty he halted his purposeless wanderings and pulled himself together long enough to analyze his situation. He had to face it: his only chance lay back at the id bloc hall. The technological and clerical staffs wouldn't have begun to show, but most of the leaders would be staking out preferred living quarters. His wristmap showed that he had drifted five miles from the hall. Suddenly terrified, he made his decision.

He flew directly back to the hall, landed on the deserted roof field, and descended to the floor of living quarters. It couldn't be put off: it was now or never.

"Come in, John," Townsand invited good-naturedly, and then his expression changed as Eggerton briefly outlined what had taken place in his office.

"You say they've already sent the final notice to your home?" Laura Townsand asked quickly. She had got up from the couch where she had been sitting and came immediately to the door. "Then it's too late!"

Eggerton tossed his overcoat to the closet and sank down in an easy chair. "Too late? Maybe ... too late to avoid the notice; but I'm not giving up."

Townsand and the other id bloc leaders came around Eggerton, faces showing curiosity, sympathy, and traces of cold amusement. "You've really got yourself into something," one of the leaders said. "If you'd let us know before the final notice was sent out maybe we could have done something. But this late. . . . "

Eggerton strangled as he felt the boom being lowered down around him. "Wait," he said thickly, "let's get this straight. We're all in this together; it's me today and you tomorrow. If I fold under this — "

"Take it easy," murmured voices came. "Let's work this out rationally or not at all."

Eggerton lay back against the chair as it adjusted to his tired body. Yes, he was glad to work it out rationally.

"As I see it," Townsand said quietly, leaning forward, his fingers pressed together, "it's not really a question of *can* we neutralize the Agency. Collectively, we're the economic battery of the niplan system; if we draw the props out from under the Agency it collapses. The real question is — do we *want* to write off the Agency?"

Eggeton croaked wildly: "Good God, it's either us or them! Can't you see they're using this net-check and probe system to undermine us?"

Townsand glanced at him and then continued for the benefit of the other leaders. "Perhaps we're forgetting something. *We* set up the Agency in the first place; that is, the id bloc before us worked out the fundamentals of random net-check inspection, use of tame telepaths, the final notice and hunt — the whole works. *The Agency is for our protection*; otherwise parakineticists would grow like weeds and finally choke us off. Of course, we must keep control of the Agency ... it's our instrument."

"Yes," another leader agreed. "We can't let it get on our backs; Eggerton is certainly right, there."

"We can assume," Townsand continued, "that some mechanism must exist at all times to detect P-K's. If the Agency goes, something must be constructed in its place. Now I tell you what, John." He gazed thoughtfully at Eggerton. "If you can think of a substitute, then maybe we'll be interested. But if not, then the Agency stands. Since the first P-K back in 2045, only females have shown immunity. Whatever we set up will have to be operated from a female policy-board ... and that's the Agency all over again."

There was silence.

Dimly, in Eggerton's mind, the ghosts of hope flickered. "You agree the Agency is on our backs?" he demanded huskily. "All right, we have to assert ourselves." He gestured around the room futilely; the leaders were watching stonily and Laura Townsand was quietly pouring coffee into half-empty cups. She shot him a glance of mute sympathy and then turned back to the kitchen. Cold silence cut down around Eggerton; he settled unhappily back in his chair and listened to Townsand drone on.

"I'm sorry you didn't inform us that your number had come up," Townsand was saying. "On the first notice we could have done something, but not now. Not unless we want to have a showdown at this time — and I don't think we're prepared for that." He pointed his authoritative finger at Eggerton. "You know, John, I don't think you really understand what these P-K individuals are. You probably think of them as lunatics, people with delusions."

"I know what they are," Eggerton answered stiffly. But he couldn't keep himself from saying, "*Aren't* they people with delusions?"

"They're lunatics who have the power to actualize their delusional systems in space-time. They warp a limited area around them to conform to their eccentric notions — understand? *The P-K makes his delusion work.* Therefore in a sense it isn't a delusion ... not unless you can stand far enough back, get a long way off and compare his warped area with the world proper. But how can the P-K himself do that? He has no objective standard; he can't very well get away from himself, and the warp follows him wherever he goes. The really dangerous P-K's are the ones who think everybody can animate stones, or change themselves into animals, or transmute base minerals. If we let a P-K get away, if we let him grow up, reproduce, have a family, a wife and children, we let this inherited parafaculty spread ... it becomes a group belief ... it becomes a socially institutionalized practice.

"Any given P-K is capable of spawning a society of P-K's built around his particular power. The great danger is this: eventually we non-P-K's may become the minority ... our rational world-view may come to be considered eccentric."

Eggerton licked his lips. The dry, languid voice made him sick; as Townsand spoke the ominous chill of death settled over him. "In other words," he muttered, "you're not going to help me."

"That's right," Townsand said, "But not because we don't *want* to help you. We feel that the danger from the Agency is less than you imagine; we consider the P-K's the real menace. Find us some way we can detect them without the Agency, and we'll go along with you — but not until then." He leaned close to Eggerton and tapped him on the shoulder with a lean, bony finger. "If females weren't clear of this stuff, we wouldn't stand a chance. We're lucky ... we could be a lot worse off than we are."

Eggerton got slowly to his feet.

"Goodnight."

Townsand also rose. There was a moment of strained, awkward silence. "However," Townsand said, "we can beat this hunt and chase rap they have on you. There's still time; the public notice hasn't been put out, yet."

"What'll I do?" Eggerton asked hopelessly.

"You have the written copy of your twenty-four notice?"

"No!" Eggerton's voice cracked hysterically. "I ran out of the office before the girl could give it to me!"

Townsand pondered. "You know who she is? You know where you can find her?"

"No."

"Make inquiries. Trace her down, accept the notice, then throw yourself on the mercy of the Agency."

Eggerton spread his hands numbly. "But that means I'll be bonded to them for the rest of my life."

"You'll be alive," Townsand said mildly, without emotion of any kind.

Laura Townsand brought steaming black coffee over to Eggerton. "Cream or sugar?" she asked gently, when she was able to attract his attention. "Or both? John, you must get something hot under your belt before you go; it's such a long trip back."

The girl's name was Doris Sorrel. Her apartment was listed under the name Harvey Sorrel, her husband. There was no one there; Eggerton carbonized the door-lock, then entered and searched the four small rooms. He rooted through the dresser drawers, tossed clothing and personal articles aside one after another, systematically rifled the closets and cupboards. In the waste disposal slot by the work desk he found what he was looking for: a not-yet incinerated note, crumpled and discarded, a jotted notation with the name Jay Richards, the date and the time, the address, and the words, *if Doris isn't too tired*. Eggerton put the note in his coat pocket and departed.

It was three-thirty in the morning when he found them. He landed on the roof of the squat Commerce Institute Building and descended the ramp to the residential floors. From the north wing light and noise came: the party was still in session. Praying silently, Eggerton raised his hand to the door and tripped the analyzer.

The man who opened the door was handsome, gray-haired, a heavy man in his late thirties. A glass in one hand, he gazed blankly at Eggerton, his eyes blurred with fatigue and alcohol. "I don't remember inviting — " he began, but Eggerton pushed past him and into the apartment.

There were plenty of people. Sitting, standing, keeping up a low murmur of talk and laughter. Liquor, soft couches, thick perfumes and fabrics, shifting color-walls, robots serving hors d'oeuvres, the muted cacophony of feminine giggles from darkened siderooms... Eggerton slid off his coat and moved aimlessly around. She was there somewhere; he glanced from face to face, saw only vacant, half-gazed eyes and slack mouths, and abruptly left the living-room and entered a bedroom.

Doris Sorrel was standing at a window gazing silently out at the lights of the city, her back to him, one arm resting on the window sill. "Oh," she murmured, turning a little. "Already?" And then she saw who it was.

"I want it," Eggerton said. "The twenty-four hour notice; I'll take it, now."

"You scared me." Trembling she moved away from the wide expanse of window. "How — long have you been here?"

"I just came."

"But — *why?* You're a strange person, Mr. Eggerton. You don't make sense." She laughed nervously. "I don't understand you at all."

From the gloom the figure of a man emerged, briefly outlined in the doorway. "Darling, here's your martini." The man made out Eggerton, and an ugly expression settled over his half-stupefied face. "Move on, buddy; this isn't for you."

Shakily, Doris caught his arm. "Harvey, this is the man I tried to serve today. Mr. Eggerton, this is my husband."

They shook hands icily. "Where is it?" Eggerton demanded bluntly. "You have it with you?"

"Yes ... it's in my purse." Doris moved away. "I'll get it. You can come along, if you want." She was regaining her composure. "I think I left it around here somewhere. Harvey, where the hell's my purse?" In the darkness she fumbled for something small and vaguely shiny. "Yes, here it is. On the bed."

She stood lighting a cigarette and watching, as Eggerton examined the twenty-four hour notice. "Why did you come back?" she asked. For the party she had changed to a knee-length silk shirt, copper bracelets, sandals, and a luminous flower in her hair. Now the flower drooped miserably; her shirt was wrinkled and unbuttoned, and she looked dead-tired. Leaning against the bedroom wall, cigarette between her stained lips, she said: "I don't see that it makes any difference what you do. The notice will be out publicly in half an hour — your personal staff has already been notified. God, I'm exhausted." She looked around impatiently for her husband. "Let's get out of here," she said to him, as he wandered up. "I have to go to work tomorrow."

"We haven't seen it," Harvey Sorrel answered sullenly.

"The hell with it!" Doris grabbed her coat from the closet. "Why all this mystery? My God, we've been here five hours and he hasn't trotted it out *yet*. Even if he's perfected time travel or squared the circle I'm not interested, not this late."

As she pushed her way through the crowded living room, Eggerton hurried to catch up with her. "Listen to me," he gasped. Holding onto her shoulder he continued rapidly, "Townsand said if I came back I could throw myself on the mercy of the Agency. He said — "

The girl shook loose. "Yes, of course; it's the law." She turned angrily to her husband who had scrambled after them. "Are you coming?"

"I'm coming," Harvey answered, bloodshot eyes blazing with indignation, "But I'm saying goodnight to Richards. And you're going to tell him it's *your* idea to leave; I'm not going to pretend it's my fault we're walking out. If you haven't got the social decency at least to say goodnight to your host ... "

The gray-haired man who had let Eggerton in broke away from a circle of guests and came smilingly over. "Harvey! Doris! Are you leaving? But you haven't seen it." Dismay flooded his heavy face. "You *can't* leave."

Doris opened her mouth to say that she damn well could. "Look," Harvey cut in desperately, "can't you show it to us now? Come on, Jay; we've waited long enough."

Richards hesitated. More people were wearily getting up and clustering over. "Come on," voices demanded, "let's get it over with."

After a moment of indecision Richards conceded. "All right," he agreed; he knew he had stalled long enough. Into the tired, experience-satiated guests a measure of anticipation trickled back. Richards raised his arms dramatically; he was still going to milk what he could from the moment. "This is it, folks! Come on along with me — it's out back."

"I wondered where it was," Harvey said, following after his host. "Come on, Doris." He seized her arm and dragged her after him. The others crowded along, through the dining room, the kitchen, to the back door.

The night was ice chill. Frigid wind blew around them as they shivered and stumbled uncertainly down the black steps, into the hyperborean gloom. John Eggerton felt a small shape push into him: as Doris savagely yanked away from her husband, Eggeton managed to follow after her. She rapidly shoved through the mass of guests, along the concrete walk to the fence that enclosed the yard. "Wait," Eggerton gasped, "listen to me. Then the Agency will take me?" He was powerless to keep the thin edge of pleading from his voice. "I can count on that? The notice will be voided?"

Doris sighed wearily. "That's right. Okay, if you want, I'll take you over to the Agency and get action on your papers; otherwise they'll sit there for a month. You know what it means, I suppose. You're indentured to the Agency for the balance of your natural life; you know that, I suppose. Do you?"

"I know."

"Do you want that?" She was distantly curious. "A man like you … I would have thought otherwise."

Eggerton twisted miserably. "Townsand said — " he began pathetically.

"What I want to know," Doris interrupted, "is why you didn't respond to your first notice? If only you'd come around … this never would have happened."

Eggerton opened his mouth to answer. He was going to say something about the principle involved, the concept of a free society, the rights of the individual, liberty and due process, the encroachment of the state. It was at that moment that Richards snapped on the powerful outdoor searchlights he had rigged up especially for the occasion; for the first time, his great achievement was revealed for everyone to see.

For a moment there was stunned silence. Then all at once they were screaming and milling from the yard. Wild-faced, dazed with terror, they scrambled over the fence, burst through the plastic wall surrounding the yard, crashed into the next yard and onto the public street.

Richards stood dumbfounded beside his masterpiece, bewildered and not yet understanding. In the artificial white glare of the searchlights the high-velocity transport was a thing of utter beauty. It was fully formed, completely ripe. Half an hour before, Richards had slipped outside with a flashlight, inspected it, and then, trembling with excitement, had cut the stem from which the ship had grown. It was now separate from the plant on which it had formed; he had rolled it to the edge of the yard, filled the fuel tank, slid back the hatch, and made it ready for flight.

On the plant were the embryonic buds of other transports, in various stages of growth. He had watered and fertilized with skill: the plant was going to turn out a dozen jet transports before the end of the summer.

Tears dribbled down Doris's tired cheeks. "You see it?" she whispered wretchedly to Eggerton. "It's — lovely. Look at it; see it sitting there?" Agonized, she turned away. "Poor Jay . . . when he understands . . . "

Richards stood, feet planted apart, gazing around at the deserted, trampled remains of his yard. He made out the shapes of Eggerton and Doris; after a moment he started hesitantly toward them. "Doris," he choked brokenly, "*what is it?* What did I do?"

Suddenly his expression changed. Bewilderment vanished; first came brute, naked terror as finally he understood what he was, and why his guests had fled. And then crazed cunning fell into place. Richards turned clumsily and began lumbering across the yard toward his ship.

Eggerton killed him with a single shot at the base of the skull. As Doris began screaming shrilly, he shot out the searchlights one by one. The yard, Richards' body, the gleaming metal transport, dissolved in the frigid gloom. He shoved the girl down and forced her face into the wet, cold vines growing up the wall of the garden.

She was able to get hold of herself, after a time. Shuddering, she lay pressed against the mashed grass and vines, arms clutched around her waist, trembling back and forth in an aimless rocking motion that gradually drained itself away.

Eggerton helped her up. "All these years and nobody suspected. He was saving it up — big secret."

"You'll be all right," Doris was saying, so low and faint that he could hardly hear her. "The Agency will be willing to write you off; you stopped him." Weak with shock, she groped blindly in the darkness for her scattered purse and cigarettes. "He would have got away. And that *plant*. What are we going to do with it?" She found her cigarettes and lit up wildly. "What about it?"

Their eyes were growing accustomed to the night gloom. Under the faint sheen of starlight the outline of the plant came dimly into focus. "It won't live," Eggerton said. "It's part of his delusion; now he's dead."

Frightened and subdued, the other guests were beginning to filter back into the yard. Harvey Sorrel crept drunkenly from the shadows and apologetically approached his wife. Somewhere far off the wail of a siren sounded; the automatic police had been called. "Do you want to come with us?" Doris asked Eggerton shakily. She indicated her husband. "We'll all drive over to the Agency together and get you straightened out; it can be fixed up. There'll be some kind of indenture, a few years at the most. Nothing more than that."

Eggerton moved away from her. "No thanks," he said. "I have something else to do. Maybe later."

"But — "

"I think I have what I want." Eggerton fumbled for the back door and entered Richards' deserted quarters. "This is what we've been looking for."

He put through his emergency call immediately. In Townsand's apartment the buzzer was sounding within thirty seconds. Sleepily, Laura roused her husband; Eggerton began talking as soon as the two men were facing each other's image.

"We have our standard," he said; "we don't need the Agency. We can pull the rug out from under them because we don't really need them to watch us."

"What?" Townsand demanded angrily, his mind fuzzy with sleep. "What are you talking about?"

Eggerton repeated what he had said, as calmly as possible.

"Then who *will* watch us?" Townsand growled. "What the hell is this?"

"We'll watch each other," Eggerton continued patiently. "Nobody will be exempt. Each of us will be the standard for the next man. Richards couldn't see himself objectively, but I could — *even though I'm not immune*. We don't need anybody over us, because we can do the job ourselves."

Townsand reflected resentfully. He yawned, pulled his night-robe around him, glanced sleepily at his wristwatch. "Lord, it's late. Maybe you have something, maybe not. Tell me more about this Richards ... what sort of P-K talent did he have?"

Eggerton told him. "You see? All these years ... and he couldn't tell. But we could tell instantly." Eggerton's voice rose excitedly. "We can run our own society, again! Consensus gentium — we've had our measuring standard all the time and none of us has realized it. Individually, each of us is fallible; *but as a group we can't go wrong*. All we have to do is make sure the random check-nets get everybody; we'll have to step the process up, get more people and get them oftener. It has to be accelerated so that everybody, sooner or later, gets hauled in."

"I see," Townsand agreed.

"We'll keep the tame telepaths, of course; so we can get out all the thoughts and subliminal material. The teeps won't evaluate; we'll handle that ourselves."

Townsand nodded dully. "Sounds good, John."

"It came to me as soon as I saw Richards' plant. It was instantaneous — I had complete certitude. How could there be error? A delusional system like his simply doesn't fit into our world." Eggerton's hand slammed down on the table in front of him; a book that had belonged to Jay Richards slipped off and landed soundlessly on the thick carpet of the apartment. "You understand? There's no equation between a P-K world and ours; all we have to do is get the P-K material up where we can see it. Where we can compare it to our own reality."

Townsand was silent a moment. "All right," he said at last. "Come on over.

If you convince the rest of the id bloc then we'll act." He made his decision. "I'll get them out of bed and over here."

"Fine." Eggerton reached quickly for the cut-off switch. "I'll hurry over; and thanks!"

He rushed from the littered, bottle-strewn apartment, now dismal and deserted without the celebrating guests. In the back yard, the police were already picking around, examining the dying plant that Jay Richards' delusional talent had brought into momentary existence.

The night air was cold and crisp, as Eggerton emerged from the ascent ramp, onto the roof field of the Commerce Building. A few voices drifted up from far below; the roof itself was deserted. He buttoned his heavy overcoat around him, extended his arms, and rose from the roof. He gained altitude and speed; in a few moments he was on his way toward Pittsburgh.

As he flew silently through the night he gulped vast lungfuls of the clean, fresh air. Satisfaction and rising excitement raced through him. He had spotted Richards immediately — and why not? How could he miss? A man who grew jet transports from a plant in his backyard was clearly a lunatic.

It was so much simpler just to flap one's arms.

A World of Talent

I

When he entered the apartment, a great number of people were making noises and flashing colors. The sudden cacophony confused him. Aware of the surge of shapes, sounds, smells, three-dimensional oblique patches, but trying to peer through and beyond, he halted at the door. With an act of will, he was able to clear the blur somewhat; the meaningless frenzy of human activity settled gradually into a quasi-orderly pattern.

"What's the matter?" his father asked sharply.

"This is what we previewed a half-hour ago," his mother said when the eight-year-old boy failed to answer. "I wish you'd let me get a Corpsman to probe him."

"I don't fully trust the Corps. And we have twelve years to handle this ourselves. If we haven't cracked it by then — "

"Later." She bent down and ordered in a crisp tone, "Go on in, Tim. Say hello to people."

"Try to hold an objective orientation," his father added gently. "At least for this evening, to the end of the party."

Tim passed silently through the crowded living room ignoring the various oblique shapes, his body tilted forward, head turned to one side. Neither of his parents followed him; they were intercepted by the host and then surrounded by Norm and Psi guests.

In the melee, the boy was forgotten. He made a brief circuit of the living room, satisfied himself that nothing existed there, and then sought a side hall. A mechanical attendant opened a bedroom door for him and he entered.

The bedroom was deserted; the party had only begun. He allowed the voices and movement behind him to fade into an indiscriminate blur. Faint perfumes of women drifted through the swank apartment, carried by the warm, Terran-like, artificial air pumped from the central ducts of the city. He raised himself up and inhaled the sweet scents, flowers, fruits, spices — and something more.

He had to go all the way into the bedroom to isolate it. There it was — sour, like spoiled milk — the warming he counted on. And it *was* in the bedroom.

Cautiously, he opened a closet. The mechanical selector tried to present him with clothing, but he ignored it. With the closet open, the scent was stronger. The Other was somewhere near the closet, if not actually in it.

Under the bed?

He crouched down and peered. Not there. He lay outstretched and stared under Fairchild's metal workdesk, typical furniture of a Colonial official's quarters. Here, the scent was stronger. Fear and excitement touched him. He jumped to his feet and pushed the desk away from the smooth plastic surface of the wall.

The Other clung against the wall in the dark shadow where the desk had rested.

It was a Right Other, of course. He had only identified one Left and that for no more than a split second. The Other hadn't managed to phase totally. He retreated warily from it, conscious that, without his cooperation, it had come as far as it could. The Other watched him calmly, aware of his negative actions, but there was little it could do. It made no attempt to communicate, for that had always failed.

Tim was safe. He halted and spent a long moment scrutinizing the Other. This was his chance to learn more about it. A space separated the two of them, across which only the visual image and odor — small vaporized particles — of the Other crossed.

It was not possible to identify this Other; many were so similar, they appeared to be multiples of the same unit. But sometimes the Other was radically different. Was it possible that various selections were being tried, alternate attempts to get across?

Again the thought struck him. The people in the living room, both Norm and Psi classes — and even the Mute-class of which he was a part — seemed to have reached a workable stalemate with their own Others. It was strange, since their Lefts would be advanced over his own ... unless the procession of Rights diminished as the Left group increased.

Was there a finite total of Others?

He went back to the frenetic living room. People murmured and swirled on all sides, gaudy opaque shapes everywhere, warm smells overpowering him with their closeness. It was clear that he would have to get information from his mother and father. He had already spun the research indices hooked to the Sol System educational transmission — spun them without results, since the circuit was not working.

"Where did you wander off to?" his mother asked him, pausing in the animated conversation that had grown up among a group of Norm-class officials blocking one side of the room. She caught the expression on his face.

"Oh," she said. "Even here?"

He was surprised at her question. Location made no difference. Didn't she know that? Floundering, he withdrew into himself to consider. He needed help; he couldn't understand without outside assistance. But a staggering verbal block existed. Was it only a problem of terminology or was it more?

As he wandered around the living room, the vague musty odor filtered to him through the heavy curtain of people-smells. The Other was still there, crouched in the darkness where the desk had been, in the shadows of the deserted bedroom. Waiting to come over. Waiting for him to take two more steps.

Julie watched her eight-year-old son move away, an expression of concern on her petite face. "We'll have to keep our eyes on him," she said to her husband. "I preview a mounting situation built around this thing of his."

Curt had caught it, too, but he kept on talking to the Norm-class officials grouped around the two Precogs. "What would you do," he demanded, "if they really opened up on us? You know Big Noodle can't handle a stepped-up shower of robot projectiles. The handful now and then are in the nature of experiments ... and he has the half-hour warnings from Julie and me."

"True." Fairchild scratched his gray nose, rubbed the stubble of beard showing below his lip. "But I don't think they'll swing to overt war operations. It would be an admission that we're getting somewhere. It would legalize us and open things up. We might collect you Psi-class people together and — " he grinned wearily — "and think the Sol System far out past the Andromache Nebula."

Curt listened without resentment, since the man's words were no surprise. As he and Julie had driven over, they had both previewed the party, its unfruitful discussions, the growing aberrations of their son. His wife's precog span was somewhat greater than his own. She was seeing, at this moment, ahead of his own vision. He wondered what the worried expression on her face indicated.

"I'm afraid," Julie said tightly, "that we're going to have a little quarrel before we get home tonight."

Well, he had also seen that. "It's the situation," he said, rejecting the topic. "Everybody here is on edge. It isn't only you and I who're going to be fighting."

Fairchild listened sympathetically. "I can see some drawbacks to being a

Precog. But knowing you're going to have a spat, can't you alter things before it begins?"

"Sure," Curtis answered, "the way we give you pre-information and you use it to alter the situation with Terra. But neither Julie nor I particularly care. It takes a huge mental effort to stave off something like this ... and neither of us has that much energy."

"I just wish you'd let me turn him over to the Corps," Julie said in a low voice. "I can't stand him wandering around, peering under things, looking in closets for God knows what!"

"For Others," Curt said.

"Whatever that might be."

Fairchild, a natural-born moderator, tried intercession. "You've got twelve years," he began. "It's no disgrace to have Tim stay in the Mute-class; every one of you starts out that way. If he has Psi powers, he'll show."

"You talk like an infinite Precog," Julie said, amused. "How do you know they'll show?"

Fairchild's good-natured face twisted with effort. Curt felt sorry for him. Fairchild had too much responsibility, too many decisions to make, too many lives on his hands. Before the Separation with Terra, he had been an appointed official, a bureaucrat with a job and clearly defined routine. Now there was nobody to tap out an inter-system memo to him early Monday morning. Fairchild was working without instructions.

"Let's see that doodad of yours," Curt said. "I'm curious about how it works."

Fairchild was astonished. "How the hell — " Then he remembered. "Sure, you must have already previewed it." He dug around in his coat. "I was going to make it the surprise of the party, but we can't have surprises with you two Precogs around."

The other Norm-class officials crowded around as their boss unwrapped a square of tissue paper and from it lifted a small glittering stone. An interested silence settled over the room as Fairchild examined the stone, his eyes close to it, like a jeweler studying a precious gem.

"An ingenious thing," Curt admitted.

"Thanks," Fairchild said. "They should start arriving any day, now. The glitter is to attract children and lower-class people who would go out for a bauble — possible wealth, you know. And women, of course. Anybody who would stop and pick up what they thought was a diamond, everybody but the Tech-classes. I'll show you."

He glanced around the hushed living room at the guests in their gay party clothes. Off to one side, Tim stood with his head turned at an angle. Fairchild hesitated, then tossed the stone across the carpet in front of the boy, almost at his feet. The boy's eyes didn't flicker. He was gazing absently through the people, unaware of the bright object at his feet.

Curt moved forward, ready to take up the social slack. "You'd have to produce something the size of a jet transport." He bent down and retrieved the stone. "It's not your fault that Tim doesn't respond to such mundane things as fifty-carat diamonds."

Fairchild was crestfallen at the collapse of his demonstration. "I forgot." He brightened. "But there aren't any Mutes on Terra any more. Listen and see what you think of the spiel. I had a hand at writing it."

In Curt's hand, the stone rested coldly. In his ears, a tiny gnatlike buzz sounded, a controlled, modulated cadence that caused a stir of murmurs around the room.

"My friends," the canned voice stated, "the causes of the conflict between Terra and the Centaurian colonies have been grossly misstated in the press."

"Is this seriously aimed at children?" Julie asked.

"Maybe he thinks Terran children are advanced over our own," a Psi-class official said as a rustle of amusement drifted through the room.

The tiny whine droned on, turning out its mixture of legalistic arguments, idealism and an almost pathetic pleading. The begging quality grated on Curt. Why did Fairchild have to get down on his knees and plead with the Terrans? As he listened, Fairchild puffed confidently on his pipe, arms folded, heavy face thick with satisfaction. Evidently Fairchild wasn't aware of the precarious *thinness* of his canned words.

It occurred to Curt that none of them — including himself — was facing how really fragile their Separation movement was. There was no use blaming the weak words wheezing from the pseudogem. Any description of their position was bound to reflect the querulous half-fear that dominated the Colonies.

"It has long been established," the stone asserted, "that freedom is the natural condition of Man. Servitude, the bondage of one man or one group of men to another, is a remnant of the past, a vicious anachronism. Men must govern themselves."

"Strange to hear a stone saying that," Julie said, half amused. "An inert lump of rock."

"You have been told that the Colonial Secessionist movement will jeopardize your lives and your standard of living. *This is not true.* The standard of living of all mankind will be raised if the colony planets are allowed to govern themselves and find their own economic markets. The mercantile system practiced by the Terran government on Terrans living outside the Sol group — "

"The children will bring this thing home," Fairchild said. "The parents will pick it up from them."

The stone droned on. "The Colonies could not remain mere supply bases for Terra, sources of raw materials and cheap labor. The Colonists could not remain second-class citizens. Colonists have as much right to determine their own society as those remaining in the Sol group. Thus, the Colonial Government has petitioned the Terran Government for a severance of those bonds to keep us from realizing our manifest destinies."

Curt and Julie exchanged glances. The academic text-book dissertation hung like a dead weight in the room. Was this the man the Colony had elected to manage the resistance movement? A pedant, a salaried official, a bureaucrat and — Curt couldn't help thinking — a man without Psi powers. A Normal.

Fairchild had probably been moved to break with Terra over some trivial miswording of a routine directive. Nobody, except perhaps the telepathic Corps, knew his motives or how long he could keep going.

"What do you think of it?" Fairchild asked when the stone had finished its monologue and had started over. "Millions of them showering down all over the Sol group. You know what the Terran press is saying about us — vicious lies — that we want to take over Sol, that we're hideous invaders from outer space, monsters, mutants, freaks. We have to counter such propaganda."

"Well," Julie said, "a third of us are freaks, so why not face it? I know my son is a useless freak."

Curt took her arm. "Nobody's calling Tim a freak, not even you!"

"But it's true!" She pulled away. "If we were back in the Sol System — if we hadn't separated — you and I would be in detention camps, waiting to be — you know." She fiercely jabbed in the direction of their son. "There wouldn't be any Tim."

From the corner a sharp-faced man spoke up. "We wouldn't be in the Sol System. We'd have broken out on our own without anybody's help. Fairchild had nothing to do with it; we brought him along. Don't ever forget that!"

Curt eyed the man hostilely. Reynolds, chief of the telepathic Corps, was drunk again. Drunk and spilling over his load of vitriolic hate for Norms.

"Possibly," Curt agreed, "but we would have had a hell of a time doing it."

"You and I know what keeps this Colony alive," Reynolds answered, his flushed face arrogant and sneering. "How long could these bureaucrats keep on going without Big Noodle and Sally, you two Precogs, the Corps and all the rest of us? Face facts — we don't need this legalistic window-dressing. We're not going to win because of any pious appeals for freedom and equality. We're going to win because there are no Psis on Terra."

The geniality of the room dwindled. Angry murmur rose from the Norm-class guests.

"Look here," Fairchild said to Reynolds, "you're still a human being, even if you can read minds. Having a talent doesn't — "

"Don't lecture me," Reynolds said. "No numbskull is going to tell me what to do."

"You're going too far," Curt told Reynolds. "Somebody's going to smack you down some day. If Fairchild doesn't do it, maybe I will."

"You and your meddling Corps," a Psi-class Resurrector said to Reynolds, grabbing hold of his collar. "You think you're above us because you can merge your minds. You think — "

"Take your hands off me," Reynolds said in an ugly voice. A glass crashed to the floor; one of the women became hysterical. Two men struggled; a third joined and, in a flash, a wild turmoil of resentment was boiling in the center of the room.

Fairchild shouted for order. "For God's sake, if we fight each other, we're finished. Don't you understand — *we have to work together!*"

It took a while before the uproar subsided. Reynolds pushed past Curt, white-faced and muttering under his breath. "I'm getting out of here." The other Telepaths trailed belligerently after him.

As he and Julie drove slowly home through the bluish darkness, one section of Fairchild's propaganda repeated itself in Curt's brain over and over again.

"You've been told a victory by the Colonist means a victory of Psis over Normal human beings. This is not true! The Separation was not planned and is not conducted by either Psis or Mutants. The revolt was a spontaneous reaction by Colonists of all classes."

"I wonder," Curt mused. "Maybe Fairchild's wrong. Maybe he's being operated by Psis without knowing it. Personally, I like him, stupid as he is."

"Yes, he's stupid," Julie agreed. In the darkness of the car's cabin, her cigarette was a bright burning coal of wrath. In the back seat, Tim lay curled up asleep, warmed by the heat from the motor. The barren, rocky landscape of Proxima III rolled out ahead of the small surface-car, a dim expanse, hostile and alien. A few Man-made roads and buildings lay here and there among crop-tanks and fields.

"I don't trust Reynolds," Curt continued, knowing he was opening the previewed scene between them, yet not willing to sidestep it. "Reynolds is smart, unscrupulous and ambitious. What he wants is prestige and status. But Fairchild is thinking of the welfare of the Colony. He means all that stuff he dictated into his stones."

"That drivel," Julie was scornful. "The Terrans will laugh their heads off. Listening to it with a straight face was more than I could manage, and God knows our lives depend on this business."

"Well," Curt said carefully, knowing what he was getting into, "there may be Terrans with more sense of justice than you and Reynolds." He turned toward her. "I can see what you're going to do and so can you. Maybe you're right, maybe we ought to get it over with. Ten years is a long time when there's no feeling. And it wasn't our idea in the first place."

"No," Julie agreed. She crushed her cigarette out and shakily lit another. "If there had been another male Precog besides you, just *one*. That's something I can't forgive Reynolds for. It was his idea, you know. I never should have agreed. For the glory of the race! Onward and upward with the Psi banner! The mystical mating of the first real Precogs in history ... and look what came of it!"

"Shut up," Curt said. "He's not asleep and he can hear you."

Julie's voice was bitter. 'Hear me, yes. Understand, no. We wanted to know what the second generation would be like — well, now we know. Precog plus Precog equals freak. Useless mutant. Monster — let's face it, the M on his card stands for monster."

Curt's hands tightened on the wheel. "That's a word neither you nor anybody else is going to use."

"Monster!" She leaned close to him, teeth white in the light from the dashboard, eyes glowing. "Maybe the Terrans are right — maybe we Precogs ought to be sterilized and put to death. Erased. I think. ... " She broke off abruptly, unwilling to finish.

"Go ahead," Curt said. "You think perhaps when the revolt is successful and we're in control of the Colonies, we should go down the line selectively. With the Corps on top naturally."

"Separate the wheat from the chaff," Julie said. "First the Colonies from Terra. Then us from them. And when he comes up, even if he is my son. ... "

"What you're doing," Curt interrupted, "is passing judgment on people according to their use. Tim isn't useful, so there's no point in letting him live, right?" His blood pressure was on the way up, but he was past caring. "Breeding people like cattle. A human hasn't a right to live; that's a privilege we dole out according to our whim."

Curt raced the car down the deserted highway. "You heard Fairchild prattle about freedom and equality. He believes it and so do I. And I believe Tim — or anybody else — has a right to exist whether we can make use of his talent or whether he even has a talent."

"He has a right to live," Julie said, "but remember he's not one of us. He's an oddity. He doesn't have our ability, our — " she ground out the words triumphantly — "superior ability."

Curt pulled the car over to the edge of the highway. He brought it to a halt and pushed open the door. Dismal, arid air billowed into the car.

"You drive on home." He leaned over the back seat and prodded Tim into wakefulness. "Come on, kid. We're getting out."

Julie reached over to get the wheel. "When will you be home? Or have you got it completely set up now? Better make sure. She might be the kind that has a few others on the string."

Curt stepped from the car and the door slammed behind him. He took his son's hand and led him down the roadway to the black square of a ramp that rose darkly in the night gloom. As they started up the steps, he heard the car roar off down the highway through the darkness toward home.

"Where are we?" Tim asked.

"You know this place. I bring you here every week. This is the school where they train people like you and me — where we Psis get our education."

II

Lights came on around them. Corridors branched off the main entrance ramp like metal vines.

"You may stay here for a few days," Curt said to his son. "Can you stand not seeing your mother for a while?"

Tim didn't answer. He had lapsed back into his usual silence as he followed along beside his father. Curt again wondered how the boy could be so withdrawn — as he obviously was — and yet be so terribly alert. The answer was written over each inch of the taut, young body. Tim was only withdrawn from contact with human beings. He maintained an almost compulsive tangency with the outside world — or, rather, an outside world. Whatever it was, it didn't include humans, although it was made up of real, external objects.

As he had already previewed, his son suddenly broke away from him. Curt let the boy hurry down a side corridor. He watched as Tim stood tugging anxiously at a supply locker, trying to get it open.

"Okay," Curt said resignedly. He followed after him and unlocked the locker with his pass key. "See? There's nothing in it."

How completely the boy lacked precog could be seen by the flood of relief that swept his face. Curt's heart sank at the sight. The precious talent that both he and Julie possessed simply hadn't been passed on. Whatever the boy was, he was not a Precog.

It was past two in the morning, but the interior departments of the School Building were alight with activity. Curt moodily greeted a couple of Corpsmen lounging around the bar, surrounded by beers and ashtrays.

"Where's Sally?" he demanded. "I want to go in and see Big Noodle."

One of the Telepaths lazily jerked a thumb. "She's around somewhere. Over that way, in the kids' quarters, probably asleep. It's late." He eyed Curt, whose thoughts were on Julie. "You ought to get rid of a wife like that. She's too old and thin, anyhow. What you'd really like is a plump young dish — "

Curt lashed a blast of mental dislike and was satisfied to see the grinning young face go hard with antagonism. The other Telepath pulled himself upright and shouted after Curt. "When you're through with your wife, send her around to us."

"I'd say you're after a girl of about twenty," another Telepath said as he admitted Curt to the sleeping quarters of the children's wing. "Dark hair — correct me it I'm wrong — and dark eyes. You have a fully formed image. Maybe there's a specific girl. Let's see, she's short, fairly pretty and her name is — "

Curt cursed at the situation that required them to turn their minds over to the Corps. Telepaths were interlaced throughout the Colonies and, in particular, throughout the School and the offices of the Colonial Government. He tightened his grip around Tim's hand and led him through the doorway.

"This kid of yours," the Telepath said as Tim passed close to him, "sure probes queer. Mind if I go down a little?"

"Keep out of his mind." Curt ordered sharply. He slammed the door shut after Tim, knowing it made no difference, but enjoying the feel of the heavy metal sliding in place. He pushed Tim down a narrow corridor and into a small room. Tim pulled away, intent on a side door; Curt savagely yanked him back. "There's nothing in there!" he reprimanded harshly. "That's only a bathroom."

Tim continued to tug away. He was still tugging when Sally appeared, fastening a robe around her, face puffy with sleep. "Hello, Mr. Purcell," she greeted Curt. "Hello, Tim." Yawning, she turned on a floor lamp and tossed herself down on a chair. "What can I do for you this time of night?"

She was thirteen, tall and gangling, with yellow cornsilk hair and freckled skin. She picked sleepily at her thumbnail and yawned again as the boy sat down across from her. To amuse him, she animated a pair of gloves lying on a sidetable. Tim laughed with delight as the gloves groped their way to the edge of the table, waved their fingers blindly and began a cautious descent to the floor.

"Fine," Curt said. "You're getting good. I'd say you're not cutting any classes."

Sally shrugged. "Mr. Purcell, the School can't teach me anything. You know I'm the most advanced Psi with the power of animation. They just let me work alone. In fact, I'm instructing a bunch of little kids, still Mutes, who might have something. I think a couple of them could work out, with practice. All they can give me is encouragement; you know, psychological stuff and lots of vitamins and fresh air. But they can't teach me anything."

"They can teach you how important you are," Curt said. He had previewed this, of course. During the last half hour, he had selected a number of possible approaches, discarded one after another, finally ended with this. "I came over to see Big Noodle. That meant I had to wake you. Do you know why?"

"Sure," Sally answered. "You're afraid of him. And since Big Noodle is afraid of me, you need me to come along." She allowed the gloves to sag into immobility as she got to her feet. "Well, let's go."

He had seen Big Noodle many times in his life, but he had never got used to the sight. Awed, in spite of his preview of this scene, Curt stood in the open space before the platform, gazing up, silent and impressed as always.

"He's fat," Sally said practically. "If he doesn't get thinner, he won't live long."

Big Noodle slumped like a gray, sickly pudding in the immense chair the Tech Department had built for him. His eyes were half-closed; his pulpy arms lay slack and inert at his sides. Wads of oozing dough hung in folds over the arms and sides of the chair. Big Noodle's egglike skull was fringed with damp, stringy hair, matted like decayed seaweed. His nails were lost in the sausage fingers. His teeth were rotting and black. His tiny plate-blue eyes flickered dully as he identified Curt and Sally, but the obese body did not stir.

"He's resting," Sally explained. "He just ate."

"Hello," Curt said.

From the swollen mouth, between rolls of pink flesh lips, a grumbled response came.

"He doesn't like to be bothered this late," Sally said yawning. "I don't blame him."

She wandered around the room, amusing herself by animating light brackets along the wall. The brackets struggled to pull free from the hot-pour plastic in which they were set.

"This seems so dumb, if you don't mind my saying so, Mr. Purcell. The Telepaths keep Terran infiltrators from coming in here, and all this business of yours is against them. That means you're helping Terra, doesn't it? If we didn't have the Corps to watch out for us — "

"I keep out Terrans," Big Noodle mumbled. "I have my wall and I turn back everything."

"You turn back projectiles," Sally said, "but you can't keep out infiltrators. A Terran infiltrator could come in here this minute and you wouldn't know. You're just a big stupid lump of lard."

Her description was accurate. But the vast mound of fat was the nexus of the Colony's defense, the most talented of the Psis. Big Noodle was the core of the Separation movement . . . and the living symbol of its problem.

Big Noodle had almost infinite parakinetic power and the mind of a moronic three-year-old. He was, specifically, an idiot savant. His legendary powers had absorbed his whole personality, withered and degenerated it, rather than expanded it. He could have swept the Colony aside years ago if his bodily lusts and fears had been accompanied by cunning. But Big Noodle was helpless and inert, totally dependent on the instructions of the Colonial Government, reduced to sullen passivity by his terror of Sally.

"I ate a whole pig." Big Noodle struggled to a quasi-position, belched, wiped feebly at his chin. "Two pigs, in fact. Right here in this room, just a little while ago. I could get more if I wanted."

The diet of the colonist consisted mainly of tank-grown artificial protein. Big Noodle was amusing himself at their expense.

"The pig," Big Noodle continued grandly, "came from Terra. The night before, I had a flock of wild ducks. And before that, I brought over some kind of animal from Betelgeuse IV. It doesn't have any name; it just runs around and eats."

"Like you," Sally said, "Only you don't run around."

Big Noodle giggled. Pride momentarily overcame his fear of the girl. "Have some candy," he offered. A shower of chocolate rattled down like hail. Curt and Sally retreated as the floor of the chamber disappeared under the deluge. With the chocolate came fragments of machinery, cardboard boxes, sections of display counter, a jagged chunk of concrete floor. "Candy factory on Terra," Big Noodle explained happily. "I've got it pinpointed pretty good."

Tim had awakened from his contemplation. He bent down and eagerly picked up a handful of chocolates.

"Go ahead," Curt said to him. "You might as well take them"

"I'm the only one that gets the candy," Big Noodle thundered, outraged. The chocolate vanished. "I sent it back," he explained peevishly. "It's mine."

There was nothing malevolent in Big Noodle, only an infinite childish selfishness. Through his power, every object in the Universe had become his possession. There was nothing outside the reach of his bloated arms; he could reach for the Moon and get it. Fortunately, most things were outside his span of comprehension. He was uninterested.

"Let's cut out these games," Curt said. "Can you say if any Telepaths are within probe range of us?"

Big Noodle made a begrudging search. He had a consciousness of objects wherever they were. Through his talent, he was in contact with the physical contents of the Universe.

"None near here," he declared after a time. "One about a hundred feet off... I'll move him back. I hate Teeps getting into my privacy."

"Everybody hates Teeps," Sally said. "It's a nasty, dirty talent. Looking into other people's minds is like watching them when they're bathing or dressing or eating. It isn't natural."

Curt grinned. "Is it any different from Precog? You wouldn't call that natural."

"Precog has to do with events, not people," Sally said. "Knowing what's going to happen isn't any worse than knowing what's already happened."

"It might even be better," Curt pointed out.

"No," Sally said emphatically. "It's got us into this trouble. I have to watch what I think all the time because of you. Every time I see a Teep, I get goose bumps, and no matter how hard I try, I can't keep from thinking about *her*, just because I know I'm not supposed to."

"My precog faculty has nothing to do with Pat," Curt said. "Precog doesn't introduce fatality. Locating Pat was an intricate job. It was a deliberate choice I made."

"Aren't you sorry?" Sally demanded.

"No."

"If it wasn't for me," Big Noodle interrupted, "you never would have got across to Pat."

"I wish we hadn't," Sally said fervently. "If it wasn't for Pat, we wouldn't be mixed up in all this business." She shot a hostile glance at Curt. "And I don't think she's pretty."

"What would you suggest?" Curt asked the child with more patience than he felt. He had previewed the futility of making a child and an idiot understand about Pat. "You know we can't pretend we never found her."

"I know," Sally admitted. "And the Teeps have got something from our minds already. That's why there're so many of them hanging around here. It's a good thing we don't know where she is."

"I know where she is," Big Noodle said. "I know exactly where."

"No, you don't," Sally answered. "You just know how to get to her and that's not the same thing. You can't explain it; you just send us over there and back."

"It's a planet," Big Noodle said angrily, "with funny plants and a lot of green things. And the air's thin. She lives in a camp. People go out and farm all day. There's only a few people there. A lot of dopey animals live there. It's cold."

"Where is it?" Curt asked.

Big Noodle sputtered. "It's ... " His pulpy arms waved. "It's some place near ... " He gave up, wheezed resentfully at Sally and then brought a tank of filthy water into being above the girl's head. As the water flowed toward her, the child made a few brief motions with her hands.

Big Noodle shrieked in terror and the water vanished. He lay panting with fright, body quivering, as Sally mopped at a wet spot on her robe. She had animated the fingers of his left hand.

"Better not do that again," Curt said to her. "His heart might give out."

"The big slob." Sally rummaged around in a supply closet. "Well, if you've made up your mind, we might as well get it over with. Only let's not stay so long. You get to talking with Pat and then the two of you go off, and you don't come back for hours. At night, it's freezing and they don't have any heating plants." She pulled down a coat from the closet. "I'll take this with me."

"We're not going," Curt told her. "This time is going to be different."

Sally blinked. "Different? How?"

Even Big Noodle was surprised. "I was just getting ready to move you across," he complained.

"I know," Curt said firmly. "But this time I want you to bring Pat here. Bring her to this room, understand? This is the time we've been talking about. The big moment's arrived."

There was only one person with Curt as he entered Fairchild's office. Sally was now in bed, back at the school. Big Noodle never stirred from his chamber. Tim was still at the School, in the hands of Psi-class authorities, not Telepaths.

Pat followed hesitantly, frightened and nervous as the men sitting around the office glanced up in annoyance.

She was perhaps nineteen, slim and copper-skinned, with large dark eyes. She wore a canvas workshirt and jeans, heavy shoes caked with mud. Her tangle of black curls was tied back and knotted with a red bandana. Her rolled-up sleeves showed tanned, competent arms. At her leather belt she carried a knife, a field telephone and an emergency pack of rations and water.

"This is the girl," Curt said. "Take a good look at her."

"Where are you from?" Fairchild asked Pat. He pushed aside a heap of directives and memotapes to find his pipe.

Pat hesitated. "I — " she began. She turned uncertainly to Curt. "You told me never to say, even to you."

"It's okay," Cut said gently. "You can tell us now." He explained to Fairchild, "I can preview what she's going to say, but I never knew before. I didn't want to get it probed out of me by the Corps."

"I was born on Proxima VI," Pat said in a low voice. "I grew up there. This is the first time I've left the planet."

Fairchild's eyes widened. "That's a wild place. In fact, about our most primitive region."

Around the office, his group of Norm and Psi consultants moved closer to watch. One wide-shouldered old man, face weathered as stone, eyes shrewd and alert, raised his hand. "Are we to understand that Big Noodle brought you here?"

Pat nodded. "I didn't know. I mean it was unexpected." She tapped her belt. "I was working, clearing the brush ... we've been trying to expand, develop more usable land."

"What's your name?" Fairchild asked her.

"Patricia Ann Connley."

"What class?"

The girl's sun-cracked lips moved. "Mute class."

A stir moved through the officials. "You're a Mutant," the old man asked her, "without Psi powers? Exactly how do you differ from the Norm?"

Pat glanced at Curt and he moved forward to answer for her. "This girl will be twenty-one in two years. You know what that means. If she's still in the Mute-class, she'll be sterilized and put in a camp. That's our Colonial policy. And if Terra whips us, she'll be sterilized in any case, as will all of us Psis and Mutants."

"Are you trying to say she has a talent?" Fairchild asked. "You want us to lift her from Mute to Psi?" His hands fumbled at the papers on the table. "We get a thousand petitions a day like this. You came down here at four in the morning just for this? There's a routine form you can fill out, a common office procedure."

The old man cleared his throat and blurted, "This girl is close to you?"

"That's right," Curt said. "I have a personal interest."

"How did you meet her?" the old man asked. "If she's never been off Proxima VI. . . . "

"Big Noodle shuttled me there and back," Curt answered. "I've made the trip about twenty times. I didn't know it was Prox VI, of course. I only knew it was a Colony planet, primitive, still wild. Originally, I came across an analysis of her personality and neural characteristics in our Mute-class files. As soon as I understood, I gave Big Noodle the identifying brain pattern and had him send me across."

"What is that pattern?" Fairchild asked. "What's different about her?"

"Pat's talent has never been acknowledged as Psi," Curt said. "In a way, it isn't, but it's going to be one of the most useful talents we've discovered. We should have known it would arise. Wherever some organism develops, so does another to prey on it."

"Get to the point," Fairchild said. He rubbed the blue stubble on his chin. "When you called me, all you said was that — "

"Consider the various Psi talents as survival weapons," Curt said. "Consider telepathic ability as evolving for the defense of an organism. It puts the Telepath head and shoulders above his enemies. Is this going to continue? Don't these things usually balance out?"

It was the old man who understood. "I see," he said with a grin of wry admiration. "This girl is opaque to telepathic probes."

"That's right," Curt said. "The first, but there'll likely be others. And not only defenses to telepathic probes. There are going to be organisms resistant to Parakineticists, to Precogs like myself, to Resurrectors, to Animators, to every and all Psi powers. Now we have a fourth class. The Anti-Psi class. It was bound to come into existence."

III

The coffee was artificial, but hot and satisfying. Like the eggs and bacon it was synthetically compounded from tank-grown meals and proteins, with a carefully regulated mix of native-grown plant fiber. As they ate, the morning sun rose outside. The barren gray landscape of Proxima III was touched with a faint tint of red.

"It looks nice," Pat said shyly, glancing out the kitchen window. "Maybe I can examine your farming equipment. You have a lot we don't have."

"We've had more time," Curt reminded her. "This planet was settled a century before your own. You'll catch up with us. In many ways Prox VI is richer and more fertile."

Julie wasn't sitting at the table. She stood leaning against the refrigerator, arms folded, her face hard and frigid. "Is she really staying here?" she demanded in a thin, clipped voice. "In this house with us?"

"That's right," Curt answered.

"How long?"

"A few days. A week. Until I can get Fairchild moving."

Faint sounds stirred beyond the house. Here and there in the residential syndrome people were waking up and preparing for the day. The kitchen was warm and cheerful; a window of clear plastic separated it from the landscape of tumbled rocks, thin trees and plants that stretched to a few hundred miles off. Cold morning wind whipped around the rubbish that littered the deserted inter-system field at the rim of the syndrome.

"That field was the link between us and the Sol System," Curt said. "The umbilical cord. Gone now, for a while at least."

"It's beautiful," Pat stated.

"The field?"

She gestured at the towers of an elaborate mining and smelting combine partly visible beyond the rows of houses. "Those, I mean. The landscape is like ours; bleak and awful. It's all the installations that mean something.... where you've pushed the landscape back." She shivered. "We've been fighting trees and rocks all my life, trying to get the soil usable, trying to make a place to live. We don't have any heavy equipment on Prox VI, just hand tools and our own backs. You know, you've seen our villages."

Curt sipped his coffee. "Are there many Psis on Prox VI?"

"A few. Mostly minor. A few Resurrectors, a handful of Animators. No one even as good as Sally." She laughed, showing her teeth. "We're rustic hicks, compared to this urban metropolis. You saw how we live. Villages stuck here and there, farms, a few isolated supply centers, one miserable field. You saw my family, my brothers and my father, our home life, if you can call that log shack a home. Three centuries behind Terra."

"They taught you about Terra?"

"Oh, yes. Tapes came direct from the Sol System until the Separation. Not that I'm sorry we separated. We should have been out working anyhow, instead of watching the tapes. But it was interesting to see the mother world, the big cities, all the billions of people. And the earlier colonies on Venus and Mars. It was amazing." Her voice throbbed with excitement. "Those colonies were like ours, once. They had to clear Mars the same way we're clearing Prox VI. We'll get Prox VI cleared, cities built up and fields laid out. And we'll all go on doing our part."

Julie detached herself from the refrigerator and began gathering dishes from the table without looking at Pat. "Maybe I'm being naive," she said to Curt, "but where's she going to sleep?"

"You know the answer," Curt answered patiently. "You've previewed all this. Tim's at the School so she can have his room."

"What am I supposed to do? Feed her, wait on her, be her maid? What am I supposed to tell people when they see her?" Julie's voice rose to a shrill. "Am I supposed to say she's my sister?"

Pat smiled across at Curt, toying with a button on her shirt. It was apparent that she was untouched, remote from Julie's harsh voice. Probably that was why the Corps couldn't probe her. Detached, almost aloof, she seemed unaffected by rancor and violence.

"She won't need any supervision," Curt said to his wife. "Leave her alone."

Julie lit a cigarette with rapid, jerky fingers. "I'll be glad to leave her alone. But she can't go around in those work clothes looking like a convict."

"Find her something of yours," Curt suggested.

Julie's face twisted. "She couldn't wear my things; she's too heavy." To Pat she said with deliberate cruelty, "What are you, about a size 30 waist? My God, what have you been doing, dragging a plow? Look at her neck and shoulders ... she looks like a fieldhorse."

Curt got abruptly to his feet and pushed his chair back from the table. "Come on," he said to Pat. It was vital to show her something besides this undercurrent of resentment. "I'll show you around."

Pat leaped up, her cheeks flushed. "I want to see everything. This is all so new." She hurried after him as he grabbed his coat and headed for the front door. "Can we see the School where you train the Psis? I want to see how you develop their abilities. And can we see how the Colonial Government is organized? I want to see how Fairchild works with the Psis."

Julie followed the two of them out onto the front porch. Cool, chill morning air billowed around them, mixed with the sounds of cars heading from the residential syndrome toward the city. "In my room you'll find skirts and blouses," she said to Pat. "Pick out something light. It's warmer here than on Prox VI."

"Thank you," Pat said. She hurried back into the house.

"She's pretty," Julie said to Curt. "When I get her washed and dressed, I guess she'll look all right. She's got a figure — in a healthy sort of way. But is there anything to her mind? To her personality?"

"Sure," Curt answered.

Julie shrugged. "Well, she's young. A lot younger than I am." She smiled wanly. "Remember when we first met? Ten years ago ... I was so curious to see you, talk to you. The only other Precog besides myself. I had so many dreams and hopes about both of us. I was her age, perhaps a little younger."

"It was hard to see how it would work out," Curt said. "Even for us. A half-hour preview isn't much, in a thing like this."

"How long has it been?" Julie asked.

"Not long."

"Have there been other girls?"

"No. Only Pat."

"When I realized there was somebody else, I hoped she was good enough for you. If I could be sure this girl had something to offer. I suppose it's her remoteness that gives an impression of emptiness. And you have more rapport with her than I do. Probably you don't feel the lack, if it is a lack. And it may be tied in with her talent, her opaqueness."

Curt fastened the cuffs of his coat. "I think it's a kind of innocence. She's not touched by a lot of things we have here in our urban, industrial society. When you were talking about her it didn't seem to reach her."

Julie touched his arm lightly. "Then take care of her. She's going to need it around here. I wonder what Reynolds' reaction is going to be."

"Do you see anything?"

"Nothing about her. You're going off . . . I'm by myself for the next interval, as far as I can preview, working around the house. As for now, I'm going into town to do some shopping, to pick up some new clothes. Maybe I can get something for her to wear."

"We'll get her things," Curt said. "She should get her clothes first-hand."

Pat appeared in a cream-colored blouse and ankle-length yellow skirt, black eyes sparkling, hair moist with morning mist. "I'm ready! Can we go now?"

Sunlight glittered down on them as they stepped eagerly onto the level ground. "We'll go over to the School first and pick up my son."

The three of them walked slowly along the gravel path that led by the white concrete School Building, by the faint sheen of wet lawn that was carefully maintained against the hostile weather of the planet. Tim scampered on ahead of Pat and Curt, listening and peering intently past the objects around him, body tensed forward, lithe and alert.

"He doesn't speak much," Pat observed.

"He's too busy to pay any attention to us."

Tim halted to gaze behind a shrub. Pat followed a little after him, curious. "What's he looking for? He's a beautiful child . . . he has Julie's hair. She has nice hair."

"Look over there," Curt said to his son. "There are plenty of children to sort over. Go play with them."

At the entrance to the main School Building, parents and their children swarmed in restless, anxious groups. Uniformed School Officials moved among them, sorting, checking, dividing the children into various sub-groups. Now and then a small sub-group was admitted through the check-system into the School Building. Apprehensive, pathetically hopeful, the mothers waited outside.

Pat said, "It's like that on Prox VI, when the School Teams come to make their census and inspection. Everybody wants to get the unclassified children put up into the Psi-class. My father tried for years to get me out of Mute. He finally gave up. That report you saw was one of his periodic requests. It was filed away somewhere, wasn't it? Gathering dust in a drawer."

"If this works out," Curt said, "many more children will have a chance to get out of the Mute-class. You won't be the only one. You're the first of many, we hope."

Pat kicked at a pebble. "I don't feel so new, so astonishingly different. I don't feel anything at all. You say I'm opaque to telepathic invasion, but I've only been scanned one or two times in my life." She touched her head with her copper-colored fingers and smiled. "If no Corpsman is scanning me, I'm just like anybody else."

"You ability is a counter-talent," Curt pointed out. "It takes the original talent to call it into being. Naturally, you're not conscious of it during your ordinary routine of living."

"A counter-talent. It seems so — so negative. I don't do anything, like you do ... I don't move objects or turn stones into bread or give birth without impregnation or bring dead people back to life. I just negate somebody else's ability. It seems like a hostile, stultifying sort of ability — to cancel out the telepathic factor."

"That could be as useful as the telepathic factor itself. Especially for all of us non-teeps."

"Suppose somebody comes along who balances your ability, Curt." She had turned dead serious, sounding discouraged and unhappy. "People will arise who balance out *all* Psi talents. We'll be back where we started from. It'll be like not having Psi at all."

"I don't think so," Curt answered. "The Anti-Psi factor is a natural restoration of balance. One insect learns to fly, so another learns to build a web to trap him. Is that the same as no flight? Clams developed hard shells to protect them; therefore birds learn to fly the clam up high in the air and drop him on a rock. In a sense you're a life-form preying on the Psis and the Psis are life-forms that prey on the Norms. That makes you a friend of the Norm-class. Balance, the full circle, predator and prey. It's an eternal system and frankly I can't see how it could be improved."

"You might be considered a traitor."

"Yes," Curt agreed. "I suppose so."

"Doesn't it bother you?"

"It bothers me that people will feel hostile toward me. But you can't live very long without arousing hostility. Julie feels hostility toward you. Reynolds feels hostility for me already. You can't please everybody, because people want different things. Please one and you displease another. In this life you have to decide which of them you want to please. I'd prefer to please Fairchild."

"He should be glad."

"If he's aware of what's going on. Fairchild's an overworked bureaucrat. He may decide I exceeded my authority in acting on your father's petition. He may want it filed back where it was, and you returned to Prox VI. He may even fine me a penalty."

They left the School and drove down the long highway to the shore of the ocean. Tim shouted with happiness at the vast stretch of deserted beach as he raced off, arms waving, his yells lost in the ceaseless lapping of the ocean waves. The red-tinted sky warmed above them. The three of them were completely isolated by the bowl of ocean and sky and beach. No other humans were visible, only a flock of indigenous birds strolling around in search of sand crustaceans.

"It's wonderful," Pat said, awed. "I guess the oceans of Terra are like this, big and bright and red."

"Blue," Curt corrected. He lay sprawled out on the warm sand, smoking his pipe and gazing moodily at the probing waves that oozed up on the beach a few yards away. The waves left heaps of steaming seaplants stranded.

Tim came hurrying back with his arms full of the dripping, slimy weeds. He dumped the coils of still quivering vegetable life in front of Pat and his father.

"He likes the ocean," Pat said.

"No hiding places for Others," Curt answered. "He can see for miles, so he knows they can't creep up on him."

"Others?" She was curious. "He's such a strange boy. So worried and busy. He takes his alternate world so seriously. Not a pleasant world, I guess. Too many responsibilities."

The sky turned hot. Tim began building an intricate structure out of wet sand lugged from the water's edge.

Pat scampered barefooted to join Tim. The two of them labored, adding infinite walls and side-buildings and towers. In the hot glare of the water, the girl's bare shoulders and back dripped perspiration. She sat up finally, gasping and exhausted, pushed her hair from her eyes and struggled to her feet.

"It's too hot," she gasped, throwing herself down beside Curt. "The weather's so different here. I'm sleepy."

Tim continued building the structure. The two of them watched him languidly, crumbling bits of dry sand between their fingers.

"I guess," Pat said after a while, "there isn't much left to your marriage. I've made it impossible for you and Julie to live together."

"It's not your fault. We were never really together. All we had in common was our talent and that has nothing to do with over-all personality. The total individual."

Pat slid off her skirt and waded down to the ocean's edge. She curled up in the swirling pink foam and began washing her hair. Half-buried in the piles of foam and seakelp, her sleek, tanned body glowed wet and healthy in the overhead sun.

"Come on!" she called to Curt. "It's so cool."

Curt knocked the ashes from his pipe into the dry sand. "We have to get back. Sooner or later I've got to have it out with Fairchild. We need a decision."

Pat strode from the water, body streaming, head tossed back, hair dripping down her shoulders. Tim attracted her attention and she halted to study his sand building.

"You're right," she said to Curt. "We shouldn't be here wading and dozing and building sand castles. Fairchild's trying to keep the Separation working, and we have real things to build up in the backward Colonies."

As she dried herself with Curt's coat she told him about Proxima VI.

"It's like the Middle Ages back on Terra. Most of our people think Psi powers are miracles. They think the Psis are saints."

"I suppose that's what the saints were," Curt agreed. "They raised the dead, turned inorganic material into organic and moved objects around. The Psi ability has probably always been present in the human race. The Psi-class individual isn't new; he's always been with us, helping here and there, sometimes doing harm when he exploited his talent against mankind."

Pat tugged on her sandals. "There's an old woman near our village, a first-rate Resurrector. She won't leave Prox VI; she won't go with the Government Teams or get mixed up with the School. She wants to stay where she is, being a witch and wise woman. People come to her and she heals the sick."

Pat fastened her blouse and started toward the car. "When I was seven I broke my arm. She put her old withered hands on it and the break repaired itself. Apparently her hands radiate some kind of generative field that affects the growth-rate of the cells. And I remember one time when a boy was drowned and she brought him back to life."

"Get an old woman who can heal, another who can precog the future, and your village is set up. We Psis have been helping longer than we realize."

"Come on, Tim!" Pat called, tanned hands to her lips. "Time to go back!"

The boy bent down one last time to peer into the depths of his structure, the elaborate inner sections and his sand building.

Suddenly he screamed, leaped back and came racing frantically toward the car.

Pat caught hold of him and he clung to her, face distorted with terror. "What is it?" Pat was frightened. "Curt, *what was it?*"

Curt came over and squatted down beside the boy. "What was in there?" he asked gently. "You built it."

The boy's lips moved. "A *Left*," he muttered almost inaudibly. "There was a Left, I know it. The first real Left. And it hung on."

Pat and Curt glanced at each other uneasily. "What's he talking about?" Pat asked.

Curt got behind the wheel of the car and pushed open the doors for the two of them. "I don't know. But I think we'd better get back to town. I'll talk to Fairchild and get this business of Anti-Psi cleared up. Once that's out of the way, you and I can devote ourselves to Tim for the rest of our lives."

Fairchild was pale and tired as he sat behind his desk in his office, hands folded in front of him, a few Norm-class advisors here and there, listening intently. Dark circles mooned under his eyes. As he listened to Curt he sipped at a glass of tomato juice.

"In other words," Fairchild muttered, "you're saying we can't really trust you Psis. It's a paradox." His voice broke with despair. "A Psi comes here and says *all Psis lie*. What the hell am I supposed to do?"

"Not all Psis." Being able to preview the scene gave Curt remarkable calmness. "I'm saying that in a way Terra is right... the existence of super-talented humans poses a problem for those without super-talents. But Terra's answer is wrong; sterilization is vicious and senseless. But cooperation isn't as easy as you imagine. You're dependent on our talents for survival and that means we have you where we want you. We can dictate to you because, without us, Terra would come in and clap you all into military prison."

"And destroy you Psis," the old man standDon't forget that."

Curt eyed the old man. It was the same wide-shouldered, gray-faced individual of the night before. There was something familiar about him. Curt peered closer and gasped, in spite of his preview.

"You're a Psi," he said.

The old man bowed slightly. "Evidently."

"Come on," Fairchild said. "All right, we've seen this girl and we'll accept your theory of Anti-Psi. *What do you want us to do?*" He wiped his forehead miserably. "I know Reynolds is a menace. But damn it, Terran infiltrators would be running all around here without the Corps!"

"I want you to create a legal fourth class," Curt stated. "The Anti-Psi class. I want you to give it status-immunity from sterilization. I want you to publicize it. Women come in here with their children from all parts of the Colonies, trying to convince you they've got Psis to offer, not Mutes. I want you to set up the Anti-Psi talents out where we can utilize them."

Fairchild licked his dry lips. "You think more exist already?"

"Very possibly. I came on Pat by accident. But get the flow started! Get the mothers hovering anxiously over their cribs for Anti-Psis.... We'll need all we can get."

There was silence.

"Consider what Mr. Purcell is doing," the old man said at last. "An Anti-Precog may arise, a person whose actions in the future can't be previewed. A sort of Heisenberg's indeterminate particle ... a man who throws off all pre-cog prediction. And yet Mr. Purcell has come here to make his suggestions. He's thinking of Separation, not himself."

Fairchild's fingers twitched. "Reynolds is going to be mad as hell."

"He's already mad," Curt said. "He undoubtedly knows about this right now."

"He'll protest!"

Curt laughed, some of the officials smiled. "Of course he'll protest. Don't you understand? *You're being eliminated.* You think Norms are going to be around much longer? Charity is damn scarce in this universe. You Norms gape at Psis like rustics at a carnival. Wonderful ... magical. You encouraged Psis, built the School, gave us our chance here in the Colonies. In fifty years you'll be slave laborers for us. You'll be doing our manual labor — unless you have sense enough to create the fourth class, the Anti-Psi class. You've got to stand up to Reynolds."

"I hate to alienate him," Fairchild muttered. "Why the hell can't we all work together?" He appealed to the others around the room. "Why can't we all be brothers?"

"Because," Curt answered, "we're not. Face facts. Brotherhood is a fine idea, but it'll come into existence sooner if we achieve a balance of social forces."

"Is it possible," the old man suggested, "that once the concept of Anti-Psi reaches Terra the sterilization program will be modified? This idea may erase the irrational terror the non-mutants have, their phobia that we're monsters about to invade and take over their world. Sit next to them in theaters. Marry their sisters."

"All right," Fairchild agreed. "I'll construct an official directive. Give me an hour to word it — I want to get all the loopholes out."

Curt got to his feet. It was over. As he had previewed, Fairchild had agreed. "We should start getting reports almost at once," he said. "As soon as routine checking of the files begins."

Fairchild nodded. "Yes, almost at once."

"I assume you'll keep me informed." Apprehension moved through Curt. He had succeeded.... or had he? He scanned the next half hour. There was nothing negative he could preview. He caught a quick scene of himself and Pat, himself and Julie and Tim. But still his uneasiness remained, an intuition deeper than his precog.

Everything looked fine, but he knew better. Something basic and chilling had gone wrong.

IV

He met Pat in a small out-of-the-way bar at the rim of the city. Darkness flickered around their table. The air was thick and pungent with the presence of people. Bursts of muted laughter broke out, muffled by the steady blur of conversation.

"How'd it go?" she asked, eyes large and dark, as he seated himself across from her. "Did Fairchild agree?"

Curt ordered a Tom Collins for her and bourbon and water for himself. Then he outlined what had taken place.

"So everything's all right." Pat reached across the table to touch his hand. "Isn't it?"

Curt sipped at his drink. "I guess so. The Anti-Psi class is being formed. But it was too easy. Too simple."

"You can see ahead, can't you? Is anything going to happen?"

Across the dark room the music machine was creating vague patterns of sound, random harmonics and rhythms in a procession of soft clusters that drifted through the room. A few couples moved languidly together in response to the shifting patterns.

Curt offered her a cigarette and the two of them lit up from the candle in the center of the table. "Now you have your status."

Pat's dark eyes flickered. "Yes, that's so. The new Anti-Psi class. I don't have to worry now. That's all over."

"We're waiting for others. If no others show, you're a member of a unique class. The only Anti-Psi in the Universe."

For a moment Pat was silent. Then she asked, "What do you see after that?" She sipped her drink. "I mean, I'm going to stay here, aren't I? Or will I be going back?"

"You'll stay here."

"With you?"

"With me. And with Tim."

"What about Julie?"

"The two of us signed mutual releases a year ago. They're on file, somewhere. Never processed. It was an agreement we made, so neither of us could block the other later on."

"I think Tim likes me. He won't mind, will he?"

"Not at all," Curt said.

"It ought to be nice, don't you think? The three of us. We can work with Tim, try to find out about his talent, what he is and what he's thinking. I'd enjoy that... he responds to me. And we have a long time; there's no hurry."

Her fingers clasped around his. In the shifting darkness of the bar her features swam close to his own. Curt leaned forward, hesitated a moment as her warm breath stained his lips and then kissed her.

Pat smiled up at him. "There're so many things for us to do. Here, and perhaps later on Prox VI. I want to go back there, sometime. Could we? Just for a while; we wouldn't have to stay. So I can see that it's still going on, all the things I worked at all my life. So I could see my world."

"Sure," Curt said. "Yes, we'll go back there."

Across from them a nervous little man had finished his garlic bread and wine. He wiped his mouth, glanced at his wristwatch and got to his feet. As he squeezed past Curt he reached into his pocket, jangled change and jerkily brought out his hand. Gripping a slender tube, he turned around, bent over Pat, and depressed the tube.

A single pellet dribbled from the tube, clung for a split second to the shiny surface of her hair, and then was gone. A dull echo of vibration rolled up toward the nearby tables. The nervous little man continued on.

Curt was on his feet, numb with shock. He was still gazing down, paralyzed, when Reynolds appeared beside him and firmly pulled him away.

"She's dead," Reynolds was saying. "Try to understand. She died instantly; there was no pain. It goes directly to the central nervous system. She wasn't even aware of it."

Nobody in the bar had stirred. They sat at their tables, faces impassive, watching as Reynolds signaled for more light. The darkness faded and the objects of the room leaped into clarity.

"Stop that machine," Reynolds ordered sharply. The music machine stumbled into silence. "These people here are Corpsmen," he explained to Curt. "We probed your thoughts about this place as you entered Fairchild's office."

"But I didn't catch it," Curt muttered. "There was no warning. No preview."

"The man who killed her is an Anti-Psi," Reynolds said. "We've known of the category for a number of years; remember, it took an initial probe to uncover Patricia Connley's shield."

"Yes," Curt agreed. "She was probed years ago. By one of you."

"We don't like the Anti-Psi idea. We wanted to keep the class out of existence, but we were interested. We've uncovered and neutralized fourteen Anti-Psis over the past decade. On this, we have virtually the whole Psi-class behind us — except you. The problem, of course, is that no Anti-Psi talent can be brought out unless matched against the Psionic talent it negates."

Curt understood. "You had to match this man against a Precog. And there's only one Precog other than myself."

"Julie was cooperative. We brought the problem to her a few months ago. We had definite proof to give her concerning your affair with this girl. I don't understand how you expected to keep Telepaths from knowing your plans, but apparently you did. In any case, the girl is dead. And there won't be any Anti-Psi class. We waited as long as possible, for we don't like to destroy talented individuals. But Fairchild was on the verge of signing the enabling legislation, so we couldn't hold off any longer."

Curt hit out frantically, knowing even as he did so that it was futile. Reynolds slid back; his foot tangled with the table and he staggered. Curt leaped on him, smashed the tall cold glass that had held Pat's drink and lifted the jagged edges over Reynolds' face.

Corpsmen pulled him off.

Curt broke away. He reached down and gathered up Pat's body. She was still warm; her face was calm, expressionless, an empty burned-out shell that mirrored nothing. He carried her from the bar and out into the frigid night-dark street. A moment later he lowered her into his car and crept behind the wheel.

He drove to the School, parked the car, and carried her into the main building. Pushing past astonished officials, he reached the children's quarters and forced open the door to Sally's rooms with his shoulder.

She was wide-awake and fully dressed. Seated on a straight-back chair the child faced him defiantly. "You see?" she shrilled. "See what you did?"

He was too dazed to answer.

"It's all your fault! You made Reynolds do it. He *had* to kill her." She leaped to her feet and ran toward him screaming hysterically. "You're an enemy! You're against us! You want to make trouble for all of us. I told Reynolds what you were doing and he — "

Her voice trailed off as he moved out of the room with his heavy armload. As he lumbered up the corridor the hysterical girl followed him.

"You want to go across — you want me to get Big Noodle to take you across!" She ran in front of him, darting here and there like a maniacal insect. Tears ran down her cheeks; her face was distorted beyond recognition. She followed him all the way to Big Noodle's chamber. "I'm not going to help you! You're against all of us and I'm never going to help you again! I'm *glad* she's dead. I wish you were dead, too. And you're going to be dead when Reynolds catches you. He told me so. He said there wasn't going to be any more like you and we would have things the way they ought to be, and nobody, not you nor any of those *numbskulls* can stop us!"

He lowered Pat's body onto the floor and moved out of the chamber. Sally raced after him.

"You know what he did to Fairchild? He had him fixed so he can't do anything ever again."

Curt tripped a locked door and entered his son's room. The door closed after him and the girl's frenzied screams died to a muffled vibration. Tim sat up in bed, surprised and half-stupefied by sleep.

"Come on," Curt said. He dragged the boy from his bed, dressed him, and hurried him outside into the hall.

Sally stopped them as they re-entered Big Noodle's chamber. "He won't do it," she screamed. "He's afraid of me and I told him not to. You understand?"

Big Noodle lay slumped in his massive chair. He lifted his great hand as Curt approached him. "What do you want?" he muttered. "What's the matter with her?" He indicated Pat's inert body. "She pass out or something?"

"Reynolds killed her!" Sally shrilled, dancing around Curt and his son. "And he's going to kill Mr. Purcell! He's going to kill everybody that tries to stop us!"

Big Noodle's thick features darkened. The wattles of bristly flesh turned a flushed, mottled crimson. "What's going on, Curt?" he muttered.

"The Corps is taking over," Curt answered.

"They killed your girl?"

"Yes."

Big Noodle strained to a sitting position and leaned forward. "Reynolds is after you?"

"Yes."

Big Noodle licked his thick lips hesitantly. "Where do you want to go?" he asked hoarsely. "I can move you out of here, to Terra, maybe. Or — "

Sally made frantic motions with her hands. Part of Big Noodle's chair writhed and became animate. The arms twisted around him, cut viciously into his puddinglike paunch. He retched and closed his eyes.

"I'll make you sorry!" Sally chanted. "I can do terrible things to you!"

"I don't want to go to Terra," Curt said. He gathered up Pat's body and motioned Tim over beside him. "I want to go to Proxima VI."

Big Noodle struggled to make up his mind. Outside the room officials and Corpsmen were in cautious motion. A bedlam of sound and uncertainty rang up and down the corridors.

Sally's shrill voice rose over the rumble of sound as she tried to attract Big Noodle's attention. "You know what I'll do! You know what will happen to you!"

Big Noodle made his decision. He tried an abortive stab at Sally before turning to Curt; a ton of molten plastic transported from some Terran factory cascaded down on her in a hissing torrent. Sally's body dissolved, one arm raised and twitching, the echo of her voice still hanging in the air.

Big Noodle had acted, but the warp directed at him from the dying girl was already in existence. As Curt felt the air of space-transformation all around him, he caught a final glimpse of Big Noodle's torment. He had never known precisely what it was Sally dangled over the big idiot's head. Now he saw it and understood Big Noodle's hesitation. A high-pitched scream rattled from Big Noodle's throat and around Curt as the chamber ebbed away. Big Noodle altered and flowed as Sally's change engulfed him.

Curt realized, then, the amount of courage buried in the vegetable rolls of fat. Big Noodle had known the risk, taken it, and accepted — more or less — the consequences.

The vast body had become a mass of crawling spiders. What had been Big Noodle was now a mound of hairy, quivering beings, thousands of them, spiders without number, dropping off and clinging again, clustering and separating and reclustering.

And then the chamber was gone. He was across.

It was early afternoon. He lay for a time, half-buried in tangled vines. Insects hummed around him, seeking moisture from the stalks of foul-smelling flowers. The red-tinted sky baked in the mounting sunlight. Far off, an animal of some kind called mournfully.

Nearby, his son stirred. The boy got to his feet, wandered about aimlessly and finally approached his father.

Curt pulled himself up. His clothes were torn. Blood oozed down his cheek, into his mouth. He shook his head, shuddered, and looked around.

Pat's body lay a few feet off. A crumpled and broken thing, it was without life of any kind. A hollow husk, abandoned and deserted.

He made his way over to her. For a time he squatted on his haunches, gazing vacantly down at her. Then he leaned over, picked her up, and struggled to his feet.

"Come on," he said to Tim. "Let's get started."

They walked a long time. Big Noodle had dropped them between villages, in the turgid chaos of the Proxima VI forests. Once he stopped in an open field and rested. Against the line of drooping trees a waver of blue smoke drifted. A kiln, perhaps. Or somebody clearing away the brush. He lifted Pat up in his arms again and continued on.

When he crashed from the underbrush and out into the road, the villagers were paralyzed with fright. Some of them raced off, a few remained, staring blankly at the man and the boy beside him.

"Who are you?" one of them demanded as he fumbled for a hack-knife. "What have you got there?"

They got a work-truck for him, allowed him to dump Pat in with the rough-cut lumber and then drove him and his son to the nearest village. He wasn't far off, only a hundred miles. From the common store of the village he was given heavy work clothes and fed. Tim was bathed and cared for, and a general conference was called.

He sat at a huge, rough table, littered with remains of the midday meal. He knew their decision; he could preview it without trouble.

"She can't fix up anybody that far gone," the leader of the village explained to him. "The girl's whole upper ganglia and brain are gone, and most of the spinal column."

He listened, but didn't speak. Afterwards, he wangled a battered truck, loaded Pat and Tim in, and started on.

Her village had been notified by short-wave radio. He was pulled from the truck by savage hands; a pandemonium of noise and fury boiled around him, excited faces distorted by grief and horror. Shouts, outraged shoves, questions, a blur of men and women milling and pushing until finally her brothers cleared a path for him to their home.

"It's useless," her father was saying to him. "And the old woman's gone, I think. That was years ago." The man gestured toward the mountains. "She lived up there — used to come down. Not for years." He grabbed Curt roughly. "It's too late, God damn it! She's dead! You can't bring her back!"

He listened to the words, still said nothing. He had no interest in predictions of any kind. When they had finished talking to him, he gathered up Pat's body, carried it back to the truck, called his son and continued on.

It grew cold and silent as the truck wheezily climbed the road into the mountains. Frigid air plucked at him; the road was obscured by dense clouds of mist that billowed up from the chalky soil. At one point a lumbering animal barred his way until he drove it off by throwing rocks at it. Finally the truck ran out of fuel and stopped. He got out, stood for a time, then woke up his son and continued on foot.

It was almost dark when he found the hut perched on a lip of rock. A fetid stench of offal and drying hides stung his nose as he staggered past heaps of discarded rubble, tin cans and boxes, rotting fabric and vermin-infested lumber.

The old woman was watering a patch of wretched vegetables. As he approached, she lowered her sprinkling can and turned toward him, wrinkled face tight with suspicion and wonder.

"I can't do it," she said flatly as she crouched over Pat's inert body. She ran her dry, leathery hands over the dead face, pulled aside the girl's shirt and kneaded the cold flesh at the base of the neck. She pushed aside the tangle of black hair and gripped the skull with her strong fingers. "No, I can't do a thing." Her voice was rusty and harsh in the night fog that billowed around them. "She's burned out. No tissue left to repair."

Curt made his cracked lips move. "Is there another?" he grated. "Any more Resurrectors here?"

The old woman struggled to her feet. "Nobody can help you, don't you understand? She's dead!"

He remained. He asked the woman again and again. Finally there was a begrudging answer. Somewhere on the other side of the planet there was supposed to be a competitor. He gave the old woman his cigarettes and lighter and fountain pen, picked up the cold body and started back. Tim trailed after him, head drooping, body bent with fatigue.

"Come on," Curt ordered harshly. The old woman watched silently as they threaded their way down by the light of Proxima VI's two sullen, yellowed moons.

He got only a quarter mile. In some way, without warning, her body was gone. He had lost her, dropped her along the way. Somewhere among the rubbish-littered rocks and weeds that fingered their way over the trail. Probably into one of the deep gorges that cut into the jagged side of the mountain.

He sat down on the ground and rested. There was nothing left. Fairchild had dwindled into the hands of the Corps. Big Noodle was destroyed by Sally. Sally was gone, too. The colonies were open to the Terrans; their wall against projectiles had dissolved when Big Noodle died. And Pat.

There was a sound behind him. Panting with despair and fatigue, he turned only slightly. For a brief second he thought it was Tim catching up with him. He strained to see; the shape that emerged from the half-light was too tall, too sure-footed. A familiar shape.

"You're right," the old man said, the ancient Psi who had stood beside Fairchild. He came up, vast and awesome in the aged yellow moonlight. "There's no use trying to bring her back. It could be done, but it's too difficult. And there are other things for you and me to think about."

Curt scrambled off. Falling, sliding, slashed by the stones under him, he made his way blindly down the trail. Dirt rattled after him while, choking, he struggled onto the level ground.

When he halted again, it was Tim who came after him. For an instant he thought it had been an illusion, a figment of his imagination. The old man was gone; he hadn't been there.

He didn't fully understand until he saw the change take place in front of him. And this time it went the other way. He realized that this one was a *Left*. And it was a familiar figure, but in a different way. A figure he remembered from the past.

Where the boy of eight had stood, a wailing, fretful baby of sixteen months struggled and groped. Now the substitution had gone in the other direction . . . and he couldn't deny what his eyes saw.

"All right," he said, when the eight-year-old Tim reappeared and the baby was gone. But the boy remained only a moment. He vanished almost at once, and this time a new shape stood on the trail. A man in his middle thirties, a man Curt had never seen before.

A familiar man.

"You're my son," Curt said.

"That's right." The man appraised him in the dim light. "You realize that she can't be brought back, don't you? We have to get that out of the way before we can proceed."

Curt nodded wearily. "I know."

"Fine." Tim advanced toward him, hand out. "Then let's get back down. We have a lot to do. We middle and extreme Rights have been trying to get through for some time. It's been difficult to come back without the approval of the Center one. And in these cases the Center is too young to understand."

"So that's what he meant," Curt murmured as the two of them made their way along the road, toward the village. "The Others are himself, along his time-track."

"Left is previous Others," Tim answered. "Right, of course, is the future. You said that Precog and Precog made nothing. Now you know. They make the ultimate Precog — the ability to move through time."

"You Others were trying to get over. He'd see you and be frightened."

"It was very hard, but we knew eventually he'd grow old enough to comprehend. He built up an elaborate mythology. That is, we did. I did." Tim laughed. "You see, there still isn't an adequate terminology. There never is for a unique happening."

"I could change the future," Curt said, "because I could see into it. But I couldn't change the present. You can change the present by going back into the past. That's why that extreme Right Other, the old man, hung around Fairchild."

"That was our first successful crossing. We were finally able to induce the Center to take his two steps Right. That switched the two, but it took time."

"What's going to happen now?" Curt asked. "The war? The Separation? All this about Reynolds?"

"As you realized before, we can alter it by going back. It's dangerous. A simple change in the past may completely alter the present. The time-traveling talent is the most critical — and the most Promethean. Every other talent, without exception, can change only what's going to happen. I could wipe out everything that stands. I precede everyone and everything. Nothing can be used against me. I am always there first. I have always been there."

Curt was silent as they passed the abandoned, rusting truck. Finally he asked. "What is Anti-Psi? What did you have to do with that?"

"Not much," his son said. "You can take credit for bringing it out into the open, since we didn't begin operating until the last few hours. We came along in time to aid it — you saw us with Fairchild. We're *sponsoring* Anti-Psi. You'd be surprised to see some of the alternate time-paths on which Anti-Psi fails to get pushed forward. Your precog was right — they're not very pleasant."

"So I've had help lately."

"We're behind you, yes. And from now on, our help will increase. Always, we try to introduce balances. Stalemates, such as Anti-Psi. Right now, Reynolds is a little out of balance, but he can easily be checked. Steps are being taken. We're not infinite in power, of course. We're limited by our life-span, about seventy years. It's a strange feeling to be outside of time. You're outside of change, subject to no laws.

"It's like suddenly being lifted off the chess board and seeing everybody as pieces — seeing the whole Universe as a game of black and white squares — with everybody and every object stuck on his space-time spot. We're off the board; we can reach down from above. Adjust, alter the position of the men, change the game without the pieces knowing. From outside."

"And you won't bring her back?" Curt appealed.

"You can't expect me to be too sympathetic toward the girl," his son said. "After all, Julie is my mother. I know now what they used to mean by *mill of the gods*. I wish we could grind less small ... I wish we could spare some of those who get caught in the gears. But if you could see it as we do, you'd understand. We have a universe hanging in the balance; it's an awfully big board."

"A board so big that one person doesn't count?" Curt asked, agonized.

His son looked concerned. Curt remembered looking like that himself when trying to explain something to the boy that was beyond the child's comprehension. He hoped Tim would do a better job than he'd been able to do.

"Not that," Tim said. "To us, she isn't gone. She's still there, on another part of the board that you can't see. She always was there. She always will be. No piece ever falls off the board ... no matter how small."

"For you," said Curt.

"Yes. We're outside the board. It may be that our talent will be shared by everybody. When that happens, there will be no misunderstanding of tragedy and death."

"And meanwhile?" Curt ached with the tension of *willing* Tim to agree. "I don't have the talent. To me, she's dead. The place she occupied on the board is empty. Julie can't fill it. Nobody can."

Tim considered. It looked like deep thought, but Curt could sense that his son was moving restlessly along the timepaths, seeking a rebuttal. His eyes focused again on his father and he nodded sadly.

"I can't show you where she is on the board," he said. "And your life is vacant along every path except one."

Curt heard someone coming through the brush. He turned — and then Pat was in his arms.

"This one," Tim said.

Psi-Man Heal My Child!

He was a lean man, middle-aged, with grease-stained hair and skin, a crumpled cigarette between his teeth, his left hand clamped around the wheel of his car. The car, an ex-commercial surface truck, rumbled noisily but smoothly as it ascended the outgoing ramp and approached the check-gate that terminated the commune area.

"Slow down," his wife said. "There's the guard sitting on that pile of crates."

Ed Garby rode the brake; the car settled grimly into a long glide that ended directly in front of the guard. In the back seat of the car the twins fretted restlessly, already bothered by the gummy heat oozing through the top and windows of the car. Down his wife's smooth neck great drops of perspiration slid. In her arms the baby twisted and struggled feebly.

"How's she?" Ed muttered to his wife, indicating the wad of gray, sickly flesh that poked from the soiled blanket. "Hot — like me."

The guard came strolling over indifferently, sleeves rolled up, rifle slung over his shoulder. "What say, mac?" Resting his big hands in the open window, he gazed dully into the interior of the car, observing the man and wife, the children, the dilapidated upholstery. "Going outside awhile? Let's see your pass."

Ed got out the crumpled pass and handed it over. "I got a sick child."

The guard examined the pass and returned it. "Better take her down to the sixth level. You got a right to use the infirmary; you live in this dump like the rest of us."

"No," Ed said. "I'm taking no child of mine down to that butchery."

The guard shook his head in disagreement. "They got good equipment, mac. High-powered stuff left over from the war. Take her down there and they'll fix her up." He waved toward the desolate expanse of dry trees and hills that lay beyond the check-gate. "What do you think you'll find out there? You going to dump her somewhere? Toss her in a creek? Down a well? It's none of my business, but I wouldn't take a dog out there, let alone a sick child."

Ed started up the motor. "I'm getting help out there. Take a child down to sixth and they make her a laboratory animal. They experiment, cut her up, throw her away and say they couldn't save her. They got used to doing that in the war; they never stopped."

"Suit yourself," the guard said, moving away from the car. "Myself, I'd sooner trust military doctors with equipment than some crazy old quack living out in the ruins. Some savage heathen tie a bag of stinking dung around her neck, mumble nonsense and wave and dance around." He shouted furiously after the car: "Damn fools — going back to barbarism, when you got doctors and X-rays and serums down on sixth! Why the hell do you want to go out in the ruins when you've got a civilization here?"

He wandered glumly back to his crates. And added, "What there is left of it."

Arid land, as dry and parched as dead skin, lay on both sides of the rutted tracks that made up the road. A harsh rattle of noonday wind shook the gaunt trees jutting here and there from the cracked, baking soil. An occasional drab bird fluttered in the thick underbrush, heavy-set gray shapes that scratched peevishly in search of grubs.

Behind the car the white concrete walls of the commune faded and were lost in the distance. Ed Garby watched them go apprehensively; his hands convulsively jerked as a twist in the road cut off the radar towers posted on the hills overlooking the commune.

"Damn it," he muttered thickly, "maybe he was right; maybe we're making a mistake." Doubts shivered through his mind. The trip was dangerous; even heavily-armed scavenger parties were attacked by predatory animals and by the wild bands of quasi-humans living in the abandoned ruins littered across the planet. All he had to protect himself and his family was his hand-operated cutting tool. He knew how to use it, of course; didn't he grind it into a moving belt of reclaimed wreckage ten hours a day every day of the week? But if the motor of the car failed . . .

"Stop worrying," Barbara said quietly. "I've been along here before, and there's nothing ever gone wrong."

He felt shame and guilt: his wife had crept outside the commune many times, along with other women and wives; and with some of the men, too. A good part of the proletariat left the commune, with and without passes . . . anything to break the monotony of work and educational lectures. But his fear returned. It wasn't the physical menace that bothered him, or even unfamiliar separation from the vast submerged tank of steel and concrete in which he had been born and in which he had grown up, spent his life, worked and married. It was the realization that the guard had been right, that he was sinking into ignorance and superstition, that made his skin turn cold and clammy, in spite of the baking midsummer heat.

"Women always lead it," he said aloud. "Men built machines, organized science, cities. Women have their potions and brews. I guess we're seeing the end of reason. We're seeing the last remnants of rational society."

"What's a city?" one of the twins asked.

"You're seeing one now," Ed answered. He pointed beyond the road. "Take a good look."

The trees had ended. The baked surface of brown earth had faded to a dull metallic glint. An uneven plain stretched out, bleak and dismal, a pocked surface of jagged heaps and pits. Dark weeds grew here and there. An occasional wall remained standing; at one point a bathtub lay on its side like a dead, toothless mouth, deprived of face and head.

The region had been picked over countless times. Everything of value had been loaded up and trucked to the various communes in the area. Along the road were neat heaps of bones, collected but never utilized. Use had been found for cement rubble, iron scrap, wiring, plastic tubing, paper and cloth — but not for bones.

"You mean people lived *there*?" the twins protested simultaneously. Disbelief and horror showed on their faces. "It's — awful."

The road divided. Ed slowed the car down and waited for his wife to direct him. "Is it far?" he demanded hoarsely. "This place gives me the creeps. You can't tell what's hanging around in those cellars. We gassed them back in '09, but it's probably worn off by now."

"To the right," Barbara said. "Beyond that hill, there."

Ed shifted into low-low and edged the car past a ditch, onto a side road. "You really think this old woman has the power?" he asked helplessly. "I hear so damn much stuff — I never know what's true and what's hogwash. There's always supposed to be some old hag that can raise the dead and read the future and cure the sick. People've been reporting that stuff for five thousand years."

"And for five thousand years such things have been happening." His wife's voice was placid, confident. "They're always there to help us. All we have to do is go to them. I saw her heal Mary Fulsome's son; remember, he had that withered leg and couldn't walk. The medics wanted to destroy him."

"According to Mary Fulsome," Ed muttered harshly.

The car nosed its way between dead branches of ancient trees. The ruins fell behind; abruptly the road plunged into a gloomy thicket of vines and shrubs that shut out the sunlight. Ed blinked, then snapped on the dim headlights. They flickered on as the car ground its way up a rutted hill, around a narrow curve ... and then the road ceased.

They had reached their destination. Four rusty cars blocked the road;

others were parked on the shoulders and among the twisted trees. Beyond the cars stood a group of silent people, men and their families, in the drab uniforms of commune workers. Ed pulled on the brake and fumbled for the ignition key; he was astounded at the variety of communes represented. All the nearby communes, and distant ones he had never encountered. Some of the waiting people had come hundreds of miles.

"There's always people waiting," Barbara said. She kicked open the bent door and carefully slid out, the baby in her arms. "People come here for all kinds of help, whenever they're in need."

Beyond the crowd was a crude wooden building, shabby and dilapidated, a patched-together shelter of war years. A gradual line of waiting persons was being conducted up the rickety steps and into the building; for the first time Ed caught sight of those whom he had come to consult.

"Is that the old woman?" he demanded, as a thin, withered shape appeared briefly at the top of the steps, glanced over the waiting people, and selected one. She conferred with a plump man, and then a muscular giant joined the discussion. "My God," Ed said, "is there an *organization* of them?"

"Different ones do different things," Barbara answered. Clutching the baby tight, she edged her way forward into the waiting mass of people. "We want to see the healer — we'll have to stand with that group over to the right, waiting by that tree."

Porter sat in the kitchen of the shelter, smoking and drinking coffee, his feet up on the windowsill, vaguely watching the shuffling line of people moving through the front door and into the various rooms.

"A lot of them, today," he said to Jack. "What we need is a flat cover-charge."

Jack grunted angrily and shook back his mane of blond hair. "Why aren't you out helping instead of sitting here guzzling coffee?"

"Nobody wants to peep into the future." Porter belched noisily; he was plump and flabby, blue-eyed, with thin, damp hair. "When somebody wants to know if they're going to strike it rich or marry a beautiful woman I'll be there in my booth to advise them."

"Fortune-telling," Jack muttered. He stood restlessly by the window, great arms folded, face stern with worry. "That's what we're down to."

"I can't help that they ask me. One old geezer asked me when he was going to die; when I told him thirty-one days he turned red as a beet and started screaming at me. One thing, I'm honest. I tell them the truth, not what they want to hear." Porter grinned. "I'm not a quack."

"How long has it been since somebody asked you something important?"

"You mean something of abstract significance?" Porter lazily searched his mind. "Last week a fellow asked me if there'd ever be interplanetary ships again. I told him not that I could see."

"Did you also tell him you can't see worth a damn? A half year at the most?"

Porter's toad-like face bloomed contentedly. "He didn't ask me that."

The thin, withered old woman entered the kitchen briefly. "Lord," Thelma gasped, sinking down in a chair and pouring herself coffee. "I'm exhausted. And there must be fifty of them out there waiting to get healed." She examined her shaking hands. "Two bone cancers in one day about finishes me. I think the baby will survive, but the other's too far gone even for me. The baby will have to come back." Her voice trailed off wearily. "Back again next week."

"It'll be slower tomorrow," Porter predicted. "Ash storm down from Canada will keep most of them at their communes. Of course, after that — " He broke off and eyed Jack curiously. "What are you upset about? Everybody's growling around, today."

"I just came from Butterford," Jack answered moodily. "I'm going back later and try again."

Thelma shuddered. Porter looked away uneasily; he disliked hearing about conversations with a man whose bones were piled in the basement of the shelter. An almost superstitious fear drifted through the plump body of the precog. It was one thing to preview the future; seeing ahead was a positive, progressive talent. But returning to the past, to men already dead, to cities now turned to ash and rubble, places erased from the maps, participating in events long since forgotten — it was a sickly, neurotic rehashing of what had already been. Picking and stirring among the bones — literally bones — of the past.

"What did he say?" Thelma asked.

"The same as always," Jack answered.

"How many times is this?"

Jack's lips twisted. "Eleven times. And he knows it — I told him."

Thelma moved from the kitchen, out into the hall. "Back to work." She lingered at the door. "Eleven times and always the same. I've been making computations. How old are you, Jack?"

"How old do I look?"

"About thirty. You were born in 1946. This is 2017. That makes you seventy-one years old. I'd say I'm talking to an entity about a third of the way along. Where's your current entity?"

"You should be able to figure that out. Back in '76."

"Doing what?"

Jack didn't answer. He knew perfectly well what his entity of this date, 2017, was doing back in the past. The old man of seventy-one years was lying in a medical hospital at one of the military centers, receiving treatment for a gradually worsening nephritis. He shot a quick glance at Porter to see if the precog was going to volunteer information previewed him from the future.

There was no expression on Porter's languid features, but that proved nothing. He'd have to get Stephen to probe into Porter if he really wanted to be sure.

Like the common workers who filed in daily to learn if they were going to strike it rich and marry happily, he wanted vitally to know the date of his own death. He *had* to know — it went beyond mere wanting.

He faced Porter squarely. "Let's have it. What do you see about me in the next six months?"

Porter yawned. "Am I supposed to orate the whole works? It'll take hours."

Jack relaxed, weak with relief. Then he would survive another six months, at least. In that he could bring to a successful completion his discussions with General Ernest Butterford, chief of staff of the armed forces of the United States. He pushed past Thelma and out of the kitchen.

"Where are you going?" she demanded.

"Back to Butterford again. I'm going to make one more try."

"You always say that," Thelma complained peevishly.

"And I always am," Jack said. *Until I'm dead*, he thought bitterly, resentfully. Until the half conscious old man lying in the hospital bed at Baltimore, Maryland, passes away or is destroyed to make room for some wounded private carted by boxcar from the front lines, charged by Soviet napalm, crippled by nerve gas, insane from metallic ash-particles. When the ancient corpse was thrown out — and it wouldn't be long — there would be no more discussion with General Butterford.

First, he descended the stairs to the supply lockers in the basement of the shelter. Doris lay asleep on her bed in the corner, dark hair like cobwebs over her coffee-colored features, one bare arm raised, a heap of clothing strewn on the chair beside the bed. She awoke sleepily, stirred, and half sat up.

"What time is it?"

Jack glanced at his wristwatch. "One-thirty in the afternoon." He began opening one of the intricate locks that sealed in their supplies. Presently he slid a metal case down a rail and onto the cement floor. He swung an overhead light around and clicked it on.

The girl watched with interest. "What are you doing?" She tossed her covers back and got to her feet, stretched, and padded barefoot over to him. "I could have brought it out for you without all that work."

From the lead-lined case Jack removed the carefully stacked heap of bones and remnants of personal possessions: wallet, identification papers, photographs, fountain pen, bits of tattered uniform, a gold wedding ring, some silver coins. "He died under difficulties," Jack murmured. He examined the data-tape, made sure it was complete, and then slammed shut the case. "I told him I would bring this. Of course, he won't remember."

"Each time erases the last?" Doris wandered over to get her clothes. "It's really the same time again and again, isn't it?"

"The same interval," Jack admitted, "but there's no repetition of material."

Doris eyed him slyly as she struggled into her jeans. "*Some* repetition ... it always comes out the same, no matter what you do. Butterford goes ahead and presents his recommendations to the President."

Jack didn't hear her. He had already moved back, taken his series of steps along the time-path. The basement, Doris' half-dressed figure, wavered and receded, as if seen through the bottom of a glass gradually filled with opaque liquid. Darkness, mixed with shifting textures of density, wavered around him as he walked sternly forward, the metal case gripped. *Backward*, actually. He was retreating along the direction in which the flow itself moved. Changing places with an earlier John Tremaine, the pimple-faced boy of sixteen who had trudged dutifully to high school, in the year 1962 A.D. in the city of Chicago, Illinois. This was a switch he had made many times. His younger entity should be resigned, by now ... but he hoped idly that Doris would be finished dressing when the boy emerged.

The darkness that was no-time dwindled, and he blinked in a sudden torrent of yellow sunlight. Still gripping his metal case he made the final step backward and found himself in the center of a vast murmuring room. People drifted on all sides; several gaped at him, paralyzed with astonishment. For a moment he couldn't place the spatial location — and then memory came, a swift bitter flood of nostalgia.

He was back in the high school library where he had spent much time. The familiar place of books and bright-faced youths, gaily-dressed girls giggling and studying and flirting ... young people totally oblivious of the approaching war. The mass death that would leave nothing of this city but dead, drifting ash.

He hurried from the library, conscious of the circle of bewilderment he had left behind. It was awkward to make a switch in which the passive entity was near other people; the abrupt transformation of a sixteen-year-old high school boy into the stern, towering figure of a thirty-year-old man was difficult to assimilate, even in a society theoretically aware of Psionic powers.

Theoretically — because at this date public consciousness was minimal. Awe and disbelief were the primary emotions; the surge of hopefulness hadn't begun. Psi-powers seemed miraculous only; the realization that these powers were at the disposal of the public wouldn't set in for a number of years.

He emerged on the busy Chicago street and hailed a taxi. The roar of buses, autos, the metallic swirl of buildings and people and signs, dazed him. Activity on all sides: the ordinary harmless routines of the common citizen, remote from the lethal planning at top levels. The people on all sides of him were about to be traded for the chimera of international prestige ... human life for metaphysical phantoms. He gave the cabdriver the address of Butterford's hotel suite and settled back to prepare himself for the familiar encounter.

The first steps were routine. He gave his identification to the battery of armed guards, was checked, searched, and processed into the suite. For fifteen minutes he sat in a luxurious anteroom smoking and restlessly waiting — as always. There were no alterations he could make here: the changes, if they were to materialize, came later.

"Do you know who I am?" he began bluntly, when the tiny, suspicious head of General Butterford was stuck from an inner office. He advanced grimly, case gripped. "This is the twelfth visit; there had better be results, this time."

Butterford's deep-set little eyes danced hostilely behind his thick glasses. "You're one of those supermen," he squeaked. "Those Psionics." He blocked the door with his wizened, uniformed body. "Well? What do you want? My time's valuable."

Jack seated himself facing the general's desk and corps of aides. "You have the analysis of my talent and history in your hands. You know what I can do."

Butterford glanced hostilely at the report. "You move into time. So?" His eyes narrowed. "What do you mean, *twelfth* time?" He grabbed up a heap of memoranda. "I've never seen you before. State what you have to say and then get out; I'm busy."

"I have a present for you," Jack said grimly. He carried the metal case to the desk, unsnapped it, and exposed the contents. "They belong to you — go ahead, take them out and run your hands over them."

Butterford gazed with revulsion at the bones. "What is this, some sort of anti-war exhibit? Are you Psis mixed up with those Jehovah's Witnesses?" His voice rose shrilly, resentfully. "Is this something you expect to pressure me with?"

"These are your goddamn bones!" Jack shouted in the man's face. He overturned the case; the contents spilled out on the desk and floor. "*Touch them*! You're going to die in this war, like everybody else. You're going to suffer and die hideously — they're going to get you with bacterial poisons one year and six days from this date. You'll live long enough to see the total destruction of organized society and then you'll go the way of everybody else!"

It would have been easier if Butterford were a coward. He sat gazing down at the tattered remains, the coins and pictures and rusting possessions, his face white, body stiff as metal. "I don't know whether to believe you," he said finally. "I never really believed any of this Psi-stuff."

"That's totally untrue," Jack answered hotly. "There isn't a government on the planet ignorant of us. You and the Soviet Union have been trying to organize us since '58, when we made ourselves known."

The discussion was on ground that Butterford understood. His eyes blazed furiously. "That's the whole point! If you Psis cooperated there wouldn't be those bones." He jabbed wildly at the pale heap on the desk. "You come here and blame me for the war. Blame yourself—you won't put your shoulders to the wheel. How can we hope to come out of this war unless everybody does his part?" He leaned meaningfully toward Jack. "You came from the future, you say. Tell me what you Psis are going to do in the war. Tell me the part you're going to play."

"No part."

Butterford settle back triumphantly. "You're going to stand idly by?"

"Absolutely."

"And you came here to blame *me*?"

"If we help," Jack said carefully, "we help at policy level, not as hired servants. Otherwise, we will stand on the sidelines, waiting. We're available, but if winning the war depends on us, we want to say how that war will be won. Or whether there'll be a war at all." He slammed the metal case shut. "Otherwise, we might become apprehensive, as the scientists did in the middle fifties. We might begin to lose *our* enthusiasm ... and also become bad security risks."

In Jack's mind a voice spoke, thin and bitter. A telepathic member of the Guild, a Psi of the present, monitoring the discussion from the New York office. "Very well-spoken. But you've lost. You lack the ability to maneuver him ... all you've done is defend our position. You haven't even brought up the possibility of changing his."

It was true. Desperately, Jack said: "I didn't come back here to state the Guild's position—you know our position! I came here to lay the facts out in front of you. I came here from 2017. The war is over. Only a remnant survives. These are the facts, events that have taken place. You're going to recommend to the President that the United States call Russia's bluff on Java." His words came out individually, icily. "It's not a bluff. It means total war. Your recommendation is in error."

Butterford bristled. "You want us to back down? Let them take over the free world?"

Twelve times: impasse. He had accomplished nothing. "You'd go into the war knowing you can't win?"

"We'll fight," Butterford said. "Better an honorable war than a dishonorable peace."

"No war is honorable. War means death, barbarism, and mass destruction."

"What does peace mean?"

"Peace means the growth of the Guild. In fifty years our presence will shift the ideology of both blocs. We're above the war; we straddle both worlds. There're Psis here and in Russia; we're part of no country. The scientists could have been that, once. But they chose to cooperate with national governments. Now it's up to us."

Butterford shook his head. "No," he said firmly. "You're not going to influence us. *We* make policy ... if you act, you act in line with our directives. Or you don't act. You stay out."

"We'll stay out."

Butterford leaped up. "*Traitors*!" he shouted as Jack left the office. "You don't have a choice! We demand your abilities! We'll hunt you out and grab you one by one. You've got to cooperate — everybody's got to cooperate. This is total war!"

The door closed, and he was in the anteroom.

"No, there isn't any hope," the voice in his mind stated bleakly. "I can prove that you've done this twelve times. And you're contemplating a thirteenth. Give up. The withdrawal order has been given out already. When the war begins we'll be aloof."

"We ought to help!" Jack said futilely. "Not the war — we ought to help *them*, the people who're going to be killed by the millions."

"We can't. We're not gods. We're only humans with paratalents. We can help, if they accept us, allow us to help. We can't force our views on them. We can't force the Guild in, if the governments don't want us."

Gripping the metal case, Jack headed numbly down the stairs, toward the street. Back to the high school library.

At the dinner table, with black night lying outside the shelter, he faced the other surviving Guild members. "So here we are. Outside society — doing nothing. Not harming and not helping. *Useless*!" He smashed his fist convulsively against the rotting wooden wall. "Peripheral and useless, and while we sit here the communes fall apart and what's left collapses."

Thelma spooned up her soup impassively. "We heal the sick, read the future, offer advice, and perform miracles."

"We've been doing that thousands of years," Jack answered bitterly. "Sibyls, witches, perched on deserted hills outside towns. *Can't we get in and help*? Do we always have to be on the outside, we who understand what's going on? Watching the blind fools lead mankind to destruction! Couldn't we have stopped the war, forced peace on them?"

Porter said languidly, "We don't want to force anything on them, Jack. You know that. We're not their masters. We want to help them, not control them."

The meal continued in gloomy silence. Doris said presently, "The trouble is with the governments. It's the politicians who're jealous of us." She smiled mournfully across the table at Jack. "They know if we had our way, a time would come when politicians wouldn't be needed."

Thelma attacked her plate of dried beans and broiled rabbit in a thin paste of gravy. "There isn't much of a government, these days. It isn't like it was before the war. You can't really call a few majors sitting around in commune offices a *government*."

"They make the decisions," Porter pointed out. "They decide what commune policy will be."

"I know of a commune up north," Stephen said, "in which the workers killed the officers and took over. They're dying out. It won't be long before they're extinct."

Jack pushed his plate away and got to his feet. "I'm going out on the porch." He left the kitchen, crossed through the deserted living room and opened the steel-reinforced front door. Cold evening wind swirled around him as he blindly felt his way to the railing and stopped, hands in his pockets, gazing sightlessly out at the vacant field.

The rusty fleet of cars was gone. Nothing stirred except the withered trees along the road, dry rustles in the restless night wind. A dismal sight; overhead a few stars glowed fitfully. Far off somewhere an animal crashed after its prey, a wild dog or perhaps a quasi-human living down in the ruined cellars of Chicago.

After a time Doris appeared behind him. Silently, she came up and stood next to him, a slim dark shape in the night gloom, her arms folded against the cold. "You're not going to try again?" she asked softly.

"Twelve is enough. I — can't change him. I don't have the ability. I'm not adroit enough." Jack spread his massive hands miserably. "He's a clever little chicken of a thing. Like Thelma — scrawny and full of talk. Again and again I get back there — and what can I do?"

Doris touched his arm wistfully. "How does it look? I never saw cities full of life, before the war. Remember, I was born in a military camp."

"You'd like it. People laughing and hurrying. Cars, signs, life everywhere. It drives me crazy. I wish I couldn't see it — to be able to step from here to there." He indicated the twisted trees. "Ten steps back from those trees, and there it is. And yet it's gone forever ... even for me. There'll be a time when I can't step there either, like the rest of you."

Doris failed to understand him. "Isn't it strange?" she murmured. "I can move anything in the world, but I can't move myself back, the way you do." She made a slight flutter of her hands; in the darkness something slapped against the rail of the porch and she bent over to retrieve it. "See the pretty bird? Stunned, not dead." She tossed the bird up and it managed to struggle off into the shrubs. "I've got so I only stun them."

Jack wasn't pleased. "That's what we do with our talents. Tricks, games. Nothing more."

"That isn't so!" Doris objected. "Today when I got up, there was a bunch of doubters. Stephen caught their thoughts and sent me out." Pride tingled in her voice. "I brought an underground spring up to the surface — it burst out everywhere and got them all soaked, before I sent it back. They were convinced."

"Did it ever occur to you," Jack said, "that you could make it possible for them to rebuild their cities?"

"They don't want to rebuild their cities."

"They don't think they can. They've given up the idea of rebuilding. It's a lost concept." He brooded unhappily. "There's too many millions of miles of ruined ash, and too few people. They don't even try to unify the communes."

"They have radios," Doris pointed out. "They can talk to each other, if they want."

"If they use them, the war will start up again. They know there're pockets of fanatics left who'd be happy to start the war, given half the chance. They'd rather sink into barbarism than get that started." He spat into the weedy bushes growing beneath the porch. "I don't blame them."

"If we controlled the communes," Doris said thoughtfully, "we wouldn't start up the war. We'd unify them on a peaceful basis."

"You're playing all sides at once," Jack said angrily. "A minute ago you were performing miracles — where'd this thought come from?"

Doris hesitated. "Well, I was just passing it on. I guess Stephen really said it, or thought it. I just spoke it out loud."

"You enjoy being a mouthpiece for Stephen?"

Doris fluttered fearfully. "My God, Jack — he can probe you. Don't say things like that!"

Jack stepped away from her and down the porch steps. He rapidly crossed the dark, silent field, away from the shelter. The girl hurried after him.

"Don't walk off," she gasped breathlessly. "Stephen's just a kid. He's not like you, grown-up and big. Mature."

Jack laughed upward at the black sky. "You damn fool. Do you know how old I am?"

"No," Doris said, "and don't say. I know you're older than I am. You've always been around; I remember you when I was just a kid. You were always big and strong and blond." She giggled nervously. "Of course, all those *others* ... those different persons, old and young. I don't really understand, but they're all you, I guess. Different yous along your time-path."

"That's right," Jack said tightly. "They're all me."

"That one today, when you switched down in the basement, when I was sleeping." Doris caught his arm and tucked her cold fingers around his wrist. "Just a kid, with books under his arm, in a green sweater and brown slacks."

"Sixteen years old," Jack muttered.

"He was cute. Shy, flustered. Younger than I am. We went upstairs and he watched the crowd; that was when Stephen called me to do the miracle. He — I mean, *you* — stood around so interested. Porter kidded him. Porter doesn't mean any harm — he likes to eat and sleep and that's about all. He's all right. Stephen kidded him, too. I don't think Stephen liked him."

"You mean he doesn't like me."

"I — guess you know how we feel. All of us, to some degree ... we wonder why you keep going back again and again, trying to patch up the past. The past is over! Maybe not to you ... but it really is over. You can't change it; the war came, this is all ruined, only remnants are left. You said it yourself: *why are we on the outside*? We could so easily be on the inside." Childish excitement thrilled through her; she pushed against him eagerly, carried away by her flow of words. "Forget the past — let's work with the present! The material is here; the people, the objects. Let's move it all around. Pick it up, set it down." She lifted a grove of trees a mile away; the whole top of a line of hills burst loose, rose high in the air, and then dissolved in booming fragments. "We can take things apart and put them back together!"

"I'm seventy-one years old," Jack said. "There isn't going to be any putting together for me. And I'm through picking over the past. I'm not going to try anymore. You can all rejoice ... I'm finished."

She tugged at him fiercely. "Then it's up to the rest of us!"

If he had Porter's talent he could see beyond his death. Porter would, at some future time, view his own corpse stretched out, view his burial, continue to live month after month, while his plump corpse rotted underground. Porter's bovine contentedness was possible in a man who could preview the future. ... Jack twisted wretchedly as anguished uncertainty ached through him. After the dying old man in the military hospital reached the inevitable end of his life-span — then what? What happened *here*, among the survivors of the Guild?

Beside him, the girl babbled on. The possibilities he had suggested: real material to work with, not tricks or miracles. For her, the possibilities of social action were swimming into existence. They were all restless, except perhaps Porter. Tired of standing idle. Impatient with the anachronistic officers who kept the communes alive, misguided remnants of a past order of incompetents who had proved their unfitness to rule by leading their block to almost total destruction.

Rule by the Guild couldn't be worse.

Or could it? Something had survived rule by power-oriented politicians, professional spellbinders recruited from smoke-dingy city halls and cheap law offices. If Psionic rule failed, if analogues of the struggle of national states arose, there might be nothing spared. The collective power of the Guild reached into all dimensions of life; for the first time a genuine totalitarian society could arise. Dominated by telepaths, precogs, healers with the power to animate inorganic matter and to wither organic matter, what ordinary person could survive?

There would be no recourse against the Guild. Man controlled by Psionic organizers would be powerless. It was merely a question of time before the maintenance of non-Psis would be seriously scrutinized, with an eye toward greater efficiency, toward the elimination of useless material. Rule by super-competents could be worse than rule by incompetents.

"Worse for whom?" Stephen's clear, treble thoughts came into his mind. Cold, confident, utterly without doubt. "You can see they're dying out. It's not a question of our eliminating them; it's a question of how long are we going to maintain their artificial preservation? We're running a zoo, Jack. We're keeping alive an extinct species. And the cage is too large ... it takes up all the world. Give them some space, if you want. A subcontinent. But we deserve the balance for our own use."

Porter sat scooping up baked rice pudding from his dish. He continued eating even after Stephen had begun screaming. It wasn't until Thelma clawed his hand loose from his spoon that he gave up and turned his attention to what was happening.

Surprise was totally unknown to him; six months earlier he had examined the scene, reflected on it, and turned his attention to later events. Reluctantly, he pushed back his chair and dragged his heavy body upright.

"He's going to kill me!" Stephen was wailing. "Why didn't you tell me?" he shouted at Porter. "You know — he's coming to kill me right now."

"For God's sake," Thelma shrilled in Porter's ear, "is it true? Can't you do something? You're a man — stop him!"

While Porter gathered a reply, Jack entered the kitchen. Stephen's shrill wails grew frantic. Doris hurried wild-eyed after Jack, her talent forgotten in the abrupt explosion of excitement. Thelma hurried around the table, between Jack and the boy, scrawny arms out, dried-up face contorted with outrage.

"I can see it!" Stephen screamed. "In his mind — he's going to kill me because he knows I want to — " He broke off. "He doesn't want us to do anything. He wants us to stay here in this old ruin, doing tricks for people." Fury broke through his terror. "I'm not going to do it. I'm through doing mind-reading tricks. Now he's thinking about killing all of us! He wants us all dead!"

Porter settled down in his chair and pawed for his spoon. He pulled his plate under his chin; eyes intently on Jack and Stephen, he continued slowly eating.

"I'm sorry," Jack said. "You shouldn't have told me your thoughts, I couldn't have read them. You could have kept them to yourself." He moved forward.

Thelma grabbed him with her skinny claws and hung on tight. The wail and babble rose in hysteria; Porter winced and bobbed his thick neck-wattles. Impassively, he watched Jack and the old woman struggle together; beyond them, Stephen stood paralyzed with childish terror, face waxen, youthful body rigid.

Doris moved forward, and Porter stopped eating. A kind of tension settled over him; but it was a finality that made him forget eating, not doubt or uncertainty. Knowing what was going to happen didn't diminish the awesomeness of it. He couldn't be surprised ... but he could be sobered.

"Leave him alone," Doris gasped. "He's just a boy. Go sit down and behave yourself." She caught hold of Jack around the waist; the two women swayed back and forth, trying to hold the immense muscular figure. "Stop it! Leave him alone!"

Jack broke away. He tottered, tried to regain his balance. The two women fluttered and clawed after him like furious birds; he reached back to push them away. ...

"Don't look," Porter said sharply.

Doris turned in his direction. And didn't see, as he anticipated. Thelma saw, and her voice suddenly died into silence. Stephen choked off, horrified, then screeched in stricken dismay.

They had seen the last entity along Jack's time-path once before. Briefly one night the withered old man had appeared, as the more youthful entity inspected the military hospital to analyze its resources. The younger Jack had returned at once, satisfied that the dying old man would be given the best treatment available. In that moment they had seen his gaunt, fever-ridden face. This time the eyes weren't bright. Lusterless, the eyes of a dead object gazed blankly at them, as the hunched figure remained briefly upright.

Thelma tried vainly to catch it as it pitched forward. Like a sack of meal it crashed into the table, scattering cups and silver. It wore a faded blue robe, knotted at the waist. Its pale-white feet were bare. From it oozed the pungent hygienic scent of the hospital, of age and illness and death.

"You did it," Porter said. "Both of you together. Doris, especially. But it would have come in the next few days, anyhow." He added, "Jack's dead. We'll have to bury him, unless you think any of you can bring him back."

Thelma stood wiping at her eyes. Tears dribbled down her shrunken cheeks, into her mouth. "It was my fault. I wanted to destroy him. My hands." She held up her claws. "He never trusted me; he never put himself in my care. And he was right."

"We both did it," Doris muttered, shaken. "Porter's telling the truth. I wanted him to go away ... I wanted him to leave. I never moved anything into time, before."

"You never will again," Porter said. "He left no descendants. He was the first and last man to move through time. It was a unique talent."

Stephen was recovering slowly, still white-faced and shaken, eyes fixed on the withered shape in its frayed blue pajamas, spread out under the table.

"Anyhow," he muttered finally, "there won't be any more picking over the past."

"I believe," Thelma said tightly, "you can follow my thoughts. Are you aware of what I'm thinking?"

Stephen blinked. "Yes."

"Now listen carefully. I'm going to put them into words so everybody will hear them."

Stephen nodded without speaking. His eyes darted frantically around the room, but he didn't stir.

"There are now four Guild members," Thelma said. Her voice was flat and low, without expression. "Some of us want to leave this place and enter the communes. Some of us think this would be a good time to impose ourselves on the communes, whether they like it or not."

Stephen nodded.

"I would say," Thelma continued, examining her ancient, dried-up hands, "that if any of us tries to leave here, I will do what Jack tried to do." She pondered. "But I don't know if I can. Maybe I'll fail, too."

"Yes," Stephen said. His voice trembled, then gained strength. "You're not strong enough. There's somebody here a lot stronger than you. She can pick you up and put you down anywhere she wants. On the other side of the world — on the moon — in the middle of the ocean."

Doris made a faint strangled sound. "I — "

"That's true," Thelma agreed. "But I'm standing only three feet from her. If I touch her first she'll be drained." She studied the smooth, frightened face of the girl. "But you're right. What happens depends not on you or me, but on what Doris wants to do."

Doris breathed rapidly, huskily. "I don't know," she said, faintly. "I don't want to stay here, just sitting around in this old ruin, day after day, doing — tricks. But Jack always said we shouldn't force ourselves on the communes." Her voice trailed off uncertainly. "All my life, as long as I can remember, when I was a little girl growing up, there was Jack saying over and over again we shouldn't force them. If they didn't want us … "

"She won't move you now," Stephen said to Thelma, "but she will eventually. Sooner or later she'll move you away from here, some night when you're sleeping. Eventually she'll make up her mind." He grinned starkly. "Remember, I can talk to her, silently in her mind. Any time I want."

"Will you?" Thelma asked the girl.

Doris faltered miserably. "I — don't know. *Will I?* … Maybe so. It's so — bewildering."

Porter sat up straight in his chair, leaned back, and belched loudly. "It's strange to hear you all conjecturing," he said. "As a matter of fact, you won't touch Thelma." To the old woman he said, "There's nothing to worry about. I can see this stalemate going on. The four of us balance each other — we'll stay where we are."

Thelma sagged. "Maybe Stephen's right. If we have to keep on living this way, doing nothing — "

"We'll be here," Porter said, "but we won't be living the way we've been living."

"What do you mean?" Thelma demanded. "How will we be living? *What's going to happen*?"

"It's hard to probe you," Stephen said to Porter peevishly. "These are things you've seen, not things you're thinking. Have the commune governments changed their position? Are they finally going to call us in?"

"The governments won't call us in," Porter said. "We'll never be invited into Washington and Moscow. We've had to stand outside waiting." He glanced up and stated enigmatically, "That waiting is about over."

It was early morning. Ed Garby brought the rumbling, battered truck into line behind the other surface cars leaving the commune. Cold, fitful sunlight filtered down on the concrete squares that made up the commune installations; today was going to be another cloudy day, exactly like the last. Even so, the exit check-gate ahead was already clogged with outgoing traffic.

"A lot of them, this morning," his wife murmured. "I guess they can't wait any longer for the ash to lift."

Ed clutched for his pass, buried in his sweat-gummed shirt pocket. "The gate's a bottleneck," he muttered resentfully. "What are they doing, getting into the cars?"

There were four guards, today, not the usual one. A squad of armed troops that moved back and forth among the stalled cars, peering and murmuring, reporting through their neck-mikes to the commune officers below surface. A massive truck loaded with workers pulled suddenly away from the line and onto a side road. Roaring and belching clouds of foul blue gas, it made a complete circle and lumbered back toward the center of the commune, away from the exit gate. Ed watched it uneasily.

"What's it doing, turning back?" Fear clutched him. "They're turning us back!"

"No, they're not," Barbara said quietly. "Look — there goes a car through."

An ancient wartime pleasure car precariously edged through the gate and out onto the plain beyond the commune. A second followed it and the two cars gathered speed to climb the long low ridge that became the first tangle of trees.

A horn honked behind Ed. Convulsively, he moved the car forward. In Barbara's lap the baby wailed anxiously; she wound its seedy cotton blanket around it and rolled up the window. "It's an awful day. If we didn't have to go — " She broke off. "Here come the guards. Get the pass out."

Ed greeted the guards apprehensively. "Morning."

Curtly, one of the guards took his pass, examined it, punched it, and filed it away in a steel-bound notebook. "Each of you prepare your thumb for prints," he instructed. A black, oozing pad was passed up. "Including the baby."

Ed was astounded. "Why? What the hell's going on?"

The twins were too terrified to move. Numbly, they allowed the guards to take their prints. Ed protested weakly, as the pad was pushed against his thumb. His wrist was grabbed and yanked forward. As the guards walked around the truck to get at Barbara, the squad leader placed his boot on the running board and addressed Ed briefly.

"Five of you. Family?"

Ed nodded mutely. "Yeah, my family."

"Complete. Any more?"

"No. Just us five."

The guard's dark eyes bored down at him. "When are you coming back?"

"Tonight." Ed indicated the metal notebook in which his pass had been filed. "It says before six."

"If you go through that gate," the guard said, "you won't be coming back. That gate only goes one way."

"Since when?" Barbara whispered, face ashen.

"Since last night. It's your choice. Go ahead out there, get your business done, consult your soothsayer. But don't come back." The guard pointed to the side road. "If you want to turn around, that road takes you to the descent ramps. Follow the truck ahead — it's turning back."

Ed licked his dry lips. "I can't. My kid — she's got bone cancer. The old woman started her healing, but she isn't well, not yet. The old woman says today she can finish."

The guard examined a dog-eared directory "Ward 9, sixth level. Go down there and they'll fix up your kid. The docs have all the equipment." He closed the book and stepped back from the car, a heavy-set man, red-faced, with bristled, beefy skin. "Let's get started, buddy. One way or the other. It's your choice."

Automatically, Ed moved the car forward. "They must have decided," he muttered, dazed. "Too many people going out. They want to scare us ... they know we can't live out there. We'd die out there!"

Barbara quietly clutched the baby. "We'll die here eventually."

"But it's nothing but ruins out there!"

"Aren't *they* out there?"

Ed choked helplessly. "We can't come back — suppose it's a mistake?"

The truck ahead wavered toward the side road. An uncertain hand signal was made; suddenly the driver yanked his hand in and wobbled the truck back toward the exit gate. A moment of confusion took place. The truck slowed almost to a stop; Ed slammed on his brakes, cursed, and shifted into low. Then the truck ahead gained speed. It rumbled through the gate and out onto the barren ground. Without thinking, Ed followed it. Cold, ash-heavy air swept into the cabin as he gained speed and pulled up beside the truck. Even with it he leaned out and shouted, "Where you going? They won't let you back!"

The driver, a skinny little man, bald and bony, shouted angrily back, "Goddamn it, I'm not coming back! The hell with them — I got all my food and bedding in here — I got every damn thing I own. Let them try to get me back!" He gunned up his truck and pulled ahead of Ed.

"Well," Barbara said quietly, "it's done. We're outside."

"Yeah," Ed agreed shakily. "We are. A yard, a thousand miles — it's all the same." In panic, he turned wildly to his wife. "What if they don't take us? I mean, what if we get there and they don't want us. All they got is that old broken-down wartime shelter. There isn't room for anybody — and look behind us."

A line of hesitant, lumbering trucks and cars was picking its way uncertainly from the gate, streaming rustily out onto the parched plain. A few pulled out and swung back; one pulled over to the side of the road and halted while its passengers argued with bitter desperation.

"They'll take us," Barbara said. "They want to help us — they always wanted to."

"But suppose they *can't*!"

"I think they can. There's a lot of power there, if we ask for it. They couldn't come to us, but we can go to them. We've been held back too long, separated from them too many years. If the government won't let them in, then we'll have to go outside."

"Can we live outside?" Ed asked hoarsely.

"Yes."

Behind them a horn honked excitedly. Ed gained speed. "It's a regular exodus. Look at them pouring out. Who'll be left?"

"There'll be plenty left," Barbara answered. "All the big shots will stay behind." She laughed breathlessly. "Maybe they'll be able to get the war going again. It'll give them something to do, while we're away."

NOTES

All notes in italics are by Philip K. Dick. The year when the note was written appears in parentheses following the note. Most of these notes were written as story notes for the collections THE BEST OF PHILIP K. DICK (published 1977) and THE GOLDEN MAN (published 1980). A few were written at the request of editors publishing or reprinting a PKD story in a book or magazine.

When there is a date following the name of a story, it is the date the manuscript of that story was first received by Dick's agent, per the records of the Scott Meredith Literary Agency. Absence of a date means no record is available. The name of a magazine followed by a month and year indicates the first published appearance of a story. An alternate name following a story indicates Dick's original name for the story, as shown in the agency records.

These five volumes include all of Philip K. Dick's short fiction, with the exception of short novels later published as or included in novels, childhood writings, and unpublished writings for which manuscripts have not been found. The stories are arranged as closely as possible in chronological order of composition; research for this chronology was done by Gregg Rickman and Paul Williams.

FAIR GAME 4/21/53. *If*, Sept 1959.

THE HANGING STRANGER 5/4/53. *Science Fiction Adventures*, Dec 1953.

THE EYES HAVE IT 5/13/53. *Science Fiction Stories*, No 1, 1953.

THE GOLDEN MAN ("The God Who Runs") 6/24/53. *If*, April 1954.

In the early Fifties much American science fiction dealt with human mutants and their glorious super-powers and super-faculties by which they would presently lead mankind to a higher state of existence, a sort of Promised Land. John W. Campbell, Jr., editor of Analog, *demanded that the stories he bought deal with such wonderful mutants, and he also insisted that the mutants always be shown as (1) good; and (2) firmly in charge. When I wrote* The Golden Man *I intended to show that (1) the mutant might not be good, at least good for the rest of mankind, for us ordinaries; and (2) not in charge but sniping at us as a bandit would, a feral mutant who potentially would do us more harm than good. This was specifically the view of psionic mutants that Campbell loathed, and the theme in fiction that he refused to publish … so my story appeared in* If.

We sf writers of the Fifties liked If *because it had high quality paper and illustrations; it was a classy magazine. And, more important, it would take a chance with unknown authors. A fairly large number of my early stories appeared in* If*; for me it was a major market. The editor of* If *at the beginning was Paul W. Fairman. He would take a badly-written story by you and rework it until it was okay — which I appreciated. Later James L. Quinn the publisher became himself the editor, and then Frederik Pohl. I sold to all three of them.*

In the issue of If *that followed the publishing of* The Golden Man *appeared a two-page editorial consisting of a letter by a lady school teacher complaining about* The Golden Man. *Her complaints consisted of John W. Campbell, Jr.'s complaint: she upbraided me for presenting mutants in a negative light and she offered the notion that certainly we could expect mutants to be (1) good; and (2) firmly in charge. So I was back to square one.*

My theory as to why people took this view is: I think these people secretly imagined they were themselves early manifestations of these kindly, wise, super-intelligent Übermenschen *who would guide the stupid — i.e. the rest of us — to the Promised Land. A power phantasy was involved here, in my opinion. The idea of the psionic superman taking over was a role that appeared originally in Stapleton's ODD JOHN and A.E. van Vogt's SLAN. "We are persecuted now," the message ran, "and despised and rejected. But later on, boy oh boy, will we show them!"*

As far as I was concerned, for psionic mutants to rule us would be to put the fox in charge of the hen house. I was reacting to what I considered a dangerous hunger for power on the part of neurotic people, a hunger which I felt John W. Campbell, Jr. was pandering to — and deliberately so. If, *on the other hand, was not committed to selling any one particular idea; it was a magazine devoted to genuinely new ideas, willing to take any side of an issue. Its several editors should be commended, inasmuch as they understood the real task of science fiction: to look in* all *directions without restraint.* (1979)

Here I am also saying that mutants are dangerous to us ordinaries, a view which John W. Campbell, Jr. deplored. We were supposed to view them as our leaders. But I always felt uneasy as to how they would view us. I mean, maybe they wouldn't want *to lead us. Maybe from their superevolved lofty level we wouldn't seem worth leading. Anyhow, even if they agreed to lead us, I felt uneasy as to where we would wind up going. It might have something to do with buildings marked SHOWERS but which really weren't.* (1978)

THE TURNING WHEEL 7/8/53. *Science Fiction Stories*, No 2, 1954.

THE LAST OF THE MASTERS ("Protection Agency") 7/15/53. *Orbit Science Fiction*, Nov-Dec 1954.

Now I show trust of robot as leader, a robot who is the suffering servant, which is to say a form of Christ. Leader as servant of man: leader who should be dispensed with — perhaps. An ambiguity hangs over the morality of this story. Should we have a leader or should we think for ourselves? Obviously the latter, in principle. But — sometimes there lies a gulf between what is theoretically right and that which is practical. It's interesting that I would trust a robot and not an android. Perhaps it's because a robot does not try to deceive you as to what it is. (1978)

THE FATHER-THING 7/21/53. *Fantasy & Science Fiction*, Dec 1954.

I always had the impression, when I was very small, that my father was two people, one good, one bad. The good father goes away and the bad father replaces him. I guess many kids have this feeling. What if it were so? This story is another instance of a normal feeling, which is in fact incorrect, somehow becoming correct... with the added misery that one cannot communicate it to others. Fortunately, there are other kids to tell it to. Kids understand: they are wiser than adults — hmmm, I almost said, "Wiser than humans." (1976)

STRANGE EDEN ("Immolation") 8/4/53. *Imagination*, Dec 1954.

TONY AND THE BEETLES 8/31/53. *Orbit Science Fiction*, No 2, 1953.

NULL-O ("Loony Lemuel") 8/31/53. *If*, Dec 1958.

TO SERVE THE MASTER ("Be As Gods!") 10/21/53. *Imagination*, Feb 1956.

EXHIBIT PIECE 10/21/53. *If*, Aug 1954.

THE CRAWLERS ("Foundling Home") 10/29/53. *Imagination*, July 1954.

SALES PITCH 11/19/53. *Future*, June 1954.

When this story first appeared, the fans detested it. I read it over, perplexed by their hostility, and could see why: it is a superdowner story, and relentlessly so. Could I rewrite it I would have it end differently, I would have the man and the robot, i.e. the fasrad, form a partnership at the end and become friends. The logic of paranoia of this story should be deconstructed into its opposite; Y, the human-against-robot theme, should have been resolved into null-Y, human-and-robot-against-the-universe. I really deplore the ending. So when you read the story, try to imagine it as it ought to have been written. The fasrad says, "Sir, I am here to help you. The hell with my sales pitch. Let's be together forever." Yes, but then I would have been criticized for a false upbeat ending, I guess. Still, this ending is not good. The fans were right. (1978)

SHELL GAME 12/22/53. *Galaxy*, Sept 1954.

UPON THE DULL EARTH 12/30/53. *Beyond Fantasy Fiction*, Nov 1954.

FOSTER, YOU'RE DEAD 12/31/53. *Star Science Fiction Stories No 3*, edited by Frederik Pohl, New York, 1955.

One day I saw a newspaper headline reporting that the President suggested that if Americans had to buy *their bomb shelters, rather than being provided with them by the government, they'd take better care of them, an idea which made me furious. Logically, each of us should own a submarine, a jet fighter, and so forth. Here I just wanted to show how cruel the authorities can be when it comes to human life, how they can think in terms of dollars, not people*. (1976)

PAY FOR THE PRINTER ("Printer's Pay") 1/28/54. *Satellite Science Fiction*, Oct 1956.

WAR VETERAN 2/17/54. *If*, March 1955.

THE CHROMIUM FENCE 4/9/54. *Imagination*, July 1955.

MISADJUSTMENT 5/14/54. *Science Fiction Quarterly*, Feb 1957.

A WORLD OF TALENT ("Two Steps Right") 6/4/54. *Galaxy*, Oct 1954.

PSI-MAN HEAL MY CHILD! ("Outside Consultant") 6/8/54. *Imaginative Tales*, Nov 1955. [Also published in a story collection as "Psi-Man."]